Love of a MARINE

BOOK TWO WOUNDED WARRIOR SERIES

Patty Campbell

This book is dedicated to wounded veteran Joseph Cameron. Thank you, Joe, for spending an afternoon with me in Naples, Florida. Your unique and terrifying experiences in the middle east were my inspiration for Cluny McPherson. Cluny battles PTSD, just like you do. I wish the very best for you, your wife and little son. Hang in there, buddy. We need men like you.

The author donates all royalties from the sale of this work to the Wounded Veteran's Relief Fund.

Information on the organization can be found at www.wvrf.org.

Chapter One

Thursday, Zuma Beach

WHO IS THAT MAN? WHY IS HE HERE EVERY DAY?

Graciella Jefferson turned her attention to her nine-year-old son, Santos, chasing wavelets at the edge of the surf on Zuma Beach. They'd been here every morning since school let out two weeks ago. He loved the ocean, but hadn't worked up the nerve to go in above his knees. She smiled, knowing he'd get there in his own good time. His father had been a genuine frogman.

"Santos, time for lunch!"

He smiled and waved, took a last flat-footed jump in the shallow water then ran to join her on the blanket under the big carnival striped umbrella. "Mama?"

"Yes?"

"See that man and his dog over there?" He tilted his head in the direction of the rocks near Point Dume.

"Yes, I see him. Why?"

"They've been here every morning this week, and they're still there when we leave. They must love the beach as much as I do."

Graciella pushed up the brim of her wide hat to get a better look. Santos was right, the man was always there. He and the dog stared out

1

to sea. Every now and then the man would reach down and rub the dog's head.

"What is the dog wearing, Mama, a T-shirt?"

"I can't be sure, but it looks like a vest, the kind service dogs wear." She squinted to get a better look.

He took a big swallow of lemonade and wiped his mouth on his forearm. "What's a service dog?"

"Use this." She handed him a faded, old cloth napkin. "A service dog is a companion that is specially trained for certain tasks."

"Like what?"

"You've seen seeing-eye dogs working with the blind."

"But that man can see. He watches the ocean a lot. His dog just sits there next to him, not doing anything." He pointed his skinny arm toward the rocks where the man sat on the sand with his hands dangling between his knees.

"It's not polite to point, Santos."

"He's not looking at us."

"It's still not polite."

"Why?"

She tousled his curly black hair. He looked so much like his late father it nearly broke her heart. "Enough questions. Eat. We have to head back in about an hour. I have a class to teach this afternoon."

Santos tucked into the rest of his sandwich, guzzled the rest of his drink and mopped his mouth with the napkin. "I'm done." He darted back to the water's edge.

Graciella watched him for a bit, then picked up her book and got comfortable in the sand chair to read. After several minutes she looked up and her heart skipped a beat when she didn't see him. She dropped her book and scanned the beach. He was walking toward the man and his dog, kicking his toes in the wet sand. He glanced back at her, a broad grin on his face, and waved.

———

Cluny and Queen had had another bad night. There had been a lot of them this past six months. He didn't understand why he could go months, even years, without the nightmares and the shaking, then they'd return. A year ago he'd gotten Queen, on the advice of his buddy, Dwayne Dempsey, and a therapist at the VA.

A skinny, dark-skinned kid about nine or ten walked in their direction. The boy and the woman had been about a quarter klik down the beach every morning. He figured it was only a matter of time before the kid got curious.

Queen stood. "Easy, girl."

"Hi, mister." The boy slowed to a stop about three yards away from him. He stood quietly, expression tentative.

"Hi." Cluny smiled. He glanced down the beach and saw the woman stand. He waved at her.

"Why is your dog wearing a vest?" He shaded his eyes from the glare of the sun.

"She's working this morning." Cluny laid his hand on Queen's back.

"I didn't see her do anything." He took a few steps closer. "What does she do?"

"Right now, she's keeping me company."

"Is she friendly? Can I pet her?"

"I'll ask her." He unbuckled Queen's vest, and she stood, shook and stretched. "Want this good lookin' boy to pet you, Queen?" She wagged her tail and took a step in the boy's direction.

Cluny smiled at the woman strolling toward them. "What's your name, son?"

The boy knelt in front of Queen. She sat on her haunches and lifted a paw. The kid giggled and grasped her foot. "Santos Jefferson, what's your name, mister?"

Cluny stood and brushed sand from the seat of his shorts. "I'm Cluny McPherson." He tilted his head toward the tall, willowy woman approaching them. "Is that your mother?"

"Yes." The boy buried both his hands in the dog's ruff and scratched vigorously. He laughed when Queen groaned with pleasure. "She likes it."

"I think we should go meet your mother. She looks concerned. Come, Queen." He stooped to pick up the dog's vest and stuffed it in his cargo pocket. The boy joined him, and they walked toward the woman.

"Mom! Isn't she beautiful? Her name is Queen. She keeps him company."

Cluny extended his hand. "Ma'am." She was almost as tall as his six-one in bare feet, her skin a luscious golden honey-brown, with eyes to match. "Cluny McPherson."

She hesitated and then took it. "Hello. Graciella Jefferson. My son was curious about your dog."

Her deep voice had a slight, intriguing accent, her handshake as firm and strong as she appeared to be. Cluny was stunned by her beauty.

He cleared his throat. "Yes, Santos asked me what she did other than stare at the water." He grinned and a thrill jolted through him when she returned his smile.

She appeared to size him up quickly, and then asked, "Would you like some lemonade? We'll be leaving soon and it'll be one less thing for me to carry back to the car."

"Yes, thank you, ma'am, I would." He followed her back down to their spot under the big umbrella, and knelt on the blanket. Queen and the boy followed close behind.

Graciella, she'd pronounced it grah-see-ay-la with an *r* roll, took a small bottle of lemonade from her cooler, shook the droplets off and handed it to him. He couldn't help noticing long, tapered fingers with bright orange polish on her short nails.

"Thanks." He opened the bottle and took a long drink. "I didn't realize I was thirsty until just now." He held the cold bottle to his forehead.

"Santos, the dog might be thirsty." She opened a thermos, poured water from it into the cup-lid and set it in the sand.

Cluny gazed at the stunning woman as she gestured to her boy. Her thick dark brown, curly hair fluttered around her shoulders in the breeze, the brim of her straw hat flapped, and she set her hand on top to keep it from blowing away. She lowered her body to sit on the blanket across from him, as graceful as a swan.

"Where'd that breeze come from all of a sudden?" She laughed and held tight to her hat.

Queen trotted to the water cup and quickly lapped it up. "Queenie was thirsty," Cluny said. "Thanks."

4

She nodded. "You're welcome." She turned to her boy. "We have to leave soon, Santos."

"Aw, gee, I just made friends with Queen." He eyed Cluny. "What does she really do when she isn't keeping you company?"

Cluny laughed. "She sleeps a lot, which is good, because her job is to help me fall asleep at night."

"I watch TV until Mama yells at me."

Cluny pressed his lips together. "That usually works for me too, but sometimes Queen helps me."

"Where'd you get her?"

"She's a genuine wounded warrior war hero. Queen is retired from the Navy SEALS. I got her from Wounded Warriors."

Santos' eyes got huge. "Are you a wounded warrior? Were you a SEAL? My dad was a SEAL. He got killed in Iraq by some bad guys. I wasn't *borned* yet, so I never even got to meet him, but I know what he looked like because I have a picture of him. Want to see it?"

"Santos." His mother put her hand on the excited boy's arm.

"It's okay." Cluny smiled at her. "Yes, I'd like to see a picture of your dad."

Santos dug through a cloth carry bag and pulled out a jacket. He soon found a laminated photo, attached to a house key, and handed it to him. "Mom says I look like him. Do you think I look like him?"

"Cluny studied the photo of a very large, very fit black man wearing standard field-issue SEAL camos. The man grinned for the photographer, a sniper rifle resting casually on this shoulder. "Yes, I see the resemblance. What was your dad's name?" He handed the photo back to the boy.

"Marvin Jefferson."

A prickly sensation crawled over Cluny's back and up his neck. The man looked familiar. He glanced at Graciella. "Where was the picture taken?"

"Fallujah. The day he was killed." Pain flashed in her soulful eyes.

"Oh, God, ma'am, I'm so sorry." His stomach twisted into a painful knot. For a moment he thought he might throw up the lemonade, but he gritted his teeth against the nausea. Queen nudged his hand.

She answered in a soft voice, "It was a long time ago."

Santos apparently hadn't noticed his discomfort. "Were you a SEAL too?"

He shook his head. "No, a Marine, but I knew some very brave SEALs in Iraq. I fought in Fallujah, too."

"What happened to you?"

Before answering the boy, Cluny glanced at his mother. He wasn't sure how comfortable she was with the conversation. She nodded slightly.

"Me and some buddies were in an M-3 Bradley that got hit by an RPG one day when we were in a convoy heading to Baghdad. One of the bad guys found us first." He swallowed and took a breath. This was something he rarely talked about, and never with a kid.

"Did any Marines get killed?" The boy's rapt face stared steadily, waiting for an answer.

"Nope. Nobody got killed, except the bad guys. Some of my buddies got wounded real bad, and I took a hard knock on the head. We were lucky."

"Is that why you can't sleep?"

"Sometimes. I don't think about it much."

"Was your dog in Fallujah, too?" Santos rested his hand on Queen's back. "What happened to her?"

"I didn't know Queen then. She was guarding Baghdad airport. She got shot by a sniper." He smiled at his dog. "You're fine now, aren't you, Queenie?" Her tail thumped the sand.

Graciella stood and folded the sand chair. "It's time we got on home, Santos. Help me pack up."

Cluny stood and pulled the umbrella stake from the sand and folded it for her. "I'll help you carry your things to the car. We're a long way from the parking area."

"We can manage."

"I'm sure you can, but I'd like to help." He slapped his leg and Queen leapt to her feet. He took her vest from his pocket and buckled it around her chest. In an instant she was back in work mode. He rested the umbrella on his shoulder and took the handle of the cooler and pulled it on its big sand tires to the parking lot.

Graciella and Santos grabbed the rest of their things and walked alongside him. She pointed to a small blue SUV. "That's our car." The back window wore a SEAL Trident decal.

He loaded the umbrella and cooler in the back hatch. She shook sand from the blanket then tossed it in on top of the folding chair. "Thank you, Cluny McPherson."

He nodded. "You're welcome, Ms. Jefferson." He put his hand on top of Santos head of tight black curls. "Nice meeting you, Santos. You do look like your dad. Have a safe trip home."

Cluny returned to the sand and waved as they climbed into the car, haunted by the eerie feeling from the photograph of the big Navy SEAL.

Queen leaned heavily against his leg, made a soft whimper, and stared into his eyes.

"I'm good, girl. I'm good."

Chapter Two

"Mr. Cluny thought I looked like Dad," Santos spoke after several moments into the drive home.

Not taking her eyes from the twisty mountain canyon road, Graciella answered, "That's because you do."

"This road doesn't look the same." Santos craned his neck.

Her observant son didn't miss much. "I'm taking Kanan Dume Road this time instead of Malibu Canyon. It's a little longer, but a change of scenery."

"Do you think Mr. Cluny knew Dad?"

"His name is Mr. McPherson. Cluny is his first name."

"Do you?" He persisted, impatient for an answer. Her little man was so like the father he'd never known.

"I doubt it. There were so many Marines, SEALs and Rangers over there at the time. They all had different tasks."

"But Dad was a SEAL sniper, and you told me SEAL sniper teams went to help the Army or the Marines whenever they could."

She sighed. "Even so, I doubt they ever met."

"He stared at Dad's picture a long time."

Yes, she'd noticed Cluny's odd expression and brief flash of puzzlement. Not exactly recognition, but she'd noticed it. The tall, dark haired man with the startling blue eyes had reacted to the photograph in an unsettling way. "I suspect he was taking a long look to answer your question, don't you?"

"Yeah, I guess." He gazed out the window. "Did you like his dog? She's like a German Shepherd, but smaller."

"Yes. Queen is magnificent and well trained."

"How do you think she helps him to fall asleep? I can't figure that out."

Graciella chuckled. "You're full of questions today, aren't you?"

"How?"

She shrugged. "I don't know. Maybe she sleeps next to him, keeps him company. Dogs have a way of comforting those who need it."

"I wish we had a dog."

He'd often expressed a desire for a dog, but their apartment complex didn't allow pets, and they wouldn't be moving any time soon. Her income from the samba school was unpredictable. She'd placed Marvin's life insurance payout into a college trust fund for her son, and her monthly survivor benefit check didn't even cover her rent.

She'd receive her monthly widow's payment until she re-married. That wasn't likely because she couldn't imagine considering marriage until her boy was on his own. Santos's payments would stop when he reached eighteen, so she conserved as much money for a rainy day as possible.

"Are we coming back to the beach tomorrow? If we do, I'll ask Mr. Macfearsome how Queen helps him fall asleep."

She smiled. "It's McPherson, and no, we can't come back tomorrow. I've got a large group of kids from the Boys and Girls Club coming in for a one-time class in the morning."

"So, I have to stay with Auntie Krystal all day?"

There was no love lost between her and Krystal. She'd stayed in California so Santos could have a relationship with his aunt and grandparents. Graciella's family lived in Sao Paulo, Brazil, where she'd met and fallen in love with Marvin.

"No, Krystal has a photo shoot tomorrow. You can help me teach the samba class. You dance with the girls, and I'll dance with the boys, how's that?"

"I guess so." His disappointment was quite clear.

"Oh, come on, you're one of my best teachers." She'd have loved to see the expression on his face, but didn't dare take her eyes off the canyon road. "I taught you to samba before you could walk."

"You taught Dad to samba, too, didn't you?"

Santos knew the answer to the question, but he loved to hear the story of how his parents met. "Yes. He and a few Navy buddies wandered into the samba club where I and a few of my girlfriends went one night in Sao Paulo. We thought they were the handsomest group of men we'd ever seen, especially Marvin, so big and tall and such a happy smile. He had all the girls giggling when he tried to talk to us."

"You were the only girl who could speak English, right?"

"Yes and no. I was the only one willing to try out my English. He asked me to teach him the samba."

"And he was a good dancer, wasn't he?"

"A natural. Every girl in the room wanted to dance with him."

"But he kept coming back to you."

She remembered the night clearly. The music, the dancing, and how the level of excitement went up in the club when the group of American Sailors wandered in, laughing and jostling one another.

"Some of the Brazilian boys were jealous, weren't they?"

She laughed. "Oh, yes, but the sailors were well behaved and respectful, so nobody could find an excuse to ask them to leave."

"And you fell in love with Dad."

"I tried not to because I knew he would only be in Sao Paulo for a few more days, and I didn't want my heart broken."

"So, you pretended not to like him very much."

"It didn't work though, did it? My parents were beside themselves when we got married five days later."

"Then Dad shipped out."

"Yes. It was very sad. I wasn't sure I'd see him again, but he called me a few days later and told me he'd started the paperwork for the Navy's permission for our marriage and before long I was on my way to his base in San Diego."

"How come you never took me to Brazil?"

"Aren't you tired of hearing this story?" She reached over the seat and squeezed his knee.

"No, because when you tell me the story it makes me feel like I really had a dad." His words sent a sharp pain through her chest.

"What say we drop in on Gunny, Queen?" Cluny took a right turn on Highway 1, then headed north on Topanga Canyon Boulevard through Canoga Park and Chatsworth. It was a little longer, but he was in no hurry to return to his plumbing business. "My guys are still on vacation." The answering service would pick up any calls. He'd check in when he got to Big D Construction in Spring Grove, outside Simi Valley.

Dwayne Dempsey's truck wasn't parked in front of the warehouse, so he probably wasn't in. He'd stop in, grab a cup of coffee and check his messages all the same.

He opened the office door and the little Yorkie, DD, came running and barking her tiny head off. She'd be no more than a snack for Queen, but she was fearless. "Hey, DD, don't hurt my dog, okay? Where's your daddy?"

Marla Danaher, Dwayne Dempsey's wife, called from the small office, "Cluny, come in. I just made a fresh pot of coffee. Dwayne will be back any time now."

Cluny grinned, rounded the desk and hugged her. "I bet Gunny doesn't go far off the reservation these days." She looked like she was ready to deliver any minute. "You're more beautiful than usual, boss lady."

Marla kissed his cheek. "Hah. I feel like a beached whale. Have a seat. I'll get your mug. I've been sitting too long." Stretching her back, she groaned. "I can't wait for little Dwayne to show up. I'm surprised I can still get behind the wheel of my car."

He held up his cell phone. "Do you mind if I check my calls? My place is still closed for a few more days, and I didn't go in this morning."

"Go ahead. I'm here to do payroll. Dwayne went to Miss Emmaline's to pick up Amber. She's learning how to knit. Did you ever hear of a baby garment called a soaker?"

"Can't say that I have, but my knowledge of all things babies is practically non-existent." He laughed when she grinned at him and set a steaming mug on the edge of the desk. "This smells great, thanks."

"I don't believe that. You were like a second dad to Amber from the day she was born. What have you been doing with yourself, Cluny? We haven't seen much of you lately." She took a manila folder from the desk and put it in a locked file cabinet.

"Queen and I've been going to Zuma Beach every morning. The weather's been perfect." He blew on his coffee and checked for messages on his cell. "No emergencies, good. I'm enjoying my short vacation and wouldn't relish crawling under somebody's house or replacing a busted toilet."

"Everything tickety-boo?"

"Yep." He put the phone back in his pocket. "What do you hear from your sister these days?" Marla's twin sister, Charlene, had married Dwayne's younger brother, Donovan. "After two years they must be acting like an old married couple."

"Char's still behaving like a newlywed. They love living in Hawaii, and they're coming to California for Christmas. Then they'll go to Wyoming to spend a few days with our mutual mother-in-law at the ranch. I can't imagine what the weather is like up there in December. I get chills just thinking about it."

"It's cold." How well he remembered winter in Wyoming. "Very cold."

She walked to the window at the side of the building. "I heard Dwayne's truck."

The entrance door opened, Amber entered, and DD took a flying leap right into her arms. "How's my little furry sister today, DD-weedie?" She hugged DD, gave Queen an affectionate pat and put her arms around Cluny's neck.

"Are you going to take me to the beach this week, Uncle Cluny?"

He hugged his tall, skinny eight-year-old god-daughter and planted a hard kiss on her cheek. "If your dad will let me."

"Hi, Mom."

"Hi, sweetie. How's the knitting?"

"I'm almost done." Amber hugged her stepmother and rested her hand on Marla's belly. "Hello, baby brother."

"I'll be so happy when you can say hello to this bruiser in person.

My back is killing me." Marla grinned when Dwayne walked in. "I need a foot rub, Dempsey."

"Soon as we get home, Danaher." He embraced her. "You ready to leave?" He smacked Cluny on the back. "How's it going, McPherson?"

"Good, Gunny."

"Amber and I'll head home, honey." Marla kissed Dwayne, then Cluny. "I've got beef stew in the slow cooker. Why don't you join us? I made more than enough."

Dinner with the Dempsey's was music to his ears. "When did I ever turn down your cooking? Thanks, I'd love it." He waved when Marla and Amber left, then gazed at his old buddy. "You are one lucky son of a bitch."

"I thank God for her every day," Dwayne answered. "When she hired me to do that apartment building renovation, heaven smiled on Amber and me."

He and Dwayne had been friends since junior high school in Buffalo, Wyoming. They'd served in the same Marine unit in Iraq. Cluny had been there all those years when Dwayne struggled to recuperate from grievous war wounds and raise Amber from infancy as a single dad.

They'd moved to California together when the senior Dempsey wanted to retire and asked Dwayne to take over his construction company. Cluny had eventually opened his own plumbing business, and they often worked together. "We've been through a lot over the years, Gunny. I couldn't be happier for you."

"What's up, soldier? I know that look."

"Do you remember that big SEAL who took out the savage with the RPG who tried to kill us outside Fallujah?"

"Marv? Sure. He saved all our asses that day. It's a crying shame he paid the ultimate price in that shithole."

"I'm pretty sure I met his wife and kid today."

"What?" Dwayne stared at him like he'd gone off the rails.

"It sounds crazy, but I was sitting on the beach today and this kid and his mom were there. They've been there for the last three mornings. The boy, his name is Santos Jefferson, got curious about Queen and wandered over."

"I don't remember Marv's last name. Did we ever hear it? What makes you think the kid was his?"

Cluny shook his head and raised his hands. "They invited me to have lemonade with them, and Santos showed me a snapshot of his dad. I recognized Marv, but didn't say anything for fear I was imagining it." His stomach clenched at the memory of the man in the photo. He still couldn't believe it.

"Amazing! I'd love to tell his wife what he did for us that day. Do you know where she lives?"

"No. I helped them load up their car and they took off. I didn't have the presence of mind to ask her. I doubt she would have told me, a total stranger, anyway. Her name is Graciella. She has an accent."

Dwayne shook his head. "Too bad. Maybe you'll run into her again."

"I doubt it. There are millions of people in this corner of California. I'm amazed to have met her in the first place." Why hadn't he asked where she lived or where she worked? He could have handed her one of his business cards.

"We better get home. I need to stay close to Marla."

"We finished that extra bedroom and bathroom on your house in the nick of time. When is she due to deliver?"

"Yesterday."

Chapter Three

Fallujah, Iraq

"Gunny!" Blood sprayed the ground outside the smoking shell of the Bradley. Cluny struggled to his knees, clutching for his weapon, the haze of blood dripping in his eyes obscured his vision. "Gunny!"

Gunny Sgt. Dempsey, screaming with shock and pain scrabbled on the ground in a frantic search for his blown off foot. Cluny raised his weapon and killed the savage aiming the next round at them just as another sprang up to take his place. In a gruesome parody of a carnival midway shooting gallery, enemy soldiers popped up one after the other. "Gunny!" he screamed and kept screaming, but couldn't hear his own voice, gunfire, anything. "Gunny!"

In the midst of the insanity, a dog barked. Cluny sprang to a sitting position, eyes wide open, drenched in cold sweat. He had to get help for Gunny before he bled out. How long had he been out? "Medic! We need a medic!" The whomp whomp of helicopter blades threw up a cloud of grit.

A heavy paw hit him in the chest. Queen, it was Queen. He pulled her close and fell back on his soaked pillows, gasping and shaking. "Fuck!" He groaned and rolled his head from side to side.

Why was this nightmare haunting him all these years after Fallujah? He'd dealt with it, dealt with the fact that when his buddies needed him to take out the next killer he'd been unable to respond. He'd covered his exploding and bloody head with his arms and curled into a protective ball.

"Jesus Christ Almighty. Stop, please stop!"

Queen nudged him with her nose and whined, crawled up and lay heavy on his chest. Finally, he stopped shaking, squeezed his eyes closed, patted her back and took deep, controlled breaths. "I'm good, Queen. I'm good, girl."

The bedside clock glowed four-thirty. Cluny rose and staggered to the bathroom. It was useless to try and go back to sleep, so he turned on the shower and stepped out of his shorts. Cold water pounded him like an Arctic blast. Head lowered, he let it lash his head, back and shoulders, punishing him for the recurring nightmare.

He had to go back to Zuma Beach. Had to find Graciella and Santos and tell them what Marv had done, how he'd saved the lives of five Marines that day.

Maybe then he could start sleeping nights, have a normal life. Dwayne's life—he wanted Gunny's life. A woman who'd worry if he was late coming home from work, a kid who'd run with joy on her face and throw her arms around him when he walked in the door. Why couldn't he have that life? Why?

Dressed in sweats, he took Queen for a hard run through the still dark and hilly streets of his neighborhood. He glanced over his shoulder at the sound of a squad car gliding in his direction. The cop put his hand out the window and waved. "Up early again, McPherson? Why would anybody in their right mind be up at this gawd awful hour?"

Cluny grinned and continued running. "Look who's talking, pal." The laughing cop was a familiar face on these dark mornings. Too many dark mornings.

Queen galloped with him stride for stride. If he stopped, she stopped and stared at him until he decided what to do next. Walk, run, sit—she followed his lead, never distracted by wildlife or a car. Cluny was her only purpose in life. "You're my best girl, Queenie." He bent and thumped her powerful chest then jogged down the next street.

At five-thirty he dumped kibble in Queen's bowl and replenished her water. Digging through the refrigerator searching for something to eat, he tipped up the orange juice carton and drank half of it. He flexed his neck and shoulders, took the waxed carton of egg whites, prepared an omelet drenched with salsa and sat at the table to eat.

"Shall we go to the beach, girl?" If Graciella and Santos were there, he'd take another look at the boy's photo of Marvin, then tell them the story.

Queen grinned and her tail dusted the floor.

————

They didn't show. He sat on the sand by the Point Dume rocks until noon, then gave up and headed home. He'd probably never see them again. Never see the boy who looked so much like his father and the breathtaking woman, his mother.

His cell sounded off. "Yo, Gunny. What's up?"

"Marla decided to have our boy today. Could you come over and sit with Amber while I'm gone? Brad and Silvia are here, but they'd like to be at the hospital with their daughter."

"Tell them I'm an hour away. I'll take over as soon as I get there."

"Okay, will do." Dwayne hung up, and Cluny raced to his car.

So, today was the day Declan Danaher Dempsey would make his appearance. *Dwayne, you lucky s.o.b.* Having a foot blown off in Iraq hadn't kept him from going after the life he wanted. At least Gunny's wound was obvious. No explanation required.

————

McDonald's restaurant, Simi Valley

Cluny and his goddaughter were about to finish dinner at McDonalds when his phone buzzed. "Yo."

"You can bring Amber to the hospital now to meet her brother and visit Marla. She's worn out, but wants to see her before she goes to sleep. Tell her the kid looks like she did, except he has my blue eyes and red hair like his mom." Relief and jubilation in his old buddy's voice poured through the phone. "Here's a picture of him."

"You're a lucky bastard, Gunny."

Amber scowled at his use of profanity.

He reached across the table and pinched her nose. "Want to wash my mouth out with soap?"

She nodded. "Yes, but I'll do it later. Let's go see Mom."

"We're on our way, pal." He held the phone for his eight—going-on-eighteen— goddaughter to see her baby brother. He grinned and winked. "Let's go meet your brother."

———

Simi Valley Hospital

Marla looked as if she'd slogged through a long mission behind enemy lines, but her face glowed with contentment. She opened her arms as Amber walked with tentative steps to her bedside.

"Give me a hug before I conk out. Did you see Declan?" She patted the bed next to her. "Come up here."

Amber boosted onto the bed and draped herself across Marla. "Not yet. I wanted to see you first, Mom. Are you tired? Did it hurt?"

Cluny and Dwayne watched from the foot of the bed. The huge grin on Dwayne's face matched his own.

Marla rubbed Amber's back. "I'm exhausted, but so happy. Did Daddy tell you Declan looks like you did the day you were born?"

"I saw his picture, but I have brown hair and light brown eyes." She sat up and asked, "When can you come home?"

"In the morning. We'll all be home tomorrow."

Dwayne leaned close to Cluny's ear and rested a hand on his shoulder. "I'd like Marla and me to have a few hours at home alone tomorrow. Do you mind picking Amber up in the morning?"

"Not at all. I'll take her to the beach for the day." He'd look for Santos and Graciella again.

"Thanks, bud." He rounded the end of the bed and lifted Amber into his arms. "What say we give Mom a rest? You and Uncle Cluny can go to the nursery and see Declan." He tipped her over the bed so she could kiss Marla goodnight.

Marla brushed a hand over Amber's cheek. "I'll see you tomorrow, sweetie. I can't keep my eyes open a minute longer."

"Goodnight, Mom. I'm so glad Daddy married you." Dwayne set her on her feet and she took Cluny's hand. "Let's go see the baby." She shook a school-teacherish finger. "And I don't want you teaching him any bad words."

Cluny winked at Dwayne and Marla. "I won't, on my honor as a Marine. Although that's where I perfected most of them. What say you stay over at my house tonight and we'll take Queen to the beach tomorrow? I'll bring you home in time for supper."

"We're going to the beach? Can I, Mom? Dad?"

Dwayne said, "You notice who she asked first? Go and have a good time, squirt. Mom and I will be all rested up when you get home."

Amber cocked her head at Dwayne. "Why do you have to rest? She did all the work."

"Good question. Try and answer that one, Gunny."

Dwayne laughed. "We'll see you at suppertime tomorrow."

"Don't cook. I'll grab Chinese on the way to your place." He pointed at his pal. "I know you need your rest." Chuckling, he took Amber's hand and left the room. "Let's take a look at this amazing new Dempsey. Nursery's that way."

———

Amber stared in the nursery window. "Did I look all red and *rill* mashed up like that when I was *borned*?" She wrinkled her nose.

Cluny ruffled her hair. "Yes, you did, but take my word for it, by tomorrow he'll look like an ad for baby food. All he needs is a chance to get used to this world. It's a big change from where he's been for the last several months."

"He looks too big to fit in Marla."

"He is, and that's why he's here now."

"Why do all the babies have hats on? It looks like his blanket is too tight."

Cluny stopped a nurse passing by. "Ma'am? This young lady is asking me questions I'm not qualified to answer. Could you help me out?"

The attractive young nurse smiled. "Sure." She glanced at his left hand. A reaction he often got from women. "Your daughter?"

Amber piped up, "He's my uncle. He's never been married and he's pretty dumb about babies. Not my dad though. He raised me all by himself since I was that big." She pointed to Declan. "Why do all the babies have hats? And why are their blankets wrapped up so tight?"

The nurse and Amber moved closer to the window. "Hats keep them calm and help them to sleep. They aren't used to air yet. Until they're born they live in warm water, so air takes some getting used to. They feel safe and cozy in a tight blanket, like someone is holding them."

Amber frowned and glanced at Cluny. "Maybe you'd sleep better if you wore a hat, Uncle Cluny. Have you ever tried that?"

Taken off guard by this kid who had a habit of throwing curve balls, Cluny shuffled his feet when the pretty nurse gave him a questioning look. "Maybe I'll try it."

"You can't sleep?" the young woman asked.

"A little insomnia, that's all." He took Amber's hand. "We'd better get going. Queen's been waiting in the car long enough." He nodded at the nurse. "Thanks."

"Sir?" The nurse hailed him, took a business card from her pocket and scribbled something on the back then brought it to him.

He read the card, saw that she'd written her phone number on it, and grinned. "Thanks."

A few steps down the hallway, Amber whispered, "You should go back and ask her for a date. She's pretty. She likes you."

"Are you sure you're only eight?" He shook his head. "I'm not in the market right now, okay?" Finding women was a problem he'd never had. His pal Dwayne teasingly compared him to a busy honeybee, bent on pollinating every flower in the garden. Keeping a woman? That was another story.

He'd curbed his social life dramatically the past several months since the nightmares had revved up. After his service in Iraq ten years ago, he hadn't spent an entire night with a willing woman, couldn't risk falling asleep. He'd had it with crawling out of a warm fragrant bed, leaving a soft compliant woman in the middle of the night.

Raised to be a gentleman, he'd never ask a woman to leave after sex, so he couldn't invite one home with him. Would he ever have a normal life, a family, kids?

"Let's stop by your house and get what you need for our sleepover and the beach. We'll go by Subway and pick up sandwiches to take with us, okay?"

"Okay." She grinned and skipped next to him. "I haven't been to the beach all summer."

He pushed through the lobby doors and into the parking lot. "Summer just started. Your dad and Marla will be busy with the baby for a few weeks, but I'll take you to the beach as often as possible."

She grumbled, "I can help them with the baby, you know, I'm big enough."

"That you are. I'm sure the boss lady's glad school is out. She'll need your help from now until it starts again. While your dad's taking a couple of weeks off to help her, let's you and me have some fun."

"Why do you call Mom the boss lady?"

He smiled at the memory. "Because she hired me and your dad to renovate the apartment building where Miss Emmaline lives, and she and Gunny argued every day over who was boss."

Cluny smiled when Amber put on her thinking face. He opened the car door, and she hopped into the passenger seat, dislodging Queen to the back. He got in on the driver's side and started the engine.

"Mom and Dad take turns being boss now. He's the boss of work and she's the boss of home. I used to be the boss of Dad before they got married."

"I know. A pretty big job for a girl, don't you think? But you can keep being my boss as long as you don't try to run my love life. Is it a deal?"

"I did a *rilly* good job running Daddy's love life, *dint* I? I told him I wanted Marla for my mom, and then he *finally* figured it out." She cast a sly look.

Two blocks later, Cluny was still laughing.

Chapter Four

Saturday, Zuma Beach

GRACIELLA RAISED A HAND TO SHIELD HER EYES WHEN SHE heard a man's voice hailing her from the far edge of the parking lot. A brown-haired girl about Santos' age, holding a battered foam belly board under her arm, trudged beside Cluny McPherson. He carried a blanket, and a small cooler. A couple of beach towels hung around his neck. His dog followed close beside him.

"Hi!" She waved back, happy to see the tall, quiet man again, and wondered about the slender young girl. Holding hands cupped around her mouth, she turned her head to the surf and yelled, "Santos!"

Her son hopped over a small receding wave and dodged through a number of teenagers playing no-net volleyball, to their umbrella as Cluny and the girl reached them.

"Macfearsome! You came back. Hi, Queen." He dug his toe in the sand. "Hi," he said to the girl, lowering his eyes.

She wrinkled her freckled nose and said, "That's not his name."

Cluny plopped his big hand on Santos's head. "You know what? I kinda like it, buddy. This is my goddaughter, Amber Dempsey. Amber, this is Graciella Jefferson and her son, Santos."

Graciella smiled at the girl. "Won't you join us?"

"Are you friends with Uncle Cluny?" She plopped down. "He comes to the beach a lot because he isn't married and doesn't have any kids and his plumbing company is on vacation, but this is the first time I got to come all summer. My mom just had a baby yesterday. His name is Declan. I'm his big sister because we have the same dad. Not the same mother though."

Graciella smiled at her son's drop-jawed expression. "Why don't you and your uncle spread your blanket next to us?"

"He's not *rilly* my uncle. I just call him that. He's my daddy's best friend from when they went to school and the Marines, and he's my godfather, but not the bad kind."

"Yes, Cluny McPherson is a new friend of ours, right Santos?"

The boy nodded, glanced briefly at Amber and said, "He let me pet his dog."

Cluny removed Queen's vest. "Want to play, Queen?"

Amber jumped to her feet and grabbed her belly board. "Queen likes to chase me when I'm skimming. Want to go?"

Heart squeezing when a brief flash of fear sparked in her son's eyes, Graciella said, "Santos doesn't know how to skim, Amber. Why don't you teach him?"

"It's easy. Come on." She and Queen raced for the water.

Santos hesitated, his brown face flushed. "Okay." He trotted after them.

Cluny shouted, "It's fun, Santos. Give it a try!" He sat next to Graciella. "Is he afraid of the water? I noticed before that he never goes out past his ankles."

"Yes. He's dying to go deeper, but so far he hasn't worked up the courage. Maybe now that he's got competition from a girl he'll overcome his fear." She watched the two children. "Will you get in trouble for letting Queen run on the beach without her leash?"

"If somebody complains, I'll put the service vest back on her. Why is Santos afraid?" Cluny's sunglasses were propped on the bill of his baseball cap today, and she noticed the contrast between the startling blue color of his eyes and his heavy black eyebrows. Not handsome in the classical sense, his angular face was masculine and quite attractive. She wondered why he wasn't married.

"When he was about three he got knocked over by a wave and

dragged under in the rip current. I ran and pulled him out. He screamed when he got the water coughed up, and has been extremely cautious ever since."

"Was he hurt?"

"No, just scared. I made light of it, but he was more frightened than I thought at the time."

"He'll get past it. Maybe playing with Amber and Queen will do the trick." He pulled his baseball cap lower releasing a fringe of black curls at the back of his neck. "Look at that dog." He laughed and pointed when Queen bounded into the surf.

"She swims like a seal."

"Didn't I tell you she's a retired Navy SEAL? She loves the water."

"Yes, I remember. What a beautiful animal. Santos would so love to have a pet." She shook her head regretfully, watching her son hop and laugh with a mixture of excitement and fear.

"Look, Graciella. I'm glad the kids are playing. I wanted to talk to you about something important."

What could this man want to talk about? They barely knew each other. Cluny shifted, raised his knees, rested on his forearms, and dangled his hands, much like she observed the past two weeks when he sat alone by the Point Dume rocks. "I may have met your husband in Iraq, Marv. Marvin, right?" His gaze locked on hers.

Shocked, she said, "You knew him?" Either this was a great coincidence, or Mr. McPherson had come up with a new and clever line. As attractive as he was, she wasn't interested in any kind of a man-woman relationship. She had her hands full with Santos and her business. Putting food on the table and getting him educated were her top priorities.

———

Cluny stared at the ocean horizon beyond the water. "Yes, I think so." Lips sucked against his teeth, he gazed at the surf, watching the kids. He raised a finger and traced it diagonally across his left eyebrow. "Did he have a thin scar here?"

Graciella stopped breathing. The pulse in her throat thudded so strong she felt and heard the swoosh and hiss of blood pumping in her ears. The photo Santos had shown Cluny was taken far enough away that Marvin's scar wasn't visible. She hadn't noticed the scar herself the first time they'd met.

She gasped. "Yes, he did. It was barely noticeable."

"If he hadn't been leaning right in my face I'd never have noticed it." Cluny sighed and shook his head.

She saw what she thought was a flash of regret in his expression. Hand on her chest, she asked, "What was he doing?"

"Shaking me. Slapping and yelling, trying to determine if I was still alive."

"*Deus!*" Were they fighting?

"He shot the Iraqi who nearly killed us in Fallujah. The first bastard's RPG hit our Bradley, and took off part of my buddy's leg. I got off a lucky shot and killed that one, but when the second one raised the launcher I was in shock from my head wound and temporarily deaf. If it wasn't for Marv we'd all be dead."

He sighed. "Amber's dad was the Marine who got his leg shot off."

She took a breath, touched his arm and blinked back threatening tears. "I don't know what to say."

Cluny hung his head and remained silent.

"When was that? That fire fight where Marvin saved you?"

"Operation Phantom Fury, November, 2004." He stared at the horizon. "I heard Marv got killed shortly after in an ambush on his sniper position atop a bombed-out building. Graciella, I'm really sorry." He turned away, but not before she saw his trembling lip.

Sitting next to her on a warm summer day at the beach in Malibu was a man who wouldn't be alive today but for her husband. The little girl playing in the water with her son might never have been born but for her husband. What a strange and unlikely series of events had brought her and Cluny McPherson together.

"I...I don't..." Words wouldn't come. She reached for a beach towel and pressed it to her face. His strong, callused hand rested lightly on her shoulder.

"I'm sorry, Graciella. I felt I owed it to Marv to tell you how grateful I am. It was a one in a million chance that you and I would ever meet. I don't know why we met except for this. My goddaughter wouldn't be here today if it weren't for Marvin Jefferson."

She rubbed her face with the towel and cleared her throat. "I'm glad you told me. I want Santos to know your story. He's desperate for details about the father he never knew."

He moved his hand from her shoulder. "I'd like to tell him, but not when Amber is around. Dwayne doesn't talk specifics about the war with her."

"Perhaps you could come to our apartment for dinner one evening. Where do you live?"

"Spring Grove. My business is in Simi Valley."

"That's not far. We live in Chatsworth, just the other side of the mountain pass." She raised her arm. "Oh, look."

Santos bobbed in water up to his waist, jumping and splashing with Amber who was showing him how to catch a wave and flop on the board to ride it in. Queen paddled next to them, barking encouragement.

"I'll be damned. I bet he manages to catch one."

As they watched, Amber gestured and shoved the board to Santos. He flopped on top with a terror stricken face and hung on for dear life. Screaming with excitement, he caught the small wave and rode it until the board jammed to a stop in the wet sand. Queen flopped down next to him.

The kids laughed, rolled in the shallow water, got to their feet and raced toward the picnic blankets. Queen shook herself and bounded after them.

"Mama, did you see me?" Santos shouted, stumbled and fell face down on the blanket then came up exuberant.

Amber dropped the board and sat. "He did it, Uncle Cluny. I taught him how to do it."

Cluny handed her a towel at the same time Graciella tossed one to Santos. "Yes, you did. It looks like so much fun," she said.

Her boy scrubbed his face with the towel and grinned at her with his father's winning smile. Her heart overflowed with love at the happiness on his face.

"I wasn't scared, either. I was brave, like my dad."

"Yes, you were."

Santos faced Amber. "You wanna see a picture of my Dad?"

"Show her later, son. I bet you kids are hungry by now."

Amber said, "I'm starved. Where are the sandwiches? Queen must be thirsty and hungry, too."

———

Cluny dragged the cooler closer and reached for the sandwiches. "We'll remedy that situation right now." He held up two sandwiches. "Who likes pastrami with Swiss?" Three hands went up. Cluny laughed and handed over those two sandwiches to Amber and Graciella, and took the last one out of the cooler and handed it to Santos.

"I brought my world-famous *bauru*," Gabriella said. "It's a good thing, too, or you'd be going hungry." His cooler contained only soft drinks and water now.

Cluny raised his eyebrows. "You read my mind and brought my favorite thing?"

The grin on her lovely golden bronze face and feisty sparkle in her chocolate brown eyes as she lifted the hefty wrapped package from her basket sent an unexpected hum of desire and longing through him.

Laughing, she handed him the package. "You don't even know what bauru is, do you?"

"Whatever this world-famous concoction is, I'm sure I'll love it." He removed the waxed paper package from the plastic bag and opened it. "Wow, it's big. I confess my ignorance. What is bauru?" He studied the crusty roll and lifted the top to peek underneath.

"It's a Brazilian sandwich. Hollowed-out French roll filled with roast beef, tomatoes, pickles and oregano, and topped with slow-melted mozzarella. My mother, in Sao Paolo, taught me to make them her special way when I was a girl. Santos loves them."

"It's huge." He turned to the boy. "Were you planning to eat this whole thing by yourself, grasshopper?"

Santos grinned through a mouthful of pastrami and nodded.

"He could eat that and more," Graciella said. "My lanky son has a hollow leg."

"So does my daddy." Amber tapped her left shin. "But he couldn't hide a sandwich in there."

Graciella's cheeks got pink at Amber's innocent comment.

"Yep, old Dwayne has a hollow leg." Cluny winked to reassure her not to be embarrassed.

Santo's eyes rounded when he spoke to Amber, "Your daddy has a hollow leg?"

"Uh huh, his rill one got blowed off in the war." She shrugged and took a big bite of sandwich.

"Did it...?"

To Graciella's apparent relief, Cluny cut him off mid-sentence. "Eat up, soldier. I'm gonna challenge you to a footrace to the rocks and back. Think you can beat me?"

———

Two hours later, Cluny packed up their beach supplies. "I'm taking Amber to her house. We gave Dwayne and Marla some alone time to rest on their first day home from the hospital. By now they'll probably be ready for Amber to take over the baby. And she will, if I know her." He grinned and shook his head.

Graciella rolled her eyes. "I have a sister in Brazil who's seven years younger than me. I know what's in store for that baby boy. Amber will be his third parent, whether he likes it or not."

"You got that right. I offered to bring take-out for dinner tonight. Marla will be back on her feet in the morning, running her household like a battlefield general. She's a terrific woman. My buddy is a lucky guy."

"Amber said you and he have known each other since school days. How wonderful to maintain such a long friendship. Is he from Spring Grove?"

"He was born there, but when he was fourteen or fifteen he and his mother moved to her dad's cattle ranch in Wyoming. That's where we met in junior high school. We're both a couple of *ah-shucks* cowboys at heart."

"I envy you. I left all my friends and family in Brazil when I married Marvin. I have many acquaintances, but the woman I see the most of here is Marvin's younger sister, Krystal. She's a royal pain in the arse, if you'll pardon my unladylike comment."

She smiled when Cluny's eyebrows went up. "I know you've heard worse, Macfearsome. I put up with Krystal for Santos' sake. My Jefferson in-laws love their grandson. He's all they have left of Marvin."

"I don't have any brothers and sisters. Dwayne is like a brother to me. That's why I followed him to California when his dad asked him to take over the family construction business. And by then I was in love with baby Amber."

"Do you work for Amber's father? I'm sorry, I shouldn't be so nosy."

"I don't mind." He stood and brushed sand from his knees. "No, I have my own plumbing company, but we often work on the same projects. I throw some business his way and he reciprocates."

"Do you have something to write on? I'll give you my address and I will make good on that dinner offer."

"No, I don't. Where's your phone?"

"Right here." She dug in her picnic basket and produced her cell phone. When she handed it over their fingers brushed, sending a buzz through him. She quickly looked away. Had she felt it too?

"I'll program in my phone number. Call me when you get time."

Chapter Five

Spring Grove

CLUNY'S HEADLIGHTS GLANCED OFF MISTY BEACHY'S JEEP parked in front of his house when he pulled into his driveway that night. She waved from the top step where she sat under the bright light on his porch.

Cluny dropped the keys in his pocket, strolled up the walk and sat next to her. Queen followed and settled at his feet. "Hey, sweet lips. What're you doing here? It's been months since you last darkened my doorstep." He and the former Marine had history.

"Hey, Mac, Queenie." She leaned in and kissed his cheek. "I'm on my way to work in San Diego after visiting my parents in Portland. Thought I'd stop in, hang out with you, and ask if I could bunk here tonight. I could use some of your TLC."

He put his arm around her shoulders. "You're welcome to stay, but I haven't been sleeping too…"

"The nightmares? Don't worry about it. I'll snuggle with you."

He squeezed her shoulder. "That's what Queen does."

"You help me and I'll help you, my old friend."

"I've missed you, Mis." He stood and unlocked his front door. "Let's go inside. Do you have a bag?"

She tilted her chin at the Jeep. "I'll get it."

"I'll put on the teapot. I could use a cup of hot chocolate. How about you?"

"Sounds good. Be right there."

A couple of minutes later she was back. "I'll put this in the bedroom, Mac. Put lots of marshmallows on mine." She walked through the bare dining room. "Hey, when are you going to put some furniture in here? You have so many empty rooms in this big house, it echoes."

"Come live with me and I'll furnish it any way you like," Cluny teased, and removed Queen's vest. "Looks like you'll be sleeping on the floor tonight, girl." He took oversized mugs from the cupboard and scooped chocolate powder mix into each one.

Misty came up behind him and put her arms around his waist and rested her cheek on his broad shoulder. "How you been, buddy? How're Gunny, Jack and Slim? Anything new?"

"Dwayne and Marla had a baby boy. Named him Declan."

"What happens when the Dempsey clan runs out of D's?"

He laughed. "Could be soon, Marla's twin sister's married to Donovan. They'll be on the baby bandwagon before long, I expect."

"They live around here?"

"No. He's a drill instructor at Kaneohe."

"Sweet duty assignment. He staying in?"

"Looks like."

Misty poured boiling water in the cups while he stirred. "Remember how we used to make cocoa late at night at FOB Fallujah?"

"Yep. We had the chow hall all to ourselves." After piling too many marshmallows on top, he gingerly carried the mugs to the table. "These are too hot. Let's catch up for a while and let 'em cool off." He turned and kissed her. "What kinda trouble you been in lately?" He pulled out a chair for her.

"The usual. I screwed up another relationship. I don't want to talk about it. Tell me how the business is going." She sat across from him at his small kitchen table and reached for his hand.

Queen lapped at her water dish, pushed through the doggie door and ambled outside.

"Business is good. We're closed for another week. I let my guys take vacation at the same time."

"Anybody I know?" She shifted in the chair and yawned.

"I doubt it. They're both ex-military, but one's army and the other's air force. They're good men. I was lucky to find them."

She grinned. "I suspect they were the lucky ones, Mac."

"You're the only person who ever called me Mac."

"It suits you."

"I met a nine-year-old kid at the beach a few days ago." He chuckled. "He calls me Macfearsome. His name is Santos Jefferson. His dad was a SEAL."

"Was?"

Lips pressed tight, he nodded. "Killed outside Fallujah. Around the same time you, Gunny and I bit it."

"Poor kid. He must not remember his dad after all these years."

"Never even met him. Carries his picture around." He shook himself. "Enough about me. How's it working out for you at Customs? What's your assignment?" He didn't ask her about the blown relationship. She'd work up to it and confide in him on her own schedule. Her attractive face carried wounds that only those who'd known her before the deadly battle in Iraq could see. Her right iris was slightly distorted and a small piece of her right ear was missing. Driving a truck in the convoy, she'd been caught in a deadly spray of shrapnel, and hearing in the right ear had been permanently damaged. Vision in her right eye was mostly restored since she'd undergone several eye surgeries. She'd disguised the scar on her shoulder with an ironic tattoo, *I believe in love.* Leave it to Beachy.

"You'll never guess, so I'll tell you. I train sniffer dogs."

"No shit?" He raised his eyebrows and reared back.

"No shit." Misty shook her head and grinned.

"I thought for sure you'd be toting a big weapon and arresting bad guys." Cluny tested his hot chocolate, sucked some marshmallows into his mouth and shook his head. "Still too hot." Misty's brown eyes contrasted with her natural blond hair in a way that stunned every man who'd ever met her. The deceptively feminine appearance hid the toughness underneath.

"Mmm." She rolled her eyes, ecstasy on her face. "Nothing is as good as melted or toasted marshmallows."

He winked. "Nothing?"

"Nope. Not since we parted friends. Slim pickings out there."

Mis closely guarded her feminine softness. He suspected he was one of a very limited number of men who'd been privileged to touch that side of her.

"You always were choosy. How'd I get so lucky?" He took a couple of careful sips of his steaming cocoa. Misty Beachy looked nothing like a battle-hardened soldier. She could have been a cover model. Instead she'd joined the U.S. Marines and served two tours in a combat zone. Nobody messed with her. Master Sgt. Beachy was tempered steel.

"Other guys lied to me. Said they loved me just to get me in the sack. You never lied, Mac. You just said what you wanted, then waited until I was ready to give it."

"You...uh, weren't too lovable as I recall." He cocked his head and smiled.

"Yeah." She huffed out a laugh. "The guys at the forward operating base weren't talking about the latest Japanese sports car when they called me Misty Bitchy behind my back."

He pointed his finger at her nose. "You always out-manned the men. That pissed them off."

She flipped her hand, dismissing his comment. "They were pissed because you were the only soldier I ever let crawl into my bunk, and you wouldn't yap about it later."

"Yeah, it drove 'em nuts." Cluny remembered those days at the base in Iraq. Most female soldiers stationed there built invisible *don't touch* barriers around themselves, but a few had a *come-and-get-it-boys* policy. Ironically, tough talking, untouchable, MSgt. Beachy took him to her bed. He'd paid for the rewards of those hot, war-desperate nights in her billet with endless hazing from the guys in his unit.

He reached for her hand. "Did I ever disrespect you, Mis?"

"No, Mac. Never." She winked and sipped the rest of the marshmallows off the top of her cup and rolled her eyes again. "You were always the perfect, appropriately grateful gentleman. I loved you for that. I still do."

He squeezed her hand. "You're the only female best friend I've ever had, and I love you for that."

"Mac, come on. I want to talk about you. Share the nightmares. It's been so many years since you got wounded. Is it getting better?"

Beachy was the only person he'd ever completely bared his soul to. Talking to her sometimes gave him a lengthy respite from the PTS, but in spite of therapy, the passing of time, and Queen, it remained a persistent struggle. A struggle that prevented him from getting on with a healthy and rewarding personal life.

"The flashbacks aren't as frequent now, thank God. But I still wake up screaming and reliving that day. I taste the blood and feel the hot sand grinding into my hands. I couldn't hear a thing for days afterward, so I don't know I'm yelling until Queen wakes me. It's a wonder my neighbors haven't called the cops."

"Still not drinking?"

"Clean as a whistle. Ancient history."

"Maybe you need more therapy. They've learned a lot since we were there. The old way was 'Suck it up, soldier,' but they're coming to grips with it now. My grandfather told me he and his buddies were ashamed to talk about it. Some of the old guys are opening up, sharing their wartime experiences, because they see their sons and grandsons with the same invisible scars."

"Christ, I'm so sick of therapists. Endless talking doesn't cut it. What scares me most is the thought of spending the night with a woman and waking up screaming."

Misty reached across the table and squeezed his hand. "Mac, there's a woman out there for you. She'll love you, she'll accept it, and she'll work with you. Don't give up. You're worth it. When you find her, she'll be the lucky one."

He nodded, squeezed back. "I want to get married. Have kids."

She sat back and stared at him. "With me!"

He nearly choked. "Heaven forbid."

"Good. You startled me for a minute. I thought you were going soft in the head." She sipped the hot cocoa. "So, who's the lucky lady?"

"Wish I knew." He reached under the table to pat Queen's head. "Nobody on the horizon."

"What say I take a shower?" She stretched. "It was a very long drive today and I'm totally wiped."

He grinned. "I'll turn on the TV. We can cuddle on the couch and watch a shoot-em-up, blow-em-up war movie."

"I need a shoulder to lean on, Mac."

"I've got two of 'em."

He carried their half-full mugs to the sink. "Bedtime, Queenie. I'll be snuggling with a different girl tonight."

Cluny followed Misty's perfect ass to the bedroom. "What say we take a shower together for old time's sake?" They weren't a couple any longer, but that didn't mean he was any less of a man. A man with a perfect memory.

"Very funny." She peeled off her shirt. "Go find a good movie."

Not surprised at her answer, he laughed and went to the living room and turned on the Military channel.

———

Sunday morning

Cluny woke on his big sofa completely rested. He'd slept straight through the night, wrapped in Beachy's arms. Not a single nightmare. "Mis?"

She called from the kitchen, "I'm making coffee. Go take your shower. I'll have breakfast ready when you're done."

Stretching, he smiled and hit the shower.

The smoke alarm blared at the same moment he turned off the water. He bolted out of the bathroom, dripping wet, and ran to the kitchen. "Jesus, what are you doing? Trying to burn down my house?" He stood on tiptoe and switched it off. Water puddled on the floor at his feet.

"I scorched some bacon." She grinned and pointed the spatula at him. "You're a magnificent specimen, Mac, but turn around now and find a bathrobe or put on some clothes. I have my limits." She turned back to the stove.

"You didn't always." He embraced her from behind. "Thank you for the best night's sleep I've had in way too long." He nipped her earlobe.

"You're entirely welcome, but you're getting me wet!" She shrugged him off. "Now beat it. These pancakes are getting cold."

He returned to his bedroom, dried off, and dragged on a pair of shorts, showed up at the table, and was quickly ordered to get a shirt. "When did you get shy?"

"Like I said, I have my limits."

He looked around the kitchen. "Where's Queen?"

"I unlocked her door and let her out. I fed her too. Now, I'd like to feed you and be on my way. I have another long drive today. Shirt!"

Cluny stood at attention, saluted, cast a snarky grin her way and said, "Yes, ma'am, Master Sergeant, ma'am."

"And don't you forget it." She poked his bare chest.

Misty's pancakes were as delicious as he remembered. Even the burned bacon tasted good. He grinned through a big mouthful.

She glared. "Don't you dare speak until you swallow. I can't believe you're turning into such a slovenly pig. You need to find a full-time woman to shape you up. That's an order."

"Hey!" He stared at her. "You want to drop in on Dwayne and Marla before you take off?"

"Nah. I gotta get on the road. I'll catch up with them at the reunion in July. Tell them I said, hi." Misty stabbed the air with her fork and smirked. "She still got that ring in Gunny Dempsey's nose?"

"Yep, and he's loving every minute of it. Never saw him happier. You might consider it sometime, if you find the right guy."

"Not for me. The idea of marriage is a total turnoff." She pinched her lips together and shrugged. "Not sure why, but as soon as the *L* word enters the conversation, I'm outta there."

"Too bad, Mis. You'd make some lucky man very happy." He winked.

"Not you, though?" She arched an eyebrow.

"You're one of my best friends. Why would I want to take a chance of screwing that up?"

"You know what? We're weird, Mac. Even if you recorded this conversation, nobody would believe it."

"I don't believe it myself. You show up every so often. No advance notice, just—there you are on my doorstep. We talk, we settle down in front of the TV, we cuddle the night away—you leave." He grasped her hand. "Being your *girlfriend* is not very flattering to my massive male ego."

She squeezed his fingers. "Every time I leave here, Mac, I don't expect there to be a next time. Then here I am, using you again. I'm really screwed up."

"Don't talk about my favorite lady friend like that. You haven't figured it out yet."

She picked up her plate and carried it to the sink. "Time to hit the road."

He carried her duffle to the Jeep, hugged her hard and kissed her forehead.

"You're the only man who ever called me a lady, Mac." She clung to him a few seconds longer than usual, then gave him a shove and punched his chest. "Remember, I've got your six."

"And I've got yours. See you July 4th." He stood at the curb and waved until her car turned the corner and disappeared from sight then murmured a quiet, "Semper fi, gorgeous."

Queen studied him with a curious stare. "Yeah, She's a mystery, huh, Queenie? Maybe I imagined the last twelve hours. Want to go for a run?"

His cell phone vibrated and he grabbed it. *Graciella Jefferson.* He felt guilty, but why should he? Nothing had happened. Misty was his pal.

———

Graciella had mixed feelings about whether she should call Cluny or not and was surprised when he answered on the first ring. "G'mornin,' Graciella."

She smiled when he pronounced her name correctly. Few Americans could get their tongues around it. "I hope I didn't wake you. It's still kind of early." Unbidden, she imagined how he'd look first thing in the morning. Rumpled curly black hair, beard growth, blue eyes smoky with sleep, bare chest? She shook herself.

"Nah, I slept in 'til seven this morning. I'm usually up about four.

So, no, it's not too early. How are you?"

"I'm fine. I called to ask if you'd be free to have dinner here with me and Santos tonight. I should have given you more notice."

"Hey, I'd love to. What time?"

His quick answer caught her off guard. "Six?"

"What can I bring?

"Just bring yourself. Our complex doesn't allow pets, so you'll have to leave Queen home."

"She'll be perfectly happy with a pan of water and a chew-bone in my car. She'll sleep the entire time I'm away. Don't worry about Queen. Are you sure I can't bring something? Wine?"

"Bring some if you like, but I don't drink."

"What a coincidence, neither do I."

"Are you just saying that?" The man probably didn't want to put her in the awkward position of explaining why she didn't drink.

"No, it's the truth. Alcohol hasn't passed my princely lips for over eight years."

She laughed. "You're teasing me. But if you're not, you can elaborate on it later."

"Why don't we get it out of the way now? While I was recovering from my head injury I started drinking too much. Amber's dad thought I was on my way to becoming an alcoholic, so he smacked me into shape and we made a pact: He'd never drink again if I didn't." He laughed. "I think Gunny spends more time explaining why he doesn't drink than I do. What's your excuse?"

"It makes me throw up." Here was a man who didn't drink and had no qualms about telling her why. She wanted to know Cluny McPherson a lot better. "Is that a good reason?"

"Excellent reason. I'll knock on your door at six. Tell Santos he and I will take Queen for a walk after dinner. She'll like that."

"Oh, he will, too. See you then." She clicked off. Suddenly excited, she didn't know where to start. She had a rough idea what she wanted to serve for dinner, but now she'd have to make sure she had what she needed.

"Santos! Are you finished dressing? We have to go to the *mercado piexe* for some fresh camarao. Macfearsome is coming to dinner."

"Camarao malaqueta, Mama?"

"Of course, it's your favorite." She jingled her car keys. "Ready?"

They drove to Rosarito Fish Market in San Fernando where she pointed to a large tray of shrimp behind the glass counter. "Is it fresh this morning?"

"Si, señora. We got these fat beauties an hour ago. How much you want?"

"Two pounds." She turned to Santos. "Go to the baking section and get a large brick of chocolate and a bag of sprinkles."

His eyes lit. "Are you making brigadeiros?"

"No, you're becoming a good Brazilian chef. Your brigaderios are just as good as my mama used to make. Now go. We have a lot to do before Mr. McPherson gets to our house tonight."

They carried their purchases to the car and Graciella put the shrimp in a small cooler. She wrapped the chocolate in a blanket. Next, they headed to a carniceria nearby. The only meat market specializing in Brazillian cuts of beef had closed, but the Mexican butcher would do. They left with a heavy package of steak. She added it to the shrimp in the cooler and returned home.

She put Santos to work on the brigadeiros, then swept quickly through their small apartment to make sure it sparkled. Why she thought Cluny would notice a little dust or stack of newspapers and magazines was silly. Men didn't notice such things. For some reason she wanted everything to be perfect for him.

"Santos, when you finish with the chocolate balls, why not find the photo album Grandma Jefferson made for you? You can show Cluny your pictures of Marvin when he was growing up."

Her adorable son grinned and stirred the melting chocolate in the double boiler. He was absolutely her pride and joy. Her reason for living. She planted a quick kiss on his head, then arranged the spices to prepare the shrimp and steak seasoning.

At six on the dot her doorbell rang. She put down a potholder and started for the front door.

Santos ran to answer. "Mom! Macfearsome is here!" He opened the door, and Cluny stood there holding a bouquet of mixed flowers. Santos grinned. "Are those for me?"

"What do you think?"

"Mom! Macfearsome brought flowers for you!"

Chapter Six

Cluny grinned at Graciella strolling to the door.

"Don't yell, son. You know I can hear you in every corner of this apartment." She returned his smile and reached for the bouquet. "Thanks. You shouldn't have."

He handed them over. "Why do women say that whenever men bring flowers?" She had her riotous curly dark brown hair piled on top her head giving the illusion that she was almost as tall as he. A few wisps had escaped at the back of her slender neck, and over her ears. If she looked this good the night Marv had walked in to that club in Sao Paolo it was no wonder he'd married her and whisked her away.

Her warm brown eyes glittered devilment. "Don't you know our mothers taught us to be wary of a man bringing flowers? It usually means they're guilty of something. So, are you, Mr. McPherson?"

"Am I what?"

"Guilty?"

He grabbed his chest, feigning shock and indignation. "Me?" For a split second he thought of last night with Misty, and actually did experience a tiny twinge of unearned guilt. "I'm extremely guilty of too many things to list. You name it, and I'm probably guilty of it."

From the corner of his eye, Cluny caught Santos, standing at his elbow listening intently, plainly wondering what this was all about. It was about playful flirting, but the kid didn't need to know. His mother was beautiful and sexy, and for some reason she wasn't hiding it from Cluny this evening. She had him turned on and seemed to enjoy every minute of it.

Santos asked, "What did you do?"

He gazed into the boy's eyes with the solemnity of a priest. "It would be ungentlemanly for me to say. You'll have to ask your mom later."

She broke the spell when she laughed and threaded her fingers through the springy black curls on her son's head. "Mr. McPherson is joking, Santos. He didn't do anything."

The boy pushed a loud exhale through his nose. "I don't get grownups sometimes." He looked out the still open door. "Where's Queen?"

"She's sleeping in the car. We'll take her for a walk after dinner, buddy. She said she was excited to come and see you tonight."

"Are you teasing me again?"

"Yep." He landed a fake punch on Santos' bony shoulder. "She's in the car, but as smart as she is, she hasn't learned to talk yet."

Graciella reached behind him to close the door. He caught a faint whiff of her hair. A warm spicy scent drifted around her. "That's nice."

She eyed him over her shoulder. "What's nice?"

"You smell good. Is it okay for me to say that?"

"Of course." She grinned. "Come in and sit down. Santos has some photos to show you while I put the finishing touches on dinner."

"Come on, Macfearsome." The boy tugged his arm. "Over there." A red photo album lay on the coffee table between glasses of sparkling water and a small plate of bruchetta.

Reluctant to take his eyes off Graciella as she sniffed the flowers and carried them into the kitchen, he turned his attention to Santos. "What have you got here, my man?"

Graciella held a vase under the faucet, added water then arranged the flowers. Her heart had skipped a beat when Cluny gave her the flowers. She shook herself. It was just a friendly gesture, or was it more?

41

Santos had set the kitchen table earlier, as he'd been taught when much younger. Their small apartment had no formal dining room, but the spacious kitchen, once she dimmed the lights over the cooking area, made presentation for their guest very pleasant.

She went about her task as quietly as possible in order to eavesdrop. Santos described each picture in his album as they went through it page by page. Cluny expressed appropriate interest and asked questions of her son as if the album were as important to him as to Santos. He had demonstrated his decency in every word and gesture since they'd met him. Still, she remained cautious, conflicted about involving herself in a relationship.

The only men who'd been in her apartment the past several years were the complex maintenance man and her father-in-law, Earl and his old buddy, Chief Williams. Hearing Cluny's deep voice, asking and answering questions, sent a warm buzz of comfort coursing through her. She'd never fooled herself into thinking that she was capable of providing the rounded parenting her son needed. He should have the influence of men. That was why she encouraged him in team sports and asked him to help her in the samba classes whenever it didn't interfere with school or other activities.

Lifting the lid off one of the pots, she inhaled and rolled her eyes at the familiar fragrance of Brazilian cooking Marvin had loved. It was perfect. She dished up the shrimp and side dishes and set them on the table, next came the steak which she placed on individual plates she'd been warming in the oven. "Dinner!"

Santos ran to the table, and Cluny followed behind, a wide smile on this face, blue eyes sparkling. "If this kitchen smelled any better I might start drooling. What is that? Heaven?"

Santos giggled, "That's what my Dad used to say. Right, Mama?"

She blushed deeply at Cluny's wink.

"You'll have to explain all these dishes to me, Santos. I can't wait to dig in." He went to the other side of the table and held Graciella's chair for her.

"Thank you, Cluny."

The heat of her blush deepened when he leaned close to her ear and said, "You're welcome." He'd been close enough for her to detect his aftershave. The sensation was not at all the same as when she danced with a male student. That was business. Cluny's masculine attention was pure pleasure, and had been missing from her life for a long time.

————

Cluny leaned back and groaned. "What can I say?" He patted first his stomach and then Santos's head. "That was the most delicious meal I've had in years. You outdid yourself, Mrs. Jefferson."

"I'm so glad you enjoyed it. I love any special occasion to cook. Santos did his part. You'll love what he made for dessert."

"I'm full up to here," and held his hand just beneath his nose. "But for Santos, no sacrifice is too great. What did you make, pal?"

The proud expression on the boy's face touched Cluny's heart. "Brigadeiros! My most favorite. Mama let me make them all by myself today."

"I can't wait to try it."

Graciella stood. "It will be better if we wait for a while. Isn't it time for you men to take Queen for that walk?" She locked eyes with Cluny, "and talk?"

Cluny rose and took his plate. "Sounds like a plan. Let's help your mom clear up the table first, okay?"

"No, please. I can accomplish it much faster without stumbling over the two of you. Go. Have your walk." She nodded. "Take your time."

He understood she expected him to use the opportunity to talk to Santos about Marv. About the war. She excluded herself from the man-to-man conversation. He set the plate down. "I never did like to pull KP duty. Let's go, sailor, before she changes her mind."

"What's KP duty, Macfearsome?"

They walked to the front door of the apartment. "Kitchen Police. It's the only part of being a Marine I didn't like." He turned and tilted his head at Graciella before closing the door.

Queen popped up at the sound of his voice when they approached his car. He unlocked the doors, let her out and attached the leash to her collar. "You hold her while I check her water." Reaching low, he lifted the nearly empty stainless steel pan from the floor of the back seat. "My water jug is empty."

"Over there." Santos pointed to the corner of the building. "Want me to show you?"

"Nope. They don't want dogs on the property, so you stay right here." He made his way to the corner of the building and found the spigot. After filling the empty plastic jug, he carried it back to the car. Santos was on his knees, scratching Queen's ears and talking nonsense to her. Her tail whipped at the boy's attention.

Cluny placed the water in the car and stood. "OK, let's take this lady for a nice long walk. I have some things to tell you."

The boy's head popped up. "You do? About what?"

"Your dad and the war." He walked ahead of them, allowing Santos to hold the leash. Queen wasn't wearing her service vest, so she knew she could enjoy the walk and the boy like a family pet. It always astounded him when she recognized the difference. The dog's intelligence was amazing. That he'd been privileged to acquire her was a blessing he did not take for granted.

He pointed to a vacant lot across the street. "Let's go over there so she can relieve herself. She drank a lot of water while waiting for us."

"Tell me about the war, Macfearsome."

"Santos, I met your father in Iraq. One day while our unit was moving outside Fallujah, we were attacked by a large contingent of..."

———

Forty minutes later he and the boy reentered the Jefferson apartment to the soft sounds of Latin music. When Graciella's eyes questioned him, Cluny pressed his lips together and nodded. Yes. They'd had the talk.

"Did you have a nice long walk with Queen?"

Santos nodded. "Yes. Macfearsome told me about the war and Dad."

She tilted her head and asked him, "Would you like to tell me about it?"

"Not now, later maybe."

"Okay. I set out the brigadeiros. The coffee is ready. Shall we go back to the table?"

Santos smiled solemnly on his way to the kitchen. "Yes. Come and taste them, Macfearsome."

"I'm looking forward to it." He touched Graciella lightly on the back and whispered, "He's fine. A little more grown up, but fine." He'd told the boy as much detail as he felt the child could absorb. At nine, he was entitled to the facts about his dad's navy service, the importance of his actions on the battlefield. He didn't glorify it because there was little glory in war, but he told the truth.

When they reached the table he said, "Santos, my man, this is the respectful way for a gentleman to behave when at the table with a lady. Doesn't matter if it's his mother, wife or sister. Let me show you." He held Graciella's chair. "After all the ladies are seated the men may sit. It's an old Wyoming cowboy custom."

"What if somebody holds the chair before I can?"

"No problem, remain standing until all the ladies are seated." Once her chair was positioned correctly, he let his fingers trail across her back when he moved to his own seat. He eyed the platter of good-sized balls of chocolate, some coated with chocolate sprinkles and others with coconut or colored sugar. "Your brigaderios? You're teasing me, you bought them. They look perfect."

Santos grinned and nodded. "I really did make them."

"Without help from your mother?" The kid's proud face lit up the room.

"Uh, huh. I learned how when I was eight, and got tall and didn't have to stand on a chair to reach the stove. Before then Mama said it was too dangerous for a child, but I'm big now." He reached for the platter and passed it to Cluny. "Take one of each and tell me what you like the best."

Cluny used the small tongs on the platter to place three balls on his dessert plate. "May I have more than three?"

"Yes, but you can't eat that many, I betcha."

"Is that a challenge?"

Graciella chuckled. "Would you like some coffee, Cluny? It's decaf. I don't drink regular coffee this late." She held an insulated pot.

"I'd love some. I'm a decaf man myself." She filled his cup. He said, "Thank you. Is he right about not eating more than three?"

"I am right, huh, Mama?" Santos placed two chocolate balls on his own plate. "I made extra for you to take home, Macfearsome. The box is in the refrigerator. Don't forget to take it when you leave."

"No chance in that happening." He started to reach with his fingers then pulled back his hand and looked to Graciella. "Fork or fingers?"

"Your choice. There's only one rule. Enjoy." She reached for the platter and placed a coconut covered confection on her plate then picked it up in her fingers and nibbled. She made a soft humming sound and rolled her eyes. "Santos, these are your best ever."

Cluny tasted the candy and sighed. "I've been completely spoiled here tonight. The first thing I'm going to do when I get home is kick down my kitchen."

They laughed at his joke and exchanged inconsequential table talk while enjoying the treat. He noted Graciella had poured coffee for her son, who then added a generous amount of cream and sipped it with aplomb. Must be a Latin custom, Cluny thought. He tipped his head in the direction of the stereo. "Is that samba music?"

"Mom!" Santos blurted.

"I'm right here, son."

"Mom, why don't we teach Macfearsome to samba? He told me he only knows the cowboy two-step."

"Is that right?" She smiled. "We'll remedy that cultural gap when we're finished here. You game, Mr. McPherson?"

"Oh, I'm game, ma'am." He was tickled when she got his double meaning. Her cheeks pinked and he warmed low in his belly. They finished the chocolate with little conversation.

———

Graciella cranked up the music and Santos nearly doubled with laughter watching Cluny try to imitate his subtle movements to the rhythm of the beat. "You're all stiff, Macfearsome. Do it like this."

"I would if I could, buddy, but I'm not as loose in the hips as you are." He shook his hands and tried again.

Clumsy in his attempt to follow her son's lead, Graciella enjoyed the big man's effort. Tall, slim and strong, he had trouble relaxing enough to do the foreign movements with grace. A good sport, he seemed to be enjoying it, wearing a big smile the entire time.

"Here." She stepped in front of him. "Let me help. Relax your back and shoulders." She put her hands on his hips and gave him a good shake then directed his movements. He loosened a bit beneath her light touch and was making progress when she suddenly stopped and stared over his shoulder. She snatched her hands away from him.

Cluny turned to see what had startled her.

A willowy young woman stared at them, shock and outrage on her flawless face.

"Krystal," Graciella said, hand to her throat. "I didn't hear you knock." She quickly turned down the stereo. "What are you doing here so late?"

"I came to see my nephew." Her glare jumped from Graciella to Santos to Cluny. "I knocked, but it seems you were having so much fun you didn't hear me."

Graciella cleared her throat. "Krystal, this is our friend Cluny McPherson. Cluny, Krystal Jefferson, Marvin's sister."

He extended his hand, but Krystal stared at him, her eyes stony and cold.

"Auntie Krystal, Macfearsome knew Dad. He told me about the war."

"Is that so?"

Cluny's hand brushed Graciella's. "Perhaps I'd better go." He touched Santos' shoulder. "Good night, buddy."

"Mama? Can I go with Macfearsome and say goodnight to Queen?"

"Yes, you may. Thank you for coming, Cluny. We enjoyed your company."

"Good night." He tipped his head at Krystal. "Ms. Jefferson. Come with me, Santos." They left the apartment.

Krystal stared at Graciella. Several seconds passed before she spoke. "Who the hell is the white guy?"

Stomach churning, Graciella clenched her fists and walked toward the kitchen. The insult stung. Krystal resented her for being of

European descent. "I told you, Krystal. He's a friend of ours. It's none of your business, but Marvin and his team saved the lives of several Marines in Iraq. Cluny was one of them. I asked him to tell Santos about it."

Krystal followed her. "I don't want him to hear any claptrap about my brother dying to save a bunch of white guys."

Graciella whirled on her. "He died saving the lives of fellow American soldiers! Not a 'bunch of white guys.' I will not have you poisoning my son's mind with your racial prejudice and rage. I've raised Santos to be color blind, just like his father and your parents. I will not allow you to teach him otherwise."

"He should be educated on the true history of African-Americans in this sewer of a country. Not sold a load of fairytale shit about equality and brotherly love!"

"I'd like you to leave."

"I came to see my nephew."

"Leave now! Do not come to our home again unless you are invited."

The hatred in the woman's eyes frightened Graciella, and not for the first time. At a loss for a solution, she thought again about taking Santos and returning to Brazil. Her son was an American citizen, but she had never completed the process. If she left the U.S. she didn't know what would happen to her veteran's pension or her son's benefits, and she might never be able to return with him to his country of birth.

"I'll leave, but I'm warning you—don't think you can get away with keeping him away from me or my parents." She stormed from the apartment, slamming the door hard. Marvin's parents were nothing like their daughter. They were decent and kind. They never spewed racial vitriol. Leaning heavily against the sink she trembled, and pressed palms to her chest to calm her racing heart.

Chapter Seven

Cluny dumped Queen's water pan in the gutter and snapped on her service vest. She crawled over the console into the front seat while Santos watched with interest.

"Is she working now?"

"Yep. She's back on the job." He shook Santos' hand. "It was good talking to you, sailor. I hope to see you again before too long."

"When I grow up I'm going to be a Frogman like my dad."

"Good for you. He'd be proud. So, would I."

"We might go to the beach again this week. Can you and Amber come?"

"Sure. I have a few vacation days left. Have your mom give me a heads up. I'll see if I can talk Amber into joining us." As if he'd have a chance in hell of going to the beach without her.

The smack of angry footsteps heading in their direction caught the boy's attention. "Uh- oh, Auntie Krystal and my mom must have had another fight." He took an unconscious side step closer to Cluny.

Krystal stopped and grabbed Santos' arm. "You're coming with me."

"No!" He yanked away from her grip.

"Do as I say!" She reached toward him again. Cluny intercepted her hand.

She gave him a murderous look. "Don't you dare touch me!"

"Santos doesn't want to go with you. If you'd like to return to the apartment, we'll ask his mother's permission first. Until then, don't put your hands on him again." Every muscle in his body tensed with anger at the woman's rough handling of the boy. There was no way he'd stand by and let her continue to scare him. He faced Santos. To give him credit, he looked more angry than frightened with his narrow shoulders thrown back and chin thrust forward.

"You'll be sorry you ever got in the middle of our family business, white boy!" She stormed past them to a dark sedan where a big man stepped out of the driver's side door. Cluny watched over the roof of his Pontiac as he held Santos to his side. The boy didn't see the unfolding drama. When Krystal got close to the guy's car, he opened the passenger door, grabbed her by the hair and thrust her inside. In seconds the car roared down the street.

"Whoa." He blew out a breath and shook his head. "What's with your aunt? Why is she so steamed up?"

"I dunno." Santos hung his head and fell back against the car. "I want to go inside with my mom."

Hand on the boy's shoulder he said, "Come on. I'll walk with you."

Santos trudged along beside him. Cluny accompanied him to the apartment where Graciella stood in the open doorway. Her face was full of stress lines and she wrung her hands.

He stopped in front of her and shoved his hands in his pockets. "Anything I can do?"

"No. I'm horribly embarrassed you were caught in the middle, Cluny."

The glimmer of pending tears wrenched his heart, so he joked, "Don't worry about me, ma'am. I'm a Marine." He embraced her in a brief hug and grinned when she pushed back and slapped his shoulder. "I can see you're okay."

She blushed and drew Santos to her side. "We're fine. Thanks for your concern."

He tipped a small salute at Santos. "See you around, bud."

Behind the wheel, he scratched Queen's bony head. "You missed all the fun tonight, girl." There had been fun, but that last ugly scene left him unsettled. Graciella had understated her sister-in-law's personality when she'd told him Krystal was a pain in the ass. If he were a betting man he'd bet she wasn't shooting with a full clip. The woman looked a good ten years younger than Graciella. That meant Krystal Jefferson had been a kid about Santos's age when her big brother, Marv, went off to war for the last time.

It was hard to imagine Santos full of such anger and resentment. A normal, happy kid, it had to be a full time job for Graciella to shield him from Krystal's radical attitude.

———

Monday

Cluny drove to his closed plumbing warehouse the next day and checked his large shop white-board calendar for the coming ninety days. He noted two big new construction jobs he and his crew would be working on with Big D Construction. Those sweet contracts would get him through to the fall with a fat bank account. It was time to hire another plumber to handle the steady stream of small re-models and repair jobs.

He started the computer and signed in to a couple of his favorite websites, VetJobs and JobsMission; posted the help-wanted ad, and then picked up the phone. Marla answered, "Big D Construction."

"Did that slave driver put you back to work already? I'll be happy to come over there and smack him into shape for you, boss lady." Amber chattered and the baby wailed in the background. "Sounds like a circus."

Marla laughed. "We were just leaving. I already had one foot out the door. What's up, Cluny?"

In the background, Amber asked, "Is it Uncle Cluny? Can I talk to him?"

"Here, hand Declan to me and take the phone." Shuffling and squalling noises assailed his ears.

"Hi, Uncle Cluny."

"Sounds like you got your hands full over there."

"Declan is cranky, and I'm getting rill tired of all his crying. Can you take me to the beach?"

"Where's your dad?"

The baby stopped crying amidst murmuring and snuffling sounds.

Amber spoke away from the phone, "Thank gunness." Back to him, she said, "He went to bid on a big job over in Simi Valley. He wants to do a bank job."

Cluny chuckled. "You mean build a bank?"

"Yes. I said that, dint I? Can we please go to the beach?"

"Not today, honey, but maybe tomorrow or Wednesday." He had a few things to get done before his men came back to work. And he wanted to wait until Graciella called him before committing to a specific time with Amber.

"I hope Santos and his mom will be there. I had fun teaching him the belly board."

"We'll see. Do me a favor, sugar. Have your dad call me when he gets back. I need to verify the next job Gunny needs me for. Got that, Madame Secretary?"

"Got it. What? Mom says we got to take Declan home so she can get some rest and put her feet up. I'll tell Daddy."

Cluny locked up the warehouse and moved his 1967 green Pontiac GTO from the carport. Queen claimed the passenger seat next to him. He needed to get to the machine shop to pick up the rebuilt motor for his old power snake.

He turned the music up and patted the steering wheel in time with the beat. After a couple of blocks he pulled to the curb and parked. "Ah, hell. Who am I kidding?" He took his cell out of his pocket and tapped *Graciella* on the contacts list. After several rings it went to voicemail. "Uh, hello, Graciella. Uh, I just wanted to call and make sure you…and Santos were okay…and uh…to thank you for dinner last night. I'll…uh…call you later. Oh, uh…this is Cluny."

What a dope! Of course she knew it was him. Who else was at her house for dinner last night? Inspiration hit him. "Let's find that damn dance school of hers, Queen. If they didn't go to the beach, she's probably working today." He tapped the Google icon and looked for samba schools in the west end of San Fernando Valley. There was one samba school in Chatsworth. He tapped the number.

"Good morning, Rio Samba."

"Santos?"

"Macfearsome?"

"Yeah. Hey buddy, is your mom there?" It made sense, school was out and she'd have the boy with her. Lively Latin music sounded in the background, reminding him of the fun he'd had with them doing their best to teach him how to dance last night.

"She's here, but she's teaching some old people how to samba. You want to come here and get another lesson?"

There was nothing he'd like more than Graciella's hands on his hips and Santos' happy laughter at his two left feet. "I don't know, maybe I'm too old for the class."

"No. I said she was teaching old people. Like you."

Kids. He shook his head and chuckled. Everybody past their teens was *old.* "Okay. It's a deal. I'll be over in about half an hour. You might want to tell her I'm coming in case she's too busy to see me."

"I can teach you if she's busy. She lets me do the beginner class sometimes."

"Okay, I'm on my way, pal." He disconnected, restarted the Green Monster and scratched Queen's chin. "Wanna learn to dance, Queenie? Yeah? Well, let's get going then. Maybe we can get a date at the beach out of this."

The small studio was located in a strip mall on Devonshire Street in what old-time residents called the Roy Rogers part of Chatsworth. The weathered center had a large parking lot, and Graciella's school, Rio Samba, occupied space between a Mexican restaurant and a dry cleaner.

Several laughing middle-aged women exited the studio as he parked his beloved muscle car. Graciella stood in the doorway smiling and chatting as they left. When Cluny closed his door, she waved.

"Bring Queen in. She doesn't need to wait in the car while you're here."

"Thanks." He nodded and opened the door again and motioned Queen to accompany him. "Come girl, you don't have to wait here for me." He grinned and approached Graciella.

"So, you want a samba lesson?" The wry expression on her face told him she didn't believe it for a minute. "Come in. We'll see if we can get those hips loosened up, although I might have more success with Queen if I recall last night correctly."

"You may be right." He suppressed a strong desire to touch her as he passed her in the doorway. "I'm game to give it another shot." His gaze swept the room. One side sported mirrors and the other a large gallery of photos and posters depicting Carnival in Rio. Scantily clad women wearing massive and intricate headdresses took up most of the space. "Any pictures of you on that wall?"

Ignoring his comment, she rolled her eyes and smiled.

Santos rushed into the large space from the back of the studio. "Macfearsome, you brought Queen!"

Cluny grinned and bumped fists with the boy. "Yep. My best girlfriend goes everywhere with me."

"Can I play with her?"

Graciella laid her hand on her son's shoulder. "It's best if Cluny leaves her vest on while she's here. We don't know who may pop in unannounced. I don't want to scare anybody away."

"She wouldn't hurt anybody! Would she, Cluny?"

"No, but your mom is right. We'll find a time for you to play with her. Maybe we'll go back to Zuma Beach one of these days." He glanced hopefully at Graciella. "Amber's been asking me when we'll go again."

Santos bounced on his toes. "We're going tomorrow, aren't we, mama? You said we could."

"Yes, I did say that, didn't I?" Eyebrows rising, she asked Cluny, "Would you and Amber like to join us?" The ironic tone of her voice didn't escape his notice.

He didn't hesitate for a split second. He'd barely been there five minutes and he'd already accomplished his goal. "Absolutely. I was planning to ask if you'd be going this week. I don't have many vacation days left. I promised Amber we'd get in a couple of trips this week."

"Well, it's settled then." Graciella flipped on the music. "Ready? Let's see if I can eek a little Latin rhythm out of those *gringo* hips of yours. Santos, stand with your back to Cluny so he can copy your moves."

A couple minutes later, Graciella threw up her hands. "I'm beginning to think you're hopeless. Change places with me, son. Watch us and see how Cluny does." She turned her back and reached behind. "Give me your hands."

She placed them on her hips. He couldn't breathe. Hands trembling, he coughed.

"Relax, think of it as an exercise in feeling the beat. Close your eyes and sense the music. Let it take over your chest and legs." She moved beneath his hands. "Follow me. Take a deep breath and let go."

The last thing he wanted to do was let go. With the music—he'd try—with his hands, no way. He did his best to concentrate on her quiet reassurances. If he wanted this to last, he had to control his libido, which seemed to have a mind of its own. He pressed his hands against her and breathed.

"He's doing it, Mama. Macfearsome's doing it."

"Good, good. See, Cluny, it's not hard."

Not yet, due to my amazing willpower. "I'm trying to concentrate on the music. I'm feeling it." Then he relaxed and smiled past Graciella's shoulder at the grinning boy. "Hey, buddy, maybe I'm not a hopeless white boy after all."

She stiffened. "I think we've made a good start. That's enough for today's lesson."

He'd have given the world to take back the words. "Graciella."

"Santos, would you fetch my handbag from the back? It's time to go home for a lunch break."

"Okay." He scampered to the back of the studio.

"Graciella, I'm sorry. I don't know why I said that. It popped out. I feel like a moron."

Santos came back, holding her bag out. "Here it is."

She took it and faced Cluny. "We have to leave now. The studio re-opens at two."

"Let me pick you up tomorrow. I'll bring the van. There's plenty of room for the four of us and anything we need to bring. Please."

"Oh, boy!" Santos' innocent eyes widened. "That sounds like fun. What time should Macfearsome and Amber come tomorrow?"

Clearly torn as to what her answer should be, Graciella shifted her feet and pushed the strap of her large cloth bag higher on her shoulder.

Cluny jumped in. "How about ten thirty? I'll bring lunch. Amber has an extra belly board Santos can use." He put on a sincere face and pleaded with his eyes. Jesus, he prayed, please, I didn't plan to spoil whatever this could be with a thoughtless comment.

She gazed deep into his eyes. "All right. We'll be ready at ten thirty. I'll supply the beverages. We really do have to leave now."

Relief flowed through him at the bullet he'd managed to dodge. "Great. Good. Come, Queen." He held the door of the studio for them and waited while she locked it. He murmured a soft, "Oh, ah, I left a dumb message on your home phone. Sorry."

"What's Macfearsome sorry about now, Mama?" Santos' childish question trailed behind them and hung in the suddenly suffocating air surrounding Cluny. He couldn't make out her answer.

———

She shouldn't have had such a silly knee-jerk reaction to Cluny's playful comment. The ugliness of last night's scene with Krystal slammed her full force. She was reaching an impasse with her sister-in-law. Krystal grew more strident in her racist comments every time they encountered her. She'd been avoiding Lillian and Earl for the past few weeks because she didn't want to encounter Krystal. Her sister-in-law's schedule was erratic and Graciella was never sure when she'd be at her parents' home. She'd call Lillian and invite them to have dinner with her and Santos.

Santos' happy talk about the planned trip to the beach didn't end until he took his first bite of lunch. "Aren't you eating, Mama?"

"I'm not very hungry. I'll have a piece of fruit and a glass of milk. That'll hold me until dinner time."

Should she have agreed to go to Zuma tomorrow? Her heart told her Cluny McPherson was interested in more than a trip to the beach, and that was a dead end. She liked him. Liked him more than any man she'd met in years. Often, decent men she met would show an interest and invite her for dinner, but she always turned them down politely, and with the unmistakable finality that she was unavailable. Some of those men she would have welcomed as friends, but true friendship between a man and a woman? A rare creature, a modern day fiction, to be sure. Why take the risk? She'd set Cluny straight tomorrow.

"Mama, why was Auntie Krystal so mad last night when she saw Macfearsome at our house? She doesn't even know him. I was sad when she was mean to him."

"I don't know. I wish I understood her." She finished her milk. "Time to get back to our samba school. Brush your teeth and see if you can find the CD you're going to use for the kid's class at the end of the week."

She waited until he ran off to the bathroom then picked up her cell phone and called Marvin's parents. "Hello, Lillian? How are you, dear?"

"We're fine, Graciella. We haven't heard from you and Santos for too long. Is everything all right?'

"Yes. We've been busy since school let out for the summer. I'm taking Santos to the beach whenever I can get away from classes. Would you and Earl be free to come to dinner on Thursday evening?"

"Let me take a look at Krystal's shooting schedule this week. I'll see if she's available."

"No...um...Lillian. I'd prefer if you and Earl came alone. Krystal dominates the conversation, and I know Santos wants to visit with you and his grandfather. Tell you about his activities and plans for the summer."

Lillian didn't answer for a couple of moments. "What should I tell Krystal?"

"Is it necessary to say anything?" The way Krystal had bullied her parents unsettled Graciella. Lillian and Earl could make their own decisions.

"She'll wonder where we're going for the evening. She worries about us driving after dark."

More likely she didn't want them out from under her thumb. Lillian and Earl were barely into their mid-sixties, both healthy and robust with all their faculties and abilities intact. Krystal had become more controlling every year since Earl had retired. Graciella sensed the stress in her mother-in-law's voice.

"Lillian, it's only four miles. Earl is a good driver, but I'd be happy to pick you up if you'd like."

"I'm being silly, dear. Of course we'd like to share a meal with you and our grandson Thursday evening. Earl promised him a new fielder's mitt. I'll have him pick one up and bring it. We'll get the men out of the house so you and I can have a gabfest."

"That sounds wonderful. Plan on coming at five. It doesn't get dark until after seven, so that will give them plenty of outdoor time. You can keep me company while I finish dinner."

"All right, dear. We'll see you on Thursday at five. I'm looking forward to it."

"Me too, Lillian."

"Was that Grandma?" Santos held the CD aloft. "I found it. It was in my room."

"Grandma and Grandpa are coming for dinner on Thursday."

"Grandpa promised to take me to a Dodger game this summer. He said it would be men only, no women allowed."

Graciella chuckled. "I suspect he doesn't want me to see all the junk the two of you will be eating all afternoon."

Chapter Eight

Tuesday morning debuted with a typical *June gloom* overcast sky. Low hanging clouds blocked out the sun, putting a chill in the air. Cluny shrugged. *Doesn't bode well for a day at the beach.* He pulled up to the Dempsey house and waved at Amber waiting impatiently on the front porch. She waved when he parked the van and hopped off the porch.

She ran to greet him. "DD made Declan laugh this morning."

"Nah. That microscopic mutt makes *me* laugh, but week-old babies don't laugh."

"They do, too. Come in and I'll show you. Anyway, he'd not like a regler baby. He's rill smart." She tugged his hand. "Hurry up."

"You're one bossy little girl."

Dwayne met them at the door with a steaming mug in his hand. "Doesn't look like beach weather."

"What're you doing hanging around the house so late? Still recovering from the birth of your son?" Cluny teased.

Marla's voice called from inside, "Come in, Cluny. He was just leaving. Do you have time for a cup of coffee with me?"

He shouldered past Dwayne, giving him a little extra bump on the way inside. "I never pass up coffee with a beautiful woman."

Dwayne snorted.

Declan reclined in his carrier on the floor next to Marla's feet. She threw her mass of strawberry blond hair over her shoulder and held up the pot. "Amber, would you get Uncle Cluny a cup from the cupboard?"

Cluny smiled at Dwayne's wife. She wore faded yoga pants, bunny slippers and an oversize sweat shirt without a smidgen of makeup on her face. He winked at the sour expression on his old buddy's face and chuckled when she puckered for his kiss. "You can leave now, Gunny. I've got everything handled here."

Amber set the cup on the table. "I'm going to get DD and prove Declan can laugh." She opened the kitchen door and called the tiny mutt.

Dwayne grinned, "You gotta see this."

Amber went to the baby carrier and knelt. She placed DD between the baby's legs, and Marla's Yorkie commenced to lick Declan's chin and hands. First a giggle then genuine laughter poured from the kid's mouth. His fat little body bounced and his arms waved like a signalman on the deck of an aircraft carrier.

Dwayne and Cluny exploded with laughter, startling the infant. He wailed pitifully, and Amber leaned in to him, cooing and snuggling until he stopped.

"I told you, dint I?" Her pixie face screwed up with satisfaction.

"I'll be da...danged." He corrected himself in time to avoid another language scolding from his goddaughter.

Dwayne leaned in to kiss Marla. "Gotta run, honey. I'm only working until two today, so you relax and I'll take care of dinner and the laundry tonight."

Cluny gagged. "You are so whipped, pal."

Dwayne grinned. "Your envy is showing, *pal.*" He grabbed his jacket from the back of the chair. "Walk me to the truck, Cluny. I need to ask you something."

What was that all about? Surely Dwayne couldn't think he had any designs on Marla. He knew better than that. He took his cup and followed.

When they got to the Big D truck, Dwayne turned. His brow wrinkled. "Did you ever meet Ollie Williams?"

"Sure, but it's been a few years, why? He must be retired by now. I know he did more than twenty with the Navy."

"He came to me looking for a job yesterday. Said the wife was going to kill him if he didn't get out of her hair." A smile twisted Dwayne's lips. "Can't say I blame her, a little of Ollie goes a long way."

Cluny remembered the old Navy Chief with the foghorn bellow and gruff personality. "Doesn't he live in San Diego? Why would he be looking around here for a job? How old is he?"

"Can't be more than sixty. He and his wife moved into half of a duplex his son owns in Thousand Oaks. They get free rent for managing the property and sitting with the grandkids after school. The old bastard can fix anything."

"You gonna hire him?"

"I don't need anybody, but aren't you looking to take on a man for routine maintenance work?"

"Yeah, I posted an ad for a plumber. I want to go after more new construction contracts. We can't keep up with the little stuff. We work off customer referrals and I can't afford to jeopardize that loyalty by turning down too much work. But, Ollie? I don't know, man. I might kill him myself."

"I know what you mean." Dwayne chuckled and unlocked the truck. "Think about it. If you want his number let me know. I didn't tell him you were looking, but I think he'd be interested." He pointed up. "Fog's burning off."

Cluny glanced at his watch. "Yep, it's time to round up Amber and get going. I'll think about Ollie and talk to you when we get back today. Am I invited to dinner?"

"Always." Dwayne fired up the engine and put the truck in reverse. "Later."

Back on the porch Cluny gathered up Amber's belly boards and the stack of towels next to them. "Amber! Get a move on. Time to go."

She came to the door carrying Declan. "Just a minute, Mom's on the phone."

He held out his arms. "Let me hold him." He lifted the baby and grinned into his fat little face. "How's it going, scrapper?" The kid looked just like Dwayne except for the red fuzz on his head. His eyes were darker than the day he was born, so maybe they wouldn't stay as blue as his dad's.

Marla reached the door. "Here's Mama." She took him from Cluny and nuzzled his face.

"We're off then," he said. "We'll be back before dark."

"Have fun. Amber, did you remember the sunscreen?" Marla raised her brows. "Make sure she puts on more when she gets out of the water, Cluny. If she gets out of the water."

"Check."

———

"They're here." Santos ran through the front door, holding his towels.

"Oh, no you don't!" Graciella said. "Take the cooler out to the van and come back for those. It's too much for me to carry in one trip."

Cluny entered the apartment. "Tote goat reporting for duty, ma'am." His happy blue-eyed grin melted any tension she'd felt about seeing him again after yesterday's little upset. "I'll carry the cooler."

"You're right on time." She returned his smile and handed over the big ice chest. "I'll get the rest. The blanket and umbrella are still in the trunk of my car." She retrieved her hat and large beach bag, locked the door to the apartment and followed them.

"Where's Amber?" Santos scanned the parking area.

"She took Queen to visit the vacant lot across the street." He lifted his chin in the direction of the van. "There she is." He turned to Graciella. "Everything okay?"

"Yes. I'm glad you twisted my arm to do this." This quiet, big man was good for her. Good for her son. "Santos has been up since the crack of dawn." She laughed. "I worry he might grow up to be a beach bum."

"What this world needs is more beach bums and fewer combat troops. He's a good kid. He'll choose his path. You've done a great job." He loaded the chest into the van through the open back doors. "You kids be sure and fasten those seat belts. Amber, hook Queen's harness to the ring or she'll slide around on that slick upholstery." To Graciella he said, "Sorry. This heap's not very fancy, but it gets the job done."

"You have it for work, right?" Was he worried she'd think less of him because he drove a utility van? "Doesn't need to be fancy, just reliable." He opened the passenger door and held it while she climbed in. "Thank you, Cluny." He'd avoided touching her. She was disappointed because even the brush of his hand warmed her in places she'd ignored for so long she'd forgotten the sensations. What happened to not wanting more than friendship from him?

He held a strong callused hand out to her. "Give me your keys and I'll get the blanket and umbrella from your car."

How would his hand feel on her bare skin? She blinked. "I'm glad you remembered. Between my front door and here I'd already forgotten about it." She dug in her bag and found the keys.

He winked and smiled, sending her heart racing. "Be right back."

She needed to tread carefully here, very carefully. "You kids all buckled up?"

They nodded and grinned back at her. Both of them had a hand on Queen's neck. She'd have sworn the dog smiled.

Cluny tossed the blanket and umbrella in the back of the van. "All set? Did anybody forget anything? Last minute pit stop before we go?"

"Get in, Uncle Cluny. We're ready. We can pee in the ocean."

Graciella grinned at Amber's comment. "Why not? The fish pee in there."

———

Her lighthearted comment wasn't missed by Cluny. Graciella's mood was nothing like yesterday when she'd dismissed him so abruptly. He was curious about Krystal Jefferson and the tension between the two women, but for now he'd avoid the subject and leave her to tell him what she wanted him to know. He wouldn't do anything to change her happy mood.

Amber and Santos talked about baseball. Cluny had encouraged her to join the park league he coached during the summer. Both boys and girls were welcome on the city park teams, and the emphasis was on fun and teamwork. A natural athlete like her father, Amber took to most sports, but she'd been nagging Dwayne to pay for gymnastics camp.

"I told my daddy I wanted to learn gymnastics. He told me it cost too much, but if I got mostly A's in fifth grade he'd pay for gymnastics camp next summer."

"Don't you get A's now?" Santos wondered.

"A'course. I get rill good report cards already. I heard him tell Mom having babies cost a lot of money. I bet that's the rill reason."

Cluny glanced at Graciella. She smiled and pressed her lips together.

He nodded to the distance. "What a sight!" The slopes in front of a hillside home up ahead flared with breathtaking amethyst of blooming ice plant.

Graciella gasped. "When we drove this way a few days ago it had barely started blooming. It takes my breath away. Santos, look to the right. Isn't that something?"

"It's the exact same color as your new bathrobe, Mama."

Cluny's heart raced at the thought of how she'd look in that robe with her smoky golden complexion and brown eyes. Chances were he wouldn't have that pleasure anytime soon, if ever. He needed to get a handle on his attraction to her. The last thing he wanted to do was rush, scare her off before they had a chance to get comfortable with each other. He wasn't sure how far he wanted this to go.

Fifty minutes after they left her apartment he turned into the large parking area at Zuma beach behind a lifeguard tower. "Okay, troops, let's figure out how to get all this stuff to a good spot without making two trips."

He put Queen's service vest on her, and she sat patiently while they portioned out who would carry what. "Atten'hun, for'ard harch!" He took the lead and they followed like a squad of raw recruits until he stopped at a nice flat stretch of sand. "Halt!"

Amber and Santos screamed with laughter, and Graciella shook her head. He snapped out the big blanket, spread it and pointed. "Towels here, picnic basket there, cooler on the other side. Snap to, soldiers."

"You're funny, Macfearsome." Santos set a smaller blanket and towels in the spot Cluny'd indicated and lifted the folded umbrella. "Where should I put this, Captain?"

"That's Sergeant to you, jarhead. Troops are dismissed. Smear on some sunscreen and take Queen for a swim."

They peeled off their T-shirts and stood impatiently while Cluny and Graciella applied sunscreen to their backs and arms then they grabbed the belly boards and ran to the water. Queen barked and galloped alongside them. To avoid a confrontation with the lifeguard, Cluny had waved, pointed to her vest, removed it, and gave her permission to go. You knew summer was finally here when the lifeguard towers were manned from early morning until dusk.

Cluny opened the large umbrella and placed it to give maximum shade on the blanket. Graciella pulled her beach caftan over her head, and his heart nearly stopped at the sight of her in a bikini. Her long slender arms and legs were in precise proportion to her sleek dancer's hips and torso.

Oh, Mama!

He swallowed, took off his jeans and T-Shirt, folded them neatly and set them to the side.

She plopped her big floppy hat on her head and leaned back on her hands. "What a perfect day."

"You got that right." Perfect day. Perfect weather. Perfect spot. Perfect kids. And the perfect woman sitting next to him. It didn't get any better than this.

———

The man had a strong, lean body. The body of a hardworking man who kept himself fit. She glanced sidewise through her dark glasses, hoping he didn't notice her gawking. His well-defined shoulders, chest and belly didn't have an ounce of flab. Cluny dangled his big hands from the raised knees of his powerful legs. She smiled at his big feet.

"You like my big feet?" He grinned. "Caught you looking. Don't be embarrassed. We got that out of the way, now we can relax and enjoy ourselves."

She sat straight. "Okay, just for the record, how big are they?"

"Size thirteen. You could use one of my sneakers for a lifeboat." He winked and pointed at her feet. "Yours are kinda big, too."

Graciella laughed and leaned back on her elbows. "I deserved that, but I'll go to my grave before I'll reveal any statistics." Her cheeks and neck warmed, and it wasn't due to the bright sun.

Cluny shifted, lay on his belly and squinted at Amber and Santos. "He's got the hang of it now. They're having a great time." He dropped his chin on his folded arms. "God, I remember the first time I saw an ocean. It was when Dwayne and I were stationed at Camp Pendleton as a couple of raw recruits. He got a charge out of my reaction. Born in California, it was old stuff to him. We were twenty years old and invincible. We knew everything."

"Cluny, do you have sunscreen on your back?" He had a beautiful, manly back. She itched to touch it.

"Only where I could reach." He rolled his head to the side. "Wanna do the honors?"

Instead of answering him she reached in her tote bag and withdrew a large bottle of SPF 30, knelt next to him and squirted a good-size dollop between his shoulder blades. She hesitated with her hand an inch from his skin, then began to massage the silky lotion over him. Cluny's back felt as wonderfully strong as it looked. She closed her eyes at the sensuous tingle she experienced when he groaned with pleasure. It had been more than ten long years since she'd put her hands on a man like this. She hadn't realized how much she'd missed it until now.

He rolled to his side, reached for the bottle and sat up. "My turn," then reached for her shoulder and pushed gently. She didn't resist and stretched out next to him waiting for the feeling of his big hands on her body.

"Graciella?"

"Yes?" *Oh, my,* his touch was wonderful. "If I ever say or do anything you don't like, please tell me. If you think I'm pressuring you or making you uncomfortable, you have to let me know."

"Okay." She relaxed into the motion of his hands. Was this time for the friends-only talk? No, she'd wait.

"Santos is a great kid. I'd like to spend time with him, invite him to join our park league baseball team. It's not far from your place to Spring Grove Park. Games are on every Saturday all summer. If you can't bring him I'll arrange transportation. I think he'd enjoy it."

She turned her head and smiled into his face. "I think he would too. He spends too much time with me. His grandfather, Earl, makes a point of encouraging him, and takes him to a Dodger game now and then. I'll ask Earl to drive him to the park."

"That would be great! I know you teach classes on Saturdays." He sat back on his heels, snapped the cap on the bottle and dropped it in her bag.

"We'll ask him… if we ever get them out of the water long enough for lunch." Cluny McPherson was a good man. She wondered if he'd ever been married. He had problems sleeping, severe enough problems to require a service dog. Was it some form of PTSD due to his head injury? He'd tell her when they became friends, when he felt he could trust her.

"What did you bring that's cold and wet?" He pointed to the cooler.

"I brought a variety of soft drinks and bottled water. Help yourself."

He dragged the cooler closer and unsnapped the lid. "Oh, my, God! Fanta Orange. I love this stuff. There are two bottles here. Want one?"

Very pleased that she'd brought something he liked, she grinned and shook her head. "No, I'll have a bottle of water."

"Coming right up." He lifted a bottle from the ice, slicked the moisture droplets off and handed it to her.

"Thank you." She held the bottle to her forehead. "It's a hot day for this early in summer." She gazed as he popped the top of the orange soda and downed about half of it. "I should have brought more."

"I'm going to get those two old sand chairs from the van. They're ugly, but we'll be more comfortable while we talk and watch the kids." He stood, dug the keys out of his jeans and jammed an Angel's baseball cap over his hair. "Be right back."

She jumped to her feet. "I'll come with you. We'll be sitting for hours." She strolled alongside him in the hot sun, waving at the lifeguard as they passed. "They get younger every year."

He chuckled. "Seems that way, doesn't it? You must be an old lady of what, thirty? I'll pass the thirty-two mark this fall. Probably start turning gray and needing a cane soon."

She laughed and playfully shoved his shoulder then jogged ahead of him to the edge of the parking lot. He made a fake grab for her as he passed and unlocked the back doors of the van. He grabbed the old sand chairs and locked up.

On the way back to the blanket, Graciella smiled, warm and relaxed. She enjoyed Cluny McPherson. She enjoyed him a lot.

He ducked his head to walk under the umbrella, unfolded the chairs and placed them out of the sun. "Your throne awaits, Mrs. Jefferson. Take a load off."

"Hmm. I'm not sure I like the sound of 'take a load off,' but thank you. This will be much more comfortable."

He sat next to her. "See, that's what I mean. If I say something you don't like, just tell me and I'll watch my mouth." He smiled and gave her the once-over. "I'll find another way to phrase it."

"Relax, I'm kidding and I'm not a fragile princess." She raised an arm in the direction of the water. "The surf is higher than when we came."

"High tide is around noon today. I'll drag 'em out for lunch soon. They should be getting tired." He stretched out his long legs, leaned back, picked up the Fanta can and took a swig. "Dwayne and I used to swill this stuff by the gallon at his mom's ranch in Wyoming when we were teenagers."

"You two spent a lot of time together."

"We were in seventh grade when we met. I lived at the ranch with him and his mother and grandfather from the time I aged out of foster care at eighteen, up until we enlisted right out of UW."

Foster care? A breathless, crushing sensation enveloped her chest. "Did you say foster care?"

"Yep, you're looking at a poor little orphan boy."

"Oh, Cluny, I'm sorry. Was it terrible for you?" She laid a hand on his arm.

He shrugged and smiled. "Nah, I had a couple of good loving families who took care of me. Ranch country isn't like the inner city. Most everybody works hard, prays hard, and spends most of their time outdoors with the animals. I had a good life."

"But what—?" He'd just revealed a powerful fact about his childhood, and she wanted to know more, but was reluctant to ask.

"Both my parents were killed in a winter avalanche when I was six. I didn't have any other relatives except my grandparents in Yellowknife, Canada. They were against my mother marrying my dad and weren't interested in raising a kid they'd never met at their age. So, I went into the foster care system. I was probably better off."

"I'm really sorry."

"I enjoyed my childhood and had a lot of friends. I made the decision early on to be happy. I am."

"I admire that, Cluny. We do have choices, don't we?" Her heart ached for the little boy he'd been.

Screams erupted from the water line. "Help! Help!"

Queen bounded to the blanket, skidded and sprayed sand on them, barked at Cluny and raced back to the water.

"Macfearsome!"

"Uncle Cluny!"

"Help my husband!"

Chapter Nine

CLUNY SPRANG UP AND DASHED ACROSS THE BEACH, HIS BARE feet pounding in the soft sand. Queen circled back and kept pace with him. He stumbled but didn't slow down. Instinct had taken over and he was homed in on the mission.

Amber and Santos hopped excitedly, arms flapping, shouting, they pointed to the water.

"My husband!" a woman screamed again. "Something happened, he's in trouble. Help him!"

Without hesitation Cluny and Queen plunged into the icy cold Pacific. He swam fast and hard through the roaring surf to the struggling man. "Gunny!" Cluny gasped. "Gunny, hang on, I'm coming."

The man went under, surfaced, and then disappeared again. "Gunny!" Cluny screamed frantically and spun in the water.

Surfacing again, the man's arms flailed. He grabbed Cluny's neck and pulled him under. Queen paddled and barked. Finally they came up and she nosed Cluny's face. He turned on his side and struggled against the undertow. Another Marine reached them and took one of Gunny's arms. They had to get him out of there before he bled to death. Between them they got to the shallow water and onto the sand, slowed down by the ankle tether still attached to the broken surfboard. Surfboard? This made no sense.

The other soldier rolled Gunny on his side and signaled a beach buggy with flashing emergency lights approaching from the far end of the parking lot. "Stand back," he ordered, throwing out an arm.

Cluny collapsed to his knees. "Gunny!" Unable to hang on to his balance, he fell forward onto his hands. The sounds of gunfire and explosions assailed him. The sickening coppery stench of blood hung heavy in the air.

"Uncle Cluny!" Amber shook his shoulder. "Uncle Cluny, that isn't Daddy."

He grabbed her at the waist and pushed her onto the sand. "Get down!" She struggled under his weight when he flopped on top of her. "Gunny's been hit. Medic! Where's the goddamn medic!"

The young Marine shouted, "You have to move back, sir!"

"Macfearsome, are you okay?" Santos knelt next to him at the edge of the shallow foamy water. "You're mashing Amber. Get up."

Dazed, Cluny stared at the boy pushing against him. Ears ringing, he blinked and tried to focus. "Santos?" He grabbed the boy. "Are you hit?" Queen barked in his face and butted him. Queen? Where was he? What the hell was happening?

The beach buggy skidded to a stop. One of the emergency crew approached Cluny. The driver assisted the lifeguard who'd helped him rescue the gasping old man who lay convulsing on the wet sand. "Everything okay here, folks? Whose dog is this?"

Lifeguard? Not a Marine, a lifeguard. Cluny squeezed his eyes shut and took a breath. "What?" He pushed himself to his feet and lifted Amber to a standing position. She sobbed and hugged him tight around the waist.

Graciella tugged Santos to his feet and stepped back, her face a wide-eyed mask of shock. "Cluny? Come away from here." She extended a hand. "Come with me."

Instead of reaching for her, he dropped his head back, hands over his ears. "Oh, shit, oh, no." Queen stood on her hind legs, her big paws planted on his chest. "Okay, girl, I'm okay."

"This your dog running loose? Unleashed dogs are not allowed on this beach."

Cluny raised his hands. "Yes, sorry. She's a service dog." He dragged the soggy vest from his pocket and held it up.

Amber took it from him. "I'll put it on her."

"Keep it on her unless you want a citation. Now move away." He turned to the crowd that had gathered, many of them more interested in Cluny and Queen than the swimmer who now sat talking to his wife. "Move away. Emergency's over. Everybody move away."

Amber grasped his hand. "Come on, Uncle Cluny. Let's go."

His head in turmoil, they slowly trudged across the warm sand toward the red-striped umbrella. Graciella and a silent Santos kept pace with them. Cluny sat heavily on the edge of the blanket and dropped his head between raised knees. Graciella draped a towel across his shoulders. "I'll get you some water."

"Did you get hurt, Macfearsome?" Santos bent close and peered at him.

"No, I... uh... I'm fine. I'm not hurt." He reached for the water bottle Graciella held for him, met her eyes, pressed his lips in a grim line and shook his head. "I'm sorry about that. I don't—"

"Drink." She placed a hand on his shoulder and sat next to him then pulled the towel down to cover his back against the blazing sun. Reaching for her caftan, she tugged it over her head. "Do you think we should leave?"

Amber knelt at his side and put her arms around his neck. "I love you, Uncle Cluny. You're so brave." Queen sat on her haunches in front of him. "Queen too." He hugged her tight and buried his nose in her damp salty hair. "Thanks, sugar. We're okay."

"You saved that man, Macfearsome, but you scared me."

———

Graciella patted the spot next to her on the blanket. "Sit here, son, beside me. Let Mr. McPherson catch his breath."

She needed to catch her own breath. Painfully aware now of the reason Cluny needed a service dog, a hard knot formed in her stomach and chest. She knew about PTS, but she'd never witnessed it. Other women at the naval base feared their husbands might return from combat with it. This big strong former Marine, with his quiet upbeat, gentlemanly manners and quirky sense of humor, carried a huge invisible wound from the same war that had killed her husband. Tears welled in her eyes, but she dashed them away and shoved on her sunglasses before he noticed.

She wouldn't cry for Cluny McPherson. He'd see it as emasculating pity. She cleared her throat. "Santos, why don't you and Amber retrieve your belly boards? They must still be down by the water. It's getting late. We should probably be getting home soon."

"We didn't have lunch, Mama."

"After lunch then, all right?"

The children walked slowly away, and she placed her hand over Cluny's. He stared straight at his feet, but didn't rebuff her. She said nothing, because she had no idea what to say. After several seconds, he turned his hand over and squeezed hers. Her heart cracked, threatened to shatter.

His voice barely above a whisper he said, "I can still smell it."

"Smell what?"

"Black powder, smoke, cordite, dirt, shit, blood. Like it just fucking happened."

Shocked at his stark answer she drew in a breath and squeezed his hand. "Tell me about it, Cluny. Marvin talked about war, what could happen. He said it was the only way to stay sane."

"It's been almost ten years. I should be over it by now." He raised his head and stared into the distance, blue eyes tragic and vacant.

"No, Cluny. There is no timetable. Please don't be afraid to tell me about it. Maybe it will help, maybe not."

He put an arm around her shoulders. "I'm afraid to scare you away."

She leaned against him "I don't scare that easy." The kids were on their way back, carrying the battered belly boards. The emergency beach buggy drove away. "I'm going to set out the sandwiches and drinks. We'll talk later."

"I'm taking a walk." He nodded in the direction of the Point Dume rocks. "I'm not hungry. Don't wait for me." He smacked his leg and Queen fell in step beside him.

Graciella's tears threatened again. No, she wouldn't let that happen. She hailed the kids and reached for towels.

His thoughts jumbled, Cluny walked to the far end of the beach, waving off a couple of comments by beachgoers who'd witnessed his actions to save the old surfer-dude. He didn't want to talk about it, and the last thing he wanted to do was accept congratulations. No hero, he didn't deserve congratulations for doing something that had required no thought on his part. An action he had no control over. Thank God for Amber and Santos. They shook him out of it before he ended up decking the lifeguard.

There were only a handful of people in the world who understood what was wrong with him; Dwayne and his family, Misty Beachy, and the former servicemen who worked for him and Dempsey. Queen didn't have the capacity to understand the nature of his *wound*; she just knew how to respond, to help him snap out of it.

A couple of years ago at the jobsite for Marla's condo project, some badasses pulled in the lot on the weekend intent on stealing tools. He, Dwayne, Jack and Slim had caught them in the act. They went after the bastards and their truck with fists and baseball bats. If Gunny hadn't shouted an order for him to *stand down* he could have done serious damage, even killed someone. He was a volcano, rumbling and ready to blow.

Now Graciella had a taste of the real Cluny. What did this mean for the possibility of them ever developing anything beyond a wary friendship? Could he ever expect to have a family of his own? Or was he destined to bear this burden until one day he'd had enough and shoot himself? He wouldn't be the first. Or the last.

Stop it, McPherson! You are one pathetic asshole!

Staring vacantly at the ocean, he was startled from his reverie when his T-shirt landed in his lap.

"You're getting sunburned." Graciella lowered herself in front of him. "Put it on." She turned and slid closer until she pushed herself backward between his raised knees and leaned into his chest. Her hands rested on his knees. Wrapping his arms around her shoulders, he rested his chin on her tangled, windblown hair.

Cluny drew a shuddering breath and closed his eyes. He'd do whatever it took not to mess this up. "Are you afraid?"

"Yes." She brushed sand off his knees then raised her hands to grasp his forearms. "I'm afraid because I just found you, Cluny. I don't want to lose you. Not unless you want me to go away."

Stunned, he was at a loss for words. Instead of speaking he kissed her on the ear and sighed. They sat quietly for several long minutes.

Then he began to rock her back and forth and hum.

———

His heart beat hard against her back. He tucked hair behind her ear and began to sing *You Send Me* in a surprisingly beautiful deep voice, and she sucked in a shuddering breath.

He brushed his lips on her neck, setting her on fire.

"Cluny."

"Yes, baby?"

She reached back and caressed his cheek. "You can sing."

"Yes, I can." He squeezed her tight. "High school musical star."

She'd never tell him Marvin sang that same love song to her. Growing up in Sao Paolo the song had been foreign to her, the tune before her time, but he said it was an old Charlie Daniels American classic his dad sang to his mom when Marvin was a boy. Her chest hurt at the memory and at the same time warmed with wonder that another warrior chose to sing it to her. Cluny didn't have the lyrics quite right, but the sentiment was unmistakable. She hoped he'd sing it to her again when they were alone.

"Mama?"

She straightened at her son's voice. "Yes?"

"The lifeguard told me and Amber to stay out of the water. He's gonna put up a red flag on the beach because the riptide is too strong for safe swimming. I said we wouldn't go in because you told us to stay at the umbrella until you came back."

Cluny helped her to her feet. "It's time to pack it in for today." He slung a long arm over her shoulders and they strolled back down the long stretch of warm sand. Amber had already started packing. Santos ran ahead to join her.

"Graciella." His hand tightened on her upper arm.

"We can't talk now, Cluny."

"I need time alone with you. When can that happen?"

She stopped and gazed into his eyes. They were no longer vacant and cold, but shone warmly under the brim of his ball cap. "Will you call me later tonight? After Santos is sleeping?"

"I'm having dinner with Amber's parents. I should be home by ten, ten-thirty. Is that too late?"

"No." She put her arm around his waist.

He pulled her closer. A wave of warm anticipation overwhelmed her senses.

Amber stomped around the blanket while Santos pulled up the umbrella stake. "This rilly stinks! We were having fun, now we have to leave."

Cluny laughed and picked her up. He swung her around and growled into her neck until she dissolved in a fit of giggles.

"You and my daddy got to stop treating me like a baby. I'm too big. It's embarrassing!"

"I keep telling you you're growing up too fast. Grab that pile of wet towels. Time to retreat, soldiers."

Graciella smiled at Amber's mercurial change of mood from angry to happy the minute her *uncle* set her on her feet and issued orders for his troops to pack up their gear and head back to base.

They were almost halfway home when Amber piped up from the back of the van. "Uncle Cluny, did you ask her?"

Graciella stopped breathing. *Ask me what?*

Cluny smacked the steering wheel. "No. I forgot." He flashed a quick grin at Graciella. "I'm under orders to invite you and Santos to Gunny Dempsey's for their annual July 4th barbecue. It's a bunch of former and active duty military and their families. And a few loose cannons like me. It's next Wednesday."

"Oh boy! Can we go, Mama? Your studio is closed that day. Grampa and Gramma are going to the VFW party for old people." He bounced in his seat hard enough to shake the van.

"Can we?"

"Oh, for goodness sake, Santos, settle down." She giggled and shook her head.

"Okay, but can we?"

Amber added her two cents, "I already invited Santos to come.

Daddy said I could bring a friend and he's the friend I want to bring, so can you come too?"

Cluny cocked an amused eyebrow. "It's potluck except for the barbecue. Whaddya say?"

Had she just been steamrolled? She pursed her lips and pretended to think about it for several seconds while the other three occupants, and Queen, of course, sat stonily silent waiting for her reply. "Yes, it sounds like fun."

Yippees and yays erupted from the back seat. Queen even added her opinion with a muted huff. Cluny slid his hand across the front seat, out of view of the kids, and squeezed her wrist. This man's touch told her she was still young and desirable and his touch was something she desired to experience.

"What should we bring?"

"I was thinking about those fan-Tas-tic brigadeiros Santos made the other night."

Amber asked, "What's that?"

"Just about the most delicious thing you ever tasted, that's what."

Graciella clamped her teeth together. Cluny had no idea how expensive they were to make, and it sounded like it would be a pretty big crowd.

He said, "Tell you what. Write down all the ingredients you'll need for about thirty people, and I'll buy everything, and you and Santos come to my house Sunday. I'll even help make them, unless it's a secret recipe you don't want to share."

She sighed because he *did* know they were expensive to make, and he'd saved her from refusing.

Santos said, "It's not a secret, Macfearsome. I can teach you. Amber told me you have a big house with a kitchen and everything, Mama. Can we?"

"Can I come too?" Amber asked.

"Everybody can come. We'll have a party. How about it, Santos's mom?"

Giggling like the schoolgirl she hadn't been for many years, she said, "I'm in!"

At her apartment, they trudged inside with the towels, blankets and the cooler. "Santos, take Amber to your room and show her your collection of Transformer comic books." Some had been his father's and were protected in sealed plastic because of their value. Her son was very proud to own something his dad had loved.

Cluny sat beside her at the kitchen counter while she wrote the list of ingredients she'd need to make the recipe for so many people. "This is going to cost a fortune, Cluny. Are you sure you want us to make them? There any number of dishes I could bring that wouldn't be so expensive."

"Don't worry about the cost. It will be worth it to watch the expressions on their faces when they bite into them. I can afford it. I want to do it." He brushed his fingers through the hair on her shoulder. "Just having you and Santos in my house will be worth it to me."

She gazed into his clear blue eyes, amazed at her good fortune to have met him. Fate had a funny way of bringing people together. Was Cluny McPherson her destiny, or was she being foolish? "I think you can find everything on this list at Trader Joe's."

"Graciella, I want to kiss you." He'd stepped away from the stool and stood close to her. Very close. "May I?"

She placed a hand on his cheek. "Cluny...I...the kids."

He gripped her upper arms and grinned. "They're busy."

The next thing she knew his mouth covered hers. At first the kiss was tentative then he deepened it and put his arms around her. She moved easily into his embrace, her hands on his neck. His soft, gentle lips against hers stirred something deep inside. Breath caught in her throat. She could easily fall in love with this man.

She drew back. "Cluny, I'm scared."

"Me too." He rested his brow on hers and stroked her cheeks with his thumbs, kissed her forehead and stepped away. "Amber! Front and center. I need to get you home before your dad sends a search party." He let his hands slide down her arms and reached for the shopping list.

"Shall I pick you up or would you rather drive yourself next Sunday?"

"Write down your address. We'll find you. What time?"

"About eleven-thirty? We'll go grab lunch then start the cooking lesson when we get back. Is that okay?" He scribbled his address on her scratch pad.

The kids walked into the kitchen. "Is what okay, Macfearsome?" Santos asked.

"We're talking about what time to meet at my house on Sunday."

"If I bring my new fielders mitt will we have time to play catch?"

"Bring it, sailor. We'll find time." He put a big hand on Amber's head. "This little trooper has a great pitching arm. Time to move out, sugar. You forgetting anything?"

"Nope. Give me your phone and I'll call Daddy and tell him we're on our way home."

"I left it in the van. We'll call from there."

Graciella and Santos stood in the open doorway and watched until they disappeared around the side of the building.

"I really like Macfearsome, Mama." Her boy peered at her. When did he get so tall? "Do you like him?"

"Yes, I do. I like him very much." She brushed a kiss on his forehead and closed the door.

"I'm going to marry Amber when I grow up."

She almost laughed but caught herself when she saw he was dead serious. "What does she think about that?"

"I didn't tell her yet. It won't be for a long time."

Not long at all the way he was growing up before her eyes. It seemed only yesterday she'd dropped him off at daycare. He'd been six weeks old, and she'd needed to find a job. Lillian and Earl had asked her to move from San Diego into their house in Chatsworth. Determined they'd be self-sufficient, she'd left her infant son and gone to work. Marvin gone, she was tired of crying, and full of anger that he'd left her alone in a foreign land with no one but her baby and a broken heart.

When he'd left for his final deployment, she'd been full of resentment. Even though her pregnancy was advanced, and he would miss the birth of their son, the SEALs came first. His job and his brother SEALs were at the top of his priority list. She and the child came second. It still hurt.

She took charge of their lives and had never looked back.

Until she'd met Cluny McPherson and begun to dream she could have a new life with a new love. Yes, she was scared. Very scared.

Chapter Ten

Over dinner at the Dempsey's, Amber peppered Marla and Dwayne with colorful descriptions of Cluny's heroics. He rolled his eyes. "Enough. It was no big deal."

Head cocked, Amber gave him a wide-eyed stare. "The lifeguard said it was a big deal."

"When did you talk to the lifeguard?"

"After you and Mrs. Jefferson hiked to the rocks. He talked to us while we were eating lunch. I gave him a brownie. He told us not to go in the water until half an hour after we ate and we told him Mrs. Jefferson already told us not to go in the water until she came back, then he put up the red flag and we couldn't go swimming anyhow." She wrinkled her nose. "Mom, you know I don't like yucky Brussels' sprouts."

Marla bounced Declan against her shoulder and shook her head. "How long is this 'I hate green stuff' going to last?" She raised her eyebrows at Dwayne.

Before her dad got a chance to insist Amber suck it up and eat the smelly little green balls, Cluny forked them off her plate and stuffed them in his mouth. He and Amber exchanged a fist bump.

"I love you, Uncle Cluny."

"I've got your six, sugar." He wrinkled his nose at Marla who'd cast a sour look in his direction, and then she rolled her eyes as if to say *I give up.*

She stood and handed the baby to him. "Here, *Uncle Cluny,* do something helpful for a change."

Dwayne dropped his napkin on the table. "Amber, help Mom clean up. Cluny and I are going to have a cigar outside." He raised his hands at Marla's skeptical look. "Relax, we won't exhale on *your* son." He lifted the empty baby carrier and led Cluny outside.

Cluny wet a finger and held it up. "Breeze going this way. We'll put the bruiser upwind. While I wouldn't object to a wrestling match with your gorgeous wife, I'm not sure you'd come to my defense, Gunny."

Pulling two fat stogies out of his shirt pocket, Dwayne said, "Nah, nah, don't sweat it. I'd step in to save your sorry ass at the last possible second. Got these from Brad after Dec was born."

Cluny held up the cigar and pointed at *It's a Boy!!* on the wrapper, "I never saw a prouder grandpop. Marla's dad must have bought a carload of these and passed them all over town."

Dwayne nodded and lit a match. They fired up the cigars. It took several long drags to get them glowing then they sat back in the two Adirondack chairs on the porch to enjoy the cooling evening breeze. Cluny caught Gunny's surreptitious, proud glances at the baby boy snoozing at his feet.

Cluny blew a perfect smoke ring, watched it float then dissipate. "I met a woman."

"What else is new? You've had more women than any man has a right to."

"This time it's different." He slid back in the chair and propped his feet on the porch railing. "Amber didn't tell the whole story. Shit hit the fan today. I nearly went nuts when I hit the water to pull that guy out. I thought he was you." Sharp chagrin lingered over the public spectacle still fresh in his mind. "I was back in the Sandbox in full combat mode.

"Amber jumped me after we dragged the guy out of the water, and told me he wasn't you. I heard enemy fire and landed on her and told her to stay down." He sighed, and thought the foul curse word rather than saying it.

"Whoa. What did she think of that?"

"She got up, brushed the sand off her face and suggested we go sit on our blanket away from the action. Not much ruffles our Amber's feathers. You're a great dad, buddy."

"I won't take all the credit. You were there from day one. Two young, torn-up vets without the first clue what to do with a newborn girl." Gunny smiled ruefully.

In Cluny's opinion, Francine Dempsey hadn't been good enough to scrape shit off the bottom of Gunny's boots. She'd deserted him three days after Amber's birth because she refused to tie herself down to a *cripple* and a baby she never wanted.

Cluny pointed his cigar. "We figured it out though."

"We did. Now I have Marla, the love of my life, and a son I know how to be a father to." He turned his head and blew a big puff of smoke away from his baby. "You were telling me about a woman. Not that you ever share any juicy details, but different, how?"

"Instead of freezing up and backing away, she followed me down the beach and sat with me. She asked me to talk about what had happened."

"Would this be the widow of Marv, the SEAL?"

"Yep." Cluny nodded. "Graciella Jefferson. I asked her if she was afraid, and she looked me right in the eye and said, 'Yes.' Honest, straightforward, no hesitation. Then she stuck right by my side. She's the most beautiful woman I've ever laid eyes on. I'm scared shitless I'll mess up before we get a chance to know each other. Her kid is something special, too."

Quiet for several seconds, Dwayne asked, "When are you going to bring her to meet me and Marla?"

"I invited them to the July 4th barbecue." He propped one ankle over the other and puffed the cigar. "I sang to her, Gunny. She made me feel so damn good that I sang a love song to her. Jesus, the last woman I sang love songs to was Esther Grossman when I was seventeen, back in Wyoming."

Dwayne chuckled and punched his arm. "Sounds serious, McPherson."

Serious, yes, but he told himself to slow down. Slow down.

———

Around ten-thirty that night he asked Queen, "What do you think, girl? Is it too late to call?" He paced for a moment then stared at the phone. Queen offered no opinion. He pressed call, and heard the smile in Graciella's voice the moment she answered. His chest expanded with a heady mixture of desire and hope.

"Am I calling too late?"

"No, I've been waiting for you."

Her words sent his heart racing. He'd rather have been holding her hand than the phone, but this would have to do for now. "What are you doing tomorrow night?"

"Marvin's mother and father are coming for dinner."

Disappointment burned in his gut. He needed to hold her. "Do you like them?"

"Yes, very much. They think of me as a daughter. Santos loves Grandpa Earl. I asked Lillian if they'd come without Krystal. I want to talk to her, find out if she has any idea what's going on with my sister-in-law. I could tell from the tone of her voice she's troubled too."

"I hope you're not walking into a minefield."

"I'll take my chances. I can't have Krystal influencing Santos with her racist rants. I have no idea what's changed her. She was a sweet child Santos's age when Marvin brought me to California."

"Dwayne's mom told me family was both a blessing and a curse, when I lived at their cattle ranch. She was Mom to me when I needed one. She did a great job raising three good men, especially Amber's dad."

"I'm anxious to meet this paragon."

"You'll meet him and his wife the day of the barbecue. You'll like them. They're good people." He gave her some details about the annual party and who would be there.

"Oh, my, do you have any idea what time it is?"

"Midnight. I don't want to, but I'll let you go." How was it possible they'd talked for so long? "Queenie is wearing out the carpet in front of the door. I didn't take her for a walk when we got home."

His chest expanded at the sound of her sexy, smoky laugh.

"Early classes tomorrow, Cluny, and then house cleaning, and laundry. I've let a lot of things slide the past couple of weeks. Santos and I'll see you on Sunday morning. You probably have plenty of pots and pans, but I'll bring my double boiler."

"Good. I don't have one of those. Thanks for staying up so late to talk."

"I asked you to call me, remember? Good night, Cluny. I hope you sleep well."

"Queen's on the job. Bye for now, beautiful." He clicked off the call, rubbed the dog's head and took her outside. The cold June night air did nothing to cool off the desire burning in him.

———

Graciella made her way to her bedroom, switching off lights and checking the front door as she went. She paused at Santos' room, carefully stepped inside and watched her son sleep. He was beginning to take on a more mature appearance. Where had all those years gone? Not her baby much longer, he'd be grown and gone from home before she knew it.

In her room, she slowly slipped out of her amethyst hued robe and studied her nude reflection in the full length mirror on the back of her closet door. She scrutinized herself, not as Santos's mother, but the young woman who'd sat on the beach in the embrace of handsome, compelling man who hadn't hidden his attraction to her. He'd rocked her in his strong arms and sung a love song. She'd never hear that song again without experiencing the same exciting sensation. When Cluny sang the words to her this afternoon, the lyrics had imprinted themselves on her heart and mind.

This man had problems and flaws she hadn't discovered, so she'd tread carefully. She had a child whose needs came before hers. But she liked what she knew of Cluny McPherson so far. The way a man related to children said worlds about his true character.

She picked up the book on her nightstand, changed her mind about reading, and snapped off the light. Settling back against her pillows, the bed seemed too big, empty and cold. She wanted Cluny's arms around her again. She knew in her heart he wanted that, too. Possibilities. She swam in a warm sea of lovely possibilities.

Thursday evening, Chatsworth

"Santos, get the door! Grandpa and Grandma are here."

She watched from the kitchen as her son ran to the door and threw it open, let out a whoop and hugged his grandparents. Earl rolled his eyes and reached behind Lillian's back to take the new fielder's mitt she'd been hiding.

This brought on another round of joyful sounds as Santos hugged it to his chest and bounced on his toes. "I knew you'd bring it, Grampa, I just knew it!"

Lillian shook her head, clearly amused at their antics, and shoved them outside. "Go! Break in your new mitt. All this excitement is too much for an old woman." They were gone before she got a chance to close the door.

"Lillian, how nice to see you." Graciella motioned for her mother-in-law to join her in the kitchen. "Let's have a glass of iced tea and talk while they work off some of that energy." She took her mother-in-law's sweater and draped it over the back of a kitchen chair. They exchanged a hug and sat at the counter. "I have dinner ready and warming and the table is set. How have you and Earl been?"

They talked about trivialities, then Graciella told Lillian that Santos had selected his future bride, and was on his way to becoming a full-fledged beach bum. "The girl and her godfather have been sharing picnics at the beach with us. We've had some good adventures this summer. Her name is Amber Dempsey, and she helped him conquer his fear of the water."

Lillian smiled and sipped her tea. "So when's the wedding?"

"That's the good news. He's decided to wait for at least ten years."

"Dempsey. That sounds Irish." Lillian's eyes took on a cloud of confusion.

"I suspect you're right. Her godfather's name is Cluny McPherson. Clearly there're Celts in the family tree." All she detected in Lillian's voice was curiosity, not a hint of alarm or concern. She breathed a silent sigh of relief.

"How did you meet them? Through Rio Samba?"

"No, Zuma beach. Santos was curious about Cluny's dog."

"He had his dog at Zuma? I'm surprised the beach patrol didn't ask him to leave."

"They allow dogs wearing a service vest."

"Oh! So the man is handicapped?"

"You wouldn't know it to look at him, but yes, he's a wounded warrior." Graciella shifted. "Lillian, I was hoping we could have a few minutes alone to talk about Krystal. There was an unpleasant confrontation in our apartment last Sunday. She came unannounced and walked right in without knocking. She was rude to our dinner guest, and she upset Santos. I was so embarrassed. I don't understand why she's changed so much lately."

Lillian lowered her forehead to her hand. "We don't know what to do."

"What's happened to her? Why is she throwing around racial epithets?"

"We believe it's the man she's seeing. He's got her convinced she's a victim of racism. That the only reason she's been unable to get her modeling career advanced beyond department store catalogs is because of her color."

"Do you believe that?"

"No, of course not! The competition for the few available slots at major modeling agencies is fierce. We've tried to reason with her. I pointed out that some of the most famous faces in major advertising are women of color, but she doesn't want to listen to us."

Graciella sighed and rested her hand on Lillian's shoulder. "I would think this attitude works against her efforts to advance. This is all so recent. It sounds as if the man has poisoned her perspective."

"Absolutely. He's convinced her to go to court to have her name changed."

That startled Graciella. "Changed to what?"

"We're not sure, but she's told us she refuses to be known by a 'slave name.' We're broken-hearted over her decision. Jefferson has been the family surname for over two hundred years. Earl is proud of his ancestry. Marvin always joked to his fellow SEALs that he had the most American name in their team." She shook her head. "It's very sad."

Shocked over Lillian's revelations, Graciella asked, "Where did she meet this man?"

"Through an online dating site. I told her she was asking for trouble. You never know what kind of person you might meet. But, she signed up anyway. She's headstrong, just like Marvin. Shortly after they first went out, she brought him home to meet us. Jamal was very courteous at first, then little-by-little he began to draw away from us. After a while he stopped coming inside the house. He comes to collect her in his car, and she leaves without a word about where they're going. We're at our wit's end."

Hair on the back of her head prickling, Graciella turned the name Jamal over in her head. "What's his last name, do you know?"

"Mujahid, but Earl and I suspect it isn't his birth name."

Graciella had become interested in Arabic names when Marvin deployed to Iraq. Krystal's boyfriend's name translated roughly to Beautiful Man Fighting. "This is unsettling, Lillian. Especially today, when we read so much about the radicalization of young American men."

"We don't know what we can do." Lillian's lips trembled. "Earl doesn't want to ask her to move out because we're afraid he might be abusing her. Two weeks ago she came in very late. We'd already gone to bed and didn't know she was home. Earl heard angry voices and scuffling sounds so he got up to investigate. Jamal was storming away from Krystal's room. Earl asked him what he was doing there, but he pushed past him and left. The next morning Krystal had bruising and swelling around her eye. She had to cancel a photo shoot."

"My God, Lillian, this is terrible! Why haven't you spoken of this to me before?"

"I'm glad we're finally talking about it." She lowered her head and rolled it from side to side then took a tissue from her pocket and dabbed her eyes.

Graciella moved closer and put an arm around her shoulder. "How did she explain what happened?"

"She made up some story about falling. We didn't believe it. When

Earl pressed her, she flew into a fury and bolted from the house." The woman's eyes sparkled with unshed tears. "She's had every advantage we were able to provide for her. She excelled in school and was popular with her classmates. Where did we go wrong?"

"Don't blame yourself, please. You—"

They were unable to continue the conversation when Earl and Santos returned. She wouldn't discuss it in her son's presence. "Is anybody hungry?" She hopped off the barstool.

"Something smells wonderful in here, daughter." Earl pecked her cheek and turned to Santos. "I don't know about you, but I'm starved. Let's get washed up so we can enjoy whatever wonderful dish your mother made for dinner."

"What can I do?" Lillian asked.

"If you'd get the salad from the refrigerator and toss it with the dressing I made, that would be a big help." She put on a pair of oven mitts and opened the oven door. "This ham is just perfect. I'll set it in front of Earl's place so he can serve us."

During dinner Graciella asked Earl if he'd drive Santos to Spring Grove Park three days a week so he could join the baseball team at the beginning of the summer season.

"I'd love to. I'll get a return on my investment in that new glove."

"Oh, boy! I'll tell Macfearsome I can come."

"What day and time?"

"I'll find out for sure on Sunday," Graciella said. "We're going to Cluny's house so Santos can show him how to make brigadeiros for a 4th of July barbecue. It will be at the home of Amber's parents next Wednesday. The annual event is attended by former and current members of the military and their families."

"Macfearsome told me practice is on Tuesday and Thursday afternoons and the games are all on Saturday." He smiled at his grandfather. "So you'll take me? And come to all the games?"

"I wouldn't miss it. You can count on me."

"We'll both come to your games." Lillian nodded at Graciella. "Will you be there on Saturdays? I know you usually have the school open."

"Yes, I'm only conducting one morning class on Saturdays all summer. The games don't start until two."

She raised her hands. "How about a round of Mexican Train Dominoes while we make room for dessert? I made *pudim*."

Earl stood and began clearing dishes. He waggled his eyebrows and grinned at Graciella. "Did I ever tell you you're my favorite daughter-in-law?"

"High praise, Earl, considering I'm your only daughter-in-law."

Chapter Eleven

Thursday, Spring Grove

CLUNY WONDERED HOW DINNER WAS GOING WITH GRACIELLA and her in-laws. He ate in front of the TV while watching a baseball game. Queen lay on her back taking up three quarters of the couch, snoring away as if she were exhausted. All she'd done was lie on the porch for hours and watch him sweat in the hot sun mowing the lawns and trimming the hedges on either side of his property. He was the one who should be snoring, but instead he was alert and restless.

He could think of nothing all day but Graciella, their kiss, and the feel of her soft mouth brushing the side his neck. She stirred something deep within him that he couldn't quite identify. She was different from any other woman he'd ever been attracted to, mature and beautiful in a very sexy womanly way. His heart pounded whenever he pictured her in that bright green bikini. All golden skin and fabulous curves. She was thoughtful, kind and laughed at his lame humor. Graciella had it all—and he wanted it all.

The woman and her son came into his life at the time when he'd reconciled to living alone, and enjoying family life vicariously through the Dempsey's.

During one of the worst, most depressing weeks he could remember, they'd appeared. First the boy, then his mother. He dared to think it possible they'd come together in some preordained way, and he feared the flame of hope struggling to ignite in his heart would be extinguished.

She'd seen what could happen. Graciella held his hand, encouraged him to talk to her, trust her. Up to this point, he'd done everything possible to hide his PTS. He desperately wanted the love and comfort of a woman. A woman to come home to. A woman he could talk to and laugh with, or sit quietly and watch TV or read without need for conversation. A woman to share those intimate, safe moments, knowing he could be himself without worrying about horrified, frightened responses leading to rejection. He dared hope Graciella was that woman.

At ten o'clock he put the popcorn bowl aside, snapped off the TV and stretched. He wanted to go to her right now. "Why not?" He pulled his loafers on, grabbed his wallet and keys and headed for the door. "Come on, Queenie, we're going for a ride."

All the way across the pass through the Santa Susana Mountains on the 118 Freeway he grinned, shook his head and asked himself what he thought he was doing. "Am I nuts, girl?"

She cocked her head from side to side, tongue hanging out of her grinning mouth.

"Is that a yes?" He bumped her nose with his fingers.

So what was he planning to do, other than cruise by her apartment building then turn around and go home? He'd see them on Sunday. He had plenty to keep him busy between now and then. His crew would return to work on Monday. They had a big job lined up starting that day. It would take most of the week to complete it, with taking the 4th off on Wednesday. "Go home, idiot!"

Queen lifted her majestic head from between her paws and stared. He laughed and patted her. "It's okay. We'll just drive past their place then leave. You're right. I'm nuts. I'll turn up ahead and we'll go home."

She sprang up and searched the area, made a small woof, put a paw on the dashboard as he turned into the parking lot of the complex, tail thumping on the seat when she recognized the building where her pal, Santos, lived.

He fully intended to drive right through to the other exit and leave. But he didn't. He parked near the stairs leading to her apartment. One small light shone from her window. He stared at it for several seconds. It went out. "Aw, hell."

Reaching for the driver's side handle, he mumbled. "Be right back," stepped out of the car and bolted up the steps. He rapped lightly on the door, and was about to turn around and avoid making a fool of himself, when the light inside blinked on. A shadow passed before the peep hole. He took a step back so he'd be well lighted under the porch lamp and waited. A wide grin, he couldn't stop, grew on his face.

The handle turned. He waited. Graciella peeked through a one-inch crack, her eyes round and wary. "Cluny?"

"Hello, gorgeous." His smile morphed into a chuckle.

She pulled open the door. Then she began to laugh. "What are you doing here?" She shook her head. "I don't know why I'm laughing, but you look so silly with that big grin on your face."

He didn't answer, just smiled wider and chuckled louder.

"What are you doing here, Cluny?" She stepped forward and put her fingers over his lips. "Shhh, you'll wake Santos." He caught her fingers between his teeth and she snatched them back squeaking with alarm.

He leaned close to her ear. "Shhh, don't want to wake Santos."

"Well, for heaven's sake. For the third time… What do you want?"

"I'm not sure, but I think I came to kiss you goodnight."

"What!" she hissed. "You came all the way over here at this hour to kiss me goodnight?"

"Sounds better when you say it." He wriggled his eyebrows, unable to take his eyes off her sexy, soft mouth and shrugged.

She crossed her arms and nodded. "Well then, what are you waiting for?"

What *was* he waiting for? He took a step forward, cupped her face in his hands and kissed her. Twice. On a sigh, he stepped back. "Nice robe."

She stared, opened her mouth to say something, but then didn't.

His hands drifted down her arms. "Goodnight, sweetheart."

Graciella wasn't sure how long she stood there in the open doorway, his kiss still warm and tingling on her lips. Her face glowed from the feel of his hands against her cheeks. She placed fingers to her mouth, smiled, and whispered, "He drove all the way from Spring Grove to Chatsworth to kiss me goodnight."

"Who did, Mama?"

She jumped and closed the door. "Santos, you startled me."

"I heard you talking to somebody. It sounded like Macfearsome. Was that him?"

Her face flushed, a deep warm buzz of embarrassment prevented her from answering for a moment. She cleared her throat and switched off the hall light. "Um…yes, it was Mr. McPherson. Now let's get you back to bed."

Santos yawned. "Did he forget something? Is that why he was here? It's kinda late."

Her hand on his shoulder, she directed him down the hall. "Yes, he forgot something."

"What?" He stopped and looked directly at her in the dimly lighted hall at his bedroom door.

There was no way she would satisfy him with anything but the truth. She wasn't in the habit of lying to her son and she wasn't going to start now.

Just answer the question, Graciella. Keep it short and simple.

"Yes. He forgot to kiss me goodnight." Her jaw clenched, waiting for his next question.

"That's nice. Night, Mama." He stumbled sleepily to his bed. Lay on his side facing the wall and pulled the blankets up to his neck.

All that worry for nothing. Santos accepted the kiss as the most natural thing for his mother and *Macfearsome.*

Graciella went back to make sure she'd locked the door, then proceeded to her bedroom. Every muscle in her body vibrated. She'd be lucky if she didn't have to read a hundred pages of her bedside book before getting sleepy.

She slipped off her robe and slid between the sheets. It was very warm. Should she turn on the air conditioner? No, it wasn't the heat of the evening she felt—it was the heat of Cluny's kiss. She sighed, hugged her upper arms and replayed the vision of his face moving close then closer to hers, the simple declaration of his purpose for being there. His smiling mouth pressing hers. His big hands gliding down her arms. His abrupt *mission accomplished* departure.

Friday morning

"We're running a little late, Santos. Finish your oatmeal and bring your toast with you."

"Why do I have to go to Grampa's house? Why can't I come with you today?"

"I told you I have some errands to run after I close the studio. I'm going to shop for a dress and you'd be bored silly. You'd distract me to the point where it would take twice as long. Just put on a happy face and spend the day with your grandparents, please." She jingled her car keys.

What she didn't say was the reason why she wanted to go shopping after work. She wanted to find something new to wear to the barbecue on the 4th. Cluny would be introducing her to his friends. It was silly, sure, because she had clothes she could wear to the party, and he'd never seen any of them, but all the same. She'd dress up for him next week; make him glad he'd invited her. And Santos, of course. He'd invited both of them.

"Bring your new mitt. You and Earl can practice. He'll help you get ready for the baseball team."

"Okay." He sighed reluctantly and went to his bedroom.

Her gaze followed him. She loved him so much, but she had to face facts—he spent far too much time with her. He needed more male companionship. She was so glad Earl had agreed to shuttle him to the park league in Spring Grove three days a week. She'd go to the games on Saturday afternoons and drive him home, but the other two afternoons he'd be with his grandfather and Cluny at the park. It was a good plan for both of them.

The day at Rio Samba dragged for her even though she'd enjoyed the classes and had a great idea to add a costume design contest for her summer students, young and old. Santos suggested a mini "Carnival at Rio Samba" in September before the start of school. Her students were on board and excited about the project. It would be a lot of work, but a lot of fun, too.

At three-thirty she locked the door and climbed into her car. First stop, Macy's.

An hour later she nearly headed back to Chatsworth, not having found anything to her liking within her budget. Instead she paused for an Orange Julius, and then drove the short distance to Nordstrom's Rack. Later she would swear she saw the dress from across the big sales floor the second she'd entered the store. It called to her like a homing beacon broadcasting in her head. It was perfect. She could afford it!

Graciella rushed to the fitting rooms and waited impatiently for one to become available.

"Let me know if you need any help," a store employee said. "Different size or anything."

"Oh, thanks. This one is a ten. I think it'll fit."

"I don't know. You look more like an eight to me. There's a smaller one on the return rack. It's the same dress, but slightly different colors. I'll get it."

The woman was right. The dress was a little roomy around the waist. Frowning she hoped the other one would fit her and she'd like it as much.

A light rap on the door then, "Here's the size eight. This label tends to run larger." She laughed. "I guess they want all their customers to feel good. I'll hang it over the door for you."

The dress fluttered over the door, and Graciella's breath caught. The colors were perfect. Shades of rose, claret, and amethyst flowers splashed over a pale lavender background. "Oh, this is lovely. I hope it fits."

The size was perfect. The strapless sundress with modest tucking of the bodice and full skirt set her figure off to the nth degree. "Oh, wow. I love this."

"Can I tell you something, honey?" The saleswoman tapped lightly on the door again. When Graciella opened it she stood back and gave her two thumbs up. "It was made for you." She reached forward and picked up the hem. "See this tiny spot of lipstick?" she whispered. "I never said this, but if you complain about it at the register, they'll give you another ten percent off."

Graciella gasped. "I never would have seen it if you hadn't pointed it out to me. Thank you so much." She tilted her head. "What have you got behind your back?"

The smiling lady held up a pair of glittery summer sandals covered with fake gems the same colors as the flowers in the dress. "Size ten. Am I right?" She handed them over. "Originally ninety bucks. I just marked them down to fifteen. They're last season's overstock of larger sizes. Want to try them on?"

Graciella stepped into the sandals and did a happy pirouette. "I'll never complain about big feet again."

"I don't know who the lucky man is, but when he sees you in this outfit he'll probably fall to his knees. Enjoy the moment, sweetie." She winked and approached another customer.

Sure enough, they took off another ten percent. She walked out of the store on a cloud of euphoria, realizing that's just what she wanted to do—bring the man who'd shown up so late on her doorstep to kiss her goodnight to his knees. *No, not really, but it would be nice.* That thought filled her with happiness all the way home.

"Okay, Queen, just like yesterday, it's time to kiss my girl goodnight." Cluny hung up the dishtowel, grabbed his wallet and keys and they left through the door between the kitchen and garage. He grinned while the door rolled up, tapping his fingertips impatiently against the steering wheel.

All the way to Chatsworth he vibrated with anticipation, probably making Queen wonder if he was all there. He grinned and rubbed her ear when they got off the freeway. She perked up, now familiar with the route.

"Yep, almost there, girl." He turned on her street and pulled into the parking lot. Bounding up the steps when he saw lights on in their apartment, his blood ran hot, his body hummed.

He knocked on her door. Waited. Santos opened it. *Dammit!*

"Macfearsome!"

"Up late, aren't you, pal?"

"Sometimes I get to stay up late on Friday night." He stepped back and yelled, "Mama! Macfearsome's here to kiss you goodnight again."

That declaration knocked him for a loop. Unable to move, he stood there shocked by the boy. Had he been awake last night? Did Graciella tell him? Before he had time to give it much more thought, she was standing in front of him with a big smile on her face.

"Are you planning on making a habit of this, Cluny?" Her laughing face had to be the most beautiful sight he'd ever seen. His heart thudded against his ribs, hands itched to touch her.

Instead of answering the question he opened his arms, and she stepped into them. He kissed her soundly, stepped back and nodded. "I am." He ran a hand down her cheek. "See you tomorrow night, baby." He turned to leave. "You too, Santos."

"'Night, Macfearsome!"

He grinned all the way home. Queen was happy because he scratched her neck and ears while he drove. Maybe he couldn't spend every waking moment with Graciella, but for the time being he'd waste some gas and an hour or less every night making the trip to Chatsworth to kiss her goodnight. It was turning into a playful game they both enjoyed.

Graciella giggled and leaned back against her front door for a few seconds after Cluny left. She rejoined Santos at the kitchen table where they had been in the middle of a game of gin rummy. Earl taught him to play, and she had to concentrate because he'd become very good at it. They used beans to bet with. His beans were brown and hers white. His jar held more than her jar and way too many of them were white.

"Do you like Macfearsome?" he asked and picked up his cards.

"Yes. Do you mind?" She had no idea what her son felt about her interest in a man. All these years, there'd been just to two of them. She'd not had so much as a date. Well, not a real date. She'd had lunch with a man a few times and her friends and students were endlessly pressing to fix her up with somebody. But she'd never been interested until they'd met Cluny McPherson at the beach a mere two weeks ago. There was such a strong masculine presence about him. A gentleness and playful nature with the children that she found deeply compelling and attractive in the man.

"No. I like him too. He'd make a good dad. I wonder why he isn't one."

She made a non-committal humming sound and drew a card. She had an idea, but it was far too early to truly know that much about him. Meeting his friends next week would give her more insight. "Gin!"

"What? You only picked up one card!" Santos squinted in disbelief when she laid down her hand.

She laughed and picked up her soda. "You dealt them, so don't blame me."

He screwed up his face then cracked a smile. "I guess I have to let you win once in a while. Or you won't want to play anymore."

"Let me win? Just for that you can load the dessert dishes in the dishwasher and go to bed. I'm not sure it's such a good idea to let you stay up this late."

"At least I got to see Macfearsome kiss you." He artfully dodged her playful smack. Giggling, he carried the two small plates and forks to the sink. "Mama has a boyfriend, Mama has a boyfriend," he sang in a rusty tenor, then dropped the dishes in the sink and ran down the hall barely missing her reach.

Graciella lowered her head in her hand and rolled it from side to side. Having a nine year old child definitely complicated a single mother's life. She loved him so much her heart ached. Did she really have room there for anyone else? This entire business, friendship, whatever it was with Cluny might be a short-lived episode. She'd be foolish to think it could amount to anything more than a playful flirtation.

If that was the case, she'd enjoy it while it lasted.

Chapter Twelve

Saturday, Rio Samba

"Mr. Ramos was a no-show for his private lesson again." Graciella sighed with resignation. She could have put another private customer in his time slot. "I'm going to have to speak with him, tell him he has to pay whether he comes or not."

Santos nodded, a wise and thoughtful expression on his young face. "You could do like the doctor's office. If you don't give twenty-four hours' notice, you have to pay."

"Good idea. Let's get to work." Saturday was the day she and Santos cleaned the studio after the last morning class. "Soon we'll have to adjust our studio cleaning schedule because you'll be playing baseball every Saturday, starting in a week. I don't plan to be slaving around here and miss any of your games." Maybe she'd consider hiring a cleaning service for the summer. She'd signed up several new students since Easter and had a little extra money in the bank.

"You could hire somebody to clean for you, Mama."

She laughed and ran her fingers through his longish mop of tight brown curls. "Were you reading my mind by any chance?"

He glanced in one of the floor to ceiling studio mirrors. "I need a haircut."

There—he'd read her mind again! "Go to the barbershop and see if Rusty is still in. He's usually open until three on Saturday. I'll finish up and meet you there."

Her cell phone played a samba tune as the door closed behind Santos. She rushed to the back of the studio and dug it out of her purse. MCPHERSON appeared on the screen. Cluny had programmed it into her contact list that day at the beach.

"Hello?"

"Hello, gorgeous. How about I take you and Santos for pizza and a movie tonight?"

"Who is this?"

"Uh-oh, I have competition. How many other guys call you gorgeous?"

She giggled softly. "Nobody but a tall, dark and handsome, blue-eyed plumber I know who lives in Spring Grove." The man who made her heart flutter like a wounded bird.

"Is that right? You scared me there for a minute. So? Wanna do it?"

"I don't have a date tonight and as far as I know Santos doesn't either, so yes."

"I'll pick you up at your apartment at five-thirty?"

"Sounds good. I'll tell him. He'll be so excited."

"Will his mother be excited?"

"No question about it. She hasn't been on a date in ten years and is afraid she won't know how to behave. It is a date, isn't it, even though she'll be accompanied by her nine year old resident *acompanhante*?"

"Even though. Just so you know," Cluny said, "I don't plan on letting him sit between us at the movies."

She heard a loud ring and shout on Cluny's end.

"Gotta go, sweetheart. The delivery I've been waiting for just got here. I'll see you in a couple of hours."

"Bye." Heart tripping, she clicked off and dropped the phone in her shoulder bag, locked the door and walked with trembling knees to the end of the strip mall to meet Santos at the barbershop, her smile growing wider with every step.

———

Simi Valley warehouse

"Whew," Cluny sighed at the rush he got whenever he heard Graciella's voice. Last night's kiss had been the best yet. His lips buzzed at the memory. "Okay, get back to work, McPherson." He approached the delivery truck, clipboard in hand.

"Where do you want this?" the burly driver asked.

"If you can back the truck farther into the warehouse it will be easier to unload. I'd like the boxes lined up next to the far wall so I can check them off my order form."

The man nodded. "Gotcha." He waved at the truck. "Doug! Move to the driver's side and I'll direct you where to back up." An annoying loud beeping filled the warehouse when the truck backed into the wide aisle. Once in place, the two men unloaded the dozen large boxes.

Cluny checked them off his inventory sheet and signed the bill of lading. The entire operation took less than half an hour. "Come on, Queenie, we've got to get ready for our big date." He locked up the shop and warehouse and headed home to shower and change.

At five-thirty on the dot he parked in front of the stairs leading to the Jefferson apartment. Queen waited for him in the car. He'd barely pressed the doorbell when Santos pulled it open for him.

"Hi, Macfearsome." The handsome boy wore jeans and a long-sleeved plaid shirt nearly identical to Cluny's outfit.

"Hey, sailor, I see you got a haircut. Lookin' good."

"You look like twins," Graciella remarked.

"I got the memo." Cluny winked.

"What memo?" Santos looked from his mother to Cluny, his face screwed up with confusion.

Graciella put her arm around her son's shoulder and pulled him close. "Cluny's joking, because you and he dressed alike. Didn't you notice?"

Santos stared at Cluny and grinned. "Oh, yeah. I got the memo too."

Cluny clamped his hand on the boy's shoulder. "You ready? I picked out a great movie tonight. It's in Imax at the Regal Sixteen."

"We're ready." Graciella grabbed their sweaters off the back of her couch.

"I'm starving, Macfearsome. Where we gonna eat?"

"Palermo Pizzeria, not far from where I live."

"Pizza! My favorite."

Queen, ears perked, stood and pawed the windshield when she spotted Santos.

"Is Queen going with us?" Santos did a double take.

Cluny opened the passenger door, shooed Queen to the back and brushed off the seat for Graciella. "No, I thought I'd kill two birds with one stone. We'll drop her off at my house on the way and you'll see how to find me tomorrow for our Brazilian cooking lesson."

Twenty minutes later Cluny drove down a tree-lined street. "That's Spring Grove Park." He pulled into his long driveway. "As you can see, I don't have far to go to coach the baseball team."

Graciella nodded. "We'll have no trouble finding you."

He hopped out of the car and called to Queen. "I'll be right back." He patted his leg and walked the dog to his front door, opened it and let her in. When he got back, Santos leaned forward.

"What if she has to go while we're gone?"

"No sweat, she's got a doggy door. After the movie tonight, we'll stop and pick her up before I take you home." The boy's concern and affection for Queen warmed Cluny's chest. He looked at Graciella and was puzzled by her expression. "What?"

"I'm surprised at the size of this place. I don't know why, but I imagined you lived in a small house on a busy residential street. This area is beautiful, and very countrified. How long have you owned the place? Do you own it?" Her cheeks pinked. "Am I too nosy?"

He squeezed her hand. "No, you're not. I'm glad you're interested."

"Tell me about this interesting house, Cluny."

"It's over forty years old. I bought it five years ago, before the park was developed. Dempsey and I did a lot of renovations right after I closed the deal. We gutted and re-did the bathrooms, then all new oak floors, new roof, modern kitchen, and painted it inside and out. I love the place."

"It's beautiful, but it's so large. You and Queen must rattle around in there all by yourselves."

"It's lonesome sometimes, and I only have half the place furnished. I've got four bedrooms, two are empty. No dining room furniture, a lot of bookshelves and a monster, man-sized TV. You'll see it tomorrow."

Santos piped up from the back seat. "Is it a man cave, Macfearsome?"

Graciella and Cluny erupted with laughter.

"You might say that, pal." He backed out of the driveway. "Pizza, here we come."

It didn't take more than ten minutes to get to the restaurant. The stand-alone pizzeria had a large parking lot filled with cars.

"It looks crowded," Graciella said, as they walked to the non-descript entrance.

"We won't have to wait long." He pulled open the entry door for them.

Quickly seated, they ordered soft drinks and studied the menu.

"See anything you like?" Cluny asked Santos. "They'll make it any way you like."

"I like jalapeños and meatballs, lots of jalapeños."

Cluny raised his eyebrows and glanced at Graciella.

"They can't make it hot enough for my son. He'd rather eat horse-radish than cake." She shrugged and wrinkled her nose. "He didn't get it from me."

"Okay, my man, how about half meatballs with black olives and half jalapeno?"

Santos extended his fist across the table. "Yes! Get the big size, I'm starving."

"Don't you ever feed this boy?" He reached for her knee and gave it a small squeeze under the table, out of Santos' view. A zing of testosterone charged excitement coursed through him when she put her hand on top of his and held it in place. His leg jittered. Holding his breath, he looked down at her slim tan fingers, remembering how they felt on his bare back at the beach.

The waiter took their order and brought a pitcher of root beer. Cluny poured their drinks in tall glasses filled with crushed ice. He leaned back in the booth and for several minutes he and Santos talked about how the park league teams were formed. He placed his hand on Graciella's knee again.

"What movie are we going to?" Santos asked, oblivious to the underlying sexual tension. He sipped soda through the tall straw and raised his eyebrows.

Cluny cleared his clogged throat, glanced at Graciella and saw her smiling at his distress. "Uh, we're, uh, I got tickets for the new Dreamspell animated film." He tightened his grip on her leg, and she sighed.

Santos' eyes got big. "Virgil the Astronaut Chipmunk and the Fairy Princess?" The boy bounced in his seat. "That one?"

"You guessed it, sailor." He reached to push the condiments to one side. "Here's our pizza. Should I ask the waitress to stand by with a fire extinguisher?" Instead of releasing his hold on her knee, he relaxed his grip, slid his hand up her leg, and then let go.

———

Graciella loved Cluny's muscled arm around her shoulders in the darkened movie theatre. He alternately squeezed and hugged her as he doubled over with laughter. She couldn't remember when she'd had so much fun in the company of a man. He was relaxed and natural with Santos, enjoying his happy giggles and sharing the jumbo popcorn tub her son held. Anyone who saw them together would assume they were a family.

Still grinning and laughing as they exited the movie, she placed herself between them. They joined hands and walked across the parking lot.

"Let's go to my house and get Queen." Cluny put the key in the door lock on his old Pontiac. He pushed the driver's seat forward so Santos could crawl into the back then he walked around the front with her and opened the passenger door. His hand drifted down her back as she slid onto the seat. Her breath caught at his intimate touch.

He took his seat behind the steering wheel.

Santos leaned forward. "How come your car doesn't have a remote lock?"

Cluny shifted in his seat so he could see her son's face. "This old gal is fourteen years older than me. They didn't have fancy remote control locks in the olden days."

"How old are you, Macfearsome?"

"Thirty-three."

Graciella could tell from Santos' expression that he was working out the numbers in his head. She thought she'd die when he said, "Mama is older than you, aren't you, Mama?"

She slapped her hands on her hot cheeks and groaned.

Cluny grasped one of her wrists, pulled her hand to his mouth and kissed her knuckles. "I've always had a thing for old houses, old cars, and older women."

"Mama will be thirty-five on her next birthday, in November."

How much worse could it get? Santos in the back seat telling her age, and Cluny chuckling at his revelations. "Why don't you tell Mr. McPherson my weight, Santos?"

"I would, but I don't know it."

By now Cluny was laughing out loud, tears sparkling on his lower lids.

Santos touched her shoulder. "Did I make a good joke?"

Through his choking laughter, Cluny said, "You're the best, Santos." He pulled Graciella to his side and whispered in her ear, "I love your kid."

He loves my kid. She believed him, because nothing he'd ever said or done had the least bit of phoniness about it. From the moment they'd met on the beach he'd spoken to Santos in a quiet, respectful, manly way. Never a single note of patronization in his voice. That was rare in a grown man. Adults could be very dismissive of children. She was guilty of it herself from time to time. Especially if she was rushed, stressed or tired.

Even when Cluny had briefly slipped into his violent past at the beach that day, he'd spoken kindly to Amber and Santos. He'd chosen to separate himself from the children for a while, and walked away. She couldn't imagine what kind of self-control it took for him to cope.

It wouldn't take more than a couple of minutes for him to retrieve his dog from the big house. "No, Santos, stay in the car. We'll see the house tomorrow." She'd barely spoken the words when Queen came bounding to the car ahead of Cluny. "There she is."

Cluny held her hand, stroking her knuckles with his thumb, all the way across the pass back to Chatsworth. Every now and then he glanced at her and smiled. She was certain she'd see his sexy smile in her dreams all night.

The man she was beginning to think of as *her* man, escorted them to their apartment door, kissed her goodnight, and shook hands with Santos.

"See you tomorrow," he called and waved goodbye. He'd no more than disappeared around the corner of the stairs than the porch light went off outside her apartment. Heart thudding in her throat, she grabbed Santos' shoulder and pulled him a few steps away from the door.

His voice quavered, "Is somebody in our house?" She stepped in front of him to shield him from whom, she didn't know. "Maybe the light bulb burned out."

"I'll run and catch Macfearsome."

"No. It's probably just the light bulb. I don't..." Her pulse raced when a shadow passed in front of the peep hole.

The door opened a crack and Krystal whispered, "Come in, quick." She stepped back and waved them inside.

Graciella looked around, fear crawling up her back and neck. She tugged Santo's arm and they entered the dimly lit apartment. "Krystal, what are you doing here?"

On a choking sob, her sister-in-law answered, "I'm hiding from Jamal."

Confusion and fear in his voice, Santos gripped his mother's hand. "What'd he do?"

Graciella placed a hand on her son's back. "Please go to your room and close the door, honey. I need to speak to your aunt privately."

"But, Mama..."

Chapter Thirteen

"PLEASE DON'T ARGUE WITH ME. GO TO YOUR ROOM AND CLOSE the door."

Santos dropped his chin and dragged his feet down the hall. Before he closed his door he glanced back, anger mixed with worry on his face.

Graciella turned on the stereo, the sound a little higher than she normally would have this late at night. She pointed to the kitchen, the furthest point in the apartment from her son's bedroom, and tilted her head for Krystal to follow her.

Leaning on the counter, she racked her brain. "Krystal, I'm sorry for your distress, but you have to go home. You can't be here."

"No! That's the first place he'll look for me."

"And this is the second. Why are you bringing this trouble to our door?" Hands on her cheeks, she paced. "How did you get in here? I know I locked the door when we left."

"I took Mom's key. A friend dropped me off. Jamal doesn't know where I am. I have to stay here. He threatened me." Pending tears sparkled in the young woman's eyes and softened Graciella's heart.

She asked for her key then said, "Have you called your parents? Do they know where you are?"

"It's better if they don't know where I am."

"You should at least send them a text message. If he's been there looking for you they're probably worried. Maybe they're in danger?"

Shaking her head, Krystal seated herself on one of the barstools. "They don't do texting. They'd never think to look for a text." The tears that threatened earlier began to slide down her cheeks. "Jamal's not who I thought he was when we first met."

"Krystal, what do you want to do? What do you want me to do?"

"I don't know." She got up paced the room.

Graciella debated with herself. Should she say what she'd thought all along? She'd brought this on herself. Once a beautiful, unspoiled young woman, she'd turned into a bitter, preachy racist, angry at everything and everyone. What good would it do to bring that up now? They needed to think of a way to diffuse the situation.

"Did you consider calling the police?"

"He didn't actually do anything, not much anyway, he threatened me."

"How? What did he say?"

"He'll kill me if I ever touched his computer again."

"His computer?" Graciella couldn't understand what Krystal meant. "What about his computer? Did you see something there you weren't supposed to see?" She squeezed her eyes closed for a second and went to the sink for a glass of water. She didn't want to be involved in this. She didn't want Santos exposed to this.

"He...uh...could I have some water too?"

Graciella gave her the glass she'd intended for herself. She spotted movement at the end of the hallway. "Santos! Stay in your room, please." She raised her hand so Krystal remained silent until his door clicked shut.

"Why were you on his computer?"

"I wasn't snooping, I swear. I wanted to Google the new dress catalog I was in to see if it had been published yet."

"I don't see anything so bad about that. Why was he upset?"

"His search history came up when I typed *catalog*. He'd been looking at websites for weapons catalogs and bomb making techniques."

Graciella closed her eyes. "Oh, good God!"

"I didn't open any of the sites. He caught me and yanked the laptop out of my hands so hard and fast that it tore off some of my nails." She held up her hand, showing Graciella the missing acrylic nails. Krystal grabbed a handful of tissues and mopped her face, ruining her makeup, or what was left of it.

Graciella whispered, "You've brought this to us, and you've put your nephew in peril. You have to leave here. Do you have a friend you can stay with? I'll drive you there or call a taxi. If Jamal's looking for you, he's likely to come here. I will not take that risk. I can't, Krystal." She handed her the cell phone. "Call somebody. I'm sorry, but you have to think of Santos's safety."

"Graciella, please. My friends...most of my friends dropped me when I started dating Jamal. They don't like him and they don't want him around."

"Can you blame them? This is all your doing, Krystal." She poured another glass of water and drank it down, taking her time to think. Setting the glass in the sink she went to her small desk and retrieved the book she kept there with the names and numbers of her students and local services she used. She tapped in a number.

Alarm covered Krystal's face. "Who are you calling?" she screeched.

"I'm calling a taxi. If you don't want me to do that, I'll call the police."

"Wait! Let me think. There may be somebody. I'll think of somebody."

Graciella set the phone down and waited.

Finally, Krystal took the phone. "I left my purse and phone when I ran. I hope I can remember Uncle Ollie's number." She tapped, stopped, erased then tapped again.

Uncle Ollie? Graciella had no idea who that was. She was sure she'd remember a name like Ollie.

Her sister-in-law drew in a sharp breath. "Chief? This is Krystal. I'm sorry to call so late. No, no, they're fine. I need your help. Could you come and get me?" She paused for a split second then said, "I'm at my sister-in-law's apartment. She lives in Chatsworth." She recited

Graciella's address. "Thank you, Uncle Ollie. I'll explain everything when you come for me. I love you, too. Twenty minutes? Okay, I'll be waiting." She clicked off and set the phone back on the counter and pressed a hand to her mouth to stifle a sob.

Graciella knew Chief. She couldn't remember ever hearing him referred to as Uncle Ollie. She'd seen him frequently over the years, first in San Diego and then after he and his wife moved to Thousand Oaks to manage their son's property. Retired Navy Chief Williams was an old friend of Earl's.

She put her hand on Krystal's arm. "Do you need anything? Clothes, toiletries? You can borrow what you need. Shall I get a bag?"

Instead of answering, Krystal fell into her arms sobbing. There was no mistaking how terrified she was. Graciella's heart ached for her and the trouble she'd walked into. "It's okay. Chief and Lu will look after you. I'm sure everything will be straightened out soon. Come to my room. We'll gather a few things to hold you over until you can return home."

She put her arm around her sister-in-law's shoulders and took her to the bedroom across the hall from Santos's. Selecting a blouse, sweater and pair of jeans, Krystal placed them and a pair of white panties in a shopping bag. Graciella found an extra brush and comb and a jar of moisturizer she hadn't opened yet. "Take this. I've been using it ever since you posed for their print ads. I have enough for a while." She didn't offer any makeup because her sister-in-law was beautiful without it.

"Can I say goodnight to Santos? I should apologize for the way I acted last time I was here."

"Go ahead, but leave the door open. I'm sure he's still awake. Please, avoid telling him details." She crossed the hall and rapped on her son's door. "Santos? Auntie Krystal would like to talk to you."

Dressed in pajamas, and still showing insult on his young face, he opened the door. "Okay, what?"

Krystal asked him if she could come in to his room to speak privately. She glanced at Graciella with a silent question in her eyes before going inside.

Graciella returned to the kitchen and turned off the stereo then filled the teapot and set it to boil. She'd make Santos a cup of hot chocolate to help him go to sleep once his aunt was gone. She sighed and shook her head, wondering why people walked right into difficult situations they could easily avoid.

The pot rumbled at the same time she heard a tap on the front door. She turned off the stove and peeked out to see who was there. They hadn't turned on the outside light after entering and it was pitch black. She held her breath and snapped it on, recognized Chief Williams and let him inside.

"Come in, Chief. You're Krystal's knight in shining armor tonight. She's talking to Santos. Let's go to the kitchen and have a seat."

He followed her. "Is she all right? Lillian is probably wringing her hands with worry."

"She's fine physically, but she's got herself in a tight corner. She needs a safe haven and some stern advice." She pointed to a chair and took the one across from him. "You're the man for the job, I think."

"I'll call the wife and tell her not to worry." The grizzled old Navy Chief took out an old-fashioned flip phone and tapped. He rolled his eyes when his wife answered. "She's fine, Lu. I'll be home in about an hour. Go to bed and we'll talk in the morning."

He hung up and smiled at Graciella. "She'll still be pacing when we get there."

"How long have you and Lu been married, Chief?"

He winked. "Forty five wonderful years."

She squinched her nose. "Wait a minute, that can't be right. I remember your forty-fifth anniversary. That was a couple of years ago."

"Forty five wonderful years out of forty seven ain't bad. The woman is driving me to distraction. I had to go get me a job so's I'd have an excuse to get out of the house."

She laughed because she knew Chief adored his wife. "Doesn't managing your son's property get you out enough?"

"Nah. I fixed everything that needed doing, and some that didn't. Collecting rent doesn't take that long. Retirement is not for me." He looked up. "Ah, here's my goddaughter." Krystal walked into his outstretched arms.

Santos followed her and shook hands with him. "Hello, Chief."

"Hello, my boy. I think you've grown a foot since Easter."

That was the last time they'd been together, a big Easter dinner at the Jefferson house. "You're right. Soon he'll be as tall as Marvin." She hugged Santos to her side. "Not too soon, I hope."

"Marvin didn't get his full growth until he was seventeen. I can still remember how it galled him to be one of the short boys on the basketball team."

Graciella couldn't imagine Marvin having been short. At six foot six he towered over every person in any room, impossible to miss.

"How tall was my dad, Mama?"

"I've told you before. Six feet and six inches."

"Is that taller than Macfearsome?"

"Oh, yes, by almost half a foot."

"But, Macfearsome is tall."

"Yes, he's a little over six foot."

"I bet my dad had to duck to keep his head from hitting the ceiling fan."

She nodded and smiled at the memory. "You're right, he did."

Chief wrinkled his brow. "Who's this Macfearsome? Anybody I know?"

Santos said, "He's our friend from the beach. We're going to his house tomorrow to make brigadeiros. He's gonna be my coach on the park league baseball team."

A flash of puzzlement crossed his face. "Ah." He jingled his car keys. "Well then, Krystal, it's late. Let's get you home and let these folks get some sleep."

Krystal hugged Graciella and whispered, "Thank you."

"I'm sorry I couldn't do more. I'll call your mom and dad and let them know where you are." Graciella locked the door and put the chain in place when they left then she called Lillian and told her briefly what had transpired.

She dropped the phone back in her bag. "How about some hot cocoa before we go to bed?"

"Oh, boy! I thought you were going to make me go right back to my room." He hurried to the kitchen and took two large mugs from the cupboard. "I'm not sleepy at all."

"That's what I was afraid of." She laughed and took milk from the refrigerator and poured it in a small pan. "I'll make it with milk tonight. This will help us sleep. Did you have a good talk with your aunt?"

"I guess so. Macfearsome stopped her when she tried to make me leave with her and Jamal, and she called him names. I told her I didn't like it that she was mean to him. She embarrassed me."

A chill went through Graciella. "Why didn't you tell me before now?" She faced Santos with her arms crossed.

He stared down at the mugs. "I didn't want to talk about it. Why was she here tonight?"

Graciella brought the milk to a simmer and considered her answer. He was old enough to understand something of adult relationships. "Sometimes we get mixed up with the wrong people and begin to doubt our true values, and then don't use good judgment. It's always best to get to know somebody for a while before you form a friendship, one that might not be the best thing for you."

"Are you mixed up with Macfearsome?"

She turned and gazed into his teasing smile. "Now, why did you ask me that?"

"He kisses you every night. So maybe you are mixed up with him." He wrinkled his brow. "Do you love him? I almost do."

"Love takes a long time, Santos." Her chest felt fluttery. She could easily love Cluny. But not so soon.

"You told me you fell in love with my dad the first night you met him."

She sighed. "I did say that, didn't I? But I was so young. As you get older you become wiser, or at least you should."

"I guess that's why I love Amber, because I'm so young. But I hope I still love her when I'm old."

"Santos, my beautiful son." She ran her fingers through his hair. "I often wonder what's going through that curly head of yours."

"Lotsa stuff."

———

The next morning, they put the double-boiler in the trunk of the car along with a grocery bag containing a few of her favorite utensils and drove across the Santa Susana Mountains to Cluny's home in Spring Grove. Santos was excited to see him and Amber again, and she had to admit, she was, too.

The slender talkative young girl with big amber brown eyes had an air of maturity about her, and at the same time she was like any eight-year-old. Perhaps it was because she was raised by a single father until a couple of years ago.

One day at the beach Amber had matter-of-factly told Santos she'd picked out her new mother, and it was a lot of work to get her dad to take the big step into a second marriage. Cluny had grinned at his goddaughter's chatter and rolled his eyes, but hadn't said anything. Later he'd told Graciella that Dwayne was a goner from the day he'd met Marla, and it had only been a matter of time.

"We're almost there." Santos sat taller in his seat and grinned. "I brought my new mitt so Amber and me can play catch."

"Amber and I," she corrected.

"You're going to play catch, too?"

"No, silly, I was correcting your English. It's Amber and I, not Amber and me."

"Oh, yeah." He pressed his lips together and nodded.

"Maybe Queen likes to play catch." She reached to tousle his hair, but he dodged her hand.

"I bet she does. I can't wait to see her again." He pointed to the park. "We're here!"

Graciella experienced a twinge of hurt when he'd ducked away from her. She had to face the fact that he was getting older, and didn't want her treating him like a baby, showing so much physical affection. She didn't like it, but it was inevitable. She'd never stop hugging and kissing him, but she'd try to give him more space.

Amber hopped off the porch and ran to their car as they came to a stop in Cluny's long driveway. "Uncle Cluny," she yelled, "they're here!" Her long legs poked out beneath a pair of bright red shorts. She wore high-top tennis shoes and a pink T-shirt with a faded Cinderella cartoon on the front.

Santos was out the door as soon as she brought the car to a full stop. Before Graciella was able to get out of the car the two kids flew through the front door of the house.

Slinging her bag over her shoulder, she opened the trunk and reached for her things. Cluny approached. "Wait." He lifted the pan from her hand and set it back in the car. "Kiss me first." He put his arms around her and pressed his smiling lips against hers.

She sighed. He deepened the kiss and held her tight. The man knew how to kiss. She dug her fingers into his back and leaned into him, her knees threatening to give way. When she finally surfaced she stared into his happy blue eyes and sexy smile. "Wow. Let me catch my breath." She inhaled deeply, then kissed him again.

"Macfearsome! Come on, it takes a long time to cook the candy."

Cluny let his hand drift down to her bottom for just an instant then stepped back. "Hold your horses, cowboy. We're going out to lunch first. Get Queen in the house and close her dog door."

"Okay." He disappeared inside.

"One of these days I'll have time to kiss you the way I really want to. Take my time and make it a good one."

Graciella tingled from head to toe, especially parts of her anatomy that had been unused for many years. "They're all good ones, Cluny. Real knee-knockers."

"Yeah?" He grinned and planted a fast peck on her lips and reached for the bag and pot. "Let's take these in. Maybe when the kids are busy this afternoon we can practice."

She followed him up the front walkway admiring his strong back and butt. He didn't have a bit of fat on his lean body. She'd seen that for herself when she'd rubbed suntan lotion on him at the beach. The familiar melting sensation warmed her body in the deepest places. She couldn't seem to exercise the will needed to keep her distance from him. Oh, please, she told herself, let him be the one.

———

Cluny joked with the kids as they finished up their hamburgers and fries at McDonalds. His hand found hers. He couldn't resist touching her.

Amber stopped chewing, ducked her head and peeked under the table. "My uncle is holding hands with your mom again."

"You know what else?" Santos said. "He comes to our house every night to kiss Mama before we go to bed. He probably has to buy gas for his old car every single day."

Graciella slid her hand away from his, leaned her elbow on the table and flushed a sexy shade of pink before she lowered her forehead to her fist. She slanted a glance at him from the corner of her eye and giggled. Catching her off guard, he leaned in and kissed her on the cheek.

"I do, sailor, but believe me, it's worth it." He rested his hand on her bare thigh. Her shorts and tank top had put his libido in an uproar when she'd stepped from the car. "Shall we go home and get started on that super-delicious Brazilian candy?" He'd find a way to be alone with her for more than a few torturing moments if it was the last thing he ever accomplished in this life.

They arrived back at his house and the candy cooking began. Santos instructed him in the fine art of stirring slowly and deliberately, covering every part of the bottom of the pan with his special wooden, chocolate-stirring spoon.

"This is not the official recipe you can find on the internet," Graciella said. "My mother always melted solid chocolate instead of using powder like the traditional way, and added less sweetened condensed milk."

"More butter too, huh, Mama?"

"Yes, more butter." Instinctively she began to reach for her son then caught herself.

"I thought this was different," Cluny said. "I compared your ingredient list with a recipe I found on a website and I thought I wasn't spelling it right." He stirred chocolate and butter while it slowly melted in the top of the double boiler.

"Hey, guess what, Macfearsome, I'm gonna be ten pretty soon. My birthday's in August. Are we going to have a party, Mama? Let's have a big party."

"My birthday's in September," Amber added. "I'll be nine. We can have a rilly big party together."

Cluny grinned. "I have a great idea. We'll have a birthday party at the beach. You can invite some friends and we'll build a big fire and roast marshmallows and make S'mores. The beach park in Ventura has nice grassy spots with picnic tables and fire pits."

The kids bounced up and down yelling, "Yippee!" and "Yay!" and "Cool!"

Graciella laughed and poked a slender finger in his ribs. "Now look what you started, McPherson."

An hour later the triple batch of chocolate candy was cooked, formed into balls, rolled in coconut, nuts and colored sprinkles, and cooling on the granite countertop. The kids grabbed their baseballs and mitts and ran to the large back yard with Queen barking at their heels.

Cluny put an arm around her and grinned. "Alone at last. What say we make some fresh coffee and carry it to the living room where we can put our feet up on the coffee table and *relax*?"

She turned in his embrace and pecked a kiss on his chin. "Sounds *relaxing*. First, where's the ladies room?"

"Sorry, you'll have to use one of the men's rooms. No ladies live in this house." He pointed down the hall. "Second door on the left." He filled the coffee maker with water and dumped fresh ground beans into a white paper filter, got it going and went to brush his teeth. He had work to do on his knee-knocker technique. He grinned all the way to the back of the big nearly-empty house.

Graciella had kicked off her sandals and waited on the big leather couch, long slender legs tucked beneath her. He let his imagination run wild with images of what it would be like the first time he made love to her, because he would make love to this woman. There was no question in his mind.

He sat next to her and pulled her onto his lap. "We have some time to kill while the coffee brews." His hand drifted down her bare leg.

"Hmm, what should we do?" She caressed his cheek and smiled. "I love your eyes, Cluny. Maybe I'll just sigh and gaze into your deep blue eyes."

"I have a better idea." He pulled her into a blazing hot kiss, then another, barely giving her a chance to breathe in between. "Do you like my idea?"

She sighed and rested her head on his shoulder. "Very much. I'm glad I'm sitting down, but what if the kids come in and we don't hear them?"

"I didn't WD-40 those screen door hinges for a very good reason."

Chapter Fourteen

Chatsworth, Wednesday, July 4th

"Settle down, for goodness sake. Cluny's not late. He said he'd pick us up at eleven-thirty and it's only eleven-fifteen." Graciella smacked Santos on the butt and turned him in the direction of his bedroom. "Brush your teeth and get your mitt."

"I already brushed my teeth after breakfast."

"Did you floss?"

Instead of answering he grumbled all the way down the hall to the bathroom.

She was nearly as anxious for Cluny to arrive as Santos was, but for entirely different reasons. Sunday's kisses still burned on her lips, even though he'd come to kiss her goodnight late Monday.

She'd insisted he not come last night because he'd be picking them up this morning for the Independence Day barbecue at the Dempsey house. He'd acceded to her wishes and she'd been sorely disappointed. She loved those late night knocks on the door and his sweet goodnight kisses that left her wanting more.

"That was quick," she remarked when Santos rejoined her, carrying his mitt and ball.

"I didn't eat anything since breakfast, so I didn't have to take long to floss."

"Hmm."

They turned at the footsteps and knock at the door. Santos ran and she followed, her heart fluttered at the thought seeing *her* man.

Santos flung it open. "Macfearsosme, you're..." He stepped back and bumped into his mother. "Jamal."

She put her arms around her son. "What do you want, Jamal?"

He had a dangerous glint in his eyes. "Where's Krystal?"

Cluny came up behind the man. "Ready to go?"

Graciella had told him about the incident on Sunday night. With Santos now behind her, she felt a wave of relief so strong it nearly did her in. "Yes, we're ready."

"Can I do something for you, pal?" Cluny directed his blunt question to Jamal. "If you've finished your business here, we're expected somewhere else."

Jamal snarled and appeared ready to say something. Instead he cast a warning glare at her then at Santos, whirled around and stalked away.

Cluny stepped forward and embraced both of them in a tight, long-armed hug. "Okay?"

"Yes." Graciella stepped back, but Santos clung tight to Cluny's waist. She patted his skinny shoulder. "We're okay now, aren't we, son?" Cluny was here and he would not let anything bad happen to them.

He nodded into Cluny's chest and said, "Uh huh."

Cluny squeezed him again. "Good. Shall we hit the road?" He glanced at her and caught his breath. "Oh, wow, wait a minute! I want to look at your mother." His smile grew huge on his lips and in his eyes. He blew a loud wolf whistle.

Santos turned and gazed at his mother. "My mama's always pretty."

Her face burned with a pleased blush. He'd noticed her new dress and sandals, and obviously liked what he saw. She did a shy pirouette. The saleswoman at The Rack had been right on the mark. Sincere appreciation shone from his breath-stealing blue eyes.

He clutched his chest dramatically and grabbed the doorframe for support. "Oh, man. You look sensational, Mrs. Jefferson." He pulled Santos back against his chest. "Take a look at the most beautiful mom this side of heaven, sailor. I won't be able to drive." He leaned close to Santos' ear. "Do you have your driver's license yet?"

She and Santos laughed. She kissed her son on top of his head and brushed a brief one on Cluny's lips, thoroughly pleased with his reaction. "I'll drive. I've wanted to try that vintage car of yours."

He handed her the keys. "It's all yours." He whispered in her ear, "So am I."

———

Santos squealed, "Eeek!" Queen banged a big paw on the back of the driver's seat to keep from flying to the floor, and Cluny winced as she ground the gears of his precious car. The Green Monster jerked to a halt. If he'd been paying attention and not staring at her chest he'd have had time to caution her when they reached the stop sign on the corner.

"Have you ever driven a stick?"

Face blazing, she jammed the clutch. The engine stopped. "Not since I was a kid in Brazil. Did I hurt your car?" She gave him a pleading look. "I'm sorry."

Cluny turned off the key. "No, this baby can handle a little abuse. Take a deep breath and try again. It'll all come back to you, sweetheart." He put her hand on the key. "Keep your foot on the clutch, turn the key and go easy."

"Maybe you'd better drive."

"Yeah, Mama, let Macfearsome drive."

Cluny turned and grinned at Santos. Queen's big-eyes and perked ears made him chuckle. If a dog could look scared, she had it down pat. "Nah. She's got it."

By the time she got on the freeway, she'd regained her confidence and was doing just fine. He told them they'd drop by his house for a few minutes to pick up the candy and put it in his cooler then head for Gunny's house. "We'll be a little early, but that will give me a chance to introduce you to my good friends, Dwayne and Marla. They've been asking about you because of Amber's ongoing reports."

Graciella glanced quickly at him. "Don't make me nervous."

He brushed his fingers on the back of her bare shoulders. "You have nothing to worry about. They'll love you. They're a great couple."

From the back seat, Santos said, "Did she tell them about me?"

"Yeah, she did. You'll meet a lot of other kids too. Most of the guys coming today have families. Last time I counted it looked like there'd be over a dozen kids there today."

Graciella asked, "Are the parents all veterans? Or are some relatives and friends?"

"Veterans, even the relatives and friends. A few are still active duty and reserve. They're a great bunch of guys and gals."

"Girl soldiers, Macfearsome?"

"Oh, yeah. They're the most feared kind. Nothing scares a bad guy more than a female with a gun." He knew this first hand. Muslim men were especially terror stricken by women in military uniform, aiming automatic weapons at them.

They made a quick stop at his house, and Cluny trotted inside. He was out with the cooler in a couple of minutes and loaded it in his trunk.

Cluny leaned forward and pointed after they'd gone about a quarter mile. "Take the first left on Orange Street, after the stop sign. Dwayne and Marla live right down the second block."

"Is Queen invited to the party, too?" Santos asked.

"Yep. She'll play with their dog. DD weighs about three pounds, and was Gunny's make-up gift after he nearly blew it with Marla. The mutt was top dog in that house before Declan came along."

"How old is the baby now? I can't imagine them hosting this big party so soon." It had been almost ten years, but she remembered clearly how tired she was for so long after Santos was born. The fact that her husband had been killed in combat shortly before, probably added to her fatigue and lethargy.

"Marla's a trooper. She was back on her feet in no time. It wouldn't surprise me if she strapped the baby on her back and went to work. She's already been to the Big D construction office to do payroll a couple of times."

"My goodness, what else does she do? You never said, but I had the impression she was a full-time mom."

Cluny had to laugh. "Everything she does is full-time. When she met Dwayne she was selling real estate and had just embarked on her first property development project. She contracted with him to renovate an old apartment building into condos. Gunny got more than he bargained for, the lucky S.O.B."

He grinned at Santos. "Hey, you're going to get in some batting practice today."

"They have a yard big enough to play baseball in?"

"It's a different kind of batting practice. Instead of baseballs we're using water balloons." He touched Graciella's arm. "It's the yellow house on the left, middle of the block. Pull in the driveway and park on the left side close to the garage door."

"What if they have to get out?"

"The door rolls up, and Gunny parks his truck on the right side of the garage. I can always move my Green Monster if necessary. That's it. Nice and tight." He opened the door and went to the driver's side to help her out. Again, she took his breath away. Every man at the barbecue would be wishing they were in his shoes.

He smiled. "You are beautiful, baby." He kissed her cheek. "Smell good too. Please tell me you wore that just for me."

Her smooth hand on his cheek, she said quietly, "I bought it just for you and I'm wearing it just for you."

Cluny was afraid his heart would stop. How was he going to keep his hands off her all day? He drew her into a kiss, not caring who saw them.

"Come on, Macfearsome. You can kiss Mama later. Open the trunk and I'll get the cooler with the candy and we can go to the party."

He had a plan for later. If Graciella agreed, they'd be alone tonight at either her apartment or his house. The wait would be an eternity.

———

Excitement roared through Graciella. If there was a way to manage it, Cluny would make love to her tonight. She was still trying to think of a solution when they entered the house and a very pretty, petite blond woman shouted, "Mac!" and flung herself into Cluny's arms.

"Mis! You made it!" He planted a kiss on her cheek and lifted her off her feet. Setting her down, he took Graciella's hand. "This is my old Marine buddy, Misty Beachy. She served in Iraq with me and Gunny. Mis, this is my special lady, Graciella Jefferson and her son Santos."

This woman was a Marine? She'd served in Iraq? Graciella gathered her thoughts and smiled at the woman. "I'm happy to meet you. Should I call you Mis or Misty?"

The woman grabbed her hand in a firm grip. "Mac's the only one on the planet who calls me Mis. The other guys always called me Beachy, or they said, 'Yes ma'am, Master Sergeant Beachy, ma'am.'" She turned to Santos. "Hi there, Amber tells me your dad was a SEAL. I'm honored to meet you."

Santos flushed a sweet shade of pink and stood taller. "Me too, thanks. Macfearsome met my dad once."

"Macfearsome? Good name for my old buddy. Let's go in, I was helping Marla rearrange the fridge so we could make room for your surprise dessert." She put her hand on his shoulder and led him through a doorway on the right. Queen bounded ahead of them.

Graciella looked up into Cluny's handsome face. "She was a Marine in Iraq? She's very pretty. I would never have guessed she was a war veteran." Determined to stifle the little twinge of jealousy she'd felt at their familiar and enthusiastic embrace, she asked, "Was she around the day you got ambushed?"

"Oh, yeah, she was right in the thick of it. The truck she was driving took a hit. She charged out the door with her M-16 blazing like a video game superhero. She was wounded and didn't even know it until later. Mis is a lot tougher than she looks."

"She was wounded?"

"Yeah, she took some shrapnel in the right shoulder, tiny fragments in the right eye and ear. Her hearing on that side was permanently damaged. That's why she turns some to the left when she's talking to you."

Graciella couldn't imagine this. She was ambivalent about women in the military, and had no idea they took such dangerous combat roles. "Is she on disability now?"

"She's eligible for ongoing medical services, but she works full time for Customs, training sniffer dogs." He put his arm around her waist. "Let's go meet Dwayne and Marla so we'll have time to talk to them before people start pouring in."

The pretty, petite woman trained dogs. Graciella wondered about the other vets she'd meet today, what kind of businesses or jobs they were in. He led her to the kitchen where a burly, dark haired man with a prosthetic leg showing below his shorts, was in the process of putting on some sort of contraption over his muscular shoulders.

"Hey, McPherson, help me with this damn thing."

"What the hell is it?" Cluny took her hand and led her to the man that had to be Dwayne Dempsey.

He looked exactly like she expected. She smiled and put out her hand. "You're Dwayne, Amber's father. I'm Graciella Jefferson."

He grinned and took her hand, and at the same time gave her a bold, appraising once- over. "McPherson should have told me you were so gorgeous. I'd have dressed better." He dipped his head. "Dwayne Dempsey at your service, ma'am." His grip was firm and his eyes danced above his big smile. She was pleased and shy by the handsome guy's unveiled admiration.

She returned his grin. "I see the problem. You've got it upside down." She reached up and pulled the papoose carrier off his shoulders, flipped it around and held it for the two men to see. "It goes this way. Otherwise the baby would fall out."

A striking red-head strolled in from the dining room. "You'd be toast if that happened, Dempsey." She stopped in front of Graciella. "I'm Marla, and you are Santos's mother. Amber talks about the two of you constantly. I'm so happy to meet you. If this big galumpff ," she pointed to Cluny, "gives you any trouble let me know."

Graciella liked her instantly. "I think I can handle him, but now I know where to go if he misbehaves. What can I do to help? I'm anxious to meet that baby of yours."

"Come right this way. Beachy's trying to dress the little squirm worm."

"You call her Beachy? Not Misty?"

"The *guys* usually call each other by their last names. Misty Beachy is one of the guys." Screams and laughter drifted in from outside as Santos and Amber played with Queen and DD. "That will have them worn out before the party even starts." She led Graciella down the hall.

Misty exited a doorway holding a lively, kicking baby in her arms. "He already kicked off his socks. I think he's a born nudist."

"Takes after Dwayne." Marla lifted the baby, nuzzled him then handed him to Graciella. "It's nice and warm today. He won't miss his socks."

Graciella sighed. "My word, except for the hair, he looks just like his daddy. I can't believe he's barely a month old. I haven't held a baby in years. Umm, the wonderful baby smell and velvety skin. "Oh, Marla, he's so precious, and so *big*."

"I expect he'll be walking by next week. We just put him in the jumper for the first time yesterday. Had to prop him up with pillows all around, but he got the hang of kicking his feet in no time."

"Gosh, babies seem to be so much stronger these days. Santos couldn't hold his head up until he was almost two weeks old."

"Declan could lift his head within a day after we brought him home from the hospital. Do you mind taking him out to his daddy?"

"Not at all. Shall I put him in the backpack?"

"Yes. Soon as Dwayne moves around he'll fall asleep. We discovered early on that it worked better than the rocking chair. I think he likes the sound of his daddy's voice too."

Graciella carried the precious baby out to the patio. She arrived in time see Santos shake hands with Dwayne and say, "I'm going to marry Amber when she grows up. Is that all right with you?"

Dwayne and Cluny, to their credit, didn't laugh. They nodded thoughtfully then Dwayne said, "It's fine with me, son. What does she think about it?"

Deadly serious, Santos answered, "I didn't tell her yet. She's too young. I'll wait for a while."

"Dwayne nodded. "Good plan. Shall we seal the deal with a beer?"

Wide-eyed, Santos said, "I don't drink beer."

"Good answer." Dwayne placed a hand on the slender boy's shoulder and smiled. "You just passed the first prospective son-in-law test."

Graciella decided she really liked Gunny Dempsey.

"In the meantime, sailor," Cluny said, "how'd you like you to meet your future brother-in-law, Declan?"

Graciella held the baby in front of Santos. "Look at this cuddly bundle. It seems to me it wasn't so long ago I was holding you at this age."

"Will he really be my brother-in-law, Macfearsome?" He touched the infant's wispy red hair and grinned.

"He's Amber's brother, so that would be a yes."

Graciella straightened and pointed her chin to the carrier on Dwayne's back. "I have orders from his mother to deposit him in the backpack."

Cluny reached for Declan. "I'll take him." He lifted the baby and tenderly threaded his legs through the holes in the seat, strapped him in and stuffed the blanket around him.

He handled him like a dad who'd raised a family of his own. He'd told her about how he and Dwayne had been left with three-day-old Amber, and were both terrified about what to do with her. They'd obviously figured it out. Both men seemed very comfortable handling Amber's baby brother.

"You do that very well, Cluny," she teased, "I'm impressed."

"A couple of the foster homes I lived in took newborns for the first couple of weeks of life while they waited for adoption. I always loved the smell of babies." He glanced at a couple of men arriving with their wives or girlfriends. "Don't let it get around."

"Your secret's safe with me." She squeezed his arm. The more she saw of this man, the more she liked. He directed a loving look to her eyes, and she warmed all over.

"I'll introduce you to these guys, then you can help me to carry out the steaks and burgers." He took her hand and led her to a small group of early arrivals.

Graciella was astonished to see Ollie and Lu Williams come through the back gate. What could he possibly be doing here? She tugged Cluny's hand and met them halfway across the lawn. "Chief, is something wrong? Is Krystal okay? How did you find me?" Her heart raced waiting for his answer.

"I wasn't looking for you. My boss invited us to the party."

"Your boss?" Confusion piled on bewilderment as she tried to understand. "Who is your boss?"

"The man you're holding hands with, Cluny McPherson." He grinned and turned to Lu. "Louella, honey, this is my new boss."

Louella offered her hand and a big smile to Cluny. "God bless you for saving our marriage, Mr. McPherson."

"Cluny, please." He laughed and kissed her cheek. "I'm happy to meet you. I may be calling on you for advice if he gives me any trouble."

"Oh, dear, you can count on that." She took Chief's arm and hugged it to her side. "I've never known this man to stay out of trouble."

Speechless, Graciella took in the exchange. Chief worked for Cluny? She squeezed his hand and asked, "Why didn't you tell me Chief worked for you?"

"I didn't know you knew Chief." He stepped back and wrinkled his brow. "How do you know him?"

Ollie shook his head. "It's a small world. I'm old pals with her father-in-law, Earl Jefferson. I've known Graciella and Santos for some ten years. She only knew a couple of people in San Diego. Marv charged me with looking in on her when he left for Iraq."

Cluny smiled his heart-melting smile. "I'll be damned. It *is* a small world." He put his arm around her shoulders and hugged her to his side.

What an astonishing coincidence.

———

This could complicate things, Cluny thought. He'd just hired a man who happened to be friends with Graciella's in-laws, and she'd known him as long as she'd been in the country as a bride. Might get a bit cozy. Too late now, the man started work tomorrow. Cluny would have to tell Gunny about this turn of events.

The old Chief directed his comments to Graciella. "Damndest thing happened. Earl called us, after you told Lillian that Krystal was staying with us, to say this hot-shot modeling agency in New York wanted Krystal to bring her portfolio and come for an in-person interview."

"Do you know the name of it?" Graciella asked.

"Can't remember, but it was a place she'd been trying to get signed by."

"So when is she leaving?"

"She left this morning. Lillian brought some of her clothes and her portfolio. Lu and I drove her to the airport at five-thirty this morning." He pressed his lips together. "That bastard boyfriend of hers won't be able to track her down now."

Graciella faced Cluny. "This is wonderful news. Krystal thought she'd be stuck doing department store catalogs forever. Lillian and I both told her if she was patient she'd get signed by a big agency."

He took her arm. "Excuse us, Chief? Mrs. Williams? I'd like to introduce Graciella to some of the people arriving." He pointed to the open side gate and the sliders leading out of the house. Partygoers were pouring in. "Circulate, Chief. You know Gunny and some of the others."

Chief nodded and led Louella to a long table where Misty Beachy was serving cold drinks and beer.

Cluny wanted to introduce Graciella to as many as possible before the festivities started. He was proud to show off *his* luscious woman.

Santos rushed up to them, breathless and excited. "Mama! See that tent way in back? Amber and her cousins are having a campout tonight. She wants me to come. Her dad has an extra sleeping bag. Can I? Can I? Please?"

This was the break he was waiting for. Before Graciella could answer Cluny said, "Hey, that sounds like a great idea, buddy." He grinned at her. "What do you think, Mama?"

"I…"

"Please, Mama. I never did a campout in my whole life. They're going to roast marshmallows and tell ghost stories." His pleading expression was so comical, Cluny had to laugh. To his great relief, she was smiling.

"If Amber's parents give their permission, it's okay with me."

"They did already, but you can ask them again."

Chapter Fifteen

GRACIELLA WANTED TO BE ALONE WITH CLUNY TONIGHT, BUT now that the perfect opportunity had presented itself, she was nervous. The look he gave her was proof he'd been thinking along the very same lines. She had a moment of hesitation, wondering if he'd planned it. No, he wouldn't trick her. That's not who Cluny McPherson was.

"Hey, here're a couple of guys I haven't seen in a while. Come, I'll introduce you."

He led her across the yard to a couple of vets who looked to be around forty. She wondered how Cluny knew them because he was much younger. One tall man was dark, the other fair. Four little girls, all toddlers, clung to their legs. The dark man's wife was a very pregnant, petite brunette and the blond man's wife was tall and also blond. Graciella smiled. The two couples made her think of the old fairy tale, Snow White and Rose Red.

Cluny made introductions all around. "Rafi and Joe own a small cargo airline in West L.A. These guys flew Queen back to the U.S. from Iraq on one of their aircraft with several other dogs being evacuated." She was amazed that there were so many connections in the large community of veterans in Southern California.

"What beautiful children," Graciella said as she bent down to the little girls. The oldest smiled shyly. "Who's your daddy?"

The tall blond man picked up the girl and kissed her on the cheek. "The two blondies are mine and Jill's, and the brown-eyed beauties are Rafi and BD's."

"You're so lucky. I wanted to have a large family, but I have just one son." She pointed to a group of kids filling small balloons with water. "He's the skinny dark boy with curly hair."

Cluny squeezed her close and kissed her cheek. "I have a hunch that situation could be remedied."

Her breath caught at his meaning. She stared into his blue gaze and blushed. The four people she'd just met got it, too. "Uh, if you'll excuse me? I'll help Marla carry out the rest of the food."

She needed some space. Her desire for Cluny unnerved her. There was no mistaking where he wanted this to go, and she was so afraid they might be moving too fast. She headed for the kitchen. "Marla, what may I do to help? I've been introduced to so many people my head is spinning."

"I know what you mean. I don't know all of them. Dwayne's been doing this party for at least seven years, and he thinks I should know everybody by osmosis. We've only been married for two years. I just smile and nod." She indicated a tray. "How about taking these condiments out and setting them on the end of the table where Beachy set up the bar? The steaks and hamburgers will be done soon. I have a big macaroni and cheese casserole in the oven for the little kids."

"Happy to." She reached for the large tray and turned to leave.

"Oh, ask Cluny if he'll unfold and set up those chairs at the side of the garage. It's hard to cut a steak if you can't balance the plate on your knees. The two picnic tables are reserved for the children."

Graciella went outside, set the tray on the end of the bar and was glad Cluny and a couple of men were already carrying the chairs and setting them up in three circles. She'd keep her distance from him for a few minutes longer.

As she made her last trip into the kitchen for a large bowl of potato salad, Marla said. "I have to retrieve DD and put her in her carrier. She's a relentless beggar and she'll annoy everyone no end. Queen will stay next to Cluny and nap during dinner."

"I'll fetch her," Graciella offered. "You need to take a breather, and anyway I've wanted to get my hands on the cute little fluff ball all afternoon." She carried out the salad and peered around the large yard. DD chased some of the children while Queen watched from the shade of a large eucalyptus. Everything about Queen indicated she thought the little dog was nothing if not boring.

Approaching the kids, Graciella stood until DD ran past her then reached down and scooped her up. "Come here you little miscreant. Your mom says it's time for your afternoon nap."

She carried the tiny dog inside.

Marla nodded her head in the direction of the hall. "Her prison cell is in Amber's room. The first one on the left. Please close the door when you leave. She'll be asleep in no time."

Graciella cuddled the little dog that was panting with exhaustion, and went down the hall to Amber's bedroom. She put her in the kennel with a final pat and locked the wire door. "Sweet dreams."

On her way back outdoors she heard some men talking and laughing. She peeked in the living room then ducked back when she heard, "Did you see the babe on McPherson's arm today? How does he do it?"

"That lucky bastard has had more women on their backs than an Arab sheik."

An icy chill settled in her stomach as she leaned back, tight against the wall.

"Do you suppose he and Beachy are still doing the nasty? They look pretty tight."

One guy snorted. "The words, Beachy and tight, don't belong in the same sentence."

"What do you know? You're just pissed because she'd never spread her legs for you."

"You either, smartass."

"She never put out for any of the guys in our unit but McPherson."

To her horror, Dwayne Dempsey walked in from the dining room and saw her cowering against the wall. She turned her head, tried to hide the dismay on her face. He glanced at the men in the living room. "You've had enough to drink. Either go out and grab some food or haul ass."

"You're not our sergeant any longer, Gunny." One of them slurred.

"This is my home, asshole. You want to take me on?"

"Nah, he's okay, Gunny. We'll get some food and coffee down him. Come on, jerk-off, before you get us thrown out of the party." The men trooped from the room. One murmured to Dwayne as he passed, "Sorry, man."

"Yeah," Dempsey answered, his voice laced with anger and skepticism. He watched them leave, then came to her. "You okay? What happened?"

Graciella squeezed her eyes closed and swallowed. "Nothing."

"What did they say, Graciella?"

She drew in a shaky breath. "They were talking about Cluny." To her horror, tears brimmed.

"Those creeps will never be invited to my home again."

"No, please don't make anything of it. They had too much to drink, that's all."

"It's not the first time. What did you hear?" He gently placed his hands on her bare upper arms. "Tell me what they said, Graciella."

She choked back a sob. "They said...they said..."

Dwayne put his arm around her shoulders and led her down the hall. "Come with me."

Marla entered carrying Declan. "Something wrong?"

He looked back over his shoulder. "She overheard those drunks, Sal, Ben and Joey, shooting off their mouths about something they probably don't know a damn thing about. In fact, they don't know shit. I'm going to go and kick their asses out of here."

Graciella gave him a pleading look. "Please, don't do that. I'll be fine."

"Great goats, please do as she asks, Dempsey, and watch your language, there are women and children present. Come with me, Graciella. I'm going to change Declan and put him down for a nap."

Not sure what to do, Graciella hesitated. Dwayne gave her a gentle push. "Sorry for my big mouth. Go on. I won't do anything. Tell Marla what happened." He left them.

Tears threatened again. She choked back a sob and followed Marla to the master bedroom, not sure what she was feeling or if she could even talk about it. "I should probably go. I should..."

"Come with me. We'll take care of the baby and get a breather from the party. I need a few minutes anyway. Please?"

Graciella sat on the side of the bed while Marla changed the infant and placed him in the bedside cradle with a pacifier in his mouth. She turned and sat next to her and took her hand. "I don't know what they said, and you don't have to tell me if you don't want to, but I'm so sorry."

"They said some things about Cluny. About him and women."

"Listen to me. Dwayne and Cluny have been like brothers for over half their lives. I don't know what you heard, but Cluny's one of the finest men I've ever known. He's our daughter's godfather. I trust him with my children. For goodness sake, I'm half in love with the big softy myself."

Marla's words took the edge off Graciella's distress, but she suspected there had to be a grain of truth in what they said, or why talk about him that way? "They said some things about him and Misty Beachy, about him having a lot of women."

Marla scooted closer and hugged her to her side. "Look. They're speculating, but I'll tell you what I know. Cluny is an attractive man. He loves and appreciates women. He likes to have fun. He likes to laugh but he's never been with anyone for more than a date or two. I doubt most of that time was much more than dinner and a movie. You're the first woman he's ever introduced to us. That says a lot."

"What about Misty? Why would they say those things if there was nothing to it?"

"That was many years ago. Dwayne told me Cluny and Misty were very close in Iraq. They looked after each other. They might have slept together back then. She was his superior officer and very much to herself as far as the men in the unit were concerned. Cluny was the only Marine she ever allowed to get close, and to this day he has never said a single word about their relationship. Dwayne said it drove the men crazy that he wouldn't dish on her, or why he was able to get close while she held every other man at arm's length."

Lingering doubt and fear persisted. "But, do you suppose they're still—?"

"No, I do not. When they came home from their deployment they went their separate ways. They have a special bond, as soldiers often do who've served in war together. Don't listen to rumors. Ask Cluny. He won't lie to you."

"Hearing those things, it really hurt because I'm falling in love with him." She covered her face with her hands and rocked back and forth. "It's just…it's been so long since I've had feelings for a man. I have a child, I have responsibilities, and I can't behave like a moonstruck teenager."

Marla chuckled. "Oh, honey, don't find trouble where there isn't any. I can give you that advice because that's what I always did before I met Dwayne. Just relax and try to have a good time tonight." She stood and tugged Graciella to her feet. "If we stay here much longer we'll miss the sing-off."

"Sing-off?"

"Let's go, you'll see. It's so much fun. Even the kids participate. Why don't you splash some cold water on your face first?"

"Yes, my eyes are probably red from crying."

Marla waited for her then checked the baby monitor, led the way from the bedroom and quietly closed the door.

Cluny spotted her when they walked out on to the covered patio. He stood and flashed a happy grin, pointed to an empty chair and motioned for her to join him. "Where you been, baby?" He kissed her cheek. "You almost missed the fun."

She forced a smile. "I was talking to Marla while she put the baby down. What fun?"

He remained standing then to her surprise began to belt out the Marine hymn. As soon as the words, "From the halls of Montezuma" left his lips about half the men joined him in a raucous version of the familiar song and finished it with a deafening "Ooh Rah!" amidst good-natured hoots and cat calls. Cluny waved his hands and sang, "Off we go into the wild blue yonder," and other men joined in, singing louder than the Marines. When they finished, laughter and applause filled the yard. Neighbors must have heard them from blocks around.

Chief bellowed, "Listen up you jarheads and flyboys!" He stood with Santos in front of him and a single other man. He sang, "Anchors away, my boys, anchors away." Santos sang along in his reedy boy's voice and the other partiers joined in. Before they'd finished the last note, the last few men in the crowd began, "Over hill, over dale, we will hit the dusty trail," and were soon joined by the rest of the company.

Cluny leaned close to her ear and shouted, "In official circles the Army song is always done first, but every year I get the jump on them." He laughed and clapped with the rest.

She smiled in spite of her bruised feelings. "This is wonderful, Cluny. Except for Chief I thought every man here was a Marine."

"The only service we don't have tonight is Coast Guard. Last year there were a couple of Born Readys here, but nobody knew the lyrics to sing along with them. They don't get no respect." He grinned. "I don't know about you, but I'm ready to cut into one of those steaks Dempsey barbecued. Let's grab a plate while the parents in the group get their kids settled. Santos and Amber can take care of themselves."

Her mood lifting, she followed him to the buffet table. Misty handed plates and wrapped silverware to them, then the others lining up behind. Graciella studied the attractive woman. Devoid of makeup she looked too young to have been a combat veteran. Misty was friendly but guarded. She joked with the guys, said things like, 'Move along, soldier," with a smile, but always seemed to have an invisible barrier between herself and others. Graciella *would* ask Cluny about her, but not tonight.

The water balloon batting contest started before everyone had finished eating. Cluny leaned in and said, "You don't want to get too close to that corner of the yard, unless you want to get your sexy new dress wet. Just watch, you'll see what I mean." He stood. "Got to take my turn behind the plate."

She admired his graceful, masculine walk as he strolled to the jerry-rigged batting cage, gathering kids as he went like the Pied Piper. Marla sat down beside her, bouncing Declan on her shoulder. Graciella held out her arms. "May I hold him?"

"Sure." She handed her a small receiving blanket. "Put this over your shoulder. He just ate like a starved piglet." She stood and put the infant in her arms. "I'll be right back; I'm going to get a Coke. Want anything?"

"No. Take your time." Graciella hugged the warm little body to her shoulder and kissed one of his fat hands then rubbed his back. In a few seconds he let fly a massive burp and kicked his legs. "My good-ness, you don't seem big enough to make a sound like that." She held him so she could examine his features, and he rewarded her with a sappy grin. "Proud of yourself, are you?"

Misty Beachy took the seat Cluny had vacated. She let out a sigh. "Wow, I'm famished. They must have had to bring a U-haul truckload of meat for this crowd."

She set the plate on her knees and sliced the huge steak on her plate. "Umm, oh, this is so good. Dempsey cooks a mean steak."

Graciella saw Marla approach, then stop, raise her eyebrows and tilt her head as if to say now's-your-chance.

Misty grinned around a bite of steak, chewed and swallowed. "Ever get the idea you and I were invited here as babysitters and serving wenches?"

Graciella returned her smile. "Now that you mention it." She put Declan on his back on her knees and patty-caked his fat little feet together. "What do you think, shorty?"

"That kid looks like he'll be bigger than his dad someday. Dempsey's the *short* one of the three brothers."

She cocked her head. "Short one?"

"You met his brother Dylan over there, and his brother Donovan is taller than both of them. I'm sorry Donovan didn't make it today. I haven't seen him in over four years. He's a lifer."

Graciella gasped. "He's in prison!"

"Oh, no, sorry, he's a career non-commissioned officer in the Marines. He's stationed in Hawaii." Her shoulders bounced when she laughed. "I've been around the military so much I forget everybody else isn't familiar with the jargon."

Here goes. "So, you've known Cluny for a long time?"

"Yeah, we served together in Iraq. We rotated out the same year."

Not much information there. "Um, you've stayed in touch."

"Not as much as we used to, but yeah, we're pretty tight."

Pretty tight? "Oh, so…"

"Okay, I'll make it easy on you because I can see where this is going, okay? I love Mac. He's the best friend I've ever had, male or female." She met Graciella's gaze. "Friend. Without benefits. That's it. Anybody who would ever hurt Mac will have me to answer to." She jabbed a bite of steak into her mouth, her expression black, she blew a breath from her nose and chewed.

Too stunned to speak, Graciella stared at the happy baby in her lap and swallowed.

"Sorry," Misty mumbled, "I didn't mean it to come out like that."

"That's okay. I get it."

"No. My dad says I lack people skills. The only thing I was ever good at is giving orders to soldiers and training dogs."

"Misty, it's okay." Graciella put the baby on her shoulder and stood. "Really."

"What's okay?" Cluny came up behind Misty, grabbed her around the neck and smacked a resounding kiss on her cheek.

"Mac! You got me all wet, you big jerk."

"That was my intention, Master Sergeant Beachy, ma'am." He let go, but not before growling into her neck. "What's okay?"

Beachy extricated herself, shoved him on the chest and said, "None of your business. Beat it!"

He held his hands up and backed away. "Yes, ma'am. I'll return when it's safer." He chuckled and walked away.

Misty huffed then began to laugh. "See what I mean?"

Graciella nodded. "Uh-huh, I do."

Marla approached them. "Holy hail, are we going to have fisticuffs here?"

Misty straightened her soggy T-shirt. "Nope. Just putting that big clown in his place. Right, Jefferson?"

"Right, Beachy." Graciella didn't try to stop the big grin growing on her face.

Misty picked up her empty plate. "I'm going to put my shirt and shorts in your dryer if that's okay. He must have taken a few direct hits with the water balloons."

"Go right ahead," Marla answered. "There's a bathrobe on the back of my bedroom door if the fireworks start before they get dry."

"Thanks." The petite blond walked away.

Marla bounced the baby on her shoulder. "So? How'd it go?"

"Good question. I'm still processing it. She's an interesting person."

Cluny returned, still wearing a sappy smile. "Can I have a hug?"

Graciella gave him a warning look. "Don't even think about it."

"Come on, McPherson, I'll get you a dry shirt." Marla handed the baby back to Graciella. "Give him to his daddy. It's his turn."

"Be right back." Cluny winked and followed Marla into the house.

Dwayne saw her coming. He took his son, held him high overhead then kissed his rosy little cheeks. "How's it goin', slugger?" He turned around so she could deposit the baby into the empty carrier he'd been wearing all day.

"All buckled up," Graciella said and patted Declan's chubby baby knees.

Dwayne touched her arm. "Graciella. I don't want to alarm you, but stay close to Cluny during the fireworks. I'll keep an eye on him, too. He'll never admit it, but I know the explosions get to him."

"You're having fireworks here?"

"No, but we're high enough we can see them from the high school football field. They're pretty spectacular. Don't worry. He'll be fine." He patted her arm and was about to leave when Amber and Santos ran up to him.

"Daddy, look. I didn't get wet."

"How'd you manage that, squirt?"

"I missed on purpose and let Uncle Cluny catch all the pitches they threw at me. He got drownded." She grinned.

"Drowned," Santos corrected.

She scowled at him. "Yeah. That." She looked up at her tall father. "When are we having ice cream?"

"After the fireworks. Would you excuse me and Santos for a minute?" He made little shooing motions with his fingers. Puzzled, Amber backed away. Dwayne leaned low next to Santos' ear so his daughter couldn't overhear. "A piece of advice, pal. If you want the relationship to last, don't correct your girlfriend's use of the language." He patted the boy's head and walked away.

Graciella smiled. "Mr. Dempsey will make a great father-in-law. Now do me a favor and go wash up. You've got mustard on your cheeks and your hands probably have enough germs to infect an entire city." She pointed to the house. "That way. Now."

He emitted a long-suffering sigh. "Okay."

"I better go, too," Amber said, and followed him. "What did my daddy say, Santos?"

"Nuthin."

Some of the men gathered up trash and set the chairs in rows facing the back fence. Moms corralled their children. A few with the smallest went to Dwayne and Marla to say their goodbyes. Graciella was about to go see if she could do anything to help with the cleanup when Cluny returned and pulled her aside.

"Come in the garage. I want to show you something."

"What?"

"You'll see." He took her hand then led her around the side to the back of the free-standing garage, next to the house. Opening the side door, he tugged her inside.

"It's too dark to see anything in here. Where's the light switch?"

"We don't need light for this." He pulled her into his arms and kissed her. "I've been dying to do this for hours." He kissed her again. This time hugging her tight to his body, he gathered up the hem of her skirt, lifted it, and then he pressed a big hand to her panty clad bottom. "God, you make me crazy."

She struggled in his arms. "Cluny, you *are* crazy." And he was making her crazy.

"Do you want me to stop?" His heavy breath warmed her ear.

"No, but..." The words died in her mouth as he kissed her deeper and with more passion. Instead of resisting, she hiked herself up and put her legs around his hips. His sexy, shaky groan turned her insides molten. She grabbed his neck then a handful of his hair and kissed him back with all she had in her.

He moved his lips from hers. "I want—"

She silenced him with a kiss. Their tongues fought for dominance in a figurative match between fencing masters. She could barely breathe, every cell of her body liquidating with a level of desire she'd never experienced. She emitted a mewling moan when his callused hand slipped inside the waistband of her panties and squeezed bare flesh. She wanted more.

Gasping, he said, "We should stop."

"Yes. Don't stop."

"Ow!"

"What's the matter?"

"You're pulling my hair out."

She released him immediately. "Sorry." She dropped her forehead on his shoulder and gasped. "You're right, we need to stop. They'll be wondering where we are." The last thing she wanted was for him to stop what he was doing.

He squeezed her bare bottom and pulled her tight against his body. "I'm coming home with you tonight."

"I want you to."

"Jesus, do you have any idea what you do to me?" He reached back and unlocked her legs then slid them down. "Go back to the party. I need a minute."

She took a deep breath and ran her hands over her hair. "I need a minute too."

"Okay." He sucked in some air and began to chuckle.

The outlines of his face and the whites of his eyes were visible in the small amount of light coming through the windows. Before she knew it they were both laughing. She reached up and put her hand over his lips. "Shush, somebody will hear us. Be quiet, be—" unable to finish the sentence, she collapsed against him, weak with laughter.

He placed his hands on her cheeks, lowered his head and kissed her gently. "Okay?"

Her long fingers wrapped his wrists. "Better than okay."

When they stepped outside the garage it was nearly dark. Her heart tripped faster than a snare drum beating a quick march.

He grabbed her hand. "Stop."

"What? Why?"

"Your hem is tucked in your panties." He tugged it free and smoothed her skirt.

"Oh, my Lord." She gasped a quiet thank you as heat burned her cheeks.

"Nobody noticed. They're waiting for the fireworks to start. Let's sit with our backs next to the garage. I'll grab a couple of chairs. He snatched two chairs and was intercepted by Dwayne and Marla on his way back to her. Dwayne carried a chair and set it next to Graciella.

"We'll sit back here with you," Marla said. "I can duck into the garage with Declan if the fireworks scare him."

Thankful her breath had returned, Graciella said, "I don't see Santos and Amber. Where are they, do you know?"

Dwayne pointed to the big eucalyptus. "Up there, sitting in the crotch of the two big limbs. Best view in the house." He motioned to Marla. "Sit, honey. I'll stand behind you."

Queen leaned against Cluny's leg. "Where'd you come from? Were you looking for me, girl?"

Dwayne grinned, "She's been right here, next to the back door of the garage, waiting for you to finish your business inside. That's a good dog. Be nice to her."

Chapter Sixteen

GRACIELLA ENJOYED THE LOUD EXCLAMATIONS FROM ADULTS AND children when the fireworks got underway. The northern sky toward Simi filled with the spectacular glow of magnificent color and continuous booming. Cluny's hand squeezed hers ever tighter. She glanced at him and saw him smiling, but his jaw twitched each time a big explosion filled the night air. His leg bounced under their joined hands.

"Cluny?" His grip had grown painful. She leaned her shoulder into his, but he seemed in another dimension. She raised her eyes to Dwayne, trepidation building inside her.

He moved behind Cluny and placed strong hands on his shoulders. "Okay, McPherson?"

"What?"

"How ya doin'?" Dwayne asked.

Queen dropped her head on Cluny's knee. When he ignored her, she whined. He patted her. "Good, Gunny, we're good."

Marla held the baby toward Cluny. "Could you hold Declan for a couple of minutes? I need to get another blanket from the house."

"Hold Declan?" He raised his eyes to Marla, let go of Graciella's hand, and reached for the infant. "Sure, I'll hold him."

Graciella noted the tender way he cuddled the baby to his chest, smiled and brushed his lips on his tiny head. Dwayne had relaxed his grip on Cluny's shoulders but remained standing behind his chair. To her relief, Cluny visibly calmed and bounced the baby against his shoulder stroking his back. He hummed a quiet tune.

Marla returned with a crocheted baby blanket, draped it over her son's back and Cluny's shoulder, but made no move to retrieve him. She took her seat next to Graciella and gave her a look that said volumes, accompanied by a small nod. She whispered in Graciella's ear. "I'll explain later."

The fireworks only lasted half an hour, but it had been spectacular all the same.

Parents gathered their kids, coolers, and other things they'd brought and began taking leave. They said their good-byes to friends and approached Dwayne and Marla to thank them for another great Independence Day party. Most of them shoved wads of bills in the big empty jar at the bar before departing. The single men folded chairs and stacked them on the side of the garage.

Beachy was one of the last to depart. She thanked her hosts, kissed Cluny on the cheek and said, "Do you want me to take Queen with me, Mac?"

"Nah, she'll stay with me. I left the key under the back steps, let yourself in, Mis."

Misty Beachy is staying at Cluny's house?

"Thanks for the bunk, Mac. I'll most likely be pulling out before you get home." She nodded to Graciella. "Nice meeting you. I hope to see you again."

Speechless for a split second, Graciella processed the fact that his former girlfriend was spending the night at Cluny's house. She wondered if this was a common occurrence. "Um, yes, Misty, me, too."

Marla picked up on Graciella's anxiety and squeezed her arm. "Don't be a stranger, Misty. Stop in next time you're in town."

Graciella's furtive glance in Cluny's direction revealed that he'd stopped paying attention to the conversation and was concentrating on the cooing infant.

"If you'll excuse me," Dwayne said, "I'm going to get the DVD player and screen set up in the tent for the kids. Honey, would you help with the ice cream?"

"I bought a huge box of drumsticks for them. It's in the freezer. All we have to do is pass them out." Marla asked, "Graciella, would you like to help me get them settled down?"

"Yes, sure." She popped out of her chair and followed Marla. Once inside the kitchen she asked, "Does she stay at his house often?"

"Whenever she passes through town. He's got plenty of room and doesn't want her to pay for a motel. It gives them a chance to catch up. I wouldn't read anything into it if I were you."

But Marla wasn't her. Graciella struggled to get her mind around it. Misty had said, "Friends, that's it." Still, she was uneasy. Could there be more to it?

Cluny strolled into the kitchen. "He's out like a light, Marla. Shall I put him in his cradle? I'd like to help Gunny put the yard back in order."

"Yes, please. I expect he'll sleep for a couple of hours before he's hungry again. Graciella and I are going to take ice cream out to the tent and make sure the kids are ready for their ghost stories. I doubt they'll close their eyes for hours. I'm so glad you installed that toilet off the laundry room last spring. At least I won't have them clomping through the house at all hours."

He brushed a quick kiss on Graciella's lips. "I'll be done shortly, sweetheart. We can head out soon."

A pile of shoes and sandals filled up an area at the side of the tent flap. The noisy kids arranged their blankets, pillows and sleeping bags around the DVD player and screen Dwayne was setting in place. They vied for the best view. The boys set up on one side of the big tent, and the girls on the other. She wondered if this had been Dwayne's idea. Santos arranged his sleeping bag across the narrow strip of canvas closest to Amber.

"Ice cream!" Graciella called out over their loud chatter, and nearly started a stampede. "One at a time, Let the girls go first." Santos offered his cone to Amber. Graciella went through the first box of drumsticks in a flash, then half the second box. She placed the remainder in the ice chest in the corner. "There's more here when you finish those."

Dwayne set up a small charcoal brazier several yards from the tent. He lit the coals and told his oldest nephews, "It'll take a while for these to start glowing. I'll leave the marshmallows, long forks and fire extinguisher on the table. You big boys are to watch the younger kids and make sure they're never unattended."

A boy of about thirteen spoke up, "You can count on me, Uncle Dwayne. I did it last year."

After bumping fists with the tall boy, he called, "You kids have fun. When you finish the ice cream and marshmallows, turn off the lanterns to save the batteries. You'll see fine with the light from the movie screen." He grinned at Graciella. "I doubt they heard a word I said."

"Are you sure they're safe toasting marshmallows on their own?"

"They won't be on their own. I'll be watching like a hawk. Don't worry. We do this every year. Soon as they've toasted all the marshmallows, I'll remove the brazier." He slung his arm around her shoulder and walked her back to the house. "You and Cluny can stay awhile or leave whenever you're ready. Marla and I've got this."

"When should I come for Santos?"

"Once they finally get to sleep they'll probably stay that way till after eight. I'll pick up a carload of breakfast sandwiches and a couple of gallons of milk and orange juice before they're up. I'm taking the day off tomorrow, so come for him whenever it's convenient."

Cluny was in the kitchen. "What say we relax and have a cup of coffee with Dwayne and Marla before we leave? You probably want to make sure Santos doesn't have second thoughts about sleeping in the tent. He said he'd never camped out before." He held a kitchen chair and took the one next to her. "Okay?"

"That sounds great. Marla, what can I do?"

"Decaf's almost done. I'm taking a breather while it perks. You stay put."

Graciella sighed. Cluny took her hand and gave her a look that sent heat scorching through her.

———

Something bothered her. They rode in silence for several minutes. Cluny racked his brain going over the day's events from start to finish. "Sweetheart?"

Graciella jerked like she'd heard a gunshot. "Yes?"

"You've been so quiet. Did I do something to upset you?" He stroked the back of her neck and kept his eyes on the road.

She didn't say a word for several seconds, then, "I don't want to spoil the rest of our evening. I'm probably too touchy and unsure of myself. Meeting all those people today was daunting to say the least. Don't worry about it."

"Please don't keep anything from me, Graciella. Tell me." He glanced at her.

Her head shook, and her glorious hair swept across the back of his hand. "It's silly really. I'm being childish."

"No, baby. Tell me."

She sighed deeply. "All right. I was shocked to learn Krystal had tried to make Santos leave with her that night she barged into our apartment while we were dancing. He told me you prevented her from taking him. Why didn't you ever say anything to me about it?"

He heard the hitch in her voice. He'd forgotten that incident, but it seemed very important to her. "God, I'm sorry, sweetheart. I wasn't keeping it from you. I thought for sure Santos would tell you after I took him back to your door."

"He said nothing and went straight to his room. I wish you'd told me. When I think of her and that awful Jamal taking him without my permission, it scares the heck out of me." She pressed her palms to her cheeks and a sob escaped her throat.

He took the off-ramp leading to her neighborhood. "I'd never met her before. It was your personal family business. I didn't think it was appropriate for me to stick my nose in." His stomach churned. The evening he'd been looking forward to was going south. "Please, baby, I had no idea."

He didn't talk again until they pulled into her parking lot a few blocks later. He turned off the engine and reached for her. "I'm sorry." Tugging her hands from her face he kissed one, and then the other.

Her expression was watery and her lips trembled, but she managed a smile. "I'm being silly. I'm spoiling everything. I'm sure you weren't deliberately keeping me in the dark about it. It's just—"

He gently kissed her lips. "Shall we go in? You said a couple of things were bothering you. We might as well clear the air."

"Yes." She dashed the tears from her cheeks and smiled again. "Yes, let's go."

"I'll pour some water in Queen's pan. She'll snooze here in the car. She's used to it."

He lowered his window an inch, stepped out of the car, and opened Graciella's door. "This will take a minute."

He lifted a gallon jug of water from behind her seat, poured some in a pan on the floor and scratched his dog's head. "Sweet dreams, Queenie." He closed and locked the car, and then he turned and embraced Graciella.

"Cluny, querido," she murmured against his chest, "I'm sorry. Can we forget it?"

His heart swelled at the first endearment she'd ever used when addressing him. "We'll finish this inside. I don't want you to keep anything from me. God, you and Santos are so important to me. You know that, right?"

She hugged his waist and they walked arm-in-arm to the stairs leading to her apartment. She had to know how important she was to him. What could he say to convince her that he wasn't only interested in making love to her, but that he wanted to be *with* her in every sense of the word?

She unlocked the door to her apartment, took his hand and led him inside. Switching on the hall light she faced him. "Hold me, amor. Can you just hold me for a moment? I want to tell you something else, but I'm losing my courage."

"Oh, baby, there's nothing I'd rather do more than hold you." He leaned back against the closed door and held her tight in his arms. His statement wasn't exactly true. He did want to hold her, but he wanted a lot more. Maybe the timing was off for tonight. He led her to the living room. "Let's sit. When you're ready, tell me what you need to say."

Once seated, she leaned into him and rested her hand on his chest. His heart pounded and he knew she could feel it. He wanted to tell her he loved her, wanted to spend the rest of his life with her, but he didn't. They'd known each other such a short time. She would mistake his declaration of love for lust, and there was plenty of that, too.

She lowered her eyes. "Some men at the party were talking about you today. They'd had too much to drink and didn't know I heard them." She stroked the front of his shirt nervously.

"What did they say?" Had they been talking about his PTS? Did they say something that scared her, made her afraid to be with him, trust him? He swallowed and steeled himself.

"They said you had a lot of…women…that you were sleeping with Misty Beachy."

He tilted her chin up and gazed directly into her eyes. "Graciella, that's not true."

"But, why would they say that?" Tears swam in her beautiful brown eyes.

"Sweetheart." He kissed her tears away. "I'll never lie to you. Misty and I were lovers for a few months when deployed in Iraq. We needed each other. That was a decade ago. It ended when we came home. We're friends."

"She's staying at your house."

"I have a big house." He clenched his fist. "Look, Beachy understands me. We went through hell over there. Those assclowns at the party didn't know what they were talking about. They always pumped me for details. Their talk today was nothing more than drunken, wishful thinking. I don't kiss and tell. It drove them nuts."

"That's what she said."

"Beachy? You talked to her about me?"

"Not by design, it just happened. She sat next to me to eat, and I asked her how long she'd known you. She's smart, she sensed my insecurity. She told me she loves you, and you're her best friend. 'Friend, period.'" Graciella gave him a weak smile. "She also told me that anybody who ever hurt you would have to answer to her, and did I get her meaning? She was fierce. That was the end of the conversation, because you came up to us at that moment and gave her a sopping wet hug."

"Timing." He stroked her cheek. "I gotta tell you, being the shallow male twit I am, I'm flattered you were jealous, but, sweetheart, you have nothing to worry about." He punctuated his declaration with a soft kiss. "Nothing."

"I want to believe you, Cluny, because I care for you and I haven't been dating all these years. I'm no kid, but my experience is limited. I know there are no guarantees, but you've been out there and I haven't."

He smiled in a way he prayed would reassure her. "It's true, I never took a vow of celibacy, but I'm far from the tireless Romeo some may think. I've had lots of dates over the years, but you're the first woman I've ever dared think might be the right one for me." Yes, he wanted her to be the one. She had it all.

"Why me?" Doubt filled her eyes.

"Why you?" He grinned and held up a fist, releasing one finger at a time. "You're smart and strong. You're self-reliant. You don't need a man to take care of you. You're beautiful and sexy, and best of all—you're a mom. Baby, you have everything I love in a woman. Believe it."

She rose to her knees and put her arms around his neck. "Kiss me, amor, because when you kiss me all my anxiety dissolves."

He didn't need any more encouragement that that. Embracing her, he laid her across his lap and smiled into her perfect face. This woman took his breath away. Having her in his arms was heaven on earth. He kissed her thoroughly, again and again. When he finally broke away, he whispered, "God, I need to make love with you, Graciella. Please tell me you want that, too."

She sighed softly. "I do."

He set her on her feet and kissed her on the mouth. "I don't only want to kiss you here," he turned her in his arms and pulled her back against his chest and cupped a breast, "but here," cupped her other breast, "and here." Her trembling sent him soaring. He slid a hand down her front and pressed against the mound at the juncture of her legs, "And here."

His heart nearly stopped beating when she pressed one of her sensuous, soft hands against the hard bulge in his jeans and whispered his name. She took his hand and led him down the short hallway to her bedroom, not bothering to turn off lights or close doors. A small lamp dimly illuminated her room.

Cluny took a deep breath, told himself to slow down. "Please, I want to undress you. I have to see you, all of you."

She shyly raised an arm, revealing a long zipper at the side of her strapless sundress. Hands trembling he lowered it and her dress drifted to the floor. She wasn't wearing a bra, just pale bikini panties. His hands covering her bare breasts, he dropped his head, groaned, and then fell to his knees and embraced her around the hips. For several seconds he stayed there brushing his lips across her abdomen. He slid her panties to her ankles; her knees trembled against his chest.

"Don't be afraid. I won't hurt you. I have protection." His last words got muffled in the thatch of dark curls where her legs met. "Oh, God, oh, my God, you're so sexy." He gazed into her face. "Am I alive? Tell me I'm still alive."

She knelt before him, smiled and said, "Very much so," while tugging his T-shirt over his head. She brushed her lips on the center of his chest. "I've wanted my mouth here ever since I smoothed sun lotion on you at the beach."

Her hands felt more wonderful sliding over his chest and shoulders than in his wildest imagination. Unable to drag out this delicious torture any longer, he stood and pulled her to her feet. Before he had a chance to unbutton his jeans, her hands were at his waist fumbling against the fastener. "Whoa, baby. I've got this." He pulled a small packet from the pocket and held it between his teeth as he kicked off his shoes and stepped out of his pants and boxers.

"Cluny, stand still so I can look at you."

He held his breath, more nervous than the last time under enemy fire. She took her time. A big grin grew on his face. "Do I pass inspection?"

She twisted her lips and tapped a tapered finger on her chin. "Um hum. You're standing at attention, I see."

"A Marine endeavors to give his all, ma'am." He winked. "You interested in finding out what my *all* is?"

She flashed a wicked smile and took him in her hand. "Would it have anything to do with this?"

She screeched when he grabbed her around the waist and lifted her high. Through a couple of caveman style grunts he carried her to the bed. "Woman! Me want you. Me have you. Now!" With that he tossed her on the bed to her scream of laughter, and pounced.

———

Graciella's excitement was nearly unbearable. When this beautiful man came down on top of her, every nerve in her body burned with a fire she felt could consume her. Where had this passion been hidden in her for so long? Her desire for Cluny was all consuming. She gasped when his teeth nipped her throat and collar bone. Mere seconds after his hand cupped her and she felt his probing fingers, she bucked against him and a massive orgasm exploded. She fell back in shock, gasped as tears welled in her eyes. "Oh, querido. Oh, Deus."

Intense blue eyes sparkled above his smiling lips. "Now that we got that one out of the way we can take it nice and slow." Kneeling between her legs, he lifted her knees and kissed her sensitive inner thighs.

Afraid she might swoon, Graciella grabbed handfuls of his hair and lifted his head. "Cluny, stop. I have to breathe. I can't…"

He lay down next to her and rolled her to face him. "It's okay, baby. I need to breathe too." His big hand stroked her back and bottom then he threaded fingers through her hair and pulled her in for a breath-stealing kiss.

She stroked his chest and sighed. "That was so fast and incredible."

"Sweetheart, you make me so happy."

"I want to make you happy, Cluny. I don't want to disappoint you."

"You can't disappoint me. You amaze me." He stroked her breast. "Every inch of you amazes me, makes me grateful to be alive, here, with you."

Against her will she thought of fierce little Misty Beachy, Cluny's former lover. How and why had she ever left him? Men like Cluny McPherson were few and far between. Graciella couldn't get her mind around why no other woman had claimed him for her own. Her heart swelled with the knowledge that he was here with her, in her bed, telling her she made him happy. Was this fleeting? Could this last?

His hand cupped her chin. "My love, look at me. Nobody is in this room but you and me. I want you. I want us. I don't want any other woman. Do you understand what I'm saying?"

Her breath stuttered. "I want to understand. I want that so much. More than anything." She stroked the stubble on his cheek. "I'm trying to stay in the moment. It's hard."

"Yes, ma'am, it is. So if you'll allow me…" He quickly sheathed himself and rose above her emitting a long groan of satisfaction as he pushed himself slowly, ever so slowly inside. "In you, Graciella. This is where I belong." His mouth covered her eager lips. And he moved.

Yes. Oh, yes. Here, he belonged here.

Chapter Seventeen

"Baby, I have to go."

"No, amor." She clung to him. "I want you to spend the night."

"I can't. I don't want to disturb your sleep. I thrash around."

Her heart cracked at the distress in his voice over his ongoing struggle with PTS. It couldn't be that bad, could it, a few nightmares? "I'm willing to lose a little sleep to have you here beside me."

"Sweetheart, I can't leave Queen in the car all night, and I have to open the shop at seven this morning. You'll need to pick up Santos in a few hours." He stroked her cheek. "I don't want to leave you, your bed. Not after what happened between us tonight. I'd rather cut off an arm than leave."

She rose on her elbow and gazed down at him. "Go get Queen and bring her in the apartment. Nobody will see you at this hour. I don't want you to leave me." She feathered her fingers across his lips. "Please?"

He sighed. "I'll do it, but against my better judgment. You have to promise me something."

"What?" She'd promise almost anything to keep him with her for a few more hours.

"If I have nightmares, you'll get up and leave me and Queen in the room. Don't try to wake me by talking or touching me. I'm afraid I might accidentally hurt you. Do you understand?"

"Yes, querido. I promise. How can we be together if you always need to leave?"

"You know I don't want to go, but I'm not willing to risk losing you before we've had a chance."

"Go get her. I'll do what you say." She slipped out of bed and donned her robe while Cluny pulled on his jeans. She could barely see him in the dim light, but didn't need to. She knew every detail of his body.

Not bothering with shoes or a shirt he padded from the room with her close behind. "I'll be a couple of minutes." When they got to the door he leaned in and kissed her. "I hope this isn't a mistake."

"It'll be okay." She wasn't as confident as she sounded, but wanted it to be true. This man had baggage, and she was willing to help him carry it. Down deep in her soul she felt he was worth it.

When the door clicked shut behind him, she went to the kitchen for a glass of water, and got a big mixing bowl to fill for Queen. A few minutes passed and she heard a loud rap on the door. Smiling, she moved with a light step to open it. "That was quick."

Jamal loomed in the semi-darkness. "Where's Krystal?"

He took a step forward and she tried desperately to close the door. "She's not here!"

Shouldering the door he knocked her back. She fell to the floor. He grabbed her by the hair. "Where is she, bitch?"

"I don't know. Stop!" Terrified, she struggled upward to keep him from pulling her hair out by the roots. "Please, stop," she screamed, "you're hurting me!"

Loud pounding footsteps sounded on the stairs and hallway followed by Queen's bark that turned into a menacing snarl. "What the hell!" Cluny threw himself forward, knocked Jamal to the floor and dragged him out the door onto the landing. Jamal screamed when Queen clamped her powerful jaws on his crotch.

Graciella heard somebody shout, "Call the police!"

Jamal yelled desperately, "Get this dog off me! Please!"

Deaf to his plea, Cluny pounded his fist over and over in Jamal's face as Queen growled and shook her head, undeterred by his flailing legs. Jamal stopped struggling. Blood gushed from his nose and mouth. Cluny pounded him relentlessly, seeming not to notice he'd stopped fighting back.

"Cluny! Stop!" Graciella shook his shoulder. "Stop, you're killing him." Terror and helplessness screamed in her brain. She was powerless to stop him from hitting the semi-conscious, bleeding man.

Shouting and footsteps rushed to her door. How had the police gotten there so fast? Three armed officers dragged Cluny off Jamal. He screamed, "You bastard! I'll kill you, you bastard!"

"Whose dog is this? Call off this dog!"

Cluny commanded, "Queen, release!"

Graciella put out a shaky hand. "It's okay, Queenie." The dog stared at her, released the torn pants and bared her teeth.

Reaching gingerly for the dog, Graciella said, "No, Queen. Good girl." In an instant the dog sat back on her haunches, ready to spring on the officers subduing Cluny. Graciella grabbed her collar, and scared to death, held on as hard as she could, Knowing she didn't have the strength to control the powerful Malinois if she charged.

Cluny stopped struggling, aware of what was happening. "Down, Queen, stand down." He tried to shake off the officers, but one of them yanked his hands behind his back, slapped on a pair of cuffs then hauled him to his feet.

When they began to drag him away, Graciella screamed, "What are you doing? He was protecting me! Wait! Where are you taking him?"

"Devonshire station." An officer held his hand in front of her face. "Take your dog and step back inside the apartment, ma'am. An officer will take your statement."

"Cluny!" She pushed against the officer blocking her way, screaming at them because they were arresting the wrong man. She was so distraught she didn't notice she'd reverted to her native Portuguese. *"Escala! Escala, por favor!"* The officer held her back.

"Graciella, call Gunny. Tell him where…" The uniforms shoved him toward the short flight of steps, and she didn't hear the rest of what he said.

She shouted, "I'll call him right now!" Shaking off the officer's restraining hand, she stepped back inside. "Come, Queen. Good girl."

She slammed the door in the man's face and turned the deadbolt. She went to the kitchen, grabbed the wall phone, and realized she didn't know Dwayne Dempsey's number.

———

Cluny struggled against the rough handling of the uniformed officers. "What's wrong with you guys? That sonofabitch attacked my girl-friend. Don't hurt my dog! You better not hurt my dog, goddammit!"

"Yeah? And what are you going to do about it? Shut up and get in the car." The man shoved Cluny's head down and pushed him into the back of the black and white and slammed the door.

Cluny leaned forward and saw two more officers dragging Jamal across the parking lot and putting him in another car. In a fury, he reared back and viciously kicked the panel protecting the front seat with the bottom of his bare foot. "Goddammit! Let me out of here!" They ignored him, got in the car and drove.

Five minutes later the patrol car pulled in the lot in front of LAPD Devonshire station. The officers went inside and left him in the car. The second car pulled in. The uniforms extracted Jamal from the back seat and hustled him inside. Cluny waited briefly and began to shout and kick again.

The door flew open. "Look, pal, so far you're not in any trouble, but if you don't stop this shit I'll have to book you. Are we clear?"

"What the hell is—?" The door slammed and the officer walked away.

Cluny slumped back against the seat, stunned and confused. If he wasn't in trouble, what was he doing in handcuffs in the back of a locked patrol car? How had the cops got to Graciella's apartment so fast? He'd barely gotten his hands on Jamal when they were all over him.

A man approached the car and stood outside staring at him for a few seconds, then opened the front door and got in. "I'm FBI agent, Jim Harris. Here's what we're going to do. Two officers will take you inside the station and make a show of booking you, and then you'll be put in a holding cell. You'll cooperate and keep your mouth shut."

"But, I...what...?"

"Jamal Mujahid is under surveillance by Homeland Security. We've been shadowing his movements and tonight followed him to the lady's apartment. If you don't cooperate, and keep your mouth shut, you'll blow our operation. Do you understand what I'm telling you?"

Homeland Security was watching his movements? "He's under surveillance?" How the hell had Graciella ended up in the middle of this crap carnival? "But, my girlfriend…she doesn't have anything to do with him."

"We know that." Harris cocked his head. "Are you ready to go in peacefully, Mr. McPherson, or do you need more time to cool off?"

"Shit, let's get it over with. I've gotta get back to my girl. She's probably scared out of her mind."

Two LAPD officers escorted him inside. They put him through the booking process, making sure Jamal Mujahid saw what was happening. After Cluny handed over his watch, wallet, and keys they fingerprinted him using a modern inkless scanner, and then took his jailhouse photos. Now he'd been moved to a different location in the building and the escorting officer removed his cuffs. He handed him a pair of disposable paper booties for his bare feet, and opened the door of a holding cell.

Cluny stepped inside and sat. "How much longer?"

The man shrugged, walked away then came back with a jail shirt and shoved it through the bars.

"What in hell am I supposed to do with this? Am I under arrest? Are they going to move me? Do I get a goddamn phone call?"

"I don't know, man. Just relax. The watch commander will come in and talk to you."

He cooled his heels for almost an hour. Nobody came. He had to keep it together, but he was ready to tear the next person he could get hold of limb-from-limb. Pacing, he raked his hair and gripped the bars on the small cell door.

Voices! The door to the outer room opened.

A tall uniformed man opened the cell door and stepped inside. He held out his hand. "Mr. McPherson, I'm Watch Commander Johnson. You'll be free to leave soon. In the meantime, there's someone here to see you." He signaled to the guard who watched from the window in the outer door.

Gunny, bleary-eyed with a dark five o'clock shadow, stepped in the room.

Johnson motioned Dwayne inside the cell. "Mr. Dempsey will take you home as soon as the FBI completes whatever-the-hell they're doing out there. Would you like coffee?"

"No."

"I'll leave you men alone then." He exited the outer room and the guard outside closed the door.

Dwayne walked in, pulled Cluny into a hard hug and thumped him on the back. "How you doin'? You sure know how to top off a good party."

Relief flooded through him. "Thanks for coming, Gunny. I'm still not sure what happened." He slumped down on one of the benches and dropped his head. "I'm worried about Graciella. And Queen. I have to know they're okay. This is a goddamn nightmare."

Dwayne took the seat across from him. "They're both fine. She called and asked me to come to her place. There're a couple of federal agents there who tried to explain what was going down. She was pretty shook up, had a couple of bruises, but otherwise she's okay. Queen's fine. She's a pro."

"Yeah, she got a good bite of that jerk's junk and wasn't about to let go."

Dwayne chuckled. "He'll probably be out of commission in that department for a while."

"Permanently, I hope. How did Graciella find you? After they hauled me in here I remembered your home phone number's unlisted."

"She called the off-hours emergency number for Big D. They phoned my home and relayed her message. Soon as I called her back she started to cry, poor kid."

Cluny looked into the face of his old pal. "What have I gotten her into?"

"From what the agents at her place told me, I don't see that it has anything to do with you."

"I went out to the car to get Queen. Graciella probably thought it was me at the door. She wouldn't have opened it if she'd been there alone."

"You're not responsible for everything that goes wrong in the world, McPherson. They're after that Jihad guy."

"Jamal."

"Yeah, him. He's on a terrorist watch list. They've been hoping he'd lead them to one of the big boys. So far, no dice."

Cluny socked a fist into his open hand. "I wanted to kill him for the way he was knocking Graciella around. What if he shows up again? What if she and Santos were alone in the apartment? How are they going to protect her?" Was he the only one worried more about protecting them than nailing some bozo on a watch list?

"What about her and the boy staying at your place for a while? You've got plenty of room."

He shook his head. "I doubt she'd go for it. She has a business to run. Except for a small pension from the Navy, it's her only source of income. Anyway, we're just getting comfortable together. Having them under my roof twenty-four-seven could put the stink eye on our connection. I don't want that. I love her. I want to marry her, but it's too soon to ask for that commitment."

"I suspected you'd seriously fallen for her. How do you think she feels?"

"She's cautious. Her first priority is Santos. I'm pretty sure she wants to see where our relationship could go, but she's wary of getting in too deep at this point. I don't blame her. She's done a good job managing life on her own since Marv was killed."

Yes, Cluny loved her. He'd never been surer of anything in his life, but was it fair of him to bring all his shit to her doorstep? He didn't want her to commit out of pity. Perhaps he should back off, let things cool down.

The watch commander entered the room and walked through the open cell door. "You're free to go, McPherson. The FBI asks you to return to Mrs. Jefferson's apartment and sit down with them."

"What for?"

"I'm not in the loop, my friend. I'm purely on a need-to-know basis with the feds. My guess is they want your cooperation to make sure you don't throw a monkey wrench in the works and blow their investigation."

"I don't give a rat's ass what the feds want. All I care about is safety for her and her boy."

The commander put his hand on Cluny's shoulder. "Piece of advice? Sit down with the feds and listen if you're really concerned and not just wanting to be a macho cowboy."

Dwayne laughed. "Officer, that's tough, because we *are* Wyoming cowboys and retired Marines to boot. I'll try to keep him reined in." He gave Cluny a light smack on the back. "Come on, Macfearsome. I'll drop you at her place and then get on home. I left Marla alone with a tent full of kids in the backyard. They'll be waking up hungry any time now, and I'm in charge of breakfast."

Cluny pulled off the jail shirt and tossed it on the bunk. "Where's my stuff?"

"Follow me. It's up front. All you have to do is sign for it and you're on your way."

———

Graciella's apartment, early Thursday morning

Graciella rushed into Cluny's arms the second he walked through her door. "Querido, I'm so happy to see you. Thank God you're safe." His embrace warmed and comforted her in the deepest places of her body and soul. She clung to her man, reluctant to let go, even for a moment. "I love you, Cluny."

He held her away so he could look directly into her eyes. "Baby, that makes me so happy. I wasn't sure you felt the same as me." He hugged her hard and kissed the top of her head. Queen leaned against his leg.

She stepped away from Cluny when he bent down to pet and talk to Queen then preceded him to the living room where two men in suits, who looked the part of FBI agents, introduced themselves.

"Amor, I'm going to make breakfast for you while you talk to these men." She went the short distance to the kitchen and returned with a steaming cup of coffee for him.

"Thank you, sweetheart." He gestured to the two men. "I need to get my shirt and shoes on, gentlemen, if you'll excuse me?"

"Sure, go right ahead, sir."

She stared at his back when he walked down the hall to her bedroom, not willing to take her eyes off him for a second. Would the road ahead be an easy one for them? Deep in her heart she wanted to try to work things out and develop a long-term relationship with this special man. He was worth it. Removing pans from the cupboard and eggs from the refrigerator, she set about cooking breakfast for the man she loved.

Once the food was ready, she carried the plate and silverware to him. One of the agents eyed the three eggs, sausage and toast as she set it in front of Cluny. She'd interrupted the conversation, but from what she'd heard, they were repeating what they'd talked about with her while waiting for him to return from police custody. "May I get you gentlemen anything?"

"No, ma'am. We're just about to leave. I reiterated to Mr. McPherson that we had instructed you to avoid contact with Krystal Jefferson and her parents during this phase of the investigation. They've received the same instructions, and our office in New York has been in touch with Ms. Jefferson. For her safety, she'll be under close watch."

"I'm glad to hear that. She's made some foolish choices, but I'd hate it if anything happened to her. Her parents have already lost their only other child, my late husband."

The two men got to their feet, gathered their briefcases and prepared to leave. "We'll show ourselves out. Don't get up, Mr. McPherson. Enjoy your breakfast. We hope this will all be over soon."

Graciella followed them to the door and shot the deadbolt. She was relieved to have them out of her apartment.

"Cluny, Queen hasn't been out of here since they took you."

"That's okay, baby. I'll take her out soon as I finish. Sit down. I need to ask you something."

Curious, and not a little unsettled, she sat across from him. "Take your time. I'll make more if you're still hungry. It's been quite a night."

Her heart tripped when he winked. "In more ways than one." She leaned back against the couch cushion and watched him devour the last of the sausage and eggs. Finally, he set the plate on the coffee table and leaned forward with his forearms on his knees. He had something on his mind and she could see he struggled with how to voice it. Maybe he was going to suggest they take a break from each other. That would probably be the wise thing to do, but something she did not want.

"Baby?" He gazed into her eyes. "Gunny made a suggestion when he came to spring me this morning. At first I thought you wouldn't go for it, but there's no way to know unless I ask you outright. So here goes." He twisted his hands as they dangled between his legs. "Would you consider moving yourself and Santos into my house in Spring Grove until this crap blows over? I know you have your business and all, but I'm not convinced the police can protect you. Take your time to think about it, you don't have to answer right now."

Flooded with happiness over his concern for her and her son, she went to him and sat on his lap. Her head on his shoulder, she said, "I can't sleep in your bedroom, amor. It wouldn't be proper."

"Does that mean you'll come?"

"Yes, I have to think of my son's safety." She would take Marla's advice and stop borrowing trouble. She wanted to be with Cluny, and didn't feel she and Santos were secure in this apartment.

He squeezed her hard. "What a relief. You can have the guest bedroom and I've got an air mattress we can put on the floor in one of the other empty rooms for Santos. Bring as much of your things as you want. I'll bring the van if you need more than you can carry in our cars."

"That wouldn't be a good idea. The name of your company is on it. Let's go get Santos and you can come back here and help us pack up what we'll need." She looked at her watch. "Oh, no, I just remembered you were supposed to open your business about now."

"I called Chief. He'll handle it today."

"Does that mean you don't have to be someplace else for the next couple of hours?" She brushed her lips on his ear.

"I know where I'd like to be, baby." He laid a sizzling kiss on her lips.

"You read my mind."

Chapter Eighteen

Same afternoon

ON THE WAY TO DWAYNE AND MARLA'S, CLUNY THOUGHT WHAT a lucky man he was to have this remarkable woman sitting beside him, the woman who'd made love with abandon, and who was presently caressing his leg.

Graciella broke the silence. "What do you think we should tell Santos, querido?"

"Tell him about what?"

"Why we're going to stay at your house for a while."

"The truth might be a good place to start."

She sniffed and removed her hand from his leg. "Says the wise father of many children."

Oh boy. Tread lightly, McPherson. "Sorry, you asked my opinion."

She put her hand back on his leg, squeezed, and sighed. "I'm more unraveled than I thought. I didn't mean to sound witchy."

He covered her hand. "Like you said, baby, it was quite a night."

She leaned across and kissed his cheek. "Yes, one I'll never forget for many reasons. I love you, Cluny. I don't know how this arrangement will go, but please have patience with me."

Queen whined from the back seat.

Graciella laughed. "You too, Queenie. We'll be encroaching on your territory."

"Don't worry about her. She loves attention, especially from Santos. She might get the idea she's a pet and forget what her real job is."

Graciella sat back. "We're almost there. I'll just answer his questions as honestly as possible. "

"Sounds like a plan."

Dwayne' house was quiet. Nobody answered when Cluny knocked on the door. "Looks like nobody's home. Let's go around the house to the back yard to make sure." He opened the gate and knocked again then took his keys from his pocket and found the one to his buddy's back door and opened it.

"Anybody home?" he called as they went inside.

"Where do you suppose they could be?"

He pointed to the table. "There's a note." He read it and handed it to Graciella. "They went to the grocery store." He turned on the light over the sink and opened the refrigerator.

"What are you doing?"

"Looking for orange juice." He reached in and pulled out a half-gallon jug and set it on the sink. "Want some?"

"Cluny, this isn't your house. Should you be helping yourself?"

He was surprised by her reaction. "Dempsey and I are like brothers. He wouldn't think anything of it."

"But it's Marla's house too. I'm not comfortable coming in here and making myself at home when they're not here."

"Marla knows how it is with me and Gunny. As long as I don't leave a mess for her to clean up, she's cool."

"I don't know, Cluny...it..." The sound of the garage door interrupted her.

"They're home. I'll put it back if it makes you feel better. Then I'll ask Marla's permission." He regretted the sharp edge to his comment.

She sniffed. "You don't have to sound so grumpy about it."

Marla walked in carrying a couple of bags of groceries. Santos and Amber followed, carrying loaded plastic sacks. "Hi, Graciella, Cluny, when did you get here?"

"Just now, gorgeous." Cluny kissed her on the mouth. "Let me help with that stuff." He took Marla's bags and set them on the kitchen counter. "I was on the receiving end of a lecture from Mrs. Jefferson about making myself too comfortable in your house when you're not here."

Marla gave Graciella a hug. "It's so nice to meet someone with manners. But, don't worry about Cluny. The way I look at it he's just another one of my kids. I'm about to make tuna sandwiches for lunch. Have you eaten?"

"Hi, Mama." Santos hugged her. "I had so much fun last night at the campout. Were you lonesome without me?"

She took a breath. "Um, no, Cluny stayed at our apartment with me." Wincing, she glanced at Marla and Cluny. He put a reassuring smile on his lips and nodded.

Santos nodded and smiled at her. "That's nice. Come on, Amber; let's let DD out of her carrier. She loves to play with Queen."

The kids ran from the room and Graciella crossed her arms and slumped down on one of the kitchen chairs. "I don't know what I was agonizing over." She glared at Cluny. "Don't laugh if you know what's good for you."

He laughed anyway. "Oh, I know what's good for me, baby, but I'll try to behave." He turned to Marla. "Where's Gunny?"

"He's looking at the engine. He thought he heard something funny and wanted to check it out. Would you bring Declan in? I left him sleeping in his car seat."

"I'm on it."

———

Graciella joined Marla at the counter and helped unload the groceries.

"My word, Graciella, Dwayne told me what happened last night. Are you okay?"

"It was frightening. I thought Cluny was going to kill Krystal's boyfriend. If the police hadn't been there so quick, I don't know what I would have done."

"I know what you mean. There's no doubt in my mind Dwayne would beat the living daylights out of anyone who harmed me or our kids. Cluny and Dwayne are warfighters, natural-born protectors and defenders. It's in the DNA. I don't know if it's possible to turn it off just because they're not active duty Marines any longer. Fortunately, Dwayne does a good job keeping it under control."

Graciella opened her mouth to say something and stopped abruptly when Cluny returned with the sleeping infant in his carrier. He held a finger to his lips, but the silence was shattered when Santos and Amber ran shrieking past them with DD on their heels barking her little head off. She skidded to a stop in front of Queen, paws on the floor, her furry butt in the air, and barked in the face of the much larger dog. Queen stood, shook herself with ennui and followed them out the door.

"Look at that," Graciella said. "Declan slept through the whole thing."

Cluny grinned at the sleeping infant. His tenderness to the baby was in sharp contrast to his fierceness with Jamal. "I'll put him in his crib. By the way that's some watchdog you've got there. She didn't make a peep when Graciella and I came in." He took the baby and left them alone.

"Marla, you said something to me at the party, about Cluny and the baby, but never finished your thought."

"Oh, that's right. Dwayne said when Amber was an infant he discovered she had a very soothing influence on Cluny whenever he held her. If he became agitated or restless, Dwayne would ask him to care for her, and it calmed him right down. I'm just speculating, but because he's an orphan I suspect he has a very special place in his heart for children."

Graciella thought about this. "He is very good with kids. That's one of the first things I liked about him, the way he is with Santos. I do wonder what he must have gone through in those foster homes after his parents died."

"He told me a while back that it wasn't so bad. Most of the foster parents were kind, if not very physically loving, to their charges. Mostly he missed the kind of love he got from his natural parents. He made up for it by holding the babies and hugging the younger ones."

"He is a hugger. I think every woman at your party yesterday managed to get a hug and a kiss from him. They acted like he was a long-lost boyfriend they were thrilled to see again."

"There's no denying it, women and kids do love him, Graciella."

"He's very special, isn't he?" She couldn't imagine what it was like for him to lose both parents at such a tender age. What would happen to Santos if he were suddenly left alone in the world without her love and care? At least he had grandparents who loved him.

"Yes. It's easy to love Cluny. He and Dwayne became fast friends when they both attended the same junior high school in Buffalo, Wyoming. Dwayne's two brothers lived with their dad here in Southern California, while he stayed with his mother at the family ranch after their parents divorced. He adopted Cluny as another brother. Kathleen welcomed him to the ranch with open arms when he aged out of foster care. They're family, however you look at it."

"I guess that's why he thinks he can just walk right into your house and help himself to whatever's in the refrigerator?"

Marla laughed. "It took some getting used to, but then I realized my sister and brothers behaved the same way at my place, and it didn't bother me a bit. Did I tell you I have identical twin brothers, and my twin sister is married to Dwayne's little brother, Donovan?"

"Oh, my word, no!" Graciella put a hand to her chest. "I'm surprised you didn't have twins."

Marla rolled her eyes. "I worried about that when I first got pregnant, but lucky for me it didn't happen. I gained a whole lot of respect for my mother after I had him. I thought I knew it all when I was a kid, but I didn't have a clue." She laughed and shrugged her shoulders.

Cluny re-entered the kitchen and embraced both of them. "I love being surrounded by beautiful, sexy women. I'm gonna go out and supervise Gunny while he repairs that engine." His knuckles grazed Graciella's bottom as he stepped away.

Graciella held up two cans of tuna. "Shall we make sandwiches, Marla?"

Fifteen minutes later they carried a tray heaped with sandwiches out to the patio. Marla went back for a pitcher of lemonade and a king-sized bag of chips. "Lunch!"

Amber and Santos ran and reached for a sandwich.

Graciella intercepted them. "Go to the hose and rinse the dog off your hands first."

She overheard Amber tell Santos, "Your mom is rill strict, isn't she?

Dwayne and Cluny joined them. Dwayne held up greasy hands. "How about a kiss from my beautiful wife first?"

Marla pointed a finger at his nose and scowled. "Not unless you want it to be the last one of your life, Dempsey."

Dwayne growled and made a fake charge. Marla screamed, and then when he turned away, she laid a hard whack on his butt. Shoulders shaking with chuckles he pulled a rag out of his back pocket and wiped his hands on the way to the garage.

Laughing at their antics, Cluny hugged Graciella from behind and nuzzled her neck. "My hands are clean. I'd like a kiss from my beautiful girlfriend."

She gave him a sidewise glance. "Santos will see us."

"I don't care. Do you?"

Did she care if Santos saw her kissing Cluny? Yes, of course she did, but what was the harm? He'd been witness to most of those goodnight kisses for a while now. She tilted her head up and gave him a light kiss on the mouth. "No, I guess not, amor. We'll just have to see how he takes it in. Now, take a sandwich and sit. It's been hours since breakfast. You'll need your strength to help us move."

He waggled his eyebrows. "And for other activities."

"How do you plan to manage that?"

"Where there's a will, baby." He winked, grabbed a sandwich and headed for the picnic table.

Santos and Amber returned, drying wet hands on the seats of their pants. "I'm starved, Mama. Can I have one too?"

"Take a sandwich and go sit with Macfearsome. I'll bring cups for the lemonade. Then you can tell us all about your campout."

Dwayne and Marla joined them. She set the baby monitor on the table. DD and Queen sat in the shade of the big eucalyptus and chewed rawhide strips.

Santos swallowed a gulp of lemonade and regaled them with recounting the scariest ghost story, and how the big kids snuck outside the tent to yell and bang on the sides of the canvas to scare the daylights out of the rest of them. "I was scared, but it was fun! Did you and Mama have fun last night, Macfearsome?"

"It was an adventure, sailor, but not nearly as exciting as yours.

Sounds like you'll be hitting the rack early tonight. I bet you didn't get much sleep, did you?"

"I don't know for sure, but we finally fell asleep. Amber did before me because she already knew the ghost story by heart."

Graciella tipped her head at Amber. "Do you like ghost stories, Amber?"

"Yeah, I guess, but they're rilly for little kids. I'm getting too big for them."

"My, aren't we growing up a little fast?" Marla asked her. "When you tricked me into marrying your dad, you promised me you'd be my little girl for a long time."

Santos' eyes got big. He stared at Amber. "Did you trick them?"

"Not rilly. They wanted to get married, but were taking too long to decide. Do you want your mom to get married again?"

Santos shrugged. "I never thought about it." He turned to his mother. "Do you want to get married again, mama? Get a new dad for me?"

Cluny smacked the table. "Hey, guess what! Baseball practice starts day after tomorrow. You both need to get your paperwork in by Saturday morning. I expect we're going to get a lot of kids signed up this summer."

"Do you have the papers, mama?"

Graciella hugged Santos and kissed his cheek. "They're in the desk at home. You can finish filling them out when Cluny takes us there." She glanced at the three adults, then put her hand on Santos's shoulder. "We're going to stay at his house for a little while, starting today."

"We are? Why?"

"I'll explain on the way home. Now, help clear up the table so we can be on our way. We have a lot to do this afternoon." She wasn't sure how she would explain why they were staying with Cluny, but would probably tell him as much of the truth as possible without frightening him.

"Hey, Santos." Amber followed him to the house. "If you stay at Uncle Cluny's I can ride my bike over there. It's not that far. We can practice baseball and go to the park and stuff. And Uncle Cluny promised he'd take some days off to go to the beach again."

Marla nodded and spoke quietly so the kids wouldn't overhear,

"That's a good decision, Graciella, especially after what happened. It's farther for you to go to and from work, though."

Graciella piled plates and cups on the tray. "I'm thinking of closing the samba studio for a few weeks. I did last summer, and it didn't hurt the bottom line that much. Many of my adult students take time off to travel and vacation with their kids as it is."

"I hope you do. That'll give the two us time to get better acquainted," Marla said. "We can take the kids to the beach if Dwayne and Cluny have a problem taking time off. I'm ready to get my mother to babysit so I can go on a real live shopping spree, and maybe you could join me for a day at the spa for some serious pampering."

Graciella pressed her lips together to suppress a smile. "Are you by any chance vetting me? Making sure I'm good enough for Cluny?"

"Am I that obvious?" Marla rested her hand on Graciella's arm.

Dwayne and Cluny exchanged amused looks but didn't comment. Cluny took the tray from her. "Let me take that, sweetheart. Gunny and I'll clean up the kitchen while you and Marla visit."

Marla shifted to the opposite bench directly across from Graciella. "I hope you're not too worried about moving into Cluny's place. He's so easy to get along with and he's got plenty of room for both of you."

"I'm very worried, Marla. Moving in together, even temporarily, is a big step. I hope we don't get off to a bad start. He'll want us to sleep together, and I told him it wouldn't be proper with Santos in the house. I'm not at all sure how to handle it."

"I hear you. It was very tricky for Dwayne and me with Amber underfoot. Fortunately, we had a few weeks by ourselves when she spent time at his mother's ranch in Wyoming. It worked out because she was scheming the whole time to get us together, and thought it was the most natural thing for us to share a bedroom. It's hard to know what a child is thinking. Sometimes we worry too much."

"I suppose you're right. We'll just have to see how it goes."

"Santos can spend the night here now and then to give you some private time. It's perfectly fine with Dwayne and me. After all, he's our future son-in-law, right?"

They enjoyed a laugh then went to join the others.

———

171

Cluny met Santos' eyes in the rearview mirror. "So, after Jamal showed up at your apartment, and behaved so badly, I asked your mother if she'd consider moving to my house for a while. He doesn't know me or where I live."

"I don't like Jamal. He scares me."

Cluny hid a small smile when he saw the boy put his arm around Queen and move closer to her. The dog sniffed Santos' ear and looked like she understood what he'd said.

"I'm going to bring my laptop to Cluny's so I can email my customers and let them know I'll be closed for a while," Graciella said. "We'll stop at the studio and put a sign in the window before we leave Chatsworth."

"Macfearsome?"

"Yeah?"

"What am I allowed to bring with me?"

"Anything you want. We've got the trunks and seats of two cars to fill up. Do you have a bike?"

"I know how to ride, but I don't have one. Grandpa taught me on his. Mama says there's too much traffic where we live to ride a bike."

Cluny grinned. "Well, I've got two of them in my garage. There are plenty of quiet streets in my neighborhood and a nice long bike trail through the park next door."

It took nearly two hours for Santos and Graciella to decide what to bring and to pack clothes for each of them. Cluny lugged the boxes and suitcases down to the cars. "Don't worry about forgetting anything. It's not that much of a trip to come back if you do."

Santo's eyelids grew heavier as the day wore on. He dozed off in the back seat of Cluny's car on the way to his house. Graciella's back seat and passenger seat were stacked with boxes.

She pulled into his driveway and parked behind him. She went to open the back door of Cluny's car. "Oh, Santos is asleep."

"Let him sleep while we haul your stuff in, baby. I'll inflate the air mattress, and you can make up his bed, then I'll carry him in." He stepped out of his green monster and embraced her for a brief kiss.

"I'm tired, too." Graciella yawned. "None of us got much sleep last night. It'll be an early bedtime all around. I could whip up an omelet for dinner. Would that be enough for you, amor?"

"That'll hit the spot, sweetheart. Now, let's get the cars unloaded."

He dragged the air mattress from a hallway cupboard and inflated it in one of the empty bedrooms. While Graciella made up the bed, Cluny made a few trips to the car and set Santos's suitcase and a few boxes of his things next to the bedroom wall.

They returned to his car together. Cluny opened the back door and lifted Santos in his arms. "He probably won't wake up for dinner. The poor kid is out like a light."

They put Santos on the airbed, removed his shoes and covered him with a sheet. He didn't move a muscle. Queen lay on the floor next to him. "Don't get any ideas about being a pampered pet, Queenie. You're still on the job." Cluny gave her a vigorous scratch between the ears and stood. "Let's leave the door open in case he comes around while we're eating."

Graciella put her arm around his waist. "Yes, I wouldn't want him to be scared when he wakes in a strange place. Come, I'll make that omelet. I'm fading fast."

After dinner Cluny led her to the living room. He lay on his back on the big sofa, pulled her down on top of him and put his arms around her. They slept through the night, and when they woke, Santos and Queen were snoozing on the carpeted floor in front of the couch.

Chapter Nineteen

Friday morning, Cluny's house

GRACIELLA RAISED HER GROGGY HEAD AND REMEMBERED WHERE she'd fallen asleep. Before she had a chance, Cluny pushed tangles of unruly hair from her eyes. He wore a broad grin on his unshaven face. She was surprised to spot a few gray bristles hiding among all the black ones.

"Good morning, babe. I slept great, how about you?"

She stared down at his chest. "Oh no, I drooled all over your shirt." Heat flushed her cheeks.

"Yeah, I know. Gross." He brushed his fingertips on her cheek.

"Why are you whispering?"

He put a finger under her chin, turned her head and pointed to the floor. "We have company."

Queen raised her head and gazed at them for a moment then lowered it between her paws next to the sleeping Santos.

Graciella smiled. "When did he come in here?"

"No idea."

She shifted. "You're poking me."

"Happens every morning." His grin grew broader. "Can't be helped."

174

She returned his sexy smile and tongued his earlobe. "By either of us, I'm afraid. Do you know what time it is?"

"Does it matter?"

She lowered her chin to his chest again. "No, I guess not. How are we going to get up from here without waking him?"

Cluny's big hand pressed down on her bottom, pushing her tight against his erection. "He found us like this, so why does it matter?"

"You better stop that, amor. Nothing can come of it."

"Pure torture, isn't it?" He pulled her head down and kissed her.

A sleepy boy's voice drifted from the floor. "Torture?"

Cluny turned his head. "Morning, sailor. We were just speculating about how to get up from here without waking you, but that's no longer a problem. How did you end up sleeping on the hard floor in here?"

Santos sat up and rubbed his eyes. "I woke up and Queen was gone. I looked in your bedrooms but couldn't find anybody. I thought you left, and then I found you in here. So I snuggled up next to Queen because you were asleep."

Graciella put her hand on his head. "Looks like we're all awake now. Shall I fix breakfast?"

Santos lay back down next to Queen. "I'm so sleepy. It's still dark out."

"Yes, it is." Graciella slid higher on Cluny's body and kissed him softly. She raised her eyes and smiled. "Maybe you should go back to bed for a while, son." She pushed off Cluny and stood. "Come on. Let's get you to a more comfortable place to sleep. Nobody is going to leave you alone." She tugged his arm.

He stumbled down the hall next to her as she led him back to his temporary bedroom and tucked him in.

"Did Queen come with us?" He said on a yawn.

"No, Cluny takes her for a run every morning before daylight. Go back to sleep. I'll wake you after a while." She kissed his cheek and pulled the blanket over his shoulders, left the room and closed the door.

Cluny was tying the laces on his running shoes when she got to the kitchen. "It's still pretty early, baby. Why don't you catch a few more winks? Queenie and I'll be out for about an hour."

"I'm awake now. If it's okay, I'll rummage around in here and find something to cook for breakfast."

"Make yourself at home." He stood and pulled her into his arms. "Sure you don't want to catch a little more sleep? It's only five."

She placed her hands on his cheeks. "Are you going to work today?"

"Got to. We're starting a big job on Monday, so I'll work a long day today. Tomorrow morning, too, but I'll be back in plenty of time to get the kids organized for the first day of baseball tryouts at the park. I'll let you in on a secret."

"What secret?" She smiled at his teasing grin.

"Every kid makes the team even if they have two left feet. We're in it for fun, not serious like Little League. I probably enjoy it the most. Wanna be the team mom?"

"That all depends." She wrapped her arms around his waist and held tight so she could lean back and gaze into his long, noble face. "What do I have to do?"

"The usual mom stuff. Have plenty of Band-aids for the boo-boos. Organize the Snack Patrol of other moms. Hugs when needed. Stuff like that."

On tiptoe, she kissed his lips. "That I can manage. Now beat it, and I'll rustle up some breakfast. I can't have you going off to work inadequately nourished. It's against my principles."

Cluny lifted her off her feet and turned in a circle. "Careful, you might spoil me."

"That I can manage too. Now, put me down so I can get to work. I need to shower first."

He ogled her, waggling his eyebrows. "I'd rather stay and watch."

Graciella held up a fist and squinted, pressing her lips tight to keep from laughing.

Cluny chuckled and backed off. Summoning Queen, he and the dog left from the kitchen door.

Graciella hugged herself and spun around in the large modern kitchen. She'd cooked in here last week when they'd made the chocolate candy for the party. It shouldn't take long for her to locate everything she'd need to put together a hearty breakfast for Cluny and Santos. But first, she'd shower and change clothes.

She walked quietly down the hall to the bedroom where Cluny had carried her suitcase and a couple of cartons. "Now where did I put those things I pulled from the dryer?" She dug through a box looking for underwear and found a freshly laundered bra and panties, and then decided to put the rest of them in a drawer of the large dresser across from the foot of the bed.

The top drawer wasn't empty. The first thing she saw was a hairbrush, a tube of hand crème and a book. It had the feel of snooping, but she touched the brush and stared at the blond hair strands. All of a sudden the presence of Misty Beachy suffocated her. Graciella dropped the brush, slammed the drawer shut and backed away. When her knees bumped into the mattress, she sat on the bed, slumped forward and put her head in her hands. "Stop this, Graciella. Stop this right now." But no matter how many times she repeated the phrase, the green-eyed monster refused taming.

Cluny pounded down the street next to Queen. He couldn't remember the last time he felt so good, so full of energy. He sucked in a deep breath of cool morning air and laughed out loud. "I don't know about you, Queenie, but I feel great." He leaned down, smacked her rump and sprinted ahead. She took off with a burst of speed and passed him easily, eager to play.

A patrol car appeared over the rise and approached him slowly. The deputy leaned out the window and grinned like a Cheshire cat. "You look like you just hit the lotto, McPherson."

Cluny stopped and bent to catch his breath. "You'd look like this too if you had a beautiful woman in your kitchen cooking breakfast, pal."

"Ah, it just so happens I do, and that's where I'm headed right now." He whacked the outside of the door with his hand. "Have a good day, my friend."

Cluny put out his hand. "Hey! You bringing your kid for baseball tomorrow?"

"Wouldn't miss it, coach."

"Good. See ya." He took off in a run. "Come on, Queen. It's time for breakfast." The last half mile went by in a flash. He passed the park and ran up his driveway, sat on the top porch step and pulled off his shirt. Growling, he played tug-of-war with an old knotted rag with her for a couple of minutes then stood. "Oops, gotta go round back, girl. This door is locked." He hadn't taken his wallet or keys when he left an hour ago.

The smell of coffee and bacon greeted him at the back screen door. Sniffing like a starved cur, he opened the door and strode into the kitchen. "It smells like heaven in here, baby."

Santos sat at the table sipping a glass of orange juice and smiled a greeting. "Macfearsome, Mama's making waffles."

"Great!" Cluny patted the boy's back. "You're up early." He embraced Graciella from behind. He sensed her stiffen, and chalked it up to the fact he probably needed a shower. "I'll be back in five, sweetheart. I'm starved."

He walked down the hall toward his bedroom. When he passed the open door of the guest room he noticed her suitcase and the still-packed boxes sitting on the bed. He shrugged off a hint of unease he couldn't explain and hit the shower.

Showered and dressed in his blue work pants and shirt with *Veteran's Plumbing* embroidered above the pocket, he sat at the table and lifted the steaming cup of coffee Graciella set in front of him, breathing deeply of the fragrant brew. "Sweetheart, you make the best coffee. Thanks for breakfast."

Graciella smiled briefly and sat across from him.

Santos dug into his syrupy waffle with gusto and poked a large piece into his mouth.

The vague feeling of unease returned. Something had changed from the time he'd left for his run and now. "Is something wrong, baby?"

Her eyes opened wide and she answered too fast. "No! Why?"

"You seem awfully quiet."

She shook her head. "I must have been preoccupied. Everything is fine. I, uh, was thinking of making a grocery list, so I could go to the store and pick up a few things, you know, for the park tomorrow."

"Good idea. The best place to check is probably the Wal-Mart in Simi. Do you know where it is?"

"Yes, Santos and I have been there a couple of times. What should I buy?"

"The practice is after lunch and we don't have anything organized yet, so maybe a couple of boxes of granola bars, some individual bags of trail mix, and a lot of bottled water. You and the other moms can talk about how you want to handle it for the rest of summer." He put his hand on hers. "Look, baby, don't go to a lot of trouble, or worry that you're getting the right snacks. It's just a bunch of sweaty kids trying out for baseball."

Santos grinned through a mouthful of food. "Mama worries about everything, Macfearsome."

Cluny laughed. "I'm beginning to see that."

"Oh, stop it, you two." Graciella waved her hands. "I do not."

They finished breakfast on a more cheery note. Cluny put down his napkin and carried his dish to the sink. "Walk out to the van with me, okay?"

She glanced at him with a tight smile and nodded. "Santos, I put some towels in the bathroom off the hall. When you finish, take a shower and put on clean clothes."

"Okay, Mama."

Cluny grabbed his wallet, phone and keys and took her hand. He led her out the front door and across the lawn to his company van and opened the driver's door so Queen could jump inside. He smoothed his hands on her upper arms. "What's bothering you? Something happened between the time I left for my run and when I got back."

She shook her head. "Nothing, I…"

"No. Please don't deny it. Talk to me." He was shocked to see tears fill her eyes. "Baby, what is it?" He wrapped his arms around her and lowered his cheek to the top of her head. His chest in a vise, he could barely breathe, but he sucked in air when her arms went around him. "I can't stand to see you cry, sweetheart. Was it something I said or did?"

"No." She shook her head against his chest.

"What then?" He stepped back and studied her face. "Let's get it in the open then we can deal with it, baby."

She sighed. "I'm embarrassed, because it's so silly." She patted his chest. "I'll get over it, don't worry."

"I am worried because you won't talk about it with me."

Her lips pressed together in a stubborn line. Cluny was afraid she wouldn't open up. He wouldn't push her if she refused to tell him.

"Promise me you won't brush it off. I already admitted it was trivial."

"I promise."

She cleared her throat. "When I went to put away my things, I found some of Misty Beachy's belongings in the dresser." Her cheeks turned pink and she put her hands to her face. "I don't want to stay in that room, amor. I can't."

Up to this point he hadn't appreciated the depth of her concern and uncertainty about his past and present relationship with Mis. He swallowed and considered his response. "Graciella, I love you so much. It kills me that you still have doubts. We can solve this." He cupped her cheeks. "Move Santos into that room, and I'll buy some furniture for the empty bedroom. It will be exclusively yours."

"I can't allow you to go to that unnecessary expense because of my insecurity, querido. I've made far too much of this. Go to work. We'll talk about it later."

"Okay, but I do need to furnish some of my rooms sooner or later. This big house echoes because of so much empty space. You could help me." He smiled to reassure her, but couldn't know what was in her mind. All he could do was be patient while she thought over his proposal.

"Queen and I'll leave now, baby. We'll be home around six." He embraced her and kissed her forehead. "I love you, and only you."

She nodded, but said nothing.

Cluny stepped into the van, closed the door and started the engine. When he looked up, she smiled and waved. He pulled out of the driveway and headed to his warehouse. It would be an intense day. His company had been subcontracted by Big D Construction, Dwayne's outfit, for a job at a new big-box store in Spring Grove. This one contract would bring in enough money to cover his overhead for the rest of summer. He'd run his plumbing business in a way that had him set comfortably as far as finances were concerned. He was ready to expand, the main reason he'd hired Chief Ollie Williams to manage the office and handle the ongoing maintenance and service part of the business.

He drove to his warehouse in Simi Valley and arrived fifteen minutes later. At this time of day he stayed off the freeway and drove the surface streets for two reasons. He avoided the rush hour traffic going east to the San Fernando Valley and the ever growing volume of traffic moving west and north into Ventura County. Second, he enjoyed watching the endless changing development between Spring Grove and Simi.

Dempsey had related stories about his and his two brothers adolescence here, long before there was a Spring Grove. The unique rocky hills and center of Simi had been a country town with acres and acres of orange and lemon groves, eucalyptus wind barriers, and cattle ranches. Gunny hardly recognized his hometown when he moved back from Wyoming.

"Look, Queenie. The new bank is almost finished. Pretty soon there will be a whole new shopping area here. Not sure if I like it, but it is what it is."

He tried to shake off his conversation with Graciella. He'd better pay close attention to her feelings about Beachy. Those loudmouths at Dempsey's party had upset her far more than he'd realized. "I wish you could talk, Queenie. I bet you'd have plenty of good advice for me."

She turned her majestic head and whimpered.

"By God, you understood everything I said. I'd swear to it." He grabbed a handful of her crest and tugged, to her obvious pleasure. "I am so lucky to have you, you miraculous creature." Touching her lightened his mood. That's what she did for him.

———

Around noon his cell sounded off. He checked the screen and Graciella's name displayed. "Hey, baby. What's happening?"

"Santos and I are having a burger for lunch. We picked up the snacks for tomorrow and I thought if it was okay with you, I'd check a couple of the furniture stores and get an idea on prices for, uh, what you mentioned."

This was a welcome surprise. "Great! Yeah, do that. In fact I have an account at Granada Furniture on L.A. Avenue. If you see something you like call me and I'll talk to the manager. They do same day delivery."

"For heaven's sake, Cluny, I can't buy furniture you haven't seen."

"Sure you can. Just take a picture of it on your phone. If I hate it, I'll tell you, and you can select something else. Besides, the manager is a friend of mine. If I don't want to keep it after it's in the house, he'll pick it up, no questions asked."

"I don't know."

"Look, if you don't want to do it that way we'll wait until Sunday and go over there together."

"Hmm, I'm not sure…"

"I just got to the head of the line at the City Building Permit office. Gotta go, sweetheart. I'll call you later." He clicked off and stepped to the counter.

The clerk, Gloria, said, "Sweetheart? Sounds serious, Cluny. Do I know the lucky lady?"

He leaned across the counter and pecked the motherly woman's cheek. "Nope."

"Careful there, blue-eyes. The others in line might suspect me of showing favoritism."

Chapter Twenty

Friday evening

CLUNY PARKED AT THE CURB. HE WAVED AT THE STORE MANAGER and his helper sitting in the furniture truck pulling away from his driveway. He went inside the house. "Honey, I'm home!" He followed his nose to the kitchen. "Something smells good in here."

Santos stood grinning behind the island stove stirring a large pot. "I'm making chicken stew, Macfearsome."

Cluny laughed. "You know how to cook more recipes than chocolate candy?"

"I can cook lots of stuff, but Mama helped me get it started."

Cluny walked to the stove and leaned down to sniff the pot. "If this tastes as good as it smells I'll think I'm on my way to Valhalla." He noticed the table set for six. "We having company?"

Santos nodded. "Amber and her mom and dad are coming for dinner."

"Cool, I need to talk to Gunny about tomorrow. He's my assistant coach again this summer." He picked up a wooden spoon with the intention of sampling the stew. "You got enough here for a battalion."

Graciella called from the back of the hallway. "Cluny, come have a look. Santos—put the biscuits in the oven."

He dropped the spoon, patted Santos's back and followed her voice. "Coming, baby." If he could return home from work every night to a domestic scene like this one he'd be a very happy man. He put on a straight face, intent on teasing her.

She waited at the open doorway to the bedroom that had contained an air mattress when he'd left for work this morning. Her smile uncertain, she twisted her hands and waited for his approval of the bedroom set. "Please tell me you like it, Cluny."

He walked to the open doorway and stood peering into the room. Arms crossed, he pressed his lips into a thin line and nodded slightly. "I don't know…"

"Darn it! I never should have bought it on my own without you being there." She stamped her foot. "I just knew it! What's wrong with it?"

He struck a pose of deep thought, hand on his chin then pointed. "The dresser is over this way about four inches too far."

"What!" She balled her fists. "You, you…,"

Cluny laughed, picked her up in a tight hug and growled into her neck. The doorbell rang and he turned, still carrying her, and hurried to answer.

"Put me down, you skunk. It's probably the Dempseys." Graciella pounded his shoulders, and he ignored her protest.

Cluny let loose with one hand and opened the door. She squirmed in his arms and tried to free herself to no avail.

The Dempsey family waited on the front porch, but hesitated to enter when they saw her struggling. Cluny further tormented his sweetheart by smooching her cheek.

Marla raised her eyebrows and grinned. "I hope we're not interrupting. Maybe we should come back later."

Amber pushed past her parents. "Santos, where are you?" Hearing his answer from the kitchen, she wrinkled her nose at her silly Uncle Cluny, and passed them. "Grownups," she muttered balefully.

Queen followed her to the kitchen.

Graciella glared at him. "Are you planning to put me down?"

He put an exaggerated pleading look on his face. "If you promise not to hit me."

"I'm not promising anything after what you just pulled."

"Okay, then." He tilted his head at the Dempsey's. "Come on in. I need to take this to the back of the house. Could get ugly, shocking even. I don't want you to see it." He stepped back as Marla entered, then instructed them, "Call the cops if I'm not back in five."

He carried Graciella back to the newly furnished bedroom, stepped inside and pushed the door closed with his foot. "You gonna behave?"

"I suppose I'll have to since our guests are in the house." She grinned. "But I'm not saying what I'll do later."

"Sounds promising." He set her on her feet but kept his arms around her slender waist. "I need a welcome-home-from-work kiss. Got one to spare?"

Her arms went around his neck. "All you want, querido." She leaned into him and sighed.

Kissing her was something he could do all day long. He'd never get enough of those luscious lips and the feel of her body against his. Instantly hard, he groaned and pressed her tighter to him then lowered his mouth to hers. It didn't end with one kiss. He backed up and fell on the bed carrying her with him. "I never wanted anyone more than I want you right this minute, sweetheart. You're killing me."

She pushed on his shoulders and rolled on top. "Killing you is the last thing I want to do, but I won't talk about the first thing I want to do because it's impossible right now."

"Yeah, I know," he said on a resigned sigh. "I'll grab a quick shower and change." He squeezed her bottom and closed his eyes.

Graciella pushed off and stood at the edge of the bed to tug him up. "Dinner will be ready in about fifteen minutes. I better check on those biscuits, if Santos hasn't already taken them out of the oven." She put a light kiss on his mouth. "I plan to punish you for teasing me."

"I can think of several things that would teach me a lesson."

"I'm sure, but I have a few ideas of my own. Now hit the shower before Marla calls the police. It's been more than five minutes."

He opened the door and strolled to his bedroom. Queen had been waiting for him, and she followed him to the back of the house. He paused to scratch her ears when he got through the door then pulled off his work clothes.

———

True to his word, in less than fifteen minutes, he walked in the living room. His wet hair gleamed almost as bright as his happy smile. "Where are the ladies, Gunny?"

"Putting the final touches on dinner, and I suspect, talking about your bad behavior." Dwayne bounced Declan on his shoulder. "What'd you do?"

Cluny told him how he teased her over the new bedroom furniture she'd bought on her own. "She was reluctant to shop for it without me, but I said to go ahead after she sent the pictures from her phone. You should have seen how nervous she was to show it to me. I couldn't resist giving her a hard time."

"I thought you had the guest room furnished."

"She had an uncomfortable *moment* when she opened a drawer and found some of Beachy's belongings. So, I suggested Santos take that room and we'd set up one of the other two for her. I hadn't checked the closet or drawers before I put Graciella's things in there. How stupid of me."

"You have to admit, you and Beachy are the *odd couple*. Graciella got a dose of nasty speculation from the drunks the other day." He lifted the baby and grinned into his fat little face. "Too bad you don't know enough to appreciate how uncomplicated your life is right now, little buddy."

Marla entered the living room, took Declan and placed him in his carrier. "Dinner's ready. It'll be cozy with all six of us around that little kitchen table of yours. Are you ever going to get a dining room set?"

He stood and pecked her cheek. "Maybe I'll send Graciella shopping again."

"Hah! Good luck with that." She rolled her eyes. "Make yourself useful, Cluny. Carry Declan for me."

Dwayne dropped his arm around Marla's shoulder. "I can carry my own kid, Danaher."

She smiled sweetly. "Yes, I know, Dempsey, but I doubt Graciella will attack Cluny if he's carrying an innocent infant."

"You've got a point."

Crowded around the table, elbow to elbow, dinner was a lively affair. Santos basked in the glow of praise for his chicken stew, and Graciella's biscuits were so fluffy they nearly floated off the plate.

Cluny's mood was sky high. He surveyed the table and listened to the conversation between the people he loved most in the world. *It doesn't get any better than this.* At least he couldn't imagine having ever felt so happy and contented.

His hand flew across the table as he beat Dwayne to the last biscuit. "You used to be quicker, Gunny." He broke the biscuit in half and handed it over. "Don't say I never did you a favor."

"Please share your recipe with me, Graciella," Marla remarked. "These are fabulous."

"They're really simple to make. I'll write it down after we clear up."

"I know how to make biscuits," Santos said, "But Mama must have a secret because hers are always the best." He held up the one on his plate and raised his eyes at Amber. "You want to share mine?"

"I'm rilly stuffed." She plopped her head on her fist. "I probly won't be able to run the bases during tryouts tomorrow."

"If you kids are finished eating, you may be excused," Cluny said. "Take Queen for a walk. She's in danger of getting fat with all the snacks you've been sneaking to her when you thought I wasn't looking."

Graciella flashed him a hesitant and concerned look.

"This is a very safe neighborhood, baby. I know everybody here and there's another hour of daylight. You don't need to worry."

Amber stood. "Can we ride your bikes, Uncle Cluny? Queen can run next to us."

"Sure, the side door to the garage is open. Stay in the park and on the path."

"Okay." The kids ran to the back door. "Queen, let's go!"

Graciella sighed. "I can't get used to allowing Santos out of my sight. I'd never think of letting him go alone in our neighborhood. I know I worry too much. Statistically it's very safe there."

Marla nodded. "Statistics aren't much comfort to a mother, are they?"

"I've got a couple of cigars in the truck," Dwayne said to Cluny. "Why don't you and I go out to the front porch and have a smoke?"

Cluny pushed his chair back. "Let's help with the cleanup first." He reached for his plate.

"No," Marla said, "We'll do this. Take those stink bombs and stroll over to the park. You can keep an eye on the kids and ease Graciella's concern. Take Declan, the stroller's in the back of the truck. Keep the smoke away from him!"

Dwayne stood at attention and saluted. "Yes, ma'am!"

"Oh, stop it." Marla embraced her husband. "When did I get so bossy?"

He hugged her hard. "Is that a trick question?"

She put her hands on his chest and pushed him away. "Get out of here."

Cluny lifted Declan's carrier and headed out. "Better make a quick exit before you venture into that mine field, Gunny. I need you to be in good shape for baseball tomorrow." He winked at Marla and threw a kiss to Graciella.

———

The red ball of the sun sank behind the mountain ridge in the cloudless sky. As it usually did during summer in California, the temperature dropped sharply. Cluny, Santos and Graciella stood on his front lawn and waved when the Dempsey's truck backed out of the long driveway. Cluny burst with warm contentment as he embraced them.

"Let's dust those bikes off and oil the chains before we put them away, sailor. They haven't been ridden in a while and need some TLC. I usually take better care of my stuff."

Santos stretched to his full height. "Grampa showed me how to oil the chain. He said if you take care of things they last almost forever." He looked at his mother. "Is Grampa coming to baseball tomorrow?"

"You remember what we told you? The police officers thought it would be best if we didn't visit for a while in case Jamal is watching them."

"Would Jamal hurt them?"

"No, I don't think so," she winced and glanced at Cluny. "He was looking for Krystal,. She's left L.A. for a job out of town, so hopefully he's given up on trying to find her. I bet Grampa will be there for the season opener."

Cluny rested his hand on Santos' head. "Let's get to those bikes, pal. I want you to get a good night's sleep so you can do your best at tryouts tomorrow." He nodded in the direction of the garage.

"I'm not very good at sports," Santos mumbled.

"You'll do just fine. It's going to be a fun summer, trust me." He nodded to Graciella. "We won't be long, baby."

"Take your time. I'm going to make up my bed. Those new sheets are ready to come out of the dryer by now. I hope you've got an extra blanket somewhere, Cluny."

"Check the top shelf in the laundry room."

He and Santos wheeled the bikes through the side door in the garage. Cluny snapped on the overhead lights and handed the boy a couple of clean rags. "You start wiping them down and I'll fill my oil can."

Santos paid close attention to him as he oiled the chains and tested them. "That's the way Grampa and Chief do it." He swiped up a drop of oil on the garage floor. "Only Grampa puts down newspaper before he starts."

"That's a great idea. We'll do it that way next time."

"Macfearsome?"

"Yeah, buddy?"

"What's in that big safe over there in the corner?"

Cluny hesitated. This could be a touchy subject with the boy's mother, but he thought it was better to speak truthfully to children. "I keep my gun collection in there. Nobody can open it except me. That's why it's called a safe."

Santos sucked in a breath and his eyes widened. "You got guns? Why?"

"Amber's dad and I like to go hunting during the season. We've been hunting ever since we were in school in Wyoming. His mother has a big freezer with bison and elk meat. They eat a lot of game at the ranch. But, mostly we like target shooting."

"I think it's sad to kill things." The look on the boy's face touched Cluny's heart.

He nodded and laid his hand on Santos' shoulder. "Humans eat meat unless they're vegetarians. All meat comes from some animal that died in order for the meat to be on the table. As long as the killing is done in a humane way I don't have a problem with it."

Santos lowered his head and sighed. "But the wild animals are so special."

"I agree, son, but hunting wild game helps keep a healthy balance of nature between the predators and the prey. State Fish and Game hands out hunting permits every year for a certain number of animals. It's a wise way to manage wildlife. It would be very sad if they slowly starved to death in the winter because there wasn't enough fodder."

"I s'pose." Santos didn't look convinced.

"That's why they introduced wolves into Yellowstone so many years ago. Man's attempt to control the growing population of grazing animals."

"Did it work?"

"The jury's still out. One thing they didn't count on was how fast the wolf packs might multiply. A lot of farmers and ranchers are upset because many packs expanded beyond the park boundary into Wyoming, Montana and Idaho. They started killing cattle and sheep. It will take a long time to see whether it was the right move."

Cluny thought it best to change the subject. He should discuss the matter with Graciella before talking about it anymore. "We're done here. What say you get your shower and into your pajamas? We'll relax and watch some TV or a movie before you hit the sack."

"I am kind of tired, Macfearsome. I got a hangover from the campout."

Cluny laughed at the child's innocent use of *hangover*. He knew hangovers first hand and it was so much worse than lack of sleep. Those days were gone forever, thank God. And thank Gunny. He doubted he'd have been able to get clean of it on his own.

He handed a rag to Santos. "We can wash the oil off at the sink in the laundry room. I've got some solvent that'll do the trick. I got a hunch your mom wouldn't look favorably on a couple of grease monkeys walking in on her."

Santos grinned and nodded. He wiped his hands and handed the rag back. "She hates dirty hands. Do you have a brush? She'll inspect my fingernails real close."

Later the three of them reclined on the couch, Santos in the middle, and watched *How It's Made.* Santos' eyes grew heavy and his head drooped against Cluny's shoulder.

Cluny peeked at his watch. "It's almost eleven. No wonder he's out."

Instead of answering, Graciella smiled fondly at her son and brushed a finger on his cheek.

Carefully extricating himself, Cluny made to get up from the couch. "I'll carry him to bed."

"No, it's better if he walks. Then if he wakes up later he'll remember where he is and how he got there." She leaned close to Santos. "It's time for bed, sweetie. We're going to your new bedroom across the hall from mine."

She stood and tugged his arms. Santos groaned getting to his feet, and she led him down the hall. Cluny leaned on the bedroom doorway and watched as she pulled back the blankets and urged him onto the bed, then covered him. A small nightlight Cluny hadn't seen before glowed from an outlet on the wall opposite the bed.

Graciella kissed her son goodnight. Her action triggered a memory in Cluny of his mother kissing him goodnight. He was younger than Santos when she died, but it seemed like yesterday. His heart squeezed painfully in his chest. He backed into the hall and waited for her to leave the room.

"Querido? Is something wrong?" She gazed at him with her beautiful chocolate eyes and laid her hand on his cheek.

Cluny sighed deeply and gave her a reassuring smile. "No, baby, I'm fine, but watching you with your boy reminded me of the many times my mother kissed me goodnight when I was a kid." He embraced her. "You're a good mom. I love you so much."

She rested her head on his chest. "Your heart is galloping." When she raised her face to him her eyes were damp. "*Amo-te.*" She brushed her lips against his.

Santos called through the open doorway, "Are you kissing Macfearsome goodnight, Mama?"

"Go to sleep, pal." Cluny kissed Graciella back. He took a side step, closed the bedroom door and deepened the kiss. He slowly walked her backwards in the direction of his bedroom.

"No you don't, Macfearsome. I decided on your punishment."

He waggled his eyebrows and grinned. "Yeah?"

"Yeah." She stepped away and entered the newly finished bedroom. "You're sleeping alone tonight." She grinned and closed the door in his face.

Well, hell.

He shoved his hands in his pockets and looked down when Queen leaned heavily against his leg. "It's just you and me again, Queenie." He scrubbed the top of her head with his fingers then walked through the house locking doors and turning off lights.

Hell. His shoulders shook with a silent chuckle.

Chapter Twenty-One

After midnight

"MEDIC! WHERE'S THE FUCKING MEDIC!" CLUNY'S SCREAM shattered the quiet. "Help!"

Graciella shot out of bed and didn't realize she was standing until she felt the cool floorboards under her bare feet. She opened her bedroom door.

Santos, owly-eyed in the dim hallway, was clearly jarred by what they'd heard. He took a couple of steps in the direction of Cluny's bedroom.

Graciella grabbed his arm. "No. Don't go in there."

"But, he needs help." He tugged against her hand. "What's wrong?"

"Shiiit!" Thrashing sounds emanated from the bedroom at the end of the hall. "No! Stop! I can't...I can't move! Somebody help!"

Santos turned stricken eyes to her. "Mama, we have to help him."

She held fast. "He'll be all right. Queen's in there, she'll help him." Her heart pounded so hard in her throat, she'd barely been able to say the words. The skin on her scalp tightened painfully.

Queen barked and a light came on in Cluny's bedroom. The screaming stopped.

"Can we go now?" Santos pleaded.

"No. Cluny warned me to stay away if he had a nightmare. He doesn't want us to come in." She fought against the instinct to rush to his side.

"But why, Mama?"

"Because he's not fully awake and it takes a while for him to get his bearings." This was far worse than she'd imagined. Cluny'd warned her, but now she had a better understanding of what he'd been trying to tell her. Her heart cracked for the man she loved and what he had to deal with.

She expressed a pent-up sigh and hugged Santos. "It's quiet now. Go back to bed." She turned him in the direction of his bedroom.

"Can I stay with you?" He clung to her waist. "I'll never go back to sleep."

"Of course." She pushed open her bedroom door. "Snuggle in with me." Graciella led him to her bed and threw back the blanket. He crawled across the bed and lay down on his side facing the opposite wall. She got in beside him and gently pulled him close. "Don't worry about Cluny. Queen will help him get back to sleep, and in the morning he'll be fine."

"I feel so sad soldiers have nightmares when they come home. I like Macfearsome a lot mostly because he's always so funny and happy. It's not fair."

No, it wasn't fair, but so little of life was fair. It wasn't fair that her son had been deprived of a father. It wasn't fair that Amber's father got his leg blown off. It wasn't fair that so many servicemen had suffered grievous wounds to body and soul.

"All we can do is love him, Santos. Make sure he knows we don't think less of him because of his struggle."

"I think *more* of him, Mama. I want to stay here forever. I want Macfearsome to be my dad."

Tears leaked from the corners of her eyes at his innocence. Children looked at life in such an uncomplicated way. It was so simple to them. Could it be as simple as he'd said? *No.* She had her demons and so did Cluny. She couldn't protect Santos from life no matter how hard she tried. It was time for her to be more open with him, allow him to experience more of life. He was soft-hearted, but also smart and strong.

"I love Cluny, sweetheart, but I don't know if we could ever be a family."

Santos squeezed her hand. "But we could try, couldn't we?"

"Yes, we could try." She kissed his head. "Now see if you can go to sleep. Baseball tryouts are tomorrow afternoon."

———

Saturday morning

Graciella put the egg carton in the refrigerator. Cluny's footsteps pounded up the driveway. In a moment she heard him open the back door, and Queen's toenails clicked on the tile floor followed by loud lapping at her water dish.

"What's cookin'?" He embraced her from behind and kissed her beneath her ear. His hard body pressed her back and his strong arms held her tight.

"French toast. Santos's most favorite."

He chuckled into her hair. "Everything is your kid's most favorite."

"Yes. It's nice to cook for someone who's easy to please."

"I'm easy to please." His big hands cupped her breasts.

"Yes, you are, querido." She turned in his arms. "Good morning."

Cluny's kiss was warm and soft. He placed a hand on either side of her face and gazed into her eyes then dived in for another.

Thrilling warmth coursed through her body and landed heavy in her lower torso. This man could melt stone with a kiss. She pressed herself against him wondering if she'd ever tire of his physicality and how it affected her.

"I can't get enough of you, baby." He placed a hand on her bottom and pressed her close.

"You read my mind, amor." She pushed back against his hand and attempted to step away.

He held her close. "I'm not done yet," he murmured into her mouth and pressed his erection against her. "God, I'll never be done."

"Good morning, Macfearsome."

They jerked apart. Graciella was glad they were on the other side of the island. Her cheeks grew hot at the thought her little boy was spared from seeing the state of Cluny's physical arousal. Arousal that disappeared as quickly as it had appeared.

Cluny's hand went down below the counter to adjust his sweat pants. "Good morning, sleepyhead. Mama's making French toast. Your most favorite." He winked at her son then patted her bottom.

Santos' face brightened. "Yay. I bet Queen likes it, too."

Cluny dragged a large bag of kibble from the pantry. "Maybe so, but because we want her to be around a long time, she'll have her usual breakfast. Hand me her food dish, will ya, buddy?"

Graciella fanned her face and jabbed Cluny in the ribs with her elbow as he brushed past her, while her son's back was turned. She gave him a stern behave-yourself look when he made a sudden fake lunge in her direction. It was frightening how much she loved him in that moment. An unwelcome wave of insecurity threatened to invade her, but she fought hard against it, silently repeating Marla's mantra, *don't borrow trouble, don't borrow trouble.*

Cluny took the big stainless steel dish proffered by Santos, set it on the sink and dumped a heaping pile of kibble in it. He looked over his shoulder as he set the pan on the floor. "Do I have time to shower?"

"Not unless you want a cold breakfast. Both of you sit down. I have everything ready."

Santos and Cluny grinned and dragged chairs from the table then flopped into them. She set a carafe of hot chocolate in front of Santos. "This is very hot. Let Cluny pour for you." Returning to the table with the coffee pot, she set it on a large hot pad next to Cluny then grabbed three mugs she'd left warming on the stovetop.

Cluny smiled up into her eyes. "Shall I pour for you, too, sweetheart?"

"Yes, please." She opened the oven, put on a mitt and slid out a large platter of French toast and sausage. Queen wasn't alone sniffing the air when she carried it to the table. Cluny and Santos wore identical big-eyed hungry faces. She had to laugh at the two men she loved so much.

When breakfast was nearly finished, Santos took a swallow and asked, "Did you have a real bad dream last night, Macfearsome?

Cluny's eyes met Graciella's. She saw hesitation in the sudden cloudiness of his usually bright blue gaze. She lowered a hand beneath the table and squeezed his knee then made a barely perceptible tilt of her chin.

For a moment Cluny didn't answer. He wiped his mouth on a napkin and put it back in his lap. "Uh, yeah, it was one of the bad ones. Did I scare you?" The regret in his face when he spoke the words so painfully crushed her heart.

Santos raised his eyebrows and bobbed his head. "Kinda. I wanted to go to your room and help you, but Mama said Queen would fix it. What did you dream about? The war?"

Graciella tamped down the urge to change the subject. Did he really need to know the details? Then she remembered the vow she'd made to herself to ease off shielding him from real life issues. "Maybe Cluny would rather not talk about it, son."

He raised a hand. "No, that's okay. It's a hateful nightmare that I have a lot. I'll tell you what I can, but remember it's not real, it's a dream. You probably have a bad dream once in a while, right? Then when you wake up and realize you're safe in your own bed, it goes away."

He exchanged a glance with Graciella that reassured her he'd only tell Santos as much as he thought he could handle.

Santos nodded gravely. "Uh, huh. I don't say bad words, though. Mama wouldn't like it."

Cluny chuckled. "I'll try to remember that." He took a sip of his coffee. "The dream takes place in a hot, dirty, smoky place I don't recognize. Bad things are happening around me, but I can't hear. For some reason I'm deaf and paralyzed, and then I see Gunny Dempsey lying on the ground. His mouth is moving and he's reaching for me. I try to get up, but I can't move. I can't help him. The next thing I know, Queen is standing or lying on my chest barking and licking my face."

Eyes big, Santos asked, "Is that when you wake up and turn on the light?"

"Queen turns on the light."

Wonder filled his eyes. "She does?" Santos stared first at Cluny then at his mother. "I didn't know she could turn on the lights."

"I have a special switch next to my bed. She bumps it with her nose or paw and the lights come on."

"Can I see it?"

"Sure." Cluny pushed back his chair. "Come on, I'll show you."

Graciella stayed at the table, but she could hear them talking at the other end of the house. The words were unclear, but the pitch of Santos' voice told her he was excited about Queen's skill. A few minutes later, he returned to the kitchen alone.

"Where's Cluny?" She poured him the last of the chocolate.

"Macfearsome is taking a shower. He said he had to get ready to go to work because there was a lot to do before he could come home in time for baseball."

"Ah, yes, I forgot he was going to work this morning." She lifted the coffee pot and swished it to see if there was any left then poured the dregs into her cup. "When you get dressed, bring me your dirty clothes. I'm doing a couple of loads of laundry this morning."

"Okay." He nodded and grinned. "Queen's light switch is just like the one we have in my bathroom at our apartment. I remember Grampa put in there for me because I couldn't work the other one very good in the middle of the night. Macfearsome put his low down on the wall next to his bed."

She'd never stepped foot in Cluny's bedroom, but she could picture the touch-switch apparatus quite clearly. "That was clever."

"The dog people told him where to put it. She already knew how to work one."

Graciella pushed back from the table. "Time for me to get dressed for work, too. I found the vacuum cleaner and cleaning supplies in a closet in the laundry room."

"What are you going to clean? Macfearsome's house looks fine to me."

"The male of the species has dust blindness." Cluny said he had a service come to clean a couple of times a month, but she saw dust everywhere. It wouldn't take long to get rid of it.

"That's what Grandma says."

"Your grandmother is a wise woman. Now, carry the dishes to the sink for me, please. I'll finish with the kitchen after I get dressed." She tousled his hair in spite of his attempt to dodge her hand. Smiling, she left the kitchen.

She went to her bedroom and dragged on a pair of shorts and a faded T-shirt with the samba school logo emblazoned on front and back. Pulling her hair into a practical ponytail, she stepped into the hall and ran smack into Cluny. "Oof."

He caught her. "You okay?" He held her at arms' length and made a low whistle. "Did I ever tell you, you have sensational legs?"

"No, but go ahead." On tiptoe, she gave him a light kiss on the lips.

"They're sensational, baby. They match the rest of sensational you." His rough hands slid up and down her bare arms. "Woof woof." In her ear he growled, "I'm going to lick my way up these legs tonight. It's a promise."

Graciella smacked his chest. "Shush. We aren't alone in the house."

"From the clatter in the kitchen, I don't think we have to worry about being overheard, do you?"

Her face hot with a combination of embarrassment and passion, she said, "Go to work."

His wink was sinfully lascivious. "I'll be home by noon. Then I need to be at the park by one so I can unlock the equipment locker before the kids get there."

"I'll have lunch ready." She put her arms around him then dropped her hands to his butt and squeezed. "Mmmm. I like."

He looked up and pointed heavenward. "Thank you, God. Thank you." He planted a stinging kiss on her lips and stepped away. "Come, Queen. We better get the hell out of here right now."

Hand over her heart, she admired his strong shoulders as he walked down the hall. He ducked his head through the kitchen archway. "See you later, pal."

"See you later, Macfearsome."

Graciella felt sure she'd be wearing her smile for at least an hour.

———

A few minutes past noon, Cluny's van pulled into the driveway. She had lunch on the table. He walked in, pasted a hurried kiss on her cheek and one on the top of Santo's head. Her breath stuttered at the spontaneous gesture of affection for her son.

"I'll get out of these work clothes and wash my hands. Be right back." He stepped from the kitchen.

Santos grinned from ear to ear. "Macfearsome kissed me, Mama."

"Yes, do you mind?"

"No, I liked it. Maybe he loves me. I hope so."

Cluny called from the hall. "I love you, Santos Jefferson."

Santos pumped his fist in the air. "Yes!"

The joy on her son's mocha-hued face brought tears to her eyes. She turned quickly, dashed them away and opened the refrigerator. "Where's the lemonade?"

"You already put it on the table."

She straightened, "Ah, so I did. Well, then go to the front porch and wait for Amber. The Dempsey's are sharing lunch with us."

"Oh boy!" He ran to the door, sneakers squeaking on the wood flooring, Queen dogging his heels. She seemed to anticipate their arrival just as much as her son. Graciella sighed, then wandered down the hall to Cluny's bedroom and leaned on the doorframe.

Water splashed in the sink, He hummed, *Take me out to the ball-game,* and stepped from the bathroom wearing sneakers, jeans and a bright green T-shirt bearing a shamrock and the words, Big D Construction.

He stopped dead in his tracks. "Faith and begorrah! I do believe I spy a magical faerie lurkin' in me doorway. Where's me pot o'gold?"

"When did you get so Irish?" His black hair, blue eyes and five-o'clock shadow cast him in the role of hero on the cover of a historical romance novel. "Do you own a kilt? I've always loved a man in a kilt."

"I'll buy one first thing Monday morning."

"Thank you for loving my son, Irish."

He rested his hands on her shoulders. "He's easy to love, just like his mom."

The warmth of his hands nearly melted her. She'd never tire of his unique touch. In spite of her natural hesitation to jump headlong into a relationship with Cluny, she knew deep down that she'd be a fool to let him get away.

Santos' voice rang down the hallway. "They're here!" Queen barked a greeting.

Graciella sighed. "Time to be parents again."

"And again." He pecked a kiss on her forehead. "And again."

"Don't get any ideas."

"Too late, baby. The idea is burned in my brain." He stepped into the hall. "Hey, Gunny, Did you remember the baseball caps?"

"In the truck. What's for lunch? I'm starving!"

Chapter Twenty-Two

Saturday afternoon at the park

HALFWAY THROUGH THE FIRST BASEBALL PRACTICE, GRACIELLA handed out juice boxes and snacks while Marla nursed Declan. "That's the last of it. I'll have to get more next time."

"The other moms will take turns bringing snacks. I'll get some for next Saturday. Last year we had different people participating, but I do recognize some of the parents here today." She waved her hand and gestured at a group of three blonde women sitting higher in the bleachers behind them. "Molly, Sonja, Diana, come down and meet Graciella Jefferson."

Marla introduced the women to Graciella then said, "Coach McPherson's girlfriend will be organizing the snack patrol this year. Why don't you write down your phone numbers and email addresses so Graciella can call you, and we'll get organized for the rest of the season?"

The tallest, who'd been talking to an awkward boy with thick glasses earlier, grinned at Graciella. "You're Coach's girlfriend? Lucky lady. If I wasn't already married with four kids, I'd be trying to land him myself. He makes the Mom Patrol drool."

The other two women bobbed their heads in agreement. One of

them put the back of her hand to her forehead, rolled her eyes. "That butt and those blue eyes," then her face went red with a deep blush.

An unwelcome coil of jealousy wrapped itself around Graciella's stomach. She wanted to like these other mothers, so she gritted her teeth against an unwise retort. "Um, now that you mention it, I guess I do qualify as his girlfriend." A quick, not-quite-smile played across her lips.

"Didn't we all know he'd get snagged sooner or later?" Marla put a hand on Graciella's forearm. "Cluny and Graciella are perfect for each other. Would you believe they met at the beach? Her son, Santos," she pointed across the infield, "was fascinated with Cluny's service dog."

The short woman's eyebrows drew together. "Whatever happened to the cute blond who was here with him a couple of times last summer? I thought they might be, uh, you know."

Graciella swallowed as heat rose in her cheeks.

"No!" Marla placed Declan on her shoulder and patted his back. "She's a Marine buddy who served in Iraq in the same unit with Dwayne and Cluny. She and Cluny are just pals. The unit's a pretty tight-knit group."

Graciella took slow breaths. Nausea threatened. *What's the matter with me?* She stood abruptly. "If you'll excuse me, I'm going to check the trunk of my car. Make sure I didn't leave any snacks behind."

As she walked away she heard one of the women ask Marla, "Did I say something wrong? I didn't mean to." Graciella didn't hear Marla's answer. She felt the perfect fool, completely undone by her reaction to their harmless girl-talk. She'd never thought of herself as a simpering, insecure boob, but she was sure acting like one. She should celebrate the fact that Cluny had chosen her, and join in the friendly banter. She didn't doubt the true nature of his commitment to her after all that had passed between them.

She returned to join Marla minutes later and leaned close. "I don't know what's wrong with me to react that way to their friendly teasing." She reached for her purse and pulled out a small notepad with pen attached then climbed up to the three women and forced a happy smile onto her face.

"If you'll put your names and contact information here, I'll call you in a few days and we'll work out a schedule. Marla's taking care of next week. Cluny dumped this week on me with very little notice. I really appreciate your help."

The blonde who hadn't spoken before tilted her head. "You have an accent I can't identify." She took the pad and scribbled her name and numbers. "We're glad to help with the kids. That's why we're here. And don't pay attention to what we say. We drool over Coach Dempsey, too." She flashed a charming and friendly grin that put Graciella at ease.

"But not Chief?"

"Oh heck yes, him too, the grizzled old grouch. We're just a bunch of harried, frustrated housewives." The three blonde women laughed. Then she asked, "Where are you from originally?"

"Brazil. Sao Paulo. I married an American sailor and he brought me to California. You think maybe I reeled Cluny in with my exotic accent?"

"Marriage didn't work out?"

"My husband was a SEAL. He was killed in action in Iraq."

"Oh, honey," The woman grabbed her hand. "I'm so sorry. How long ago?"

"Marvin died before Santos was born. He'll be ten soon." The woman's sincere reaction, her sad watery eyes, almost had Graciella tearing up. "It was a long time ago." She squeezed the woman's hand. "Sonja, right? I'm so happy to meet all of you."

The three began talking all at once, reassuring her how happy they were to make her acquaintance and apologizing again for teasing her.

"Don't give it another thought." She raised her eyebrows. "But hands off my boyfriend, okay?" She playfully raised a fist.

They exchanged relieved smiles, and Graciella returned to her seat next to Marla. "Disaster averted. I can't imagine why I reacted the way I did. I'm either in love or crazy."

"Love makes one do crazy things. For instance..." She rolled her eyes. "I'm pregnant."

Graciella jerked back. "You're...? But Declan's only—"

Marla sighed. "So much for breast feeding preventing conception. I nearly fainted when the doctor told me yesterday."

"How did Dwayne react?" She was still wrapping her head around Marla's revelation.

"He doesn't know yet, but he'll be crowing and strutting like a rooster when I tell him. It's entirely my doing. Good grapes, I can't keep my hands off him. It's been that way since the first time he kissed me."

Graciella stared across the diamond at Dwayne. "Gosh."

"Yes. There I was, smart, unflappable, independent business woman. I had big plans that didn't include a man. Then in walks Dempsey oozing testosterone, teasing me relentlessly, hitting on me every five minutes. I wanted to kill him. Instead, I fell in love. What do you think of that?"

Graciella put her arm around Marla and hugged her tight. "Oh, Marla, I think it's wonderful. It's obvious to everyone how much you love each other and your kids." She reached out her hands. "Let me hold the Dec. I love cuddling a baby in my arms."

Marla handed him over. "Thanks, I need to get to the restroom. Seems I have to pee every thirty minutes." She stood and checked to make sure her blouse was properly buttoned. "Remind me when I get back; I have a favor to ask you." She hurried to the cinder block building housing the toilets.

Cluny wandered over and sat next to Graciella. He dropped an arm over her shoulder and kissed her cheek. Graciella imagined she could hear Sonja, Molly and Diana sighing. She giggled.

"What's so funny?" He put his index finger in Declan's tiny hand and made a silly face for the baby.

"Nothing, other than the fact I'm burning for you and want to kill every woman within fifty feet."

"Yeah?" He pecked her cheek again. "I like that."

"I'm going to beg the Dempsey's to take Santos home with them because if I don't get you to myself for a few hours, I'll need to be locked up."

"Holy cr...!" He pressed his hand in his lap. "Don't tell me that in a public park where children are present. You want to get me ejected?" He tightened his grip on her shoulder.

She leaned into his side. "Are you totally, miserably frustrated?"

"Shit, yes, baby."

"Me too. Now do me a favor and go away." She nudged him with her shoulder until he stood and walked to the dugout.

"Lover's quarrel?" Marla slid onto the bench next to her.

"Just the opposite." She cast imploring eyes at her friend. "I need a big favor. Could you please take Santos home with you for a few hours after practice?" She held her breath and mouthed *please*.

"Sure, but I also have something to ask of you."

"Anything." Graciella got up and lowered the sleeping baby into his carrier. "Ask."

"It's something you might enjoy." She shifted the carrier to keep the afternoon sun off her son's face. "I really want to do it because I have a feeling it'll be another year before I can squeeze into a sexy dress."

"What is it?" Sexy dress probably meant Marla needed a babysitter so she could go on a date with her husband. Graciella would love to babysit little Declan for an evening.

"I'd be so grateful if you and Cluny would attend a black tie event with us for the Wounded Warriors of Ventura County. It's next Saturday night. Dwayne knows several people there, and if I know him he'll wander away to shoot the breeze about the good ole days, and leave me sitting there like a frog on a log. I'd like you to come and keep me company. How about it?"

"I'd love to go." Graciella clapped her hands. "I haven't been to a dressy affair in forever. I'll need to shop for a new dress though. When is it? Will Cluny have to rent a tuxedo?" Excitement at the prospect sent her blood racing. "Oh, but who will watch the kids?"

"My parents have already volunteered. Adding Santos to the mix will be great for Amber." Marla put her hand on Graciella's arm. "May I go shopping with you? Hey, the malls are open until ten every night. Dwayne and Cluny could watch the kids." She sighed. "I really need this."

"Tuxedos?"

"The vets have a choice of black tie, or their dress uniforms. Dwayne will wear his uniform. I'm not sure about Cluny. There's a bridal shop on L.A. Avenue that can do a turnaround in twenty-four hours if he decides on the tux."

Graciella grinned. "You and I can pretend like we're having so much fun at the party without them they'll be curious and spend more time with us." Graciella pointed. "Looks like they're breaking up for the day. Do you want a ride back to the house with me?"

"It's only a couple of blocks. I need to walk. The stroller is under the bleachers. Dwayne and I'll meet you at your house. We'll take Santos home with us. He'll stay for supper. You can pick him up between eight and nine, okay?"

"Thank you, Marla. I'll owe you."

"I'm sure I'll find a way to collect." She waved at her approaching husband and step-daughter. "Amber, invite Santos to share dinner with us tonight."

"Rilly?" She skipped off to tell Santos.

Other parents made their way down the bleachers to fetch their tired and sweaty kids. When the three blondes reached the bottom, Dwayne winked. "Ladies. Nice to see you again this summer."

Sonja smiled and brushed past them. "You too, coach."

"See you next Saturday," Molly called over her shoulder.

Diana fluttered her fingers.

"Graciella." Chief joined them. "Earl and Lillian will come next Saturday. The detectives told them Jamal's left town, but he's on their radar. The stubborn bastard's trying to track down Krystal in New York, but she's on a photo shoot in Tel Aviv."

"Tel Aviv!" Krystal was achieving her dream of the glamorous life of a super model. She felt happy for her, in spite of recent events. "When did she leave New York?"

"A few days ago. There's no way he'll go after her now, because they've put him on an international no-fly list, and her agency never divulges the whereabouts of their models."

"Do you know what the shoot is for?"

"Lucille told Lu they were creating an international La Perla Lingerie calendar. They've set up several locations in Israel, and then they're moving on to Greece. We won't be seeing Miss Krystal for some time. Her folks are breathing a sigh of relief, I can tell you."

But this news also meant she and Santos could probably return to their apartment. She had mixed feelings about that. She'd talk it over with Cluny. Not this afternoon, though. They'd be too busy to talk.

No more than half an hour later, Dwayne's vehicle backed out of the driveway. Graciella and Cluny waved until the big black truck turned the corner. He took her hand and led her inside. "Queen's out back, baby. Could be a long boring afternoon with just the two of us," he teased.

Instead of answering him, she tugged on his arm and raced down the hall to his bedroom. "Get your clothes off and hit the shower, Marine."

He pulled her around, grabbed her hips, lifted her off her feet and wrapped her legs around his waist. "Not unless you take your clothes off, too. What's fair is fair."

Graciella panted with all-consuming desire when he walked backwards to the master bathroom holding her tight against him. The heat from his body, added to hers, seared her flesh like a branding iron. Clutching handfuls of his hair, she pulled him in for a scorching kiss. He detoured to the bed, fell back, and pulled her down on top.

"Baby," he gasped between kisses, "I didn't realize until a few weeks ago that before I met you I was only half alive. I'll never get enough of you." He flipped over, pinning her underneath. "I'm going to make love to you right now. The shower can wait."

She stared into his serious blue gaze and nodded. "Yes, now. I don't want to wait, either."

He eased off her, unbuttoned her shorts and slid down the zipper. "Wiggle out of these, sugar. I'm in a hurry." He reached across the bed and took a box of condoms from the bedside table, scattering them over the bed and floor in his haste. Catching one, he ripped it open, went up on his knees and undid his jeans.

"Aren't you going to...?"

"Nope. Like I said, I'm in a hurry. No nice. Down and dirty. You with me?"

Raising herself on an elbow, she answered. "All the way."

"God, baby, you're scary. I love it." He put his hands on her shoulders and eased her flat on the bed.

She put a palm on his cheek. "Remember this morning you promised me you were going to...oof!" He slammed into her so fast and hard the breath left her body in a whoosh. "Oh, Cluny, oh, Cluny, amor." Before she could utter another word, he covered her mouth with his and speared inside with his tongue to the rhythm of his hips.

Her excitement rose to such a high pitch she feared she might faint. *This man. This man. Oh Deus, this man.*

Cluny raised his head and stared into her face, teeth clenched, urging her on with every thrust. Her muted scream started at the knees and shot up to her throat. Only then did he allow his own release, slumping heavily on her. "God in heaven."

She could barely breathe, but she clutched him around the waist as tight as she could and held him close. "Don't move, please don't move."

"I don't ever want to move from here, but I also don't want to crush you." His forehead pressed to hers, he whispered, "You blow me away, sweetheart."

"Amo-te, Cluny."

He kissed the tears from her cheeks then repeated her words, "Amo-te, my Graciella, amo-te." He rolled on his back, carrying her with him.

She dropped her head on his chest and listened to his thundering heart, fearing she loved him too much, too soon.

He quietly sang to her. And when he got to the lyrics, "*I wanna love you till I die,*" her tears flowed anew.

———

Warm water pounded down and against them in Cluny's made-for-a-man shower. He'd installed specialized showerheads on two levels at both ends. It was a luxury she'd never experienced. "Aaaah, this is wonderful. I'll never be satisfied with my shower again."

"No reason you should be. Make this your shower."

"Don't tease me. We both know I'm only here temporarily."

"It doesn't have to be temporary, baby. I'm serious. I want you and Santos to stay here for a long time." He massaged her shoulders and back. "God, you're so soft. I'll never be satisfied to shower alone again."

It hadn't escaped her notice that he'd said 'long time,' not forever. *For the love of Deus, Graciella, stop it. Do you want to end it now?*

"Amor, Earl told Chief the detectives thought it would be all right

for them to come to the baseball games on Saturdays. It would probably be a good time for me to think about returning home."

His hands went still. "He told me, too, but I don't think so.
Not yet."

"Why not?" She leaned back so her shoulders touched his chest.

"That Jamal creep will probably return to L.A. when he gives up
on finding Krystal in New York. He might show up on your doorstep.
It's not safe for you to go home yet, I don't care what the detectives
said. It's too soon." His hands slid across her breasts as he pulled her
tight. "Give it a little more time, baby. Give it a month at least." He
turned off the water and took the two towels hanging over the glass,
handing her one of them. "It's after seven. We should get over to
Gunny's and bring our boy home."

Her breath caught at his use of *our* boy. Cluny's affection for
Santos was sincere, and her son returned it in kind. She hated herself
for being so full of doubt, so anxious. Either things would work out
for the three of them, or they wouldn't. Her constant anxiety
prevented her from enjoying their wondrous love affair in the
moment.

As if he'd read her mind, he added, "Take a breath, baby. Take
your time making the best decision." He pulled the towel away from
his face and gave her a husbandly peck on the nose and stepped out of
the shower.

Driving to the Dempsey home he smacked a hand to his forehead.
"Damn, I forgot to tell you something. I bought tickets to the
Wounded Warriors formal dinner-dance for next Saturday night.
Dwayne and Marla are going. Is it too late for you to decide? I'd really
like us to go."

She laughed and squeezed his knee. "Marla already told me about
it. We made plans to go shopping for new dresses Tuesday or
Wednesday night. You and Dwayne will have babysitting duty. I
haven't been to a formal affair in years."

He pulled into Dempsey's driveway. The Big D truck wasn't there.
The house was dark. He turned off the ignition and stepped out of the
Green Monster. "I wonder where they are." He ducked his head back
in the car. "Do you have your phone?"

She handed it to him. "Yes. What are you going to do?"

"Call Gunny." He punched in the number and waited. "No answer, it went to voicemail. Hey, Gunny, where are ya? We're here to pick up Santos and nobody's home. Call back this number, it's Graciella's cell."

"What should we do?"

"Give it a few minutes and see if he calls back." He knocked on the roof of the car. "I'm going to check the back door."

She hopped from the car and Queen leaped out after her. "I'll go with you." Icy fingers skittered up her back and neck. They'd probably just gone to the store or fast food place, but the frigid fingers crept through her hair and over her scalp.

Chapter Twenty-Three

CLUNY, CONCERNED, BUT NOT WORRIED, WENT TO THE BACK OF the house. He stopped on the porch when the fixture lit up. Was somebody home? No, that light was on an automatic timer.

"Are they here?" Graciella asked, breathless. Her anxious eyes widened.

"No, but we're on the early side." He slapped his leg. "Come, Queen." He put his arm around Graciella's shoulder and turned her toward the gate. "Let's wait in the car." They walked to the Green Monster and got in.

Cluny cocked his head at the sound of an approaching vehicle. "I bet that's them now, yep, I recognize the sound of Dwayne's truck." He stepped out of his car for the second time.

Graciella flung open the passenger door. She met Dwayne's truck as it pulled in the driveway. Marla rolled down the window and smiled. "You're early."

"Where have you been!" Graciella clasped her hands around her waist and bent forward. She gasped and sobbed.

Marla stepped out of the truck and reached for her. "Graciella, what is it?"

Cluny put his arm around her. "Baby, are you okay?" At a loss, he glanced to Marla.

Santos wiggled out of the back seat of the extended cab. "Mama?" He touched her shoulder gingerly. "Mama, what's wrong?"

Graciella's body wracked with sobs and she collapsed to her knees.

Cluny went down on his heels beside her. "Baby, talk to me." He tried to tug her to her feet.

She lashed out with her arm. "Get away from me!"

Cluny staggered back. Mouth open and eyebrows drawn together, he stood frozen. Fear gripped his belly. The woman he loved was suffering and she wouldn't let him touch her.

"Mama!" Santos cried. "Mama, what's wrong?"

Amber, Dwayne and Santos hovered next to Graciella.

Marla waved them back. "Everybody go. Leave."

Cluny stepped forward. Dwayne put out his arm. "No, let Marla handle it."

Cluny pushed away from Dwayne, doubled his fist and directed a glare at his buddy.

"Don't." Hands up, Dwayne shook his head. "Don't."

"Uncle Cluny." Amber threw her arms around him. "Listen to Daddy. Let's go in the house." She tilted her head and gazed up at him. "Uncle Cluny?"

Pent-up breath left his lungs like a pricked balloon and he lifted her in his arms. He buried his nose in her hair. Amber's long legs dangled below his knees. She tightened her arms around his neck.

"Yes, sugar, let's go in the house. I didn't mean to upset you. I'm sorry."

"I know you dint," she whispered and hugged him tighter.

Dwayne put his hands on Santos shoulders. "Come on, son. Marla will take care of your mom. You get Queen out of Cluny's car, and I'll get Declan. Listen, I hear DD barking. She knows we're here."

Cluny caught Santos' distressed expression and put Amber on her feet. "Okay, let's get Queen and go inside, pal." He hugged Santos to his side, and they went to the car and opened the door.

Queen bounded out and stood on her hind legs in front of Santos, her big paws on his shoulders.

Startled at first, a weak smile bloomed on his face. "Hi, Queenie." He put his fingers through her ruff and tugged her muzzle close to his face then giggled when her long tongue lapped at his mouth. "Yick."

"Down girl," Cluny and Santos glanced over their shoulders at Marla and Graciella before going in the house. He wanted to tell the boy everything would be okay, but because he was at a loss, he kept silent, and patted Santos' back instead.

"Do you know what's wrong with Mama, Macfearsome?"

"I wish I did. She was worried when nobody was home, then she had a meltdown when you got here. I hope she'll talk to Marla. I can't stand to see her hurting, but she didn't want my help."

"I don't understand. Mama loves you. She told me."

"Hey, kids," Dwayne put the baby carrier on the floor and pointed to the kitchen. "Let's get some of that ice cream I promised you after Grampa Brad's swimming lesson."

"We can do it ourselves, Daddy." Amber took Santos' hand. "Come on. We have your most favorite, mint chip. Mom bought it especially for you."

Instead of following them to the kitchen, Cluny went to the living room and collapsed on the couch. DD leaped into his lap and Queen dropped her heavy head on his knee. "Jesus H suffering Christ," he groaned.

Dwayne sat at the other end of the sofa. "What did you do, brother?"

Cluny shot forward and glared at his lifelong pal. "What the hell kind of a question is that?"

"Shhh. The kids." Dwayne waved his hands. "I'm just trying to figure out what's going on with you and Graciella."

"That makes two of us."

———

Mortified at her breakdown, Graciella took deliberate, slow breaths. She squeezed Marla's hand. "I'm okay, I'm okay."

"Stand up." Marla tugged her to her feet. "What happened? What did Cluny do? Tell me."

She shook her head and smeared the tears from her cheeks. "He didn't do anything."

Marla reached in her pocket and took a small packet of Kleenex and handed it to her. "Let's take a walk." She placed a hand in the crook of Graciella's elbow and directed her toward the sidewalk at the end of the long driveway.

She mopped her face and blew her nose. She'd never behaved like this in her entire life and was deeply embarrassed. Marla's quiet closeness comforted her. She hadn't had a woman friend to confide in since she'd left Sao Paolo, barely out of her teens. A deep sigh escaped her lips.

"Take your time. When you're ready, tell me what happened."

They'd covered nearly half a block before Graciella could speak. "It makes no sense, but I was terrified you weren't home when we got here and…and then didn't answer Cluny's phone call. Why didn't you answer the call?"

"We were almost home when Dwayne realized he'd left his phone at my parent's house. I didn't take mine when we went there after dinner. It's still on my kitchen counter. Don't you trust us to take good care of Santos?"

"It's not a matter of trust. I do trust you, but I've barely had him out of my sight since he was born. On rare occasions my sister-in-law or Marvin's parents watch him for a couple of hours. When we got here tonight, and you weren't home, I imagined every awful thing that could have happened to him, to you. I was drowning in guilt because I'd thought only of wanting to be with Cluny."

Yes, she'd left Santos to go shopping for a dress to impress Cluny. She'd left him overnight after the Independence Day barbecue so she could sleep with Cluny. Left him again this afternoon for the same reason. At the park she'd made plans with Marla to go shopping again, and to the dinner-dance next weekend, which meant leaving him yet again. What kind of a mother was she?

"I don't know what to say, Graciella. I won't presume to tell you how to feel, but it seems perfectly normal to me to want to spend private time with the man you love. It's not as if we only have so much love to give, and then there's none left for anybody else. Did Cluny say or do something to set you off?"

Graciella laughed quietly. "Other than make beautiful passionate love to me, transport me to a level of emotion I've never experienced, express a tenderness I've never known. No."

"That bastard!" Marla stopped walking and scowled. "How could he?" She perched her hands on her hips.

Graciella twisted her lips to suppress a smile. "Exactly. So tell me what's wrong with me, Marla. Am I crazy?"

"Crazy in love maybe, and thinking you don't deserve to be?"

"I do feel that way, and I know I shouldn't. Santos asked me the other day if Cluny could be his dad."

"Oh, dear." Marla brushed windblown auburn hair off her face.

"I'm afraid of filling him with false hope, so I said it might never be possible for us to be a family."

"What did he say to that?"

"He asked me if we could try." A tear tracked down her cheek and she quickly wiped it away.

"That sweet kid. It's so simple for them isn't it? They think if you love somebody enough everything will work out just fine."

Graciella sighed. "I know I'm too protective of him. I've been trying to talk myself into letting him stretch his wings, but obviously I'm not doing a great job of it. He's such a happy, confident child. I don't want him to ever be hurt or disillusioned."

"You already know that's unrealistic." Marla pointed to a bus bench. "Let's sit here for a few minutes. It's a long walk back."

Graciella's shoulders slumped. "So where do I start? How do I stop feeling insecure and guilty? What am I afraid of?"

"I wish I had the answers. You need to have a frank talk with Cluny. He's a man, and he's far from perfect, but he'd never say or do anything to deliberately hurt either of you. He's a good man, Graciella."

"I believe that in my heart, but we've known each other such a short time. Am I really in love with him? Is he in love with me, or is it merely physical?" Unable to sort her feelings, or even to trust them, her brain in turmoil, she swallowed threatening tears.

She must stop acting like an air-headed teenager, get her thoughts under control, and do what was best for the three of them. Cluny deserved a chance at happiness as much as she and Santos did. She'd quit throwing up chimeras, quit dwelling on scenarios of failure, quit acting on fool-headed emotion and use her brain.

Before you make failure a self-fulfilling prophecy, Graciella Jefferson.

"Thank you for taking me under your wing." She touched Marla's arm. "I want so much for it to work out between us. But it unsettles me that I fell in love with him so quick. How can I be sure it's real?"

"My dad gave me a nice piece of wisdom when I was in turmoil, questioning my feelings over falling in love with Dwayne. He said, 'You know when you know.'" She rubbed her arms against the chill in the air. "You do know."

"That's where children have it all over us, isn't it? They don't question their feelings. They just act on them."

Marla nodded and said, "It's getting cold. Shall we go back before Dwayne and Cluny come looking for us?"

"Yes." Graciella walked alongside Marla. "Poor Cluny, he must be wondering if he's got a crazy woman living under his roof. Earlier I told him Santos and I should go home now that Jamal isn't around to threaten to us, but he said no, he wanted us to stay longer. He probably wishes he hadn't said so now."

"You do worry about every little thing, don't you, my friend?" Marla bumped her lightly with an elbow. "You don't need to be concerned about 'poor Cluny.' He's a big boy who's weathered a lot worse than a woman in distress. He's paid a heavy price, but he's solid."

"You're right." She reached in her pocket for a scrunchy and pulled her blowing hair into a ponytail. "I upset Santos too. I'm a mess."

"Yes, you are, but trust me it's temporary, you'll figure it out." Marla stooped to pick up a newspaper on the sidewalk in front of a neighbor's house. She stepped across the lawn and tossed it to the porch. "Mr. Johnson's knees are bothering him. He'll appreciate not having to walk so far."

"You're so thoughtful, Marla." Graciella felt fortunate to have made such a friend. Marla's confession about how conflicted she'd been when she'd fallen in love was encouraging. Everyone had fears and conflicts. "So, are we going shopping for sexy dresses Wednesday after our guys get home from work?"

"Absolutely. Now that I don't have to be concerned about keeping my hands off Dwayne to avoid pregnancy, I plan to live it up. Watch out, Dempsey, you'll never know what hit you."

Graciella laughed. "You're a very bad girl and he's a lucky man."

"We're both lucky. We love each other and we have two great kids."

Cluny, Santos and Queen were waiting for her on the front porch when they got back to Marla's. They wore identical wrinkled-brow expressions. She smiled, and it was comical how quickly they relaxed. She shouldn't have put them through this drama. She'd do better because they deserved better.

Marla passed them without a word and went inside the house.

Graciella sighed and stepped into Cluny's embrace then pulled Santos in with them. "Shall we go home?"

"Guess what, Mama? Amber's grandpa gave me a swimming lesson. He said if I was going to be a SEAL I'd have to be a strong swimmer. They have a swimming pool and everything, and he said me and Amber can come over there any time we want to. Oh, and her grandma made popcorn for us when we got out of the water."

"Isn't that nice? How did you do?" She kissed his forehead, noticing she didn't have to bend much because he'd grown taller in the past couple of months.

"Pretty good. I even opened my eyes under the water, and I wasn't scared."

A stab of fear sliced into her at the thought of him going into a swimming pool without her there to watch out for him. He was afraid of the water.

Stop it! He's fine!

Cluny held his arms around their shoulders and walked them to his car. He opened the passenger door and pushed the seat forward to allow Queen and Santos into the back. He whispered in her ear. "I love you, baby."

"Amo-te," she whispered back.

Cluny jumped in the driver's seat and turned the key. "We'll be home before you know it." He headed down the dark street to his house a few blocks away.

Aware of him turning his head to glance at her every few seconds, Graciella put her hand on his leg and squeezed, and then she shivered and hugged her upper arms.

"Are you cold, baby?"

"I got chilled when walking with Marla. I'll be fine."

"Santos? Is my denim jacket back there?"

"Yes, it's rolled up in the pocket behind Mama's seat. Do you want it?"

"Thanks, buddy. Hand it to your mom, she's cold." He brushed his knuckles across her cheek.

She turned in the seat. "Never mind. We'll be home before I can get into it." She rubbed Cluny's thigh. His muscles were hard and tense. "I'm fine. You can warm me up when we get there."

He flicked his eyes away from the road and let out a pent up breath. "Ooh-rah."

It was so good to see him relax and smile. She berated herself for putting him through distress when it was so unnecessary.

"Santos, I'll bet you're exhausted after playing baseball all afternoon and then your swimming lesson."

"I am. Macfearsome said we could sleep late in the morning because it's Sunday, and he'll make blueberry waffles for breakfast. They're my most favorite. Then we're going to watch the Dodger's game, then the Angel's game on his giant TV in the afternoon, and maybe grill steaks for dinner after." He yawned. "I'm sleepy."

"Ah hah, I can see my men have a strenuous day planned." She poked Cluny's arm. "If you wake up in the night and see my bedroom door open, don't worry. I'll be with Cluny in his room."

Cluny drew a sharp breath and turned into his driveway.

Santos yawned again. "Okay, but I'm so tired I won't wake up until tomorrow."

Cluny caught Santos' eye in the rear view mirror. "Before we go in the house, let's you and I take Queen for a short walk, sailor. Mom can take a warm shower and put on her pretty purple robe while we're out."

"That'll make you all toasty, won't it, Mama?"

"Yes it will, but come in and grab your sweater off the hook in the hall." She stepped out of the car. "You too, Cluny. The temperature is dropping fast tonight."

Cluny grinned at Santos. "Guess we better do what Mom says."

———

"Why does Queen have her nose up and wiggling like that, Macfearsome. I don't smell anything, do you?"

Cluny let Queen off leash. "She's scenting. Old habits are hard to break. Part of her training as a war dog was sniffing out explosives and finding bad guys. There's little chance she'll find either in this town. Sometimes she forgets she's retired."

"Oh." Santos looked into his eyes. "Do you know why Mama was crying today?"

He was pretty sure the question was coming and Cluny had chased several responses around in his head. "She's not used to you being away from her. I imagine she got real anxious when nobody was home at Dempsey's and they didn't answer my phone call."

"Gee whiz, I'm not a *baby* anymore. I don't know why she worries about me so much. I almost hardly never ever do anything bad. Auntie Krystal says I'm a goody-two-shoes, and Grandpa Earl says I'm just like my dad when he was a boy. He never got in trouble, either."

Cluny stopped and whistled for Queen. "Well, buddy, moms are supposed to protect their children, so that's why they worry. As long as you don't give her reason to be concerned, she'll gradually come around to the idea that you're growing up and you know how to be responsible."

"Do you love Mama? Do you want to sleep with her? Amber said grownups who love each other like to cuddle together in the same bed every night."

Oh boy! Leave it to Amber.

The hair on the back of Cluny's neck prickled.

"Yes, son, I do love your mother and I like to have her close to me. Let's get back home now so you can get to bed." First chance he got he'd tell Dwayne and Marla about Amber's *imparted wisdom*. They'd all share a good laugh over that one.

In the meantime, he and Graciella would have a discussion about what happened today, before Santos came up with more pointed questions they hadn't prepared answers for.

Chapter Twenty-Four

"You comfortable, baby?"

Graciella shifted and laid her leg over his. She snuggled deeper into his side. "Yes, but we've been talking for hours. We should get some sleep."

He stroked her bare hip wanting this new level of intimacy to go on and on. "We're sleeping late tomorrow, remember?" The mass of her hair lay strewn across his neck, shoulder and chest. He threaded his fingers through the silken strands, stuck his nose deep in her tresses and sniffed. "You smell good enough to eat. I think I'll—"

She smacked his hand. "If there's one thing I've learned since we moved in here, it's that you *never* sleep in. You and that dog—she's sleeping on my foot—are up running the hills around here while it's still dark every morning. I could set my watch by the time you two close the front door."

"You know all my secrets, huh? I should have thought of that before I invited you to move in, but it's too late now."

"Yes, poor you." Her fingers fluttered across his lips.

Any secrets he'd lose were a small price to pay for having this woman in his arms. That day at the beach, when he looked into the sun and watched her strolling toward him like a vision, seemed a dream now. From that day to this night was proof miracles do happen.

"Amor?"

"Hmm?"

"Are you sure I can't sleep here with you?"

"You remember what happened the other night."

"I also remember we slept through the night on your couch. You didn't have a nightmare then."

He chuckled. "It was a fluke." No way was he getting his hopes up to the possibility that having her in his bed was a solution to the unpredictable and recurring dreams. "That's because you were on top of me and had me pinned down."

She raised her head and crawled on top of him. "Let's try it again."

His arousal was spontaneous. "I don't know if this is a good way to fall asleep. I'm…uh…well, it's obvious what I am."

"Ignore it. Go to sleep."

"Never happen."

"It's an order, Marine."

"You've been spending too much time with Marla."

"Shut up and go to sleep."

"Sheesh. Another order."

She nipped his collar bone. "Get used to it."

He grinned into the darkness, put his arms around her and rocked from side to side. "I'll give it a shot, but no promises." Get used to it? There was nothing he wanted more.

Queen's nose sniffing his ear was the next thing to penetrate his awareness. Her barely audible whine had him alert and awake. Rolling his head to the side he read the digital display on his clock. Five-fifty. "I'll be damned." He'd slept nearly five hours without so much as a twitch. Queen hopped off the bed and stood staring at him in the early light. *Time for our run,* she told him.

Very gently, he slipped out from under Graciella. She murmured and rolled to her side exposing her bare back and bottom. Grinning, resisting the urge to wake her with a kiss, he pulled the sheet up and over her shoulder. It wouldn't be good if Santos came looking for her and found her half naked.

He took his running clothes from the hook on the back of the closet door and crept down the hall to the living room. The only sound in the house had been Queen's toenails tapping on the hall floor when she followed him. "Time for you to visit the groomer, girl."

He sat on the front porch step to put on his running shoes, breathed in the cold early morning air, stood and stretched. Taking off at a lope, he laughed when Queen tore out ahead of him claiming the lead in the familiar five mile route. "What's your hurry?" He shook his head at her joy in exercising her boundless energy. He had a good deal of extra vigor himself this morning.

Cluny wasn't naïve enough to think sleeping with Graciella was the simple solution to his ongoing struggle with the *paralyzed-and-helpless* nightmare. His tension rested on a knife edge. No matter which way he moved, somebody was going to get hurt. Graciella was fragile. She put up the front of a strong and self-sufficient single mom, but underneath something wasn't adding up. They'd had a good long talk last night, but she held something back.

She'd been more stressed over Jamal than she'd let on, hence her breakdown yesterday. Cluny had restrained from underestimating her concerns or offering meaningless platitudes to soothe her. He knew the phenomenon of continuous tension and how it could erupt without warning. Living a *normal* life since he'd left the Marines had taken a toll on him.

Maybe he should find a desolate mountaintop where they could go and scream into the wind at the top of their voices until they got it all out.

Long quiet talks like the one they'd had last night would be more beneficial to them in the long run. And he certainly wanted that *long run* with Graciella. They'd open up to each other little by little, he hoped. If that *long run* didn't work out his heart would break.

He whistled for Queen then bent over and rested his hands on his knees. Glancing at his watch, he grinned. They'd surpassed his goal. Cut a good five minutes off their usual time. He jogged down the hill and waved to a grandmotherly woman who lived two doors away from him.

She held the Sunday paper. Shaking her head in a disapproving fashion, she called, "Keep that damn mutt of yours on a leash!"

"Kiss my ass, Bertie."

"I would, but you run too fast." She grinned and waved. "Slow down for an old woman, why don't you?"

Cluny laughed and slowed to a walk. "How's this?"

"Still too fast, but I'll catch you one of these mornings."

"Eat your Wheaties, Bertie. I'm looking forward to it." He waved over his shoulder and smacked his leg for Queen to get in step with him.

Lights glowed from the kitchen window. He wondered who was up, opened the gate and ushered Queen into the back yard. He tapped on the window.

Santos peeked out.

"Unlock the back door, son."

Santos opened the door and stepped out in his bare feet. "You and Queen finished your run already? I'm still making the coffee. I didn't remember the filters were in the dishtowel drawer. When are you going to cook the waffles?"

Cluny kicked off his shoes in the laundry room and followed Santos to the kitchen. "Take that package of blueberries out of the freezer and let them thaw while I take my shower. Where's Mom?"

"She's asleep in your bed. I've been real quiet." He put a finger to his lips. "She must be tired."

"Yeah, we talked late into the night. I'll sneak in the bedroom for my robe then take my shower in your bathroom so I won't disturb her. Between us we'll have breakfast ready when she decides to get up." He turned to go and stopped. "Do me a favor, pal. I didn't fill Queen's water pan by the outside faucet. Will you do that for me?"

"I'll do it now before I finish the coffee, Macfearsome."

"Good man. Leave her outside, okay?"

He walked quietly in his stocking feet, avoiding the one squeaky board in front of his bedroom door. He'd left it like that on purpose as a Mickey Mouse alert warning. It gave him a sense of security when he turned out the lights at night.

He slipped sidewise through the partially open door with the squeaky hinge for the same reason, and tiptoed to his closet to lift his robe from the hook. Graciella was out like a light and didn't even alter her breathing. If they'd been alone in the house he'd have been tempted to slip under the sheets and wish her a proper good morning. Lord knew the sight of her in his bed had him locked and loaded.

Cluny and Santos were having a cup of coffee at the small kitchen table when Graciella shuffled in, hair sleep-tossed. She looked so luscious and sexy. It was all he could do to breathe. "Good morning, beautiful. Sit and have a cup of coffee."

She yawned. "Are you drinking coffee, Santos?"

"Yes, Mama." He jumped up and brought a mug and the pot to the table.

"How many cups have you had?" She wrapped a hand around the back of her head and pulled the mountain of wavy hair over one shoulder then wrinkled her nose in Cluny's direction.

Cluny raised his mug. "This is our first cup. Right, sailor?"

"Right, Macfearsome."

Graciella filled her mug, picked it up with both hands and inhaled the strong aroma. "Why do I sense a conspiracy?"

Instead of answering, Cluny stared at her with wide-eyed innocence, exchanged a look with Santos and concentrated on their nearly full mugs.

Graciella took a long slow sip and sighed. "Next thing I know you'll be letting him drink beer."

"Macfearsome only has root beer in the refrigerator."

Cluny bumped fists with him. "That's right, buddy. The only beer drinker in this house is her."

Graciella's eyes slitted. "Hmm."

———

Her man and her boy ganged up on her with their easy familiarity. You'd think they'd been together for years. They shared a hidden language she wasn't privy to. A male thing she was more than happy to let Santos share with Cluny. She didn't need to insert herself between them, to protect her son from growing up. He would anyway, with or without Cluny's masculine influence. Influence Santos craved and emulated. It pained her to admit he was a more positive male role model than Marvin. But Santos didn't need to have his hero worship of Marvin tarnished.

"So why am I sitting here drinking coffee when there's no sign of breakfast, huh?" She widened her eyes at Cluny first then Santos. "Get cracking. I'm hungry."

Cluny pushed back his chair. He rounded the table and kissed her on the lips. "Yes, ma'am, we've got you covered. Blueberry waffles coming right up."

Santos followed him to the big island. "What do you want me to do?"

"Empty those blueberries into a cereal bowl and find the bacon. I think it's in the fridge deli drawer. Do you know how to cook bacon in the microwave?"

"No, but you can tell me. I'll make another pot of coffee."

"Make it decaf," Graciella instructed.

"Good thinking." Cluny lifted a waffle iron from a drawer in the island and cleaned the surface with a paper towel. Graciella pushed back her chair. "Where do you think you're going?"

"The shower?"

"Sit yourself right back down in that chair. No way am I going to allow you to take away my view of the real Graciella Jefferson. You're my inspiration."

"I must look like a car wreck. I didn't even have the courage to check in the mirror before I walked in here."

Santos giggled. "Mama always says that in the morning."

"Women say dumb stuff like that all the time. It's best not to confirm or deny anything they say when they first wake up. Unless you like wandering through a minefield." Cluny shared the joke with her grinning son.

Graciella stuck out her tongue. She loved both of them so much. She lifted a napkin to her lips so they couldn't see her smile. Nothing could spoil this day.

The doorbell rang.

Graciella smoothed the front of her robe and went to the door. She peeked through the peephole and saw a teenage girl standing on the porch. She opened the door. "Hello."

The girl's face turned scarlet. She took a step back. "Oh!"

"Yes?" The girl looked familiar. "Ah, didn't I see you at baseball yesterday?"

Her face got redder and she shifted her feet. "Um, yes, my, um, my brother is on Coach's team." She clutched a shoe box next to her chest.

"Would you like to come in?"

The pretty girl shook her head so hard, Graciella worried she might give herself whiplash. "No! I, um, I brought something for Coach McPherson. Here, you take it."

"Cluny, *honey*, there's a little girl here who has something for you."

Oh, Graciella, that was cruel. Shame on you.

Cluny, in his bathrobe, strolled into the hallway. "Hey, Kaylin. What have you got there?" He nodded at the box.

Kaylin thrust it toward him. "Here, take it." She turned and ran down the driveway.

"What the hell?" Cluny's chin bobbed. He blinked at Graciella.

"Don't look at me. Is she one of your groupies?" She pressed her lips tight to muffle a giggle at his perplexed expression.

Santos joined them. "Who was that?"

"Kaylin. Leo's sister. She brought me something."

"What is it?"

Cluny lifted the top off the shoebox.

Santos grinned. "Oh boy, sticky buns, my most favorite." He took the box. "Sticky buns *and* blueberry waffles. This is my lucky day!"

Cluny scrubbed his hands over his unshaven face. "For the love of God, just what I need, a pubescent teenager making a move on me." He jammed his hands in his pockets. "You don't have to enjoy it so much."

"I love eliminating my competition." She slid her hand inside his robe and stroked his chest. "She's so mortified you'll probably never see her again, poor young thing."

He'd snorted at the word *competition*. "Enjoy it all you want now, baby, because you're going to pay later."

"Mmm." She sashayed away, adding an extra swing to her hips. "Can't wait."

Chapter Twenty-Five

Wednesday evening

"Here's Marla. I don't know when we'll be back from shopping." Graciella heard no answer. "We'll make the rounds of a few bars then go to a male strip club before we come home. Magic Mike is making a special appearance." She stuck her head through the living room doorway. "Are either of you listening to me?"

Two males, one tall blue-eyed and handsome, and the other, skinny dark and cute, stared at whatever sporting event they were fixated on, but shook their heads. Graciella shrugged and walked out the front door to Marla's car.

Marla smiled when she opened the passenger door. "Everybody all set to spend the evening without Mom?"

"They won't even notice I'm gone." Graciella fastened her seat belt.

"I doubt that." She laughed. "Dwayne will miss me. I left Amber in charge."

"You married into an interesting family, Marla." Graciella had enjoyed the many tidbits she'd heard about the Dempsey clan. Marla's family was unique, too. Twin daughters and twin sons!

"What about your family? I don't mean your late husband's parents and sister. Do you have family in Brazil?"

"My parents are both still living and I have a younger sister. We stay in touch by phone. I haven't been back since I married Marvin."

"How come?"

"I'm not an American citizen."

"I didn't know that."

"When Marvin got killed in Iraq, and I was left to raise Santos on my own, I let the naturalization steps slip into the background. I really should start the process again. Even though I married an American and Santos is an American, I've been wary of leaving the country for fear they wouldn't let me return."

"Do you think that could happen?"

Graciella sighed. "I don't know, but I'm not willing to risk it. My father's a rabble rouser. He's a communist with strident political opinions. My poor mother has had to put up with more and more as he's grown older. My sister, Catia, was Amber's age when I left Brazil, so I've never had a close relationship with her like you have with Charlene. I love them, but not enough to risk losing our life here."

"Gosh. Does Cluny know?"

"It's never come up. Why?"

"I think he'd do anything to keep that from happening."

"Like marry me, maybe?" She wanted Cluny to propose because he loved her and wanted to spend the rest of their lives together. Not because she needed a permanent green card.

"He's crazy about you and Santos, Graciella. I have a hunch he's going slow, afraid to rush you into marriage." Marla took surface streets in the direction of Simi Valley.

Graciella changed the subject. "Where are we going to shop?"

"We'll start at Simi Town Center. If we can't find what we like tonight, we'll head over the pass to the Valley tomorrow night."

Cluny said he loved her every day, but she had no intention of giving up her apartment to live in his house. She'd be reopening Rio Samba in less than two weeks, and unless more trouble with Jamal reared its ugly head, she and Santos would go back to their apartment in Chatsworth. Being apart would be a more reliable test of their relationship than living together. What kind of example was she setting for her son? She believed in marriage and everything, good and bad, that went with it. And she wanted Santos to understand that.

Graciella dug through her shoulder bag. "I saw an ad from one of the stores, maybe it was Chico's. Where did I put it? They had a very dressy black silk, ankle-length pants outfit with a shimmery silver tunic. I'd like to try it on. I know it's not a sexy dress, but it really looked good in the print ad."

"Sounds like it would be perfect for you. I don't have your willowy figure, so I'll definitely be shopping for a dress. Dwayne will love anything that shows off my cleavage, and Lord knows I have plenty of that at the moment."

"Marla, you have a glamorous figure. I'd kill for some of your curves."

"Pooh. I'm lucky to have a husband who appreciates them because I don't see myself slimming down anytime soon."

"I doubt he'd want you to." She was hyperaware of the way Dwayne looked at his wife. The man ate her up with his eyes. It also hadn't missed her notice that Cluny loved putting his arms around Marla's curves in a nice hug whenever he got the chance. But then, he was a huggy kind of man.

"Dempsey's very diplomatic with his comments. When I complained about the extra ten pounds I'd kept on after Declan was born, he said, 'Honey, it's all the more of you to love.'"

Graciella drew in a breath and put hands over her heart. "Aw, Marla, that's so romantic."

Marla grinned. "Yeah, it is." She took the street for the main entrance to the mall. "We're here. Let's get shopping!"

Graciella found the black and silver silk pants outfit and it was perfect. The pants hugged her long slim legs, and the way Marla and the saleswoman exclaimed when she exited the dressing room convinced her it was the right choice. "I do love it. Now I need some silver spike heel sandals and a matching evening bag."

Marla held her cell phone aloft. "I'm going to program nine-one-one on my speed dial because Cluny may have a heart attack when he sees you in that. Turn around, so I get the full effect. Wow. It was made for you."

Graciella gulped, paid with her credit card and pushed the guilt out of her mind. "He'd better have a heart attack, because I'm going to have one when I get my bill." She grinned in spite of it. His reaction to her would be worth the cost. They left with her purchases.

"I just found the perfect dress!" Marla pointed to a low cut, emerald green dress in the window of a small boutique. "I hope they have it in a twelve." She sighed. "I hope I can get into a twelve, if they do."

They entered the shop, found the dress rack and pushed hangers back and forth looking for a size twelve. Marla grabbed it and ran to the dressing room. She stepped out in less than five minutes. "What do you think, Graciella?"

"Oh, Marla, you look like a movie star walking down the red carpet at the Oscars."

Graciella stood back and admired how the dress emphasized every luscious curve. "Turn around." She drew a breath when she saw the back of the dress.

Marla wore a look of mild panic on her face. "Is it too slutty?"

"No! You have a sexy back. There won't be a man at the party who'll want to miss a chance of dancing with you, so he can get his hand on it." She rolled her eyes. "Oh, Deus, your hair color compliments the dress to perfection. Wear it down around your shoulders the way you have it now. You're stunning, Marla."

"If I look too slutty, Dwayne will reluctantly let me dance with some of the other guys, but he won't be a good sport about it. Because of his leg, his version of dancing is to hold me tight and sway. It's very sexy really." She brought her hands to her cheeks. "Oh, God, I am slutty. I'll be lucky if I'm not pregnant for the next ten years."

Graciella giggled and pointed to the next dressing room where another shopper laughed at the remark.

She'd never had such a frank conversation with another woman, or so much fun shopping. "Shoes next, my friend."

———

Carrying their bags and hangers, they flopped in chairs at a bistro table outside a coffee bar. "We made great time, Marla." Graciella glanced at her watch. "It's nine on the dot. You guard the packages and I'll go in and get a couple of pick-me-ups. What would you like?"

Marla groaned and kicked off her shoes. "Decaf cappuccino would be great, thanks. I'd prefer the real stuff, but I've been avoiding caffeine while I'm breast feeding."

"I'll be right back." She went inside the quaint shop, ordered the drinks and was told the attendant would bring them out. She added a couple of macadamia, white chocolate chip cookies to the order and rejoined her new friend.

The spike-haired, nose-ringed barista delivered their order. Graciella and Marla sipped in silence and enjoyed people-watching.

"Marla, I want to tell you something I've never told anyone."

Marla held up her hand. "Don't tell me anything I can't tell Dwayne. We have no secrets from each other."

Graciella thought about this before she answered. "I don't want Cluny to know. I do plan to tell him soon, but I'm not ready now." She prayed she wasn't making a mistake she'd be sorry for later.

"If I tell Dempsey you don't want Cluny to know, he won't say anything." Marla's forehead creased and she sat forward. "Be honest with me, Graciella. Has Cluny done something he shouldn't have?"

"No! This is something that happened a long time ago and it still hurts. It's affecting my relationship with the man I love." Her breath caught and she looked away. "I have to tell somebody."

Marla reached across the small table and squeezed her wrist.

"Um…" Graciella cleared the clog from her throat. "I loved Marvin so much. I left my family and my country behind to be with him. Then he cheated on me. I felt like a naïve young fool when I found out. It destroyed me. Some of his fellow SEALs, their wives, and even Chief knew before I did. It's not a subject Chief would ever bring up." It was hard for her to believe Earl and Lillian didn't know what kind of man their son was, but she'd never said anything to them.

The pained expression on Marla's face and the increase in pressure from her hand had Graciella swallowing back tears.

"It wasn't just once. He was shacked-up with a woman in his apartment after we were married, while he was waiting for my paperwork to clear so I could join him in San Diego. I found something of hers when I moved in. He looked me straight in the eye, and told me they were Krystal's, but ten year old girls don't wear that style undergarments. I was so broken-hearted and lost. I thought about killing myself." She swallowed a sob and hung precariously to her fractured composure.

"I can't begin to imagine…"

"He hadn't had the decency to make sure there was no evidence for his new bride to find. He lied and said it had been over for a long time, and I shouldn't freak out about it."

Marla breathed through her nose; lips pinched, and shook her head.

"I got pregnant with Santos right away. I had horrible morning sickness and migraines. Instead of comforting me, he stayed away for days at a time, telling me he was on assignment for the Navy. I wanted desperately to believe him. Then I asked one of the other wives if she knew where the men were that kept them away from home at night. The poor woman didn't want to tell me, but finally admitted the team was still on shore leave, waiting for their next deployment, and were home every night. Marvin had taken up with a bimbo he'd picked up in a bar."

"My God, Graciella. I don't know what to say."

Graciella held up a hand. "Here's the best part. Right before he shipped out, the last thing he said to me was he hoped by the time he got home to meet his son, I'd have my act together." Involuntary tears brimmed on her lower lashes. She dabbed them with a paper napkin.

"God, I'm so sorry that happened to you." Tears of sympathy sparkled in Marla's eyes.

"It's been extra hard for me because I've let Santos believe Marvin was this virtuous, noble war hero." She blew her nose. "He was a war hero. I won't take that away from him. I've never discussed this with anybody because I was afraid it might get back to my son. I never want Santos to know the truth about his father. He'd be devastated.

"The shameful thing is…when he was killed, I momentarily felt a jolt of savage justice, that he'd been punished. I have a lot of guilt about that, Marla."

"Oh, honey, don't blame yourself. You were just a kid."

"I blame myself for being so foolish. For falling in love with him at first sight, leaving my life and everyone I loved behind to be with him. Marvin was handsome and charming. His smile could stop traffic. He was the kind of man everybody enjoyed, he made those around him laugh. His fellow SEALs had him on a pedestal and they trusted him with their lives. I'm trying so hard not to let this spoil my chance of happiness with Cluny."

Marla pushed aside the dregs of her cappuccino. "Don't you think it would help if Cluny knew this? You'll have to tell him eventually, won't you?"

"Yes, I will tell him, but what I don't want is to make him feel pressured to rush into marriage as a way to *fix* me." Her stomach cramped with indecision. It was a secret she'd have to share with him. She knew that, but not yet. "I need for him to understand that protecting Santos is my primary concern."

Marla gathered her packages. "Trust Cluny. He'll protect your son no matter what." She glanced at her watch. "It's time we got home. I'll keep your confidence and Dwayne will never breathe a word of it without your permission. I wish I could do more."

"Just sharing it with you has been a relief." She retrieved her hanger and bags. "I can think less emotionally about it now and decide the right time to tell him."

———

Marla drove into Cluny's long driveway and turned off the engine. She reached for Graciella and kissed her cheek. "For now, let's concentrate on how great we're both going to look at that big party Saturday night. It will be a happy occasion for the four of us to share. I'm so glad I met you, Graciella. I hope we'll be friends for many years, until we're old and gray. You can always tell me anything. I'll never betray your trust, I promise."

"That means a lot to me, Marla. And I do feel better."

"I suppose the men will have a plan for one or two cars on Saturday night. I'll put my two cents in with Dempsey about driving two cars. That way if for any reason one of us has to leave early, we won't have to spoil the party for all of us."

"That's a good idea. I'll plant the seed in Cluny's mind, too. Will we be taking the kids to your parent's house, or will they come to yours?"

"Dad will pick them up from our house. He's planning a cookout for them and he's erecting the pup tents in the family room so they can sleep over at their place if we're late. It all depends on my mother. We'll check with them when we're ready to leave the party to see if she's okay keeping Dec overnight. I'll be pumping breast milk for the next two days. Ick."

Graciella grinned. "Or maybe for the next ten years?"

Cluny and Santos were asleep in front of the TV. A partially eaten bowl of popcorn sat precariously close to the edge of the coffee table. Graciella tiptoed to her bedroom and hung up her new outfit and hid the shoe box in the closet. She had no intention of giving him a peek until Saturday night.

Queen wandered in to investigate. "Don't say anything, Queenie. I'm counting on you." She knelt down and gave the dog a vigorous back scratch, giggling at her twitching leg and moans of pleasure.

"Are you spoiling my dog?"

"Cluny! You scared me to death!" She dropped her forehead on Queen's back.

He chuckled and pulled her to her feet. "How's about a kiss? I missed you."

"Oh, pooh, I don't believe that for a minute, but I'll take the kiss anyway."

Drawing her tight against his lean body, he came up with a real knee-knocker. "Believe me now, baby?"

She trembled in his arms. "Oh, yes. Do that again."

He kissed her again, and this time his hands caressed her sides and back. He groaned and yanked her tight. "Let's go to bed."

"We can't leave Santos in the living room." She pushed back. "I'll take him to his room."

His head fell back and his fingers dug into her bottom. "Okay." He blew a breath. "I'll take Queen out back for a few minutes. I have something special in mind for you tonight. Could take hours. We'll start in the shower." His grin was so deliciously sinful, her heart tripped wildly.

Oh, Deus. This man.

Chapter Twenty-Six

Ventura Greens Country Club, Saturday night.

"WHAT A GREAT TURNOUT, I DIDN'T EXPECT SO MANY PEOPLE here," Cluny handed her shoulder wrap to the coat-check clerk and took the ticket. "Do you see Gunny and Marla?"

"No, but we're assigned to the same table. They're sharing with us and another couple. Do you know who they are?" Graciella craned her neck as she looked around the large ballroom then took Cluny's arm.

"No, but I expect it'll be a veteran I've met in the past." He led her across the dance floor surrounded by tables for six. "We're over here, baby. Oh great, I recognize Joey Hamilton at our table. One of your favorite vets."

Graciella's eyebrows drew together. "I've met him?"

"He's one of the boys who had too much to drink at Gunny's party and shot off his mouth."

"Oh." She tightened her grip on Cluny's arm. "I don't recognize him, but I didn't get a good look. Maybe he won't remember the incident. Who's the woman he's with? She wasn't at the party." Her stomach cramped, but she was determined not to let Joey Hamilton spoil the evening. It had to have been the alcohol talking. If the man had had his wits about him he wouldn't have been so obnoxious. She'd give him the benefit of doubt.

Cluny whispered in her ear. "I'll ask them to change our table."

"No, amor, please. I don't want to make anything of it." She held his uniform-clad arm and continued in the direction of the couple who'd just noticed their approach.

The good-looking man with a military haircut stood. "Hey, McPherson, we're at the same table."

Cluny's face was unreadable. "I believe you've met my lady, Graciella Jefferson." He gave a polite nod to the brunette sitting next to Hamilton.

"Yes, I've had the pleasure. Nice to see you again, Graciella." He indicated the brunette. "This is my sister, Liz."

"Your sister?" Cluny didn't look convinced. "She can't be the same Liz I met when she was this high." He held a hand at waist level.

The young woman smiled. "Yes, I really am the same Liz. Joey calls me whenever he can't get a date, so I get to go out a lot."

Joey rolled his eyes. "Thanks, sis." He pulled back the vacant chair next to him. "Graciella?"

She hesitated for a split second then smiled and took the seat. She leaned past Joey. "It's a pleasure to meet you, Liz."

Cluny, who'd been silent, rounded the table to Joey's sister. "Liz, give us a kiss." He put his hand on her arm and pecked her cheek then took the chair next to her, across the table from Graciella.

Joey stood again. Graciella looked over her shoulder. Dwayne and Marla made their way to the table. Dwayne gave a warning evil-eye to Joey and the man lowered his eyes and cleared his throat.

Cluny embraced Marla. "You get more beautiful every day, Ms. Danaher. You *are* dancing with me tonight, no matter what Gunny says." He turned and spoke to the other couple. "Joey, you remember Dempsey's wife. Marla, this brave young lady, who appears far too decent to be seen in public with Hamilton, is his sister, Liz."

"Nice to meet you, Liz." Marla smiled and took the chair next to Cluny.

Dwayne remained standing, leaned past Graciella's ear to kiss her cheek. "How you doing, gorgeous? Looks like you and Red had a very successful shopping trip." He briefly fingered the sheer silver tunic at her shoulder. "Nice, very nice."

She reached up and patted his hand. "Thank you, Dwayne."

"Back off, Gunny," Cluny teased.

After a few minutes a waiter in white livery arrived at their table with a tray of champagne flutes.

Dwayne told him, "The men here will have sparkling cider or soft drinks. You can bring them after you've served the ladies." He looked pointedly at Joey.

"I'll have club soda, please, with lemon." Joey said.

"Very good sir." He lowered the tray and the three women accepted the proffered champagne. "Any specific requests for you gentlemen?" He looked at Dwayne first, then Cluny.

"I'm good with club soda," Cluny said.

"Make it three," Dwayne added.

Graciella felt a wave of gratitude toward Dwayne's making sure there would be no further incident of embarrassing drunken talk. She patted his arm and sighed. "You're very handsome tonight, Mr. Dempsey. I couldn't believe my eyes when Cluny walked into the living room in his dress blues. For a minute I thought a stranger was in the house."

"We clean up pretty good when the occasion calls for it." Dwayne grinned and nodded his head in Joey's direction. "The uniform does wonders for us, even Boozy over there."

"Okay." Joey raised his hands. "I get the message, Gunny. I'm on my best behavior. Anyway, I'm off the sauce and I reenlisted. I didn't like the nickname anymore, and my dad would have my hide if I didn't bring Liz home safely."

"Glad to hear it," Cluny said as the waiter returned with the club sodas. He picked up his glass. "Here's hoping they raise a ton of bucks tonight. I hear they brought in a great orchestra. Liz, save a spot on your dance card for me."

Liz sighed dramatically and put a hand over her heart.

The tables filled quickly, and the wait-staff rushed efficiently through the room placing salads and French rolls on the tables. Graciella relaxed as Joey engaged her in pleasant small talk. Joey impressed her as an intelligent man with a sweet sense of humor.

Dwayne was seated at her other side and Cluny sat between Marla and Liz. Liz laughed and blushed at something Cluny said. Yes. It promised to be a pleasant evening, and worth what she'd spent on her outfit.

She'd also indulged in a mani-pedi this morning. But instead of visiting the hairdresser she'd let her hair fall in natural waves and curls over her shoulders, the way Cluny liked it best. She smiled to herself when she remembered his last-minute suggestion they stay home, get naked, make love all night, and forget about the party.

Soft music began to play near the end of the main course. A few couples made their way to the dance floor. Cluny stood and reached for her hand. "Let's dance, baby."

She moved easily into his arms and they joined the other dancers. In her spike heels she was nearly as tall as Cluny. She tilted back her head and looked into his twinkling blue eyes. "What?"

He pulled her tighter and nipped her earlobe. "I want to grab your ass and take a bite out of your neck, but they'd frown on it here. Marines must maintain a certain level of decorum when in uniform. There are at least two generals in the room."

Her blood raced as his hand slid low on her back. "Watch it, Marine. I don't want you to end up in the brig. What would I tell Santos?"

"He understands a lot more than you think he does. He stopped me dead in my tracks with a few of his questions lately."

"Such as?" She stroked the back of his neck, knowing it only added fuel to his fiery libido. How nice it was to wield such power over him.

He chuckled. "He asked me if I wanted to make a baby with you."

"What!" she hissed. "Oh, Deus. What did you say?"

"I said no."

"Thank goodness." She was shocked that her little boy had asked him such a question. Had even *thought* to ask such a question.

"Yeah, I said no, not *a* baby, several babies." She groaned and dropped her head on his shoulder. His chest bumped against hers in silent laughter. "Take it easy. He's just an innocent kid. If a kid asks questions it means they're old enough to get an honest answer. I didn't elaborate and he didn't probe deeper."

"What did he say?"

"He said, 'That's nice,' and went back to the popcorn and the ballgame."

Deep in her heart, she sensed Cluny was a natural-born father. His easy manner with her son, the way he respected what Santos had to say, and the adoration and enthusiasm of the boys and girls he coached at the park spoke to that. Someday she'd question him more about his parents and his life in foster homes. She wanted to know everything about this man she loved.

A senior officer wearing the uniform of a different service tapped on the microphone. The dance floor quickly emptied as guests returned to their tables and resumed their seats. He announced the program for the evening and promised there'd be no long-winded boring speeches, and then introduced a woman, identifying her as the chairman of the Wounded Warriors of Ventura County.

The tiny, gray-haired lady lowered the mic. "Good evening, ladies and gentlemen. Our thanks to all of you for attending tonight. Our ticket sales increased fifty percent over last year." She paused for polite applause. "That's the conclusion of my speech." She smiled at the laughter and enthusiastic applause. "In a few minutes volunteers will be approaching your tables to sell raffle tickets. We've received many generous donations from several of our supporters, the value of the prizes greatly exceed the ten-dollar ticket price. So, buy more tickets! Thank you for coming and for your financial support."

The musicians took a break and the conversation level in the ballroom increased as ticket sellers went from table to table, while the wait-staff cleared away dinner and served dessert. Drinks around the table were refreshed.

"Hey, guys."

Heads turned at Misty Beachy's greeting. Graciella's breath caught. She saw the perplexed look on Joey's face when his eyes flicked from her to Misty to Cluny. Graciella met Joey's eyes and his cheeks reddened. He stared at his club soda.

"What are you doing here, Mis?" Cluny was clearly flabbergasted. "We didn't know you were coming, or we'd have asked you to sit with us."

"I'm working tonight, Mac. I'm at one of the single's tables. Got five men all to myself." She held up a large roll of raffle tickets. "Pony up, Marines. I happen to know what some of the prizes are. And if you don't win, you *do* win because the money we raise will help a lot of vets and their families."

Misty, like the men, wore full dress uniform and had her hair in a neat bun at the back of her neck. Except for a tinge of color on her lips, she wore no makeup. Graciella remembered Sgt. Beachy didn't need makeup. Naturally attractive and feminine, Misty appeared particularly young tonight.

Graciella was comforted by the thought that there'd been no communication between Cluny and Misty. He was as surprised to see her as she was.

Joey recovered quickly and grinned. "I'll take five tickets, Master Sergeant, and I challenge McPherson and Dempsey to match me."

"Good man, Boozy." She looked askance at Liz. "Do you know about this man's checkered past?" She peeled tickets off the strip, separated them in half and gave Liz the stubs. The fifty dollars he handed over went into a small basket she carried on her wrist. It already had a good-sized stack of bills.

Liz grinned. "Oh, yes, he's my big brother."

Dwayne pulled out his wallet. "Boozy has reformed, Master Sergeant. As of tonight he's to be known as Joe. He's sworn off the sauce, joined the ranks of us teetotalers, and reenlisted." He passed her a hundred dollar bill. "I'll take ten."

Misty handed Marla his stubs. "That's good news, Gunny. We'll start calling him Hambone again."

Cluny grumbled, "Show-off," and directed a grin at Dwayne. "I'll take ten tickets, Mis. Can't let Gunny show me up."

"Okay," Joey said. "Give me five more."

Liz laughed. "Oh, good, I want to win that spa vacation."

Good natured laughter followed Misty Beachy's move to the next table, and they sampled their desserts. The orchestra returned to the ballroom and this time the music was a bit louder. One by one, men rose from tables and wandered to the *Smoking Room*, which was in reality an outdoor balcony. Several non-smokers and a few women joined them, but most, like Graciella, Marla and Liz remained behind.

Liz asked Graciella, "How long have you known Cluny? Joey

warned me he had a beautiful girlfriend, so I should give up the crush I've had on him since I was eleven and move on."

Graciella and Marla exchanged smiles.

"We've been together since the beginning of summer. I have my son to thank for it. He made friends with Cluny at the beach in early June."

"Yes," Marla said. "Her son, Santos, told Dwayne he was going to marry Amber when he grows up. So, we already know the future father of our grandchildren."

Liz giggled. "Oh, that's sweet. How old is he?"

"He'll be ten in September. Amber will be nine. Just the right age difference, don't you think?"

"Perfect." Liz stood. "If you'll excuse me, I'll head to the ladies room. You won't hate me if I dance with Cluny, will you?"

"Don't be silly." Graciella waved as the sweet young woman left the table.

"How are you doing?" Marla asked. "I noticed you were startled when Misty came to the table to sell tickets."

"I'm fine. I'm trying very hard not to let Marvin's infidelity intrude on my relationship with Cluny. Any flirting he does is natural and playful. You don't notice me getting upset whenever he hugs or kisses you." There was a definite difference in her mind, but the knowledge that Cluny and Misty had once been lovers continued to nag like an evil, slithering vermin working to worm its way into her heart.

She and Marla followed Liz to the ladies' room. A short time later, the men, having heard the orchestra resume music for dancing, slowly drifted back into the ballroom. Cluny entered among a small knot of laughing veterans, including Misty Beachy. He spoke to her for a few seconds, kissed her cheek and made his way to their table. He leaned close to Graciella's ear. "I'm going to ask Liz for that dance."

She reached up and patted his cheek. "Okay. You know where to find me."

Dwayne led Marla to the dance floor, leaving Graciella and Joe alone at the table. After an awkward few seconds he stood. "May I have this dance?"

A blush warmed her cheeks. She nodded, smiled, and answered, "Yes, of course." She accepted because she didn't know what else to do.

He'd been very polite all evening, How could she refuse? She took his hand and followed him to the center of the room.

An accomplished dancer, Joe didn't hold her stiffly away, or uncomfortably close. She slowed her breathing and relaxed. *Amazing, the power of booze to facilitate bad behavior.* She knew Cluny stopped drinking alcohol because he'd recognized how pernicious it was for his PTS. She decided she wouldn't drink when she was with him. Temptation was an insidious creature. She loved the man and she'd behave in a way that was best for both of them.

"You're a great dance partner, Graciella," Joe remarked. "If they play any Latin music before the evening is out, I'd love to have another dance with you."

She laughed softly, "Are you saying that because Cluny told you I'm a dance teacher?"

He stopped for a split second. "You are? Wow. Where do you teach?"

"I own Rio Samba in Chatsworth. I met my late husband at a samba club in Sao Paulo, Brazil."

"I'll be damned. My sister talked me into taking some Latin dance lessons at a studio in Thousand Oaks a few months ago. I loved it." He raised an eyebrow. "I'm pretty good at it, too." Joe had a very charming smile.

"Is that right? Why don't we ask the orchestra leader to play a couple of songs? Do you know the samba and the tango?"

Instead of answering her he took her hand and walked the short distance to the orchestra and requested the bandleader to play some Latin music before the evening was over. The man answered, "Why not now?" As soon as they finished the piece they were playing, they began a dramatic tango.

"Ma'am?" Joe extended his hand and led Graciella back to the center of the floor.

Joe had told the truth. He was an excellent Latin dancer. Graciella laughed and joined freely in the masculine, sensuous tango with him. About half the dancers left the floor, apparently not adept at tango. Soon, others backed away from them and enjoyed watching. Graciella spotted Liz and Cluny grinning on the sidelines. The orchestra eased expertly from the sedate tango into a lively and delightful bossanova samba. At the conclusion of the dance, she and Joe acknowledged scattered applause and laughter. He led her to the edge of the floor and handed her off to Cluny.

Cluny's arm around her waist, he whispered in her ear as he led her back to their table, "You gotta give me some more dance lessons, baby. I shoulda been the guy out there dancing with you. I have no choice now but to kill Hambone." His grin belied his comment.

"What Joe probably doesn't know," she confided, "is tango originated in the brothels of the poor sections of Buenos Aires. I won't tell him, if you won't."

Cluny squeezed her waist. "He's on a strictly need-to-know basis."

The dancing went on for another hour. Graciella accepted many invitations to dance, one from an elderly general, who, when he approached their table, had the three men instantly on their feet. Cluny danced with Marla, and then a matronly woman Graciella hadn't met. Then he led Misty Beachy in a brief foxtrot.

The master of ceremonies tapped the microphone to announce the winners of the prize drawings and the amount of money they'd raised for the evening.

Graciella enjoyed Cluny's surprise when one of the prize winners won six private lessons at Rio Samba. To her relief, Joe didn't win the private lessons. Liz showed her disappointment at not winning the coveted spa vacation. In fact, there were no raffle winners at their table, but the evening ended on a happy and upbeat note.

"I have to call my mother." Marla took out her phone while they walked to the front of the club and waited for the valets to bring their cars. She sighed and snapped her cell closed. "Mom is not up to keeping Dec all night, so we're going to head over there and pick him up. Amber and Santos have already settled into their family-room campout. Dad said he'd bring them home after breakfast."

Cluny waved. "Ask Brad to get them to my house by noon. We're going to the beach tomorrow."

Graciella cocked her head and drew in her eyebrows. "We are?"

"Yep. Sound like a plan to you?"

Chapter Twenty-Seven

Sunday morning, Cluny's kitchen

GRACIELLA SCRAMBLED EGGS AT THE BIG ISLAND STOVETOP. SHE glanced up when Cluny entered the kitchen. "I put the paper on the table for you, amor." She raised an eyebrow. "Shirts are required at the table."

He grinned and turned on his heel. "Be right back."

Men—why did they like to run around half naked all the time?

Cluny returned, pulling an old T-shirt over his head. "That better?" He stepped behind her to pour himself a mug of coffee then leaned in and kissed her neck. "Good morning."

"Good morning. Sit. These will be done in a few seconds."

Cluny unfolded the big Sunday edition and separated the sections while sipping his coffee. Graciella brought his plate of eggs and toast then took the chair adjacent to him. "I'll pack a lunch for the beach so we'll be ready to leave when Santos and Amber get here."

He hummed a response while sprinkling a generous amount of pepper on the eggs. He stared at the page and his fork stopped halfway to his mouth. "Holy crap!"

"What is it?"

He put down his fork and held up the front page. "Isn't this Jamal?"

Graciella jumped to her feet and leaned over his shoulder. "Yes, it looks like him. What does it say?"

Cluny read, "The FBI, after a lengthy investigation, has taken several Los Angeles residents into custody as part of a greater operation to crack a suspected terrorist cell. The alleged leader of the group, a UC Irvine assistant-professor of Middle Eastern studies, whose name has been withheld, is reported to have cooperated with the Department of Homeland Security, in exchange for having charges against him reduced. A few of the suspects arrested are foreigners studying at the university on student visas, but most are American citizens. The total number arrested early this morning, is nine. The charges are serious enough that bail has been denied. According to our confidential sources, two Chechen men fled the country before they could be apprehended. The investigation is ongoing."

Graciella slumped into her chair and dropped her forehead on a shaking hand. Her heart pounded so hard in her throat she could barely breathe.

Cluny put the paper down and moved behind her chair. He put his strong hands on her shoulders, squeezing gently. "You okay, baby?" He kissed the top of her head. "This is good news, right?"

Unable to form words, she nodded then reached up and stroked his bristled cheek when his lips brushed her ear. Greatly relieved to see Jamal in handcuffs, the other side of this news story was…she now had no excuse to stay in Cluny's house. It was time for her and Santos to return home. She only had a few days to get the studio ready before she reopened for business. Not wanting to put a damper on their planned day at the beach, she decided not to mention it just yet. "Yes, I'm fine. This just took me by surprise."

He returned to his chair and swallowed some coffee, a look of relief mixed with confusion on his face. He seemed to be waiting for her to talk, to tell him what else was on her mind, but instead of saying anything further, she picked up her fork and began to eat her breakfast.

Before they finished, the back door banged open and Santos and Amber ran in. "When are we leaving?" she asked.

Cluny grinned at their eager faces. "And good morning to you too." He folded the paper and tucked it next to his plate. "Have you had breakfast?"

Queen followed the kids inside and nose in the air, she sniffed the cooking smells. She nosed around the floor for any fallen morsel. Cluny rose and retrieved her big stainless bowl. He took the bag of kibble from the cupboard and filled her dish to the top.

"Cluny asked you a question, Santos." Graciella brushed the hair out of his eyes. "You need a haircut."

He took a step back out of her reach, his cheeks pinking at her touch. She reminded herself of her pledge to quit treating him like a baby, but it was hard to break the old habit.

Amber piped up, "We ate at Grampa's house. When are we leaving? I left all my beach things on the front porch."

Cluny chuckled. "Is it okay if we finish our breakfast first?"

She sighed, "Yeah, I guess so. Come on, Santos; let's get your towel and stuff. Which car are we going in, Uncle Cluny?"

"The plumbing van, but I have to clear some equipment out of the back first. Take Queen for a walk so she can do her business. There's a bunch of plastic bags in a box next to the washing machine."

Amber put her fists on her nonexistent hips. "Do you know how big her poop is?"

"Take two bags." He winked and picked up his coffee mug. "We'll pack lunch after we eat. The sun is barely up."

She stared at him like he was nuts. "Nuh uh. It's after ten already." She turned. "Come on, Santos. Uncle Cluny likes to tease me. We'll get your things then take Queen out."

As they shuffled down the hall, Graciella and Cluny heard Santos say, "You don't have to pick up the poop. I'll do it."

Graciella bit her lip and exchanged an amused look with Cluny.

"It's love," he whispered.

She knew the feeling.

———

At the Beach

Cluny lay on his stomach, chin on his hands, watching the kids on their belly boards. He stole a quick glance at Graciella from the side of his shades. She'd been unusually quiet all day. She had something on her mind. "Want to take a walk, baby?"

"Okay." He enjoyed the view when she stood and brushed sand off her bottom. She shaded her eyes and peered at the lifeguard tower. "He's there. The kids will be fine. The surf's very quiet today." She picked up his T-shirt and handed it to him, then pulled on her cover-up.

He took her hand and they headed to the Point Dume rocks. After they'd walked a couple of hundred yards he squeezed her fingers. "Are you still troubled about Jamal? You haven't said much all afternoon."

"I'm sorry. No, I'm relieved he was arrested, but that means it's time for us to go home, amor. I'm opening the studio a week from tomorrow." She stared straight ahead. "There's no good reason for us to stay."

"I can think of a very good reason." He stopped walking and drew her into his arms. "I don't want you to go."

She placed her hands flat on his chest. "Cluny, the arrangement was temporary. I can't go on living with you. It isn't right. I have business and family responsibilities."

He ran his hands up and down her back. "I don't know how to sleep alone anymore, baby." He knew this day would come, but he wasn't ready for it. "I want you in my life." Teeth clenched, he couldn't manage a smile.

"I am in your life, and you're in mine. I'm not breaking up with you. It's been two months since we met. That's not enough time to know each other, querido."

He tried to put a happy expression on his face. "Can Santos stay?"

She grinned and pushed back. "Oh, stop it. Why don't we do this? We'll spend the weekends together. I'm not planning any Saturday classes until after school starts in the fall. You can come over for dinner once in a while. We'll go out as a family every so often. I'll ask the Dempsey's to have Santos spend the night with them some Saturdays and we'll reciprocate with Amber and Declan. Can we try that until the end of summer?"

He took her hand. They strolled closer to the point. "Do I have a choice?"

She matched his stride and put her arm around his waist. He felt she was on the verge of telling him something then changed her mind. He hugged her close, wary of pressuring her.

The sun lowered near the ocean horizon. They watched silently when it went behind a cloud. The Pacific undulated, silvery and dark. "We better get back. I have an early call in the morning. I'll be up and gone before you and Santos are awake." Holding hands, they strolled slowly back to their umbrella.

She raised his workingman's hand to her cheek. "I'll get up and make breakfast for you."

"No, it'll be too early. I'll grab a couple of Egg McMuffins on my way to Valencia. I'll be out there most of the day. I'm bidding on a big job worth a hefty paycheck for me and my guys."

Might as well get used to the bachelor life again.

She dropped the side of her head on his shoulder. "I'll have dinner ready around six. Will you be home by them?"

"I'll make sure of it."

Queen languished on the blanket watching their approach. Her hair was damp and coated in sand. "It's a good thing I have a stiff brush in the van. You're a soggy mess, girl." She thumped her tail as if he'd given her a great compliment.

Graciella picked up two beach towels. "I'll get Santos and Amber out of the water."

"Yep." He pulled up the umbrella stake and carried it and the picnic cooler across the wide beach to the van. The kids were toweling off and pulling on shirts when he got back. "I'll take the wet towels and belly boards. Amber, fold up the blanket and bring it. Santos, do you know where Queen's vest is?"

"I put it in Mama's beach bag, Macfearsome. Shall I put it on her?"

"No. I just wanted to make sure we don't leave it behind. Help Mom with the rest of our things. Amber and I'll meet you at the van."

He and his goddaughter trudged through the deep warm sand. She waved at the lifeguard when they passed the tower. "Are you mad, Uncle Cluny?"

"No, sugar. Why would you say that?"

"Your face is rilly serious. Did you and Mrs. Jefferson have a fight? Daddy gets that face when he and Mom argue." She stopped at the back of the van and stared up at him.

He dropped the towels and belly boards on the asphalt behind the van, bent low and put his hands on her cheeks and kissed her forehead. "I'm not mad and Graciella and I did not have a fight, okay? Everything is good." He found the brush. "Get some of that sand off Queen before she climbs in. "I'll go help with the rest of the gear."

Graciella and Santos had almost reached the parking lot. "Let me take that." He lifted the heavy beach bag from her shoulder and put it over his own then brushed sand off Santo's wet butt. "Hold up, sailor. You need to go over to that faucet and wash the sand off your legs and feet. I'll carry this."

Santos trotted to the shower pole and foot washer faucet. Graciella laughed. "It'll take a fire hose to get these kids clean."

"They can rinse the rest off with the hose when we get home." The word *home* rang hollow in his ears. Once she and her son were gone, it would be nothing but a big empty house again.

Back in Spring Grove, they emptied the van and Cluny swept the sand out before placing his equipment inside. "You kids go out back and hose as much sand off as you can before you go in the house."

"I left some clean towels on top of the dryer." Graciella led them and the dog through the back gate. She waved to Cluny as they disappeared around the corner of the house. The plan was for all of them to take showers and change then have a light meal before they took Amber home.

By the time he entered the house through the back door Graciella had finished unpacking and was putting the finishing touches on a big tuna salad. "Would you like some iced tea, amor? I put a fresh pitcher in the refrigerator before we left this morning."

"Yes, thanks." He took two tall glasses from the cupboard. "Shall I pour one for you?"

"No." She removed the pitcher and handed it to him then put the salad bowl inside. "I'll shower first." She put her arms around his neck then kissed him. "Thank you for last night."

Her words gratified him, predictably setting him on fire. He pulled her hard against his body and kissed her slowly. "You're welcome, baby, but I should be the one thanking you."

Santos called from the hall. "I'm done with Macfearsome's shower, Mama. You can go in now."

"Thank you, sweetie." She pulled away from his arms. "I won't take long. You can get in there when I'm done."

"I don't think so."

"You want to go first?"

"That's not what I had in mind. You need help getting out of what few clothes you're wearing. I'm the man to do it." For the rest of his life, he hoped. He took her by the shoulders and marched her down the hall. As they passed the guest bathroom, he rapped and called, "Amber, don't use all the hot water."

The shower went off. "I'm done, Uncle Cluny."

He closed and locked his bedroom door, took Graciella's hand and led her to his bathroom.

She whispered, "Do you think we should?"

He whispered back, "Yes, I think we should."

"But, the kids."

"They'll be glued to the TV as soon as they hit the living room. The Dodgers and Angels are playing the Freeway Series. They talked about missing the start of the game on the way home from the beach, remember? No more protests. You're mine, baby."

Tonight would have to last them for a while. She was going, no matter what. For now, maybe this separation was the right thing for her to do. Maybe after they lived separately for a while she'd be ready to consider a marriage proposal.

He wasn't convinced, but it was her call. Might as well face it, like going on a mission. Gear up, get your head straight and just do it.

Chapter Twenty-Eight

Cluny's Kitchen, Next Evening at Supper

"I DON'T WANT TO GO HOME." SANTOS SCOWLED AT HIS PLATE. "I want to stay here." He stared pointedly at Cluny.

Silent, Cluny lifted a glass to his lips and drank some iced tea.

Graciella touched Santos' shoulder. "We talked about this. You haven't visited your grandparents in weeks. They were so happy I was bringing you to spend the day with them tomorrow. You don't want to disappoint them, do you?"

He lowered his head and mumbled, "I guess not." He put his elbows on the table and dropped his chin against his fists.

She stopped herself a split second before berating him about elbows on the table. Now was not the time to discuss table manners. He and Cluny had grown close, complicating her own confusion about how to proceed with their relationship. She had to pay attention to Santos's feelings. She'd brought him into the middle of this. The very last thing she wanted to do was drive a wedge between herself and her son because of her own uncertainties.

"Look, you have baseball every Saturday for the rest of summer. Cluny will spend weekends with us, at our apartment or here. We'll do things together. It won't be so bad, you'll see." At the same time she reassured him, she tried to reassure herself that going home was the right thing to do.

"It's so boring at the dance studio and our apartment. At least when we're here I can ride my bike to Amber's house if I want. I can play with Queen. We can go to the beach."

Cluny dabbed his lips with the napkin. "We'll still go to the beach. How about if I bring Amber with me sometimes when I come to dinner?" He put his hand on Santo's shoulder. "Mom needs you to cooperate with her. You can do that, can't you?"

Santos took a moment to answer. A variety of emotions flickered on his young face. Finally, he sighed, resignation in his body language. "I guess."

"Okay then," Cluny answered, "how about some of that ice cream?"

Graciella cleared the table and loaded the dishwasher when Cluny and Santos carried their dessert to the living room. He didn't turn on the TV; instead she heard them talking quietly. She wanted so badly to eavesdrop on their conversation, but willed herself to let them have this private time. Her heart was heavy at the prospect of leaving. She loved both of them so much and questioned separating them, separating herself from Cluny.

But it was time for them to go home. If she thought unemotionally it was the right thing to do. She had a business to run. Admittedly, she could commute easily from Spring Grove to Chatsworth. It would only add half an hour in each direction to her work day. She could enroll Santos in the Boys and Girls club if he didn't want to accompany her to the studio each day. She had to take him to work with her. It was out of the question to leave him alone either here or at her apartment. Marla would keep him for the day, anytime. He and Amber had a lot of fun together, always finding endless things to keep them occupied.

Queen lay between the kitchen and the dining room, giving herself a clear view in either direction. Perhaps the dog couldn't decide who needed her the most. Sometimes the way Queen gazed at her was unnerving, like she could see right through to her soul. If only she could talk. Graciella put down the dishtowel and knelt next to her. "What's your advice, girl?"

She raised her head at Cluny's footsteps. He'd heard the question, but he only nodded and carried the dessert bowls to the sink and put them in the dishwasher. "You need help packing?"

She got to her feet, shook the dishtowel and hung it up. "No, I've got everything ready to go, except for what we take in the morning. You could help me carry the boxes out to my car though, if you don't mind." She brushed hair back from her face, shy for some reason. It unsettled her, considering their deep level of intimacy. Why was she speaking to him as if he were a polite stranger instead of the man who knew every inch of her body, the man who made her laugh, cry and sigh with deep satisfying passion?

Expressionless, he tilted his head in the direction of the hall. "Lead the way."

"Santos, would you get your shower while Cluny and I pack up the car?"

He'd followed Cluny to the kitchen and had observed the tension between them. "Yes, Mama."

———

Cluny set the last box on the back seat of her little blue car. "That it?"

She forced a smile. "That's it."

"I have another long today tomorrow. I'm going to hit the sack. I'll be leaving early again."

"Oh." She heard withdrawal in his words. He might as well have punched her in the stomach because she felt breathless and sick. She'd taken for granted they'd sleep together this last night. "We'll, uh, we'll see you at the park on Saturday?"

He shrugged and grunted an unintelligible response and walked to the front door. He and Queen entered, leaving her standing alone by the side of her car. Too rattled to move, she stayed there, her mind and heart in chaos. She'd made light of how deeply he felt about them leaving. Anxiety and anger burned in the deepest recesses of her chest. He'd known they weren't going to stay here permanently. Why was he behaving like an ass?

Instead of entering the house she wandered to the end of the driveway and turned at the sidewalk. She clenched her fists and continued in the direction of the park. In the growing darkness, she dropped on a bench and gritted her teeth against impending tears. Not sure how long she'd been sitting, she jerked when she heard Santos calling, "Mama?"

The beam of his flashlight bounced on the pathway. "Mama?"

She wiped her eyes and cheeks with the hem of her blouse. "I'm here, sweetie."

"Why didn't you come in the house with Macfearsome?" He stopped and directed the weak beam at her face.

"Don't shine that in my eyes, please." She gently pushed the light away. "I wanted to get some air before bedtime. I'm sorry if I worried you. Let's go back. We have a lot to do tomorrow." She rose and put her arm around his bony shoulders.

"I don't think Macfearsome feels well."

"Why do you say that?"

"He didn't even say goodnight, he just took Queen and went to his bedroom and shut the door. Did you have a fight or something?"

"No." They hadn't had a fight, not in the true meaning of the word. Cluny had merely shut her out and left her by the side of the car. A good argument would have been better; at least they could have cleared the air. "He probably thought you'd already gone to bed."

"I left my bedroom door open and my light was on. He knew I was still up. I don't get it."

"Oh, honey, don't fret over it. He was most likely distracted. He's got an important business meeting in the morning. I'm sure he didn't mean to ignore you."

But he *had* ignored her son. Hurting for him, she kept her disappointment in Cluny's behavior to herself.

"I guess." He flicked off the flashlight and opened the front door. "I'm going to bed."

"Sweet dreams."

"Yeah." He dragged his feet down the hallway, went in his bedroom and closed the door.

Heart heavy in her chest, she locked the front door, turned off the lights. Was she doing the right thing by leaving? She hadn't expected

Cluny to close up that way. All of a sudden she was freezing. She put on her robe and crawled in bed without washing her face or brushing her teeth. She'd never done that before. Not in her most devastated moments with Marvin. Not ever.

————

2:00 a.m.

His horrified scream echoed through the house. She leapt from bed and opened her bedroom door at the same moment Santos stepped into the hall. They froze, staring at each other in the dim light. She was about to go to Cluny when his bedroom light popped on. Deep silence descended on the house. Without a word, Santos returned to his room and closed the door. Her heart hammered against her ribs so fiercely she sucked in a deep breath. She went to the kitchen and filled a tall glass with iced water. Sweating in the warm robe, she shrugged out of it and let it fall on the floor.

Cluny's wartime nightmares had nothing to do with her. He'd struggled with them for years and would most likely have them in the future. But, it was true…he'd only had a few restless nights since they'd been sleeping together. She told herself not to feel guilty. It was his battle. She was merely a supportive observer. She hated it when he suffered, but what was her obligation? He'd be disgusted if she showed pity. That much he'd made clear from the beginning.

She downed the entire glass of water, recoiling at the stab of pain in her forehead. Retrieving her robe, she turned out the light and went back to bed. She'd get up early. She didn't want to leave until she'd had a chance to speak to Cluny, to tell him how much she loved him. That everything was all right between them.

————

5:30 a.m.

The sound of the van's engine firing to life woke her. She jumped from her bed and ran to the front door and flung it open, but he'd already made his turn at the end of the driveway and was headed down the street away from the house.

———

10:00 a.m.

She'd finished the note to Cluny and propped it against the salt shaker when Santos entered the kitchen with his backpack over his shoulder. "Got everything, honey?"

"I think so, but it doesn't matter if I forgot something. Macfearsome will keep it for me or bring it to our apartment when he comes over."

"Yes, he will. Anyway, we'll be back on Saturday for baseball. If you left anything behind, you can get it then."

She double-checked the back door lock, turned off the kitchen light and locked the front. Santos yawned and didn't have much to say on the drive over the mountain pass to Chatsworth. She parked as close to the apartment as she could and smiled to see Earl waiting for them.

"Grandpa!" Santos threw open the passenger door.

"There's my two kids." Earl grinned broadly, white teeth gleaming in sharp contrast to his deep brown face. Santos whooped, ran to him and jumped into his arms.

Graciella enjoyed the warm reunion between grandson and grandfather. She joined them, and Earl put his arm around her shoulder and hugged them tight.

Santos squeaked, "Help, I can't breathe. I'm the bologna in a sandwich!"

Earl chuckled, dropped his arms and opened the door to the back seat of the car. He removed a heavy box. "Santos, run ahead and open the door for me. We'll get this car unloaded in no time."

True to his word, Earl and Santos had all their belongings in the apartment in a few minutes time. "That's the last box." Graciella closed the trunk. "Take those two to your room, Santos then you can go home with Grandpa."

Earl put his hand on her shoulder and leaned close. "Lillian is expecting you to join us for dinner. She's busy making Santos' most favorite."

They enjoyed a laugh at the family joke. Santos was easy to please. He loved to eat and his *most favorite* changed from day to day.

"I'm ready, Grandpa. Wait till you see how good I am at catching. You can come to all the games on Saturday now. Macfearsome taught me how to hit, too."

"Macfearsome?" Earl cocked his head and put his hand on his grandson's head.

Graciella cleared her throat. "That would be Coach McPherson. We've been staying at his house in Spring Grove. You never made it to any of the games yet, but I'm sure Chief told you."

"Ah, yes, Chief's boss, the plumbing contractor. Chief says he's a good man."

"He is." She was self-conscious under her father-in-law's gaze. A grown woman, she didn't need to explain herself to him, but he was bound to know she and Cluny were in deep.

"Macfearsome loves us, Grandpa. I wanted to live at his house. He has a dog and a big yard and lives by the park. My girlfriend, Amber, and me like to ride our bikes on the park trails. I can't ride a bike around here, but it's safe to ride where Macfearsome lives. I can ride to Amber's house by myself. Macfearsome takes us to the beach, too."

"Well, I'm glad you enjoyed your time there, and Grandma and I are looking forward to coming to the games on Saturdays from here on out."

"Macfearsome is going to come home with us on Saturdays after the games so we can be a family again. I hope we don't get in trouble for letting Queen stay here when Macfearsome sleeps over."

Her son's innocent chatter brought on a chill of loneliness and uncertainty. Cluny had never mentioned marriage. If he had asked her to marry him, what would she have said? Coming back to this apartment didn't feel like coming home. Where Cluny lived was home. For both of them, but especially Santos.

Earl cocked his head then spoke to his grandchild, "Queen? Ah, yes, Chief told me about that wonder dog. I look forward to meeting her and her master."

Graciella was grateful to Earl for ignoring Santos' comment about

Cluny spending the night. She had no idea how he felt about it, but she suspected he had few illusions about her remaining single indefinitely. It had been ten years since Marvin was killed. No matter what happened, she'd never let her son lose his relationship to his grandparents.

She took a breath and opened the refrigerator as soon as they left. It wasn't so bad. She got a garbage bag and discarded several items that were marginal or past dated. She'd need to replace what they'd taken from the pantry when they moved out. "Time to make that grocery list," she mumbled, "and quit working myself into a tizzy over Cluny."

She drove past the small center where her studio was on her way to the market. She was glad to see that all the merchants were open and the vacant space at the end, next to the barber shop had been leased. Busy workmen installed a large German Bakery sign above the doors. She smiled thinking how Santos would love visiting the bakery and discovering new *most favorites*.

The afternoon went quickly. On the way to the Jefferson's house she realized she'd been so busy today that she'd temporarily put out of her mind the deep unhappiness she'd felt last night and this morning. She hoped her dear Cluny had been able to put some of it behind him also. She'd get a read on his feelings when he stopped in later to kiss her goodnight.

He might not come. They were well beyond the courting stage. Why would he drive all the way over here after a long day to perpetuate that old ritual?

———

Cluny's house, 8:30 p.m.

"Hold still." Cluny put Queen's harness on her and opened the driver's side door on the Green Monster. She leapt across the seat to take her place on the passenger side. "You know where we're going, girl?" He fastened the seat clip to her harness. Her ears perked up when he took the on-ramp to the 118 Freeway heading east and her tail thumped on the seat. Cluny laughed and patted her back. "Yeah, you know."

Chief had given him the address to the senior Jefferson's house, and he knew Graciella and Santos would be there. It was time he met Marvin's parents.

He drove on the quiet residential street where they lived. The old house was set back behind a wide lawn and shaded by large trees on both sides. Lights shone from every front window. Graciella's car was parked in the driveway.

"You stay here, girl."

He knocked on the front door. An elderly black woman with white hair answered the door. She gave him a curious look. "Yes?"

"Good evening, ma'am. My name is Cluny McPherson. I'm here to kiss Graciella and Santos goodnight."

Her face broke into a feisty smile. She opened the door and gestured. "Won't you come in, Macfearsome? They're in the living room. I'm Mrs. Earl Jefferson. Please call me Lillian."

He grinned at her welcome and stepped inside. "Please call me Cluny. I'm happy to meet you, ma'am."

"But wait. You have a dog. I believe her name is Queen. Is she with you?" Lillian peered around him.

"She's in the car, ma'am."

"Well, my goodness, she doesn't have to wait for you in the car. Bring her in, please."

"Are you sure?"

"Certainly." Lillian stepped onto the front porch and nodded toward Cluny's car parked at the curb. "That your automobile?"

"Yes, ma'am. The Green Monster."

"Oh, my. Earl will be in raptures over that vehicle." She stepped off the porch and followed him. "Umm, mmm, mmm. This is some car, and look at that beauty staring at me through the window."

Cluny opened the door, unsnapped the restraint and Queen jumped out. He gestured for her to sit. "Shake hands with Lillian, Queen. She's Santos's grandmother."

Lillian bent forward with her hands on her knees. "Hello, you marvelous creature, you."

On her best behavior, Queen approached Mrs. Jefferson, sat and held up a paw.

"How do you do, young lady?" Lillian grasped the paw and shook it. "She's everything Santos told us. Do come in now before they come looking for me." She walked back to the front porch, Queen trotting along beside her.

Cluny followed close behind them shaking his head. "You're a fickle girl, Queenie."

"Lillian?" The profile of a large man darkened the open door.

"I'm here, Earl. This is Cluny McPherson and Queen. He's come to kiss Graciella and Santos goodnight."

"Is that so?" Earl stepped forward and shook Cluny's proffered hand. His eyes swept Cluny from head to toe. "Nice to meet you, son."

Cluny was aware of Earl Jefferson sizing him up. "Yes, sir. I'm happy to meet you."

"Macfearsome!" Santos squealed, "Mama, come quick!" He threw himself on Cluny. He'd never done that before. Cluny was gratified, and floored.

"Whoa, sailor. You nearly knocked me down." His instinct was to give the boy a hard hug, but Santos stepped back, face red with embarrassment.

Queen stood on her hind legs and put her big paws on Santos's shoulders then covered his face with dog kisses. Santos giggled, grabbed her ruff to pull her off and they both tumbled to the floor. The boy laughed and kicked while Queen bounced around him.

"What's all the fuss?" Graciella stopped and stared. "Cluny?"

"Hey, baby." He shrugged when her hands flew to her wide-eyed face. "It's time for your goodnight kiss."

Lillian stepped aside as her daughter-in-law walked into his arms and crumpled against him. "Let's go in, Earl. These young people need a moment of privacy." She closed the door, leaving them alone on the dimly lit porch.

Graciella's cheek was pressed tight against his shoulder. He stroked her hair. "You didn't think I'd forget, did you?"

She raised her face. "Kiss me, then I'll tell you what I think."

"You got it." He lowered his head and put his lips softly against hers. Her arms floated up and settled around his neck. His kiss deepened and he pressed her close. "I love you, baby. I'm so sorry I was in a crappy mood last night. I'm…"

"Shhh, querido. You don't need to apologize. Amo-te." Her lips were on his again. Her long slender fingers slid into his hair. "Amo-te."

Cluny's heart soared. Her ardent profession of love for him was more than he'd hoped for. This woman was everything he wanted. Everything he desired. He couldn't imagine living without her.

Chapter Twenty-Nine

Saturday, two weeks later, Spring Grove Park

"Were you watching, Mama? I got two hits!" Santos smiled from ear to ear. Graciella grinned at her adorable son.

"I certainly did. Your best game yet." She wanted to grab and kiss him but knew he'd be embarrassed in front of the other kids if she did. Sighing inwardly, she mourned her loss.

"I was watching too." Lillian held Declan against her shoulder while Marla packed up the snack litter and stuffed it in a net bag on the baby stroller. "A single and a double."

Earl, Dwayne, Chief and Cluny gathered near the dugout. Parents and kids drifted to the parking lot. "Santos, why don't you help the coaches pack up the equipment bags?"

Amber plopped next to Lillian and swiped sweat from her forehead with the back of her forearm. "Do you think my baby brother looks like me, Miz Jefferson?"

Lillian leaned back and studied Amber. "Well, let's see now. He's got your mama's red hair and your daddy's blue eyes, and your button nose." She nodded sagely. "There's definitely a family resemblance."

Amber's eyes widened. "Rilly? My nose? I didn't think he looked like me at all." She planted a kiss on Dec's cheek and ran to join Santos and some other players gathering bats and balls.

Marla straightened her back with a groan. "Thank you for that, Lillian."

Graciella eyed the very slight baby bump. "Dwayne knows, doesn't he?"

"Yes, I told him." She took a long drink from her water bottle.

"What did he say?"

"At first he was speechless, then he grinned, and then laughed like a lunatic. He couldn't wait to tell my parents, so we went over there after dinner. He and Dad had a high old time smoking smelly cigars and indulging in man talk while Mom and I watched them from a safe distance."

"So he's happy about it." Graciella glanced across the field where the men talked and laughed. Brawny Dwayne stood tallest, his transtibial metal and plastic prosthesis gleaming in the hot sun. Cluny reacted to something he said by punching him playfully then dodging back.

"Happy, yes. He told me later we might as well have all our kids, whatever he means by 'all,' and have done with it. Says it'll be easier to do things as a family. Amber took it in stride. She knows she's looking at several years of being Mom's little helper, poor kid."

"Yes, she informed Santos in a matter-of-fact way that men and women who love each other spend a lot of time trying to make babies after the children go to bed." Graciella rolled her eyes and covered her mouth.

Lillian didn't bother to mask her smile. "Lord a'mercy."

Marla slapped her forehead. "Great goats! That child will say anything." She took Declan. "You're a jewel, Lillian. My son has been very content in your arms this afternoon. I may ask you to move in with us."

"Think nothing of it, honey. I love babies, and I'm here every Saturday." She got up and adjusted her dress. "I think Earl is ready to go." She kissed Graciella's cheek and went to meet her husband.

"They are the nicest people, Graciella. And they seem to have accepted Cluny without reservation."

"Yes. What a relief that was. It makes life so much easier. I wasn't sure how they'd feel about me being with another man. Or how Cluny behaves like a father to Santos."

Marla stretched again. "I'm going to take Dec and walk home. Dempsey and Amber can catch up with me." She lowered the canopy on the stroller and adjusted her wide sunhat. "We still on for dinner at our house on Wednesday?"

"Yes, we'll be there. I'll dream up dessert."

"Okay, but ice cream is always a hit in summer."

"Thanks, I'll bring ice cream." Graciella waved goodbye to Marla and gathered her seat cushion and parasol. She covered her light olive skin with sunscreen and hid beneath the small umbrella most Saturday afternoons.

Cluny and Santos made their way across the diamond with two large bags, to stow in the back of the Green Monster because the lock on the park equipment shed hadn't been repaired.

Santos ran to her. "I'm gonna ride home with Macfearsome, Mama. We'll put the gear in his garage then come to the apartment."

Cluny reached for her. "I'd give you a hug with this kiss, but I'm too sweaty. Mind if I grab a change of clothes and shower at your place?"

"Of course not, amor, but you've got clean clothes in the apartment. I washed a pair of chinos and a couple of T-shirts the last time I did laundry." She'd never confess she loved doing his laundry and folding his underwear. He already knew how much she enjoyed cooking for him.

"Great!" He kissed her cheek. "We'll be right behind you. Come on, bud. Queen's probably mad at me for leaving her home."

"Why'd you leave her?"

"She's got a sore foot. She stepped on a piece of glass when we were out running a couple of mornings ago. I left her home because she loves charging around like mad with the kids before the games."

"Oh, guess what?" Graciella said. "Even though our complex has a no-pet policy, the lease allows for service animals. It's illegal to exclude them. As long as she wears her vest when you bring her over, they can't complain."

"Well, whaddaya know? That saves a lot of sneaking around after dark, doesn't it?" He closed the trunk. "We'll be there shortly." He put his hand on Santos' shoulder and nudged him toward the passenger side. "Hop in, son."

———

By the time her *men* arrived, she'd turned off the slow cooker and was preparing a Brazilian potato salad. Santos had set the table before they'd gone this morning. All that was left for her to do was squeeze fresh lemons for sweet lemonade. She'd just removed the lemons from the refrigerator when Cluny, Santos and Queen bounded noisily through the front door.

"Honey, we're ho-ome," Cluny sang, even though they had a clear view of each other in the small apartment. He dropped his overnight kit on the hall table.

"Yes, I see that. Dinner is almost ready. You two hit the showers and make it quick."

They stood at attention, saluted and said in military unison, "Yes, ma'am." She pressed her lips together and shook her head as they headed down the hallway. Santos loved to mimic Cluny's gestures. Not that he did it consciously, but he'd even altered the way he walked. He idolized the man.

Tonight after Santos went to bed she'd have that long overdue talk with Cluny about Marvin's infidelity. She'd mentally rehearsed what she'd say for the past couple of weeks. She couldn't hold things back from him if the relationship was to move forward without avoidable bumps. He'd been open with her. She owed him the same measure of trust.

———

Graciella's incredible story blindsided and stunned Cluny. Her facial expressions and body language said almost as much as her agonized words. Helpless in the face of her deep wounding, all he could think of was how much he hated that bastard, Marvin Jefferson. How much he wished the man was there in the room so he could beat the living shit out of him. He'd feel a whole lot better, but it was not what Graciella needed from him. She'd buried her feelings all these years for the sake of her son. The strength of her character left him awestruck.

He pulled her across his lap and stroked her back as she wept. Kissing her hair and forehead, he muttered, "I'm so sorry, baby. I'm so sorry." How any man could have disrespected this woman so callously was foreign to his senses, leaving him incapable of offering other words of comfort. Her pain was every bit as bad as his *paralyzed-and-helpless* nightmares.

"Promise me, amor." She sobbed against his neck. "Promise me you will *never* say a word of this to Santos. He'd feel betrayed and brokenhearted."

"Baby, I'd never do that to him. You know I wouldn't." He couldn't imagine he could love his own biological children, if they ever had them, any more than he loved the wiry brown innocent asleep down the hall. "I love him. He's my boy. He's our boy."

Graciella clutched him. Her sobs grew more savage. She raised her wretched face and kissed him. There wasn't a hint of sexual passion in her kiss. It was a kiss of deep gratitude and relief. He rocked her from side to side and hummed softly. Slowly she calmed and expressed a deep sigh. Her steady breathing told him it was bedtime. Using all the strength he could muster in his legs, he managed to get to his feet while holding her.

"Cluny?"

"Yes, baby?" He was nearly to her bedroom door.

"Is it all right if you just hold me tonight?"

"Exactly what I had in mind."

———

Wednesday evening, Dempsey's home

Graciella and Marla cleared the residue of dinner while Dwayne and Amber teamed up against Cluny and Santos in a game of hoops at the back of the garage. Their raucous shrieks of laughter echoed in the gloaming.

"I'm so glad you finally told him."

"Yes, I am, too. I can't explain why it took me so long to work up my nerve. I trusted Cluny, but I couldn't risk Santos learning the truth."

They worked silently for several moments.

Marla closed the dishwasher door. "Declan is finally sleeping through the night. Can you imagine that little stinker taking so long? Some mornings Dwayne and I look like a couple of zombies at breakfast."

Graciella relaxed. She was certain Marla changed the subject to lift her spirits. "Enjoy your reprieve. You'll only have it for about the next six months."

"Oh, thanks for reminding me." Marla's voiced dripped sarcasm despite her grin.

The back screen door banged open. "Ice cream!" Amber, then Santos, shouted.

Graciella crossed her arms. "Step outside and re-enter this house when you can behave like a proper guest, Santos Jefferson."

He hung his head and walked out. Amber giggled.

"You too, Miss Dempsey," Graciella added.

Amber raised her eyebrows in surprise at Graciella's order.

Marla pointed to the door. "You heard her. Scat."

The moms exchanged a wry look. They nodded with approval when two contrite youngsters stepped politely inside. "That's more like it." Graciella pointed to the dessert bowls on the table. "Have a seat and I'll dish it up."

Dwayne stepped to the door. "May we come in, please, Sergeant Mom?"

Cluny nudged him. "Uh, I'd go easy on the Sergeant Mom stuff, Gunny. You're about to ace me out of my ice cream." He sat at the table and hummed with approval when Graciella heaped his dish. "Hey, Gunny, you remember Hot Stick don't you?"

"Sure. What about him?"

"He's in San Diego. I'd like to get down to see him. He's thinking of retiring next year. You don't mind doing the coaching Saturday without me, do you?"

Dwayne smirked. "No, Chief and I'll try to handle it. When are you leaving?"

"The early train out of Simi Friday morning. He'll pick me up at

Oceanside. He called Beachy. The three of us will go to the Camp Pendleton Iron Dog Trials on Saturday. I'll spend Saturday night in San Diego, and she'll give me a lift home on Sunday on her way to the Bay Area to meet up with her parents for a family wedding."

A cold knot formed in Graciella's chest. "I didn't know you'd be gone for the weekend."

Marla tried to hide her jarred reaction to Cluny's announcement by concentrating on her ice cream, but Graciella had caught her eye before she looked away.

Oblivious to the stiffness in her question, Cluny shrugged. "Did we have something planned that I forgot about? I can cancel. It was just a lucky chance to catch two old friends in the same place on the same weekend."

Graciella slowed her breathing. She would not overreact. It sounded innocent enough. "Um, who is Hot Stick? And what kind of a name is that?"

"He's a close-air-ground-support A-10 pilot. We met him in Iraq after he saved our, a...uh, our squad one day when we got surrounded by hostiles outside the FOB wire. Those pilots and their warthogs are amazingly skilled at getting ground troops out of tight spots. He got the nickname Hot Stick during the Afghanistan war. He's what? About forty or so, Dwayne?"

"Has to be. I'm sure he's already put in twenty."

Marla put her spoon down. "Outside the FOB wire?"

Dwayne raised his eyebrows and eyed Santos and Amber who were all ears. "You kids finished with your ice cream? How about leashing up DD and Queen and taking a walk to the corner? If there're any free Spring Grove papers left in the box, you can bring me one."

Amber pouted. "Do we have to?"

"Yes."

"Put on your hoodies," Marla added. The adults remained silent until the kids had gone out and closed the door. "Sorry, I know better than to ask questions about Iraq in front of Amber."

"That's okay, honey. Outside the wire means the danger zones beyond the perimeter of the forward operating base. We got in a fire-fight one day and we called for air support. Hot Stick to the rescue.

The Warthog is one ugly airplane, but it flies close to the ground and their firepower is super accurate. He's one of the best."

Unable to shake herself loose from the fact that Cluny was planning to see Misty Beachy and spend Saturday night in San Diego, Graciella couldn't help herself. "Does, uh, Misty know him?"

"Yeah, they met a couple of times in de-brief sessions over there." Cluny squinted at Dwayne. "Do you remember when she met him?"

"Not exactly, no. As I recall, they didn't like each other much."

Graciella reached across the table and took their empty bowls. "I'll put these in the dishwasher, Marla. We should probably be getting home as soon as Amber and Santos return."

The men got up from the table and wandered out to the front porch. Marla joined Graciella at the sink. "Are you all right?"

"I'll be okay. He took me off guard. I'm trying, Marla. I'm trying."

"You don't need to worry about him. They're just warriors with something in common. They like to catch up and reminisce every once in a while, that's all."

It was that *something in common* that tore at Graciella.

———

Around midnight, Graciella's apartment

"What are you doing?" Graciella sat up and tugged the sheet to cover her chest.

"I'm heading home. I have to be in early in the morning so I can get Chief set for tomorrow and Friday. The bid I gave for the job in Valencia needs some explanation; on the chance he gets a phone call from the developer. He can always call me, but I want to make sure he's up to speed on the specs, terms and conditions."

"You can't stay the night?" She hated the plaintive note in her voice. "I mean, I won't see you again until next week."

He sat on the side of the bed and tied his shoes. "I'd like to stay, but it isn't practical, baby. I have a shitload of paperwork to go through. I haven't been in for days." He leaned across the bed and kissed her. "I'll call when I get back on Sunday. Let's plan a date for just the two of us next week." His fingers trailed down her neck and across her breast. "Oh man, I'll miss this."

But not enough to stay.

She put a smile on her face. "And I'll miss you, amor."

He gave her a husbandly peck on the cheek and slapped his knee. "Come, Queen. I'll lock the door. Tell Santos goodbye for me. I'll see you in a few." He opened the bedroom door and they slipped out.

Was it her imagination, or couldn't he get out of there fast enough?

Chapter Thirty

Thursday, Rio Samba

GRACIELLA STRETCHED HER BACK AND TIGHTENED HER ponytail. "We got so much done this morning we won't need more than an hour after lunch."

"I'm pooped." Santos sat on the floor. "I'm hungry too."

She poked his leg with her toe. "You're always hungry. I'm still trying to figure out which of your legs is hollow." She carried the dust mop to the corner. "Tell you what. Go to the deli, order us a sandwich and see if you can get that nice table by the window. I have a couple of things to do here, and then I'll join you in about fifteen minutes." She handed him enough money to pay for lunch.

"What do you want to drink?" He hitched up his pants and stuffed the bills in his pocket.

"I'll have a crème soda. I haven't had one in ages."

The minute he left, Graciella dug her cell phone from her bag and tapped the icon for Cluny's office.

"Veteran's Plumbing. What's your problem?"

She grinned at Chief's terse answer. "Hello, Chief. It's Graciella. Is Cluny there?" Not sure how she'd open the conversation with Cluny, she gripped the phone and paced.

"He might've already bailed for lunch. I'll take a look. Hang on." She heard him holler, "McPherson! You still here? Harry, can you waylay him? Hang on, looks like we caught him."

"Thanks." The lump in her throat grew thicker.

"Hey, baby." Cluny, breathless, answered faster than she'd expected.

"I, um, I wanted to talk to you before you left in the morning. Is now a good time?"

"Good as any. What's up?"

"I didn't want you to leave town without telling you something...I wanted to, uh...tell you." *Oh, heck, I'm rambling.* "You know what, amor? It can wait until you get back."

"No way. Tell me, or I'll be speculating about it all weekend."

"I, uh, have no problem with you going to Camp Pendleton to visit your friend, the pilot, but it really bothers me that you're planning on spending the night in San Diego...with Misty."

Say something, Cluny. This silence is killing me.

"Cluny? Are you still there?"

"Don't do this, Graciella."

"Don't do what?"

"I'm not him. You're projecting his infidelity onto me. It's not fair."

Is that what she was doing? "I know, but..."

"No, I don't think you do. You have no reason to distrust me. None. Mis and I have told you about our past. We're good friends. Don't tell me who I'm allowed to have as friends."

Her heart sank. "Oh, no, I don't mean it like that."

"Then explain it to me."

She didn't know what to say. Her brain told her one thing and her heart told her the opposite. "I admit it, uh, I'm having a hard time, you know, trusting." That wasn't what she'd planned to say. She wasn't sure now what she *had* planned to say.

"What do you want from me, Graciella? Your fears are unfounded. I've told you, and shown you how much I love you. What more can I do?" His use of her name instead of his usual endearment said volumes about his reaction to her confession.

"I'm torn, Cluny. I love you. I want to trust you. I do. But your past with her…I can't help how I feel."

"We both have pasts. We have to trust each other or we don't stand a chance."

Could this have gone any worse? "I shouldn't have called. I have to go."

"Oh, no you don't. We can't leave it like this. I want an answer. Will you trust me? Or will you punish me for what he did, and ruin what we have?"

She clutched her stomach. "That's not fair, Cluny."

"Fair? You're the one not being fair." She didn't miss the slow burn of anger in his voice.

Damn him!

"Like I said, this phone call was a bad idea. Go ahead with your plans and just forget I called." She turned her phone off and stormed out of the studio. When she approached the deli, she slowed her step and took deep breaths. Santos didn't need to see her fuming. She pasted a calm expression on her face, opened the door to the small deli and stepped inside.

Santos smiled and waved from across the small eat-in area. Tall drinks sat on the table. "I got your crème soda, Mama. Roast beef sandwiches will be up in a minute. I got mine with extra horseradish and yours with a side of sauerkraut."

"Perfect." She hung her shoulder bag on the back of her chair and took her seat. "I'm hungry." She felt her composure slipping and picked up her drink to mask it. To her horror, tears puddled on her lower lashes. She picked up her napkin, blew her nose and wiped her eyes.

"Are you crying, Mama?" His alarm was exactly what she'd wanted to avoid.

"Um, no, It's must be allergies. My eyes started to burn as soon as I stepped outside and locked the door at the studio."

He was about to speak when the man behind the counter shouted the number on the ticket in the middle of their table. Santos bounced up and went to the register. He paid the check and carried the plates to the table. She had a tight grip on her emotions by the time he returned.

"Dammit to hell!" He picked up the stapler and hurled it across the room. He slammed the top of the desk with his fist. "Ow!"

Chief peeked around the doorframe. "Safe to come in?" He bent over and picked up scattered pieces of the innocent, now violated, desk accessory. "Somebody has his skivvies in a knot."

"What?" Cluny glared. "What the hell are you talking about?"

"Female trouble would be my guess."

Is the old man slipping?

"Yep. Women. You can't live with'em and you can't live with'em." He directed a wry smile at Cluny.

Cluny dropped his booted feet on top the scarred desk. "You're full of wisdom, old man."

"Been married to the same woman for over forty years, jarhead, and I have yet to determine what makes her tick." He chuckled and dropped the shattered corpse of the stapler in the overflowing waste-basket at the corner of the desk.

"That's encouraging."

"Wasn't meant to be. Had to happen sooner or later, you know. The first big fight. There'll be plenty more if you two stick it out. Don't mean you don't love each other. It's the way living with a woman is. Can't be helped."

Cluny's chair bounded forward with a painful squeak and his work boots hit the floor. "I'm going to get some lunch before you bestow any more of your *sageness* on me, Chief." He slammed the ball cap on his head. "Hold down the fort."

"Don't I always?"

Cluny went back to his car. He got in and grabbed a handful of Queen's hair and gave it a good shake. "I didn't forget you, Queenie. Let's go get that hamburger." He turned out of the industrial neigh-borhood and headed to McDonalds, gave his order at the drive through, paid, and then parked under a big oak tree.

Queen's panting increased when she smelled the food. Her tail thumped on the passenger door in anticipation of her favorite not-good-for-dogs treat.

Graciella's call played havoc in Cluny's head. He took his time eating. Queen downed her burger in two gulps and was nosing his soft drink. "Hey! Get out of there." He took the top off the paper cup containing water. "That's yours."

Should he have been less quick to react? Spent more time putting her at ease about his weekend? *No, dammit!* She had no reason to mistrust him. She had plenty of reason to feel insecure, he supposed, but not with him. She was irrational. He rolled his eyes and groaned. Graciella hadn't exactly demanded anything from him; she'd expressed herself supposing she was safe telling him her feelings, her fear. He took his cell phone out of his pocket and touched her picture on the display. No answer, so he tapped a text: *Sorry. U hav nthng 2 worry abt. I'll call when I gt bak Sun nt. I luv u. C.*

His thumb hovered over Send. He pushed Cancel. He'd give her time to settle down, try her again later. He squeezed his eyes closed and wondered if he'd have a repeat performance of the nightmare tonight. He missed being able to reach across the bed for her, missed pulling her close, missed holding her. Sleeping together once or twice a week just didn't cut it. Something had to give.

He considered calling Hot Stick to say he'd changed plans and going online to cancel his train reservation. Instead he grabbed the trash from lunch and carried it to a big waste can. He watched while Queen sniffed the low growing junipers at the perimeter, deciding which one to honor with her urine.

"Shake a leg, girl. We got a lot more to do this afternoon." He clapped. "Car!"

Doubts assailed him on the drive to the warehouse. He immediately plunged into paperwork and returned several phone calls.

"Knocking off, boss." Chief stood in the doorway wiping his gnarled hands on a shop towel. "Me and the boys are done for the day. Enjoy your trip. We'll see you bright and early Monday morning."

"I'll call the answering service and remind them to call you for emergencies."

"Already done." Chief stuffed the towel in his back pocket and waved. "G'night."

"Give Lu a kiss for me."

"If I tell her it's from you, she'll probably allow it. She's got her book club this evening. Looks like I'll get some peace and quiet."

The old man wasn't fooling Cluny. Those two were completely devoted to each other. They'd weathered many storms and long deployments, but the love in their eyes gleamed every time he'd seen them together. "Turn off the lights in the warehouse. I'll go out the side door soon as I'm done here."

"Aye, aye, captain."

Quiet descended on the warehouse in the lowering sunlight. Against his wishes he thought of Graciella again and wondered how he could have handled it differently. What more could he do? It was her problem. She'd have to come to terms with his friendship with Mis. If he gave up their friendship to put Graciella at ease, eventually he'd resent her for it.

What a mess.

Were men and women ever meant to live together? Why couldn't he and Graciella be more like Dwayne and Marla? He gave himself a mental slap. *Grow up.* Nobody ever knew what went on behind closed doors. Every couple had problems.

He blew a resigned sigh, straightened up the desk and grabbed his keys.

———

The next morning he boarded the early train south. He tried to read the newspaper, think of anything but their phone conversation. He stared out the window, seeing nothing. Queen, wearing her service vest, snoozed at his feet. That's what he should do, catch a nap after the lousy night they'd both had. He closed his eyes and leaned back. First Graciella's face, then Santos' face stared back at him. Cluny remembered the kid's joyful expression when he hit that double. The sweet boy's moment of jubilation was infectious. The team and the coaches enjoyed it almost as much as Santos. Cluny had experienced a real sense of satisfaction and accomplishment. That was why he loved coaching every summer. To be there when a kid reached an important milestone was something impossible to put a price on.

He remembered a deer hunting trip many years ago near Sheridan, Wyoming with Dwayne and his little brother, Donovan. They were in their teens. The Dempsey boys had been hunting since adolescence, but this had been the first time Cluny had gone with them. He'd proven himself at the gun range, but had never hunted wild game. He bagged a beautiful buck with his first shot. Donovan jumped on his back whooping and hollering at his success as if he'd made the shot himself.

Later when they brought the field-dressed carcass back to the ranch, Kathleen had danced him around the smoke house, congratulating him on providing the family and the ranch hands with enough meat to get them through winter. He knew exactly what it was like to accomplish something and to bask in the congratulations of those you cared for.

———

Saturday afternoon ballgame

Graciella and Marla handed out treats during the seventh inning stretch while Lillian walked back and forth behind the bleachers with a feverish, fussy Declan.

"Poor baby, he's trying to cut teeth already," Marla said. "He's an overachiever just like his daddy."

"I remember those days. I spent many a night pacing the floor with an inconsolable Santos in my arms. Before long I was doing as much crying as he was. It wasn't post-partum depression. It was exhaustion, pure and simple."

"Ouch. At least I have Dwayne to take turns with me. Last night he wouldn't let me get up. I heard him in that squeaky rocker in the living room, trying his best to let me get some sleep." Marla buttoned up the canvas bag holding what was left of the energy bars and apples. "How are you doing with Cluny gone?"

"I screwed things up by calling him Thursday to say how uncomfortable I felt about him spending two days with you-know-who. All I accomplished was getting his back up about trying to pick his friends. We were both mad by the time I hung up on him."

"Uh-oh. Well, it was bound to happen sooner or later." Marla sat next to her and squeezed her arm. "It's not the end of the world."

"I should have known better. He was offended that I didn't trust him. I'm sure we'll get it smoothed over when he calls me tomorrow night." She fanned her face and neck against the afternoon heat.

———

Sunday night, Beachy's car

Beachy angled her head and said, "I want to know why you've been down in the dumps all weekend, and you might as well tell me," she warned, "because I'm fed up with your lousy mood and long face. Either open up or walk back."

Cluny tried to make a joke of it. "You'd make Queen walk all the way home?"

"Cut the crap, Mac. What's going on? Did you have a fight with her?"

"You mean Graciella?"

"God, you're such a smartass. I wasn't talking about your dog."

Was that what it was? A fight? He didn't think it met the level of a fight, but emotions had run high on both sides of their conversation. How much would he reveal to Mis, if anything? He changed the subject. "What do you think of Hot Stick?"

"He's a jerk. Don't try to change the subject."

"Why's he a jerk?"

"He just is. Ever since the first time I met him ten years ago in the sandbox, he's made it clear he doesn't think much of women in the military. He keeps it under wraps, but it's always there, just beneath the surface. His attitude hasn't changed."

He chuckled inwardly at her sour expression, but knew better than to get her started, so a brief smile was the only thing that could give him away. "He's a little old school. Give the guy a break."

"Old school? He can't be more than forty-two forty-three at the most."

"I wasn't referring to his age. He's got no wife and a teenage daughter. I get the impression she's a handful."

"Where's her mother?" She glanced quickly at him then turned her eyes to the perpetually jammed freeway.

"She bailed on them about three years ago. Said she never liked being a military wife, so she divorced him and a year later married another grunt and followed him overseas. Face it, Mis, your species has always been a mystery to us lesser beings."

"No kidding. You're about the closest to a girl of any guy I've ever known."

"Wow. What a compliment, I love being your girlfriend." He tinged his remark with sarcasm.

"You should. I'm very choosy, Mac." She stared straight ahead with a wide feisty grin on her face. He reached across the seat and tugged on her earlobe. "Ouch." She laughed and pulled away.

Maybe she was on to something. Cluny had always sought the company of women. It must have been his craving for the softness of his mother's love. When that love was ripped away at such an early age, he gravitated to the girls in the foster homes and to the foster moms who had a little bit to spare for their temporary children.

His dating history was steady and spotty. He loved to laugh, loved fun dates, and when he could manage it, good sex. Even mediocre sex was good sex. He'd just never connected on a level as deep as he'd achieved with Graciella. She was the first—scratch that—only woman he'd ever met who he'd thought of spending the rest of his life with. He'd tell her when they patched things up.

"Enough stalling, Mac, did you have a fight with her?"

He gave up. "I wouldn't exactly call it a fight. I saw a side of her I hadn't noticed before and had a knee-jerk response. I suppose it was inevitable." He had no intention of telling Beachy about Graciella's history with Marvin. Considering how long it had taken her to confide in him, no way would he further complicate things by violating her trust.

"Side of her?"

"She told me she didn't like me to spending the weekend with you. She doesn't trust me."

"Heck, she probably doesn't trust *me*. I told her I loved you. I'm not so sure any woman would want to hear that from a woman who'd slept with her boyfriend. Especially if she was in love with the guy. Try and see it from her viewpoint, Mac. Our situation," She wagged her finger between them, "is pretty unusual, you've got to admit."

"Yeah, but I told her the sex was over years ago and so did you. I don't know what else I'm supposed to do. I said it wasn't up to her to decide who I can have as friends. She hung up on me." Graciella had to let go of her past. If she couldn't trust him they were doomed. He wouldn't go ballistic if she had a close male friend. At least he was pretty sure he wouldn't.

"I take back what I said, Mac. You're as clueless as most men. Face it; you're so in love with that woman and her son, your thinking processes have been damaged. Why didn't you call me and cancel? Would that have been so hard, macho guy?"

"First, I'm a girl and now I'm macho guy? Make up your mind, woman. Jeez. No wonder guys are so confused about the mysteries of the female brain. Are you going to sit there and tell me that if I'd called to cancel—if I'd told you Graciella didn't want me to spend time with you—it would have been okay?"

"I'd have been temporarily pissed, sure, but I'd get over it. Looking at it from her side, I'd be very wary of any woman who showed the slightest interest in you. Men like you are hard to come by, Mac, as hard as it is for me to admit."

"God Almighty, Mis. That's the nicest thing you've ever said to me!" The smile on his face threatened to split his cheeks. Beachy was unique for sure. He pitied any man who took a serious interest in her but would be the first in line to congratulate him on getting past her armor.

"Don't get used to it."

"Not likely, since it took you over ten years to say so." He leaned across the gap between them and planted a smooch on her cheek. "So I'm a catch?"

She rubbed it off like a child who'd received an unwelcome kiss from a fat old uncle. "Don't let it go to your head."

He laughed and leaned back in the seat.

She continued to needle him, "Are you going to call her?"

"No, I'll let her stew for a while. I'll see her next Saturday at the park league baseball game. She'll probably have cooled off by then." He hoped so, because he wasn't sure what his next step should be if she hadn't.

"Don't mess up, Mac."

Quiet for several minutes, their conversation for the last half hour of the long drive centered on the dog trials. She'd enjoyed training the sniffer dogs, but was so intrigued at the Iron Dog Trials she said she might want to go into that line.

"You'd have to quit your job with Customs if you did that. There go all your government benefits."

"Yeah. I need to give it a lot more thought. I'm not so sure I want to keep working for the government." She turned down his street and pulled into his driveway, parked and opened her door. "I'll stretch for a few minutes before I head out."

"You should spend the night here."

She snorted. "And take the chance on her showing up? You're even dumber than I thought."

He let her little insult pass. "How much farther are you planning on driving tonight? Don't tell me you're pulling an all-nighter, dead-heading all the way to Frisco."

"I'm only going as far as Santa Barbara. I made a reservation at a motel just off PCH for the night. I've stayed there before. A guy I once knew in Seattle owns it."

"A guy?" Cluny surprised himself with the question. Where she stayed and with whom was none of his business.

"Yes, a guy. And his wife. She and I were in high school together. They've been married forever. Did I detect a hint of jealousy, Marine?" She faced him with her arms crossed.

"More like concern."

"I can take care of myself, Mac."

"So you've made abundantly clear." He reached inside for his bag. Queen bounded over the back seat and out of the Jeep. Setting the duffle on the ground, he embraced her. "Ease up, soldier. I'm allowed to be concerned about my friends. Give us a goodbye kiss."

Beachy sighed and rested her forehead in the center of his chest for a second then raised her face to his. "The squad didn't call me Misty Bitchy for nothing." She kissed him lightly on the lips and hugged him hard. "I'll be seeing you, Mac."

"Love you, Mis." He held her face in his hands and ran his thumbs over her lovely cheekbones, remembering their unique past, and how they'd saved each other over there.

"Love you back. So long, Queenie. If you have to, give Mac a bite on the ass. He can be a stubborn S.O.B."

Cluny stood on his front porch watching the taillights of her car until they winked out of sight. He shook his head and put his key in the lock to open the door to his empty house.

———

Graciella's kitchen, same evening

"I'll do that." Earl carried Graciella's made-from-scratch Brazilian Coconut Cake with lighted candles to the table and placed it in front of Lillian. "You'll blow coconut flakes all the way to the front door, but go ahead and make your birthday wish, Lil."

"Wait! We have to sing Happy Birthday to Grandma first."

Lillian covered her ears at the loud off-tune chorus.

"Come on, Mama. We have to hold hands when Grandma makes her wish."

Lillian stared at the candles, took a big breath then blew them out.

"What did you wish for, Grandma?"

"I have to keep it secret or it might not come true," Lillian said, "but I'll give you a hint. It had to do with your mama and that fine looking baseball coach of yours."

Graciella gripped the back of the chair. She'd been able to hold it together for days now, but that happy comment from Marvin's mother was all it took to undo her. "I'm sorry, will you excuse me? Don't wait for me, Lillian. Cut the cake. I'll just be a minute." She rushed from the room on shaky legs making a beeline to her bathroom. Sweat beaded on her upper lip. She made it to the toilet in the nick of time, and then vomited up her supper. On her knees she held hair away from her face. For a stark fearful moment the possibility she might be pregnant clutched her belly. No, she told herself, that wasn't possible. They'd always been careful. Heaving violently she lowered her head close to the toilet bowl and threw up what little was left.

"Graciella? Are you ill?" Lillian tapped on the bathroom door then cracked it open. "Oh, dear, you are, aren't you?" She took a cloth from the stack on the shelf and wrung it out in cold water then pressed it to Graciella's forehead.

"I'm sorry to spoil your party, Lillian."

"Don't be silly, dear." She laid her palm to her daughter-in-law's cheek. "You don't seem feverish. Did this come on suddenly, or have you been poorly before tonight?"

Graciella shook her head. "I was a little queasy at the park yesterday afternoon. I probably got too much sun. It's been blazing hot all week." That was it. Too much sun. "I'm okay, Lillian. Just give me a couple of minutes to splash water on my face. Does everyone else feel okay?"

"We're fine, honey. I'll go on out and let the boys know you're all right. Take your time."

The nausea passed as quickly as it had come. Graciella washed her face. She pinned her hair back on the sides, smoothed her blouse and returned to the table. Earl held her chair and squeezed her shoulders as she sat down.

She stared at the small slice of cake on the plate in front of her, suddenly famished. Lifting her fork, she smiled across the table at Santos and took a small bite. "Mmm, one of my best."

"It certainly is." Lillian agreed. "Earl's taking some to Cluny's warehouse in the morning so we can share it with Chief and the other boys. He was planning to stop in and go to lunch with Chief anyway."

Santos bounced in his seat. "I made a wish on Grandma's candles, too, Mama, but I'm not telling you because I really want it to come true. I'll wish it again at the birthday party next month for me and Amber just to make sure."

She swallowed the bite of cake and smiled. Her precious son.

When she woke the next morning, she cried with relief because she'd started her period right on schedule. Then she cried because Cluny hadn't called her when he got home from San Diego.

Chapter Thirty-One

Friday evening, five days later

GRACIELLA COULDN'T FACE HIM. NOT AFTER HE'D FAILED TO CALL her. She phoned Earl. "Could you take Santos to the game tomorrow? I have a private lesson with a new couple who recently signed up for a series. The only time they can come is on Saturday afternoons." She glanced at Santos, sitting morosely across the kitchen counter. "You can? Thanks, Earl. He'll be ready to leave at one."

Santos frowned. "What should I tell Macfearsome?"

"Tell him the truth."

It was mostly the truth. She'd asked the couple to come in on Saturday afternoon instead of Friday evening. They hadn't been thrilled about changing their plans, but she assured them they'd be doing her a great one-time favor, and in return she'd give them a nice discount on the package. She now needed a valid excuse not to go to any of the games for the rest of the summer season.

———

Thursday evening

Marla called. "We missed you on Saturday. I hope everything is okay."

"Yes, everything's fine. I picked up a new couple who wanted their private lesson on Saturday afternoon. It's a very nice fee. I couldn't afford to pass up the income."

"Oh, that's too bad. At least Santos' grandparents stood in for you."

Graciella thought Marla had a suspicion something was not right between her and Cluny, but all she said was, "Yes, I'm so glad they're there for him. Oh, Marla, I have to go. The last group for this evening just came into the studio. We'll talk later."

"Okay, let's try and get together for dinner soon."

"Yes, let's. Bye." A sick feeling filled her chest. She hated brushing off Marla, but until Cluny made some effort to put things right between them, she saw no reason to discuss their differences with anyone.

Not only had he failed to called that Sunday evening as he'd promised, she'd heard nothing from him all week. She'd analyzed and re-analyzed her feelings before and after the fateful phone call eleven days ago. She was entitled to her feelings! Why was that so difficult for him to understand? He shouldn't have accused her of wanting to pick his friends. He'd picked apart her words to make them suit his interpretation, not what she'd actually meant. How was she to know how prickly he could be?

The Amber-Santos birthday party was in two weeks. She had no idea how she'd handle the day. The kids had been looking forward to it all summer. The entire baseball team had been invited. If something didn't give between her and Cluny, it was destined to be very awkward. At some point she'd have to confide in Marla. It would be much better to tell her the truth instead of leaving events open to speculation. She'd promised Marla she'd do her share to make the party a success. And she'd keep her word.

If only he'd callled.

Santos's conversation had consisted of one word answers or grunts. It was increasingly difficult to overlook his moods and to find excuses why he couldn't spend a day at Amber's house. She practically had to drag him out of bed to get them to the studio on time in the mornings. He used to enjoy going to work with her during school vacations, helping at the studio, answering the phone. Now he resented every minute of it.

"Why doesn't Macfearsome come here anymore."

She didn't meet his gaze. "He's very busy."

"Don't answer me like I'm a baby! I have a brain, Mama." His face brick red with anger, he scowled and put down his fork. "I'm going to my room."

"No, sweetie, wait, I'm sorry. Finish your dessert. It's complicated to explain." She extended her hand and nodded at his chair.

He stood rooted to the floor. Finally, he took his seat, but didn't pick up his fork. "Why do grownups always say 'it's complicated' when they don't want to tell the truth?" Santos had never taken this belligerent tone of voice with her before.

Her heart ached. And not just because she'd been so unprepared to discuss this with him. "The truth is, it *is* complicated. Cluny and I had a misunderstanding."

"What kind of misunderstanding? Do you still love him?"

"I—"

"Does he love you?" He'd leaned forward challenging with his chin. "I know he loves me because he told me so when I asked him why he didn't come here anymore, why we couldn't be a family anymore." His freckled nose wrinkled and tears filled his eyes. "He told me 'it's complicated.' I hate you! I hate him!" With that, he shoved back from the table and ran to his room. His door slammed so hard the TV wobbled on its stand.

Her son's bitter outburst hurt deep down. Graciella clenched her fists and squeezed her eyes shut. She was the adult here. She would not react like a wounded child. She'd drawn her son into the budding love affair. He was innocent, his life turned upside down, and it was her doing. She'd been so filled with passion for Cluny that she'd neglected her responsibility as a mother.

If it were possible to go back in time she wouldn't have invited Cluny to join them for a cool drink on their beach blanket that day. She'd never have known what it was like to be with him, to love him, to anticipate him coming through the door. Even now, if she closed her eyes and held her breath, she could feel the heat of Cluny's bare skin under her hands.

The doorbell rang.

Her heart leapt. It must be Cluny. It had to be Cluny. She flew to the door and pulled it open. The hopeful smile died on her face. "What do you want?"

Misty Beachy stared stonily. "We need to talk."

The last human being on the planet Graciella had anything to say to would be this woman. "I have nothing to say to you."

"I'm not leaving until you either let me in so we can speak in a civilized manner, or you can shut the door in my face and I'll shout from out here. What's it going to be?"

Graciella got a glimpse of Misty's steel. A hint of the way she must have spoken to the men under her command. "My son is in the apartment. He's still awake."

"Then step outside and we'll go for a walk or sit in my car. Make up your mind."

Graciella gritted her teeth. "I have to let Santos know I'm stepping outside." She made to close the door.

"Leave the door open. Tell him. I'll wait here."

Hands to her hot cheeks, Graciela hesitated then whipped around and strode down the short hallway. At the door to Santos' room she knocked. "Santos? Honey, I'm stepping outside. I won't be far away." She heard nothing. "Santos, did you hear me?"

"Yes. Leave. I don't care."

This was a nightmare. Graciella turned on her heel, grabbed her keys and stepped outside. She locked the door and followed Beachy to the parking area.

Beachy crossed her arms and leaned her hip against the front fender of her Jeep. "In the car or walk?"

"In the car so I can keep an eye on my front door."

Misty opened the driver's side and pointed across the hood. "Get in."

Graciella got in the car and sat as far away from Misty as possible. Angry words spewed from her mouth, "Tell me what you want. Do you want Cluny? Take him. There's nothing I can do about it."

"God! The two of you are beyond pathetic." She pursed her lips and gripped the steering wheel. "If I didn't love Mac, I'd tell both of you to go to hell, but I do love him so I have something to say to you, and then I'll leave."

"I'd rather you —"

"Oh, shut up!" She slammed her fist on the steering wheel. "I'm only going to say this once, so listen up!"

Stunned by Misty's hot temper and the command in the small blonde woman's voice, Graciella held her tongue. Pulse thundered in her ears. She'd let Beachy have her say then get out of there as fast as she could.

"Are you listening?" Misty stared hard into Graciella's eyes.

Instead of answering she glared. Who did the woman think she was?

"This is not easy for me to tell you. Mac and I served several months in a forward operating base in the middle of an active battle zone in Iraq. Dempsey and some of the other guys you met were there, too. It's impossible to feel safe, ever. Even inside the wire. You never knew when an RPG would detonate, or whether or not it was headed right for you. We were under mortar fire twenty-four-seven. You could be watching a movie or writing a letter, or standing in the mess line. The threat of sudden death was constant. I felt my humanity slipping away inch by inch. It was impossible to sleep when the sirens went off at all hours of the day and night.

"One night warning sirens screamed for about the tenth time. I was shaking in every part of my body. I stepped outside the mess tent and slammed into Mac. I ripped into him from start to finish just because he was there. I choked and started to cry. He put his arms around me. I slapped and punched him, but he wouldn't let go. When I got hold of myself, he walked me to my tent. He never said a word. At the door he turned to leave. I grabbed his hand and pulled him inside. It was wrong, but I didn't care because I knew if I stayed alone I'd come unglued."

Gasping, Graciella tried to picture what Beachy described. Acid reflux burned the back of her throat.

"We sat on the edge of my cot holding hands. Finally, Mac gently lowered me on the cot and held me. There was nothing sexual about it. We fell asleep. When I woke a few hours later he was gone."

"But, I thought…"

Misty held her palm out. "Let me finish. Not long after that night we began to sleep together. What you need to understand is that it wasn't passion or even love. It was one human reaching out to another human on the most primal level. Sex was how we maintained our sanity in the raging chaos around us. You have no inkling what it's like to be a woman in a war zone during a long dangerous deployment. We both could have been busted in rank for it, but a few of the men in the unit, like Gunny Dempsey, deflected the gossip. Mac never said word one to anyone about me. It's easy for basic kindness and decency to deteriorate, even among the people you depend on for your very life.

"The day of the RPG ambush, the day Dempsey lost his leg, we were in a convoy heading back to Baghdad. Several of us got wounded." She touched her ear unconsciously. "And a couple of guys in my squad were killed. It was indescribably ugly. I didn't expect to get out of there alive. An A-10 Warthog came in low and held off the bad guys until we could be extracted by a SEAL fire team. The one your husband was part of. Marv was killed within twenty four hours of that incident."

Tears clogged Graciella's throat.

"Mac and I were on the same Medevac plane to Germany, but we didn't see each other again for about three months. It was just before he was on his way to Walter Reed with Dempsey and I was shipping out to a facility on the west coast. The only thing that existed between us by then was a melancholy, a deep respect. We'd saved each other over there. Mac is responsible for me not being a total crazy bitch, a total lost cause. He'll always be my best and most trusted friend."

Graciella raised her hands to cover her face. Moaning softly, she shook her head for what they'd gone through. All of them, including Marvin. Finally, she understood why she had no reason to distrust the man she loved. He and this woman had connected during a nightmarish situation she could never imagine. Their devotion to each other was no threat to her. Had never been a threat to her.

"I had no idea. I'm sorry. I don't know what else to say."

"Do you love Mac? Because if you do, get off your ass and figure out a way to patch it up with him. If you don't love him, then end it. I can't stand to see him suffering like this. He's one of the finest men I've ever known. Your kid would be lucky to have him for a father."

A tear trickled down Graciella's cheek. "I do love him. I just don't know how to..."

"Then figure it out!" Misty pointed to the door. "I'm done. You can go back to your kid now." Misty put the key in the ignition and started the Jeep.

The second Graciella closed the car door Misty backed out and sped away.

She hugged herself against the chilly night air. Slowly, she walked back to her apartment. Santos' bedroom door was closed and there was no light shining under it. She rapped softly.

"Santos? May I come in?"

His voice, muffled and sullen was barely audible. "Why?"

"I want to talk to you. "

"I'm asleep."

Her lips twisted in a rueful smile. "Please?" She turned the knob ever so slightly. He hadn't locked it. "Sweetheart?"

He was fully clothed, sitting on his bed, leaning against the headboard. The vertical blinds on his window facing the parking area were open. "Who was that lady?"

Graciella crossed the room and sat on the edge of his bed. "Cluny's old friend from the Marines, Sergeant Beachy."

"Why did you go out to her car?" He crossed his arms and scowled. "What were you talking about?"

"Were you watching me?" She put her hand on his leg. "I went outside because I wasn't sure if I wanted you to hear our conversation."

"Because you were talking about '*it's complicated*' grownup stuff?"

"Um hum. That was it."

"So, you're not going to tell me." He turned his head to face the window.

"No, honey, not tonight, but I promise I will soon." She shook his foot. "Why don't you take your shower and get ready for bed? I need to call Marla before it gets too late."

"When can you take me to visit Amber?"

"Tomorrow's Friday. I'll ask her parents if it's okay to bring you over to spend the night. How's that?"

His face broke into a happy grin. "I know what I want for my birthday."

"What?" She gave him encouraging smile.

"Macfearsome."

"I can't give you Macfearsome."

"Why not? You took him away from me and I want him back."

Everything was so simple to a child. Perhaps they had the right idea. "I want him back, too. I'll see what I can do. I won't make any promises."

"Okay." Resigned, he scooted off the bed, got his pajamas from the dresser and headed to the bathroom.

The minute Graciella heard the shower running she called the Dempsey house. Dwayne answered. "Dwayne? It's Graciella here. Is it too late to talk to Marla?"

"No, she's right here. Give me the boy, honey, Graciella's on the phone."

"Hey! What are you up to?"

"Do you have a few minutes to talk, Marla?"

"Sure, hold on a minute." A chair scraped. "I'm going to take Graciella's call in the den." Footsteps, then a door closing. "There. We have privacy."

"Could you keep Santos tomorrow night?"

"Sure. Are you and Cluny going out?"

"Not exactly. I'm going to his house and see if he'll talk to me."

"Finally! Are you going to let him know you're coming?"

"I hadn't planned to. I thought I'd just show up, not give him a chance to find an excuse not to see me."

"He wouldn't do that. He's miserable. I've never seen him so down in the mouth. I hope you're going over there to make up with him. If you're feeling as rotten as he is, it's time to talk it out." Marla sighed. "I'm one to talk. I have Amber to thank for being so single-minded in getting us back together after we split up."

"You'll have to tell me about that sometime."

Marla laughed. "She'd be happy to share with very little prompting. What time will you be by?"

"Around three?"

"That works. He can have dinner with us. You, too."

"No, I want to get to Cluny's house before he gets home. If it works out, we'll have dinner together."

Marla didn't answer her. "Marla?"

"I'm here. I, uh… Oh, heck, Graciella. Misty Beachy is at his place. She stopped on her way back to San Diego. We went out for pizza with them tonight. But they're not…he's not…"

"I know. That's okay. I talked with her an hour ago. She was here."

"What?"

"I won't go into detail. Let's just say she gave me a verbal slapping. I needed it."

"I'll keep my fingers crossed, my friend. You and Cluny and Santos are very special to Dwayne and me. We want nothing but the best for you."

"Thank you, Marla. I'll see you tomorrow afternoon, and keep those fingers crossed."

Graciella clicked off and slumped against the couch cushions. Now she'd worry for the next several hours about how to break the ice with the man she loved. She'd be turning the words around in her head all night.

Cluny's house, next afternoon

Cluny lounged against his porch railing. "Sure you can't stay another night?"

"Yes, Mac, I'm sure. I have to get back to work." Misty pointed to the duffle bag next to the door. "Would you carry that to the Jeep? I'll make one more sweep through the bedroom and bathroom to make sure I don't leave anything behind. You never know when your girlfriend might show up."

"You referring to my ex-girlfriend?" The words stabbed a pain in his chest and a choking lump in his throat.

Misty nodded to the street. "You mean her?"

Cluny's back went stiff and he whipped his head around. Graciella's car crept down his driveway. She stopped behind the plumbing van and turned off the engine, but didn't open her door. The front screen snapped shut when Beachy went inside the house. "Oh, shit," he groaned. "Oh, shit."

Graciella opened the door and stood next to her car. She gazed at him with unreadable eyes.

Beachy stepped outside, and lifted her duffle. "I'm outta here, Mac."

"You don't have to leave, Mis." But if she didn't, what was he to do?

"There are times, Mac, when I can't believe what a numbskull you can be. Go talk to her. What are you waiting for?"

He reached for Misty's bag and yanked it from her hand. "I'll walk you to your car."

"You're an idiot, but let's get it over with." She waved at Graciella.

"What are you doing, for chrissake?"

"Waving goodbye to your girlfriend." Misty opened the passenger door and rounded the front of Jeep to the driver's side. "Throw my bag on the seat."

He did as instructed, slammed the door and followed her. From the corner of his eye he saw Graciella watching his every move. His neck and shoulders cramped, and he asked himself why he was pushing it. "Give us a goodbye kiss, Mis." He leaned close to her door.

"I carry a gun, knothead, and unless you have a death wish, you'll step away from the car. I resign as your relationship therapist. Now back up or I swear to God I'll drive right over you." She glared and started the Jeep's engine then threw it into first.

He jumped to avoid the back wheels when she accelerated. She wasn't kidding about running over him. He might as well have been naked, standing there in the street, the dust kicked up by the Jeep swirling around his battered work-boots. He hadn't felt so vulnerable since the evac from Fallujah. Graciella hadn't moved, but he thought he detected the lowering sun glint off what could be a tear on her cheek. *Oh, God no, Graciella, please don't cry.* He was mush when faced with female tears. He threw up his hands helplessly and stepped in her direction.

She moved around the back of her car toward him, swiped her

cheeks and clutched her arms around her midsection. The pain on her face destroyed him as effectively as a bayonet slicing slowly into his belly. Instinctively, he moved forward and opened his arms. She hesitated at first then took a tentative step, both eyes streaming now.

She was in his arms, clutching his back, holding him so tight against her that he could feel her heartbeat. It matched his. "Baby, sweetheart, my love. Please don't cry." Cluny rested his cheek against her head, buried his nose in her hair and breathed in her scent. Her scent meant home to him, life to him, the future to him. "I love you, my Graciella."

"I love you so much, querido. I love you so much it hurts every cell in my body. Please forgive me." Her lips brushed the side of his neck, nearly undoing him. "Please."

A noisy, obnoxious car with bass pounding, full of young guys, slowed in the street. The smartass driver yelled, "Get a room!" Cluny smiled and lifted his middle finger without loosening the hold on his woman. He kissed the top of Graciella's head, took the profane hand and lifted her chin to kiss her. Loud catcalls emanated from the rowdies as they sped away.

"Let's go inside, baby." He urged her up the driveway to the front walk, luxuriating in the feel of her arm around his waist, her hand clamping his side. The thought of being without this woman was like being without air. He couldn't live without either. Whatever it took, he'd fix it with her. Leading her inside, he closed the door, leaned back against it and pulled her to his chest. "Graciella. Mis and I…"

Her fingers against his lips stopped the words. "No, amor, no. You don't need to explain. I trust you. It was me. All me. I've never been so sorry in my life. I was afraid of being hurt by you, of Santos being hurt by you, and so I hurt you instead. I know you aren't like *him*. It was my fear, not you, never you. Please believe me."

His heart reared like a Wyoming mustang. A sob racked his chest. There were no words. By way of answer, he lowered his mouth to hers, brushed his lips across her mouth then deepened the kiss. He'd swear he could sense their bodies melting into one. He raised his face from hers and pressed her head against his chest in an effort to breathe. They stood like that for a full minute, not moving, holding tight.

Graciella placed her hands on his chest and put an inch between them. She raised her gaze to his. Cluny let his hands loosen on her back and slide down to her hips, holding her firmly in place. The whisper of a smile flitted on her luscious mouth. Unable to resist, he lowered his head for another kiss, a soft kiss this time, a sweet kiss.

"Cluny," she breathed against his mouth, "I want you to make love to me, but I have to ask you something first."

"Anything." He barely got the words out of his mouth because of the surge of blood draining south from his brain. "Ask me, baby."

"If you don't want to answer, I'll leave to give you time to think it over."

Over my dead body. Leave? No way in hell was she leaving. "Ask me."

"Will you marry me?" She gazed shyly through her thick fringe of eyelashes, her cheeks flushing bright pink, hand trembling on his chest.

"Marry you? I was afraid you were going to ask me a hard question." He grinned and pressed her pelvis against his. "Come with me. I have something for you." When she hesitated slightly, he added, "And, by the way, my answer is yes."

Taking her hand he tugged her in the direction of the couch and sat her down. "Stay right there." He had to force himself not to run to his bedroom. He yanked open his dresser drawer and rooted through his socks and shorts. Snatched the package he was looking for and returned to the living room.

"Close your eyes."

"Why?"

"Not a good way to start. Close your eyes."

She twisted her fingers. "Okay, they're closed."

He gently lifted her fist. "Open your hand." When her fingers uncurled, he placed a small brown paper envelope there. "Okay, look."

Eyes full of trepidation; she stared at the battered envelope. "What is it?"

"Open it. It won't bite you." He knelt before her. "Go ahead."

Graciella turned the package over and lifted the flap. Squeezing the sides, she peeked inside then retrieved a small tissue-wrapped lump. She raised her eyes to his. He nodded and smiled. She dropped the envelope and slowly undid the yellowed tissue. "It's a ring," she gasped.

"A plain gold wedding ring." She turned it in her fingers and raised her eyes to his face.

"My mother's." He took it from her and slid it onto her ring finger. "I've been saving it for you. For the last twenty five years, I've been saving it for you."

Her hands flew to her mouth and she slumped forward against him.

"It comes with one condition." Cluny straightened her and smiled. She didn't answer, just stared with huge swimming milk-chocolate eyes. "The deal has to include my boy, Santos." He grinned. "And a few siblings, yet unknown."

Hands tight to her face, she nodded then lowered them, leaving red finger marks around her mouth. After a quick indrawn breath, she answered, "Yes, amor." She gripped his forearms. "Now I have a condition."

"Shoot." He was beginning to have fun.

"We'd like permission to move back in here. In your house. With you."

He pressed his lips together, delaying the answer, keeping her in suspense. "I'm nixing the separate bedrooms. We'll need it for the siblings." Cluny raised a finger. "One more condition."

She raised her tawny eyebrows.

"The three of us drive up to Vegas tomorrow and seal the deal."

"The three of us? What about my step-daughter, the one with four legs?"

"Okay, the four of us." Definitely fun.

"Anything else?" Graciella raised her chin and wrinkled her nose. "Hmm?"

"We should get a head start on the sibling thing. Like now. My biological clock is ticking."

She stood and tugged him to his feet. "Mine too."

She took a step toward his bedroom. "Tick."

Crooking her finger, she smiled over her shoulder. "Tick."

Cluny suspected he was in for a wild ride with this spirited woman as his wife. He smiled and breathed. He planned to enjoy every minute of it for the rest of their lives.

Graciella collapsed into shrieks and giggles when he raced after her and lifted her off her feet.

THE END

———

Don't miss out on your next favorite book!

Join the Satin Romance mailing list
www.satinromance.com/mail.html

Chapter Thirty-Two

Friday evening, five days later

GRACIELLA COULDN'T FACE HIM. NOT AFTER HE'D FAILED TO CALL her. She phoned Earl. "Could you take Santos to the game tomorrow? I have a private lesson with a new couple who recently signed up for a series. The only time they can come is on Saturday afternoons." She glanced at Santos, sitting morosely across the kitchen counter. "You can? Thanks, Earl. He'll be ready to leave at one."

Santos frowned. "What should I tell Macfearsome?"

"Tell him the truth."

It was mostly the truth. She'd asked the couple to come in on Saturday afternoon instead of Friday evening. They hadn't been thrilled about changing their plans, but she assured them they'd be doing her a great one-time favor, and in return she'd give them a nice discount on the package. She now needed a valid excuse not to go to any of the games for the rest of the summer season.

Thursday evening

Marla called. "We missed you on Saturday. I hope everything is okay."

"Yes, everything's fine. I picked up a new couple who wanted their private lesson on Saturday afternoon. It's a very nice fee. I couldn't afford to pass up the income."

"Oh, that's too bad. At least Santos' grandparents stood in for you."

Graciella thought Marla had a suspicion something was not right between her and Cluny, but all she said was, "Yes, I'm so glad they're there for him. Oh, Marla, I have to go. The last group for this evening just came into the studio. We'll talk later."

"Okay, let's try and get together for dinner soon."

"Yes, let's. Bye." A sick feeling filled her chest. She hated brushing off Marla, but until Cluny made some effort to put things right between them, she saw no reason to discuss their differences with anyone.

Not only had he failed to called that Sunday evening as he'd promised, she'd heard nothing from him all week. She'd analyzed and re-analyzed her feelings before and after the fateful phone call eleven days ago. She was entitled to her feelings! Why was that so difficult for him to understand? He shouldn't have accused her of wanting to pick his friends. He'd picked apart her words to make them suit his interpretation, not what she'd actually meant. How was she to know how prickly he could be?

The Amber-Santos birthday party was in two weeks. She had no idea how she'd handle the day. The kids had been looking forward to it all summer. The entire baseball team had been invited. If something didn't give between her and Cluny, it was destined to be very awkward. At some point she'd have to confide in Marla. It would be much better to tell her the truth instead of leaving events open to speculation. She'd promised Marla she'd do her share to make the party a success. And she'd keep her word.

If only he'd callled.

Santos's conversation had consisted of one word answers or grunts. It was increasingly difficult to overlook his moods and to find excuses why he couldn't spend a day at Amber's house. She practically had to drag him out of bed to get them to the studio on time in the mornings. He used to enjoy going to work with her during school vacations, helping at the studio, answering the phone. Now he resented every minute of it.

"Why doesn't Macfearsome come here anymore."

She didn't meet his gaze. "He's very busy."

"Don't answer me like I'm a baby! I have a brain, Mama." His face brick red with anger, he scowled and put down his fork. "I'm going to my room."

"No, sweetie, wait, I'm sorry. Finish your dessert. It's complicated to explain." She extended her hand and nodded at his chair.

He stood rooted to the floor. Finally, he took his seat, but didn't pick up his fork. "Why do grownups always say 'it's complicated' when they don't want to tell the truth?" Santos had never taken this belligerent tone of voice with her before.

Her heart ached. And not just because she'd been so unprepared to discuss this with him. "The truth is, it *is* complicated. Cluny and I had a misunderstanding."

"What kind of misunderstanding? Do you still love him?"

"I—"

"Does he love you?" He'd leaned forward challenging with his chin. "I know he loves me because he told me so when I asked him why he didn't come here anymore, why we couldn't be a family anymore." His freckled nose wrinkled and tears filled his eyes. "He told me 'it's complicated.' I hate you! I hate him!" With that, he shoved back from the table and ran to his room. His door slammed so hard the TV wobbled on its stand.

Her son's bitter outburst hurt deep down. Graciella clenched her fists and squeezed her eyes shut. She was the adult here. She would not react like a wounded child. She'd drawn her son into the budding love affair. He was innocent, his life turned upside down, and it was her doing. She'd been so filled with passion for Cluny that she'd neglected her responsibility as a mother.

If it were possible to go back in time she wouldn't have invited Cluny to join them for a cool drink on their beach blanket that day. She'd never have known what it was like to be with him, to love him, to anticipate him coming through the door. Even now, if she closed her eyes and held her breath, she could feel the heat of Cluny's bare skin under her hands.

The doorbell rang.

Her heart leapt. It must be Cluny. It had to be Cluny. She flew to the door and pulled it open. The hopeful smile died on her face. "What do you want?"

Misty Beachy stared stonily. "We need to talk."

The last human being on the planet Graciella had anything to say to would be this woman. "I have nothing to say to you."

"I'm not leaving until you either let me in so we can speak in a civilized manner, or you can shut the door in my face and I'll shout from out here. What's it going to be?"

Graciella got a glimpse of Misty's steel. A hint of the way she must have spoken to the men under her command. "My son is in the apartment. He's still awake."

"Then step outside and we'll go for a walk or sit in my car. Make up your mind."

Graciella gritted her teeth. "I have to let Santos know I'm stepping outside." She made to close the door.

"Leave the door open. Tell him. I'll wait here."

Hands to her hot cheeks, Graciela hesitated then whipped around and strode down the short hallway. At the door to Santos' room she knocked. "Santos? Honey, I'm stepping outside. I won't be far away." She heard nothing. "Santos, did you hear me?"

"Yes. Leave. I don't care."

This was a nightmare. Graciella turned on her heel, grabbed her keys and stepped outside. She locked the door and followed Beachy to the parking area.

Beachy crossed her arms and leaned her hip against the front fender of her Jeep. "In the car or walk?"

"In the car so I can keep an eye on my front door."

Misty opened the driver's side and pointed across the hood. "Get in."

Graciella got in the car and sat as far away from Misty as possible. Angry words spewed from her mouth, "Tell me what you want. Do you want Cluny? Take him. There's nothing I can do about it."

"God! The two of you are beyond pathetic." She pursed her lips and gripped the steering wheel. "If I didn't love Mac, I'd tell both of you to go to hell, but I do love him so I have something to say to you, and then I'll leave."

"I'd rather you —"

"Oh, shut up!" She slammed her fist on the steering wheel. "I'm only going to say this once, so listen up!"

Stunned by Misty's hot temper and the command in the small blonde woman's voice, Graciella held her tongue. Pulse thundered in her ears. She'd let Beachy have her say then get out of there as fast as she could.

"Are you listening?" Misty stared hard into Graciella's eyes.

Instead of answering she glared. Who did the woman think she was?

"This is not easy for me to tell you. Mac and I served several months in a forward operating base in the middle of an active battle zone in Iraq. Dempsey and some of the other guys you met were there, too. It's impossible to feel safe, ever. Even inside the wire. You never knew when an RPG would detonate, or whether or not it was headed right for you. We were under mortar fire twenty-four-seven. You could be watching a movie or writing a letter, or standing in the mess line. The threat of sudden death was constant. I felt my humanity slipping away inch by inch. It was impossible to sleep when the sirens went off at all hours of the day and night.

"One night warning sirens screamed for about the tenth time. I was shaking in every part of my body. I stepped outside the mess tent and slammed into Mac. I ripped into him from start to finish just because he was there. I choked and started to cry. He put his arms around me. I slapped and punched him, but he wouldn't let go. When I got hold of myself, he walked me to my tent. He never said a word. At the door he turned to leave. I grabbed his hand and pulled him inside. It was wrong, but I didn't care because I knew if I stayed alone I'd come unglued."

Gasping, Graciella tried to picture what Beachy described. Acid reflux burned the back of her throat.

"We sat on the edge of my cot holding hands. Finally, Mac gently lowered me on the cot and held me. There was nothing sexual about it. We fell asleep. When I woke a few hours later he was gone."

"But, I thought…"

Misty held her palm out. "Let me finish. Not long after that night we began to sleep together. What you need to understand is that it wasn't passion or even love. It was one human reaching out to another human on the most primal level. Sex was how we maintained our sanity in the raging chaos around us. You have no inkling what it's like to be a woman in a war zone during a long dangerous deployment. We both could have been busted in rank for it, but a few of the men in the unit, like Gunny Dempsey, deflected the gossip. Mac never said word one to anyone about me. It's easy for basic kindness and decency to deteriorate, even among the people you depend on for your very life.

"The day of the RPG ambush, the day Dempsey lost his leg, we were in a convoy heading back to Baghdad. Several of us got wounded." She touched her ear unconsciously. "And a couple of guys in my squad were killed. It was indescribably ugly. I didn't expect to get out of there alive. An A-10 Warthog came in low and held off the bad guys until we could be extracted by a SEAL fire team. The one your husband was part of. Marv was killed within twenty four hours of that incident."

Tears clogged Graciella's throat.

"Mac and I were on the same Medevac plane to Germany, but we didn't see each other again for about three months. It was just before he was on his way to Walter Reed with Dempsey and I was shipping out to a facility on the west coast. The only thing that existed between us by then was a melancholy, a deep respect. We'd saved each other over there. Mac is responsible for me not being a total crazy bitch, a total lost cause. He'll always be my best and most trusted friend."

Graciella raised her hands to cover her face. Moaning softly, she shook her head for what they'd gone through. All of them, including Marvin. Finally, she understood why she had no reason to distrust the man she loved. He and this woman had connected during a nightmarish situation she could never imagine. Their devotion to each other was no threat to her. Had never been a threat to her.

"I had no idea. I'm sorry. I don't know what else to say."

"Do you love Mac? Because if you do, get off your ass and figure out a way to patch it up with him. If you don't love him, then end it. I can't stand to see him suffering like this. He's one of the finest men I've ever known. Your kid would be lucky to have him for a father."

A tear trickled down Graciella's cheek. "I do love him. I just don't know how to…"

"Then figure it out!" Misty pointed to the door. "I'm done. You can go back to your kid now." Misty put the key in the ignition and started the Jeep.

The second Graciella closed the car door Misty backed out and sped away.

She hugged herself against the chilly night air. Slowly, she walked back to her apartment. Santos' bedroom door was closed and there was no light shining under it. She rapped softly.

"Santos? May I come in?"

His voice, muffled and sullen was barely audible. "Why?"

"I want to talk to you. "

"I'm asleep."

Her lips twisted in a rueful smile. "Please?" She turned the knob ever so slightly. He hadn't locked it. "Sweetheart?"

He was fully clothed, sitting on his bed, leaning against the head-board. The vertical blinds on his window facing the parking area were open. "Who was that lady?"

Graciella crossed the room and sat on the edge of his bed. "Cluny's old friend from the Marines, Sergeant Beachy."

"Why did you go out to her car?" He crossed his arms and scowled. "What were you talking about?"

"Were you watching me?" She put her hand on his leg. "I went outside because I wasn't sure if I wanted you to hear our conversation."

"Because you were talking about *'it's complicated'* grownup stuff?"

"Um hum. That was it."

"So, you're not going to tell me." He turned his head to face the window.

"No, honey, not tonight, but I promise I will soon." She shook his foot. "Why don't you take your shower and get ready for bed? I need to call Marla before it gets too late."

"When can you take me to visit Amber?"

"Tomorrow's Friday. I'll ask her parents if it's okay to bring you over to spend the night. How's that?"

His face broke into a happy grin. "I know what I want for my birthday."

"What?" She gave him encouraging smile.

"Macfearsome."

"I can't give you Macfearsome."

"Why not? You took him away from me and I want him back."

Everything was so simple to a child. Perhaps they had the right idea. "I want him back, too. I'll see what I can do. I won't make any promises."

"Okay." Resigned, he scooted off the bed, got his pajamas from the dresser and headed to the bathroom.

The minute Graciella heard the shower running she called the Dempsey house. Dwayne answered. "Dwayne? It's Graciella here. Is it too late to talk to Marla?"

"No, she's right here. Give me the boy, honey, Graciella's on the phone."

"Hey! What are you up to?"

"Do you have a few minutes to talk, Marla?"

"Sure, hold on a minute." A chair scraped. "I'm going to take Graciella's call in the den." Footsteps, then a door closing. "There. We have privacy."

"Could you keep Santos tomorrow night?"

"Sure. Are you and Cluny going out?"

"Not exactly. I'm going to his house and see if he'll talk to me."

"Finally! Are you going to let him know you're coming?"

"I hadn't planned to. I thought I'd just show up, not give him a chance to find an excuse not to see me."

"He wouldn't do that. He's miserable. I've never seen him so down in the mouth. I hope you're going over there to make up with him. If you're feeling as rotten as he is, it's time to talk it out." Marla sighed. "I'm one to talk. I have Amber to thank for being so single-minded in getting us back together after we split up."

"You'll have to tell me about that sometime."

Marla laughed. "She'd be happy to share with very little prompting. What time will you be by?"

"Around three?"

"That works. He can have dinner with us. You, too."

"No, I want to get to Cluny's house before he gets home. If it works out, we'll have dinner together."

Marla didn't answer her. "Marla?"

"I'm here. I, uh... Oh, heck, Graciella. Misty Beachy is at his place. She stopped on her way back to San Diego. We went out for pizza with them tonight. But they're not...he's not..."

"I know. That's okay. I talked with her an hour ago. She was here."

"What?"

"I won't go into detail. Let's just say she gave me a verbal slapping. I needed it."

"I'll keep my fingers crossed, my friend. You and Cluny and Santos are very special to Dwayne and me. We want nothing but the best for you."

"Thank you, Marla. I'll see you tomorrow afternoon, and keep those fingers crossed."

Graciella clicked off and slumped against the couch cushions. Now she'd worry for the next several hours about how to break the ice with the man she loved. She'd be turning the words around in her head all night.

———

Cluny's house, next afternoon

Cluny lounged against his porch railing. "Sure you can't stay another night?"

"Yes, Mac, I'm sure. I have to get back to work." Misty pointed to the duffle bag next to the door. "Would you carry that to the Jeep? I'll make one more sweep through the bedroom and bathroom to make sure I don't leave anything behind. You never know when your girl-friend might show up."

"You referring to my ex-girlfriend?" The words stabbed a pain in his chest and a choking lump in his throat.

Misty nodded to the street. "You mean her?"

Cluny's back went stiff and he whipped his head around. Graciella's car crept down his driveway. She stopped behind the plumbing van and turned off the engine, but didn't open her door. The front screen snapped shut when Beachy went inside the house. "Oh, shit," he groaned. "Oh, shit."

Graciella opened the door and stood next to her car. She gazed at him with unreadable eyes.

Beachy stepped outside, and lifted her duffle. "I'm outta here, Mac."

"You don't have to leave, Mis." But if she didn't, what was he to do?

"There are times, Mac, when I can't believe what a numbskull you can be. Go talk to her. What are you waiting for?"

He reached for Misty's bag and yanked it from her hand. "I'll walk you to your car."

"You're an idiot, but let's get it over with." She waved at Graciella.

"What are you doing, for chrissake?"

"Waving goodbye to your girlfriend." Misty opened the passenger door and rounded the front of Jeep to the driver's side. "Throw my bag on the seat."

He did as instructed, slammed the door and followed her. From the corner of his eye he saw Graciella watching his every move. His neck and shoulders cramped, and he asked himself why he was pushing it. "Give us a goodbye kiss, Mis." He leaned close to her door.

"I carry a gun, knothead, and unless you have a death wish, you'll step away from the car. I resign as your relationship therapist. Now back up or I swear to God I'll drive right over you." She glared and started the Jeep's engine then threw it into first.

He jumped to avoid the back wheels when she accelerated. She wasn't kidding about running over him. He might as well have been naked, standing there in the street, the dust kicked up by the Jeep swirling around his battered work-boots. He hadn't felt so vulnerable since the evac from Fallujah. Graciella hadn't moved, but he thought he detected the lowering sun glint off what could be a tear on her cheek. *Oh, God no, Graciella, please don't cry.* He was mush when faced with female tears. He threw up his hands helplessly and stepped in her direction.

She moved around the back of her car toward him, swiped her

cheeks and clutched her arms around her midsection. The pain on her face destroyed him as effectively as a bayonet slicing slowly into his belly. Instinctively, he moved forward and opened his arms. She hesitated at first then took a tentative step, both eyes streaming now.

She was in his arms, clutching his back, holding him so tight against her that he could feel her heartbeat. It matched his. "Baby, sweetheart, my love. Please don't cry." Cluny rested his cheek against her head, buried his nose in her hair and breathed in her scent. Her scent meant home to him, life to him, the future to him. "I love you, my Graciella."

"I love you so much, querido. I love you so much it hurts every cell in my body. Please forgive me." Her lips brushed the side of his neck, nearly undoing him. "Please."

A noisy, obnoxious car with bass pounding, full of young guys, slowed in the street. The smartass driver yelled, "Get a room!" Cluny smiled and lifted his middle finger without loosening the hold on his woman. He kissed the top of Graciella's head, took the profane hand and lifted her chin to kiss her. Loud catcalls emanated from the rowdies as they sped away.

"Let's go inside, baby." He urged her up the driveway to the front walk, luxuriating in the feel of her arm around his waist, her hand clamping his side. The thought of being without this woman was like being without air. He couldn't live without either. Whatever it took, he'd fix it with her. Leading her inside, he closed the door, leaned back against it and pulled her to his chest. "Graciella. Mis and I..."

Her fingers against his lips stopped the words. "No, amor, no. You don't need to explain. I trust you. It was me. All me. I've never been so sorry in my life. I was afraid of being hurt by you, of Santos being hurt by you, and so I hurt you instead. I know you aren't like *him*. It was my fear, not you, never you. Please believe me."

His heart reared like a Wyoming mustang. A sob racked his chest. There were no words. By way of answer, he lowered his mouth to hers, brushed his lips across her mouth then deepened the kiss. He'd swear he could sense their bodies melting into one. He raised his face from hers and pressed her head against his chest in an effort to breathe. They stood like that for a full minute, not moving, holding tight.

Graciella placed her hands on his chest and put an inch between them. She raised her gaze to his. Cluny let his hands loosen on her back and slide down to her hips, holding her firmly in place. The whisper of a smile flitted on her luscious mouth. Unable to resist, he lowered his head for another kiss, a soft kiss this time, a sweet kiss.

"Cluny," she breathed against his mouth, "I want you to make love to me, but I have to ask you something first."

"Anything." He barely got the words out of his mouth because of the surge of blood draining south from his brain. "Ask me, baby."

"If you don't want to answer, I'll leave to give you time to think it over."

Over my dead body. Leave? No way in hell was she leaving. "Ask me."

"Will you marry me?" She gazed shyly through her thick fringe of eyelashes, her cheeks flushing bright pink, hand trembling on his chest.

"Marry you? I was afraid you were going to ask me a hard question." He grinned and pressed her pelvis against his. "Come with me. I have something for you." When she hesitated slightly, he added, "And, by the way, my answer is yes."

Taking her hand he tugged her in the direction of the couch and sat her down. "Stay right there." He had to force himself not to run to his bedroom. He yanked open his dresser drawer and rooted through his socks and shorts. Snatched the package he was looking for and returned to the living room.

"Close your eyes."

"Why?"

"Not a good way to start. Close your eyes."

She twisted her fingers. "Okay, they're closed."

He gently lifted her fist. "Open your hand." When her fingers uncurled, he placed a small brown paper envelope there. "Okay, look."

Eyes full of trepidation; she stared at the battered envelope. "What is it?"

"Open it. It won't bite you." He knelt before her. "Go ahead."

Graciella turned the package over and lifted the flap. Squeezing the sides, she peeked inside then retrieved a small tissue-wrapped lump. She raised her eyes to his. He nodded and smiled. She dropped the envelope and slowly undid the yellowed tissue. "It's a ring," she gasped.

"A plain gold wedding ring." She turned it in her fingers and raised her eyes to his face.

"My mother's." He took it from her and slid it onto her ring finger. "I've been saving it for you. For the last twenty five years, I've been saving it for you."

Her hands flew to her mouth and she slumped forward against him.

"It comes with one condition." Cluny straightened her and smiled. She didn't answer, just stared with huge swimming milk-chocolate eyes. "The deal has to include my boy, Santos." He grinned. "And a few siblings, yet unknown."

Hands tight to her face, she nodded then lowered them, leaving red finger marks around her mouth. After a quick indrawn breath, she answered, "Yes, amor." She gripped his forearms. "Now I have a condition."

"Shoot." He was beginning to have fun.

"We'd like permission to move back in here. In your house. With you."

He pressed his lips together, delaying the answer, keeping her in suspense. "I'm nixing the separate bedrooms. We'll need it for the siblings." Cluny raised a finger. "One more condition."

She raised her tawny eyebrows.

"The three of us drive up to Vegas tomorrow and seal the deal."

"The three of us? What about my step-daughter, the one with four legs?"

"Okay, the four of us." Definitely fun.

"Anything else?" Graciella raised her chin and wrinkled her nose. "Hmm?"

"We should get a head start on the sibling thing. Like now. My biological clock is ticking."

She stood and tugged him to his feet. "Mine too."

She took a step toward his bedroom. "Tick."

Crooking her finger, she smiled over her shoulder. "Tick."

Cluny suspected he was in for a wild ride with this spirited woman as his wife. He smiled and breathed. He planned to enjoy every minute of it for the rest of their lives.

Graciella collapsed into shrieks and giggles when he raced after her and lifted her off her feet.

THE END

———

Don't miss out on your next favorite book!

Join the Satin Romance mailing list
www.satinromance.com/mail.html

THANK YOU FOR READING

Did you enjoy this book?

We invite you to leave a review at the website of your choice, such as Goodreads, Amazon, Barnes & Noble, etc.

DID YOU KNOW THAT LEAVING A REVIEW…

- Helps other readers find books they may enjoy.
- Gives you a chance to let your voice be heard.
- Gives authors recognition for their hard work.
- Doesn't have to be long. A sentence or two about why you liked the book will do.

About the Author

I wrote my first novel at the age of six. It was titled "The Mouse," and was two pages long—including illustrations! My mother saved that *first edition* and every now and then, I take it out and smile over it.

When my beloved husband of many years suddenly died, I'd come home after a long day of work and write. Writing allowed me to pour out all my sadness. Then, the more I wrote, the more I realized I would go on. I would be happy, I had a lot of living to do, and love stories to tell.

I'm published now in Romance novels and an anthology of short stories. But my first two manuscripts still reside on a CD somewhere in my house. I can't bear to erase them because they're mine, they're loved, and like a crazy relative one hides in the attic, they reside in a quiet, safe place.

www.pattycampbell.com
pattycampbellauthor.blogspot.com

facebook.com/Patty-Campbell-Author-536855299661241

goodreads.com/goodreadscomuser_PattyCampbell

Also by Patty Campbell

WITH MELANGE BOOKS

Risky Business

www.ingramcontent.com/pod-product-compliance
Lightning Source LLC
Chambersburg PA
CBHW031159020726
47499CB00002B/420